HOUSE OF CARDS

'This very readable blood-and-thunder tale, lifelike and thoroughly cynical, certainly carries the ring of authenticity . . . a great triumph.'
ANTHONY HOWARD, *Independent*

'A well-written and well-constructed political thriller. Let's hope it is the first of many.' *Sunday Times*

'A triumph . . . Dobbs's genius as a novelist is the same as his advertising slogans: take an essence and distil it . . . I loved it.' AUSTIN MITCHELL MP

'A rollicking plot . . . a hugely enjoyable read.'
Evening Standard

'It has pace, a beguiling authenticity and a cast of Achilles heels.' JULIAN CRITCHLEY MP

'Watergate set in Westminster . . . set cabinet pulses racing . . . *House of Cards* must not be allowed to fall into the hands of impressionable Tory backbenchers.'
Daily Telegraph

'Intrigue and financial scandal . . . written by a seasoned insider, this well-paced and marvellously authentic thriller translates Watergate into Westminster and comes up with a fiery winner.' *Wales on Sunday*

'Unspeakable dirty tricks, blackmail, drug addiction and murder.' *Bristol Evening Post*

'A cracking political thriller that shows his marvellous inside track knowledge of government. A roller coaster that culminates in a thrilling finale. For thriller lovers – political or otherwise – *House of Cards* does not fall down on any count.' *Irish News*

MICHAEL DOBBS

Michael Dobbs has spent many years at the most senior levels of British politics, advising Mrs Thatcher, Norman Tebbit and many other leading politicians. He worked as a journalist in the United States throughout the Watergate crisis, and after returning to London in 1975 played major roles in the general elections of 1979 and 1983, and was Chief of Staff at Conservative Party headquarters during the 1987 elections. He has a doctorate in defence studies. He lives in London with his wife and two young sons.

Michael Dobbs's first novel, *House of Cards*, was published to great success in 1989 and has been serialized by BBC TV. He has recently published his third novel, *Last Man to Die*.

MICHAEL DOBBS

Wall Games

Fontana

An Imprint of HarperCollins*Publishers*

For Michael Joseph.
And, as always, for his mother.

First published in 1990 by Collins

A continental edition first issued in 1990 by Fontana,
an imprint of HarperCollins Publishers,
77–85 Fulham Palace Road,
Hammersmith, London W6 8JB

This Fontana edition first issued 1991

9 8 7 6 5 4 3 2 1

Printed and bound in Great Britain by
HarperCollins Book Manufacturing, Glasgow

ACKNOWLEDGEMENTS

One of the characteristics which makes writing such a pleasure is the help and encouragement so freely given by many friends, old and new. In a world which seemed to be changing beyond recognition with every edition of the morning newspaper and requiring changes to this book with it, their support has been particularly invaluable. *Wall Games* was started in the era of Cold War and was finished just a few months later in a time which promised freedom and release for millions throughout Eastern Europe. Yet promises are so often broken, and I suspect that the collapse of the Soviet Empire will not be a smooth and painless process. It is still too soon to pronounce 'peace on earth, goodwill to all men'. In any event, the challenges of love, ambition and betrayal on which this plot is based are perpetual, no matter what the political backcloth.

So thank you Sara McLean, who helped get me started; Ed Schumacher, who bravely lent me his name; Peter Frank, who gave freely of his advice and expertise even while he was so busy; Jeffery Tolman, who allowed me to destroy one of his delightful dinner parties by investigating women's views of younger men; Andrei Vandoros, who is a perpetual source of encouragement and rude good humour; and many other individuals who instructed me about Berlin but who prefer to avoid the guilt of association.

In Berlin itself I have been showered with kindness by both British and American friends, and in particular by Alan Patterson, Major Glyn Taylor and other of their colleagues at Headquarters Berlin (British Sector).

Most of all, I owe a debt to the kindness of Berliners over many years. It is possible both to love and hate the city itself, but for its people I have only the greatest admiration. As a teenager in the 1960s I used to run errands across the Wall for refugees whose families had been torn apart by its construction. I met people who had braved the bullets to cross. They, and the many who didn't make it, saw something in the West they thought was worth risking death for. It would be insulting to dedicate a work of fiction, essentially a work of entertainment, to them. Yet I hope we shall not forget them.

M.J.D.

PROLOGUE

Berlin, January 1970

She stood trembling in the freezing air, hugging the shadows of the Berlin night. It had been many hours since they had stolen into their hiding place – too many hours, she thought. They were numbed by the January chill and by the fear which had been following them around every corner for weeks. They had gambled on waiting until a couple of hours before dawn in the hope that the border guards in their unheated watch towers might be seduced into carelessness. It was probably a mistake. The long wait was confusing her, undermining her morale. And mistakes in Berlin cost lives.

She kept looking at the baby to reassure herself, to give her back the courage which the night tried to drain from her. It was the baby which had changed everything for them. She and Peter might have been able to tolerate the mindless anonymity of East Berlin, like the tens of thousands of other couples who shuffled about their lives in quiet resentment beneath the huge red banners of the State, listening to the proclamations of working-class victory even while they were forced to forage for clothing and fuel like medieval peasants in the ruins. All she and Peter had ever known were the empty streets of East Berlin with its bomb-cracked walls, missing roofs and constant suspicion. Like all children born into the post-war shambles of Berlin they had played amid the crumble and decay of the once-great city and had listened to the whispered memories among the women of what had happened when the Russians arrived.

Somehow she and Peter survived, and even found reason to laugh and time to love. But when the baby arrived they both knew it was not enough, and could never be enough any longer. They had to get out.

And that meant the Wall. That angry fist of bricks and barbed wire which smashed its way across the streets of Berlin and straight through the centre of homes, cutting off East from West, children from their grandparents and the cold realities of socialism from materialist temptation and deception. What had at first been no more than a tangle of barbed wire had grown into a mess of bricks and mortar, hurriedly thrown together as the steady trickle of *Flüchtlinge* – escapees from East to West – threatened to turn into a tide and swamp the economic dreams of the master planners in East Berlin. Yet even that had not been enough to foil the inventiveness and desperation of Berliners, and so the original Wall was being replaced along its length by great slabs of concrete, up to twelve feet high, defended by a no-man's-land of trip wires, dog runs, searchlights and minefields which formed a killing field for the border guards. German now hunted German; the sentries were reminded every night before going on duty that they would be rewarded handsomely for preventing any escape – and punished harshly if they didn't. The Wall had not only broken the back of Berlin, but also its heart.

Now it lay directly ahead of them, the floodlights illuminating the piles of rubble and concrete which poked through the fresh layer of snow in no-man's-land like monuments to the dead.

Peter squeezed her hand. 'It's time,' he whispered. He was still wearing the conscript's uniform worn by all men over the age of eighteen and which had helped to smuggle them past the prying eyes of the guards along the Koepenicker Strasse into the shadows of a deserted school, just fifty yards from the forbidden zone. She took the baby from her breast where he had stayed all night, warm, content and quiet. She kissed his forehead before wrapping him carefully in his christening shawl and a woollen blanket, and handing him to Peter. She said nothing. What was there to say?

Peter pointed once more to the loose fold in the barbed wire he had spotted several days before. It was their door to freedom, a mass of greedy iron teeth which had sprung a gap scarcely eighteen inches across and which would, with luck, allow them to squeeze through without delay and reach the Wall. Yet from 200 yards away it looked impossibly small . . . were the helpers waiting on the other side as promised, ready to throw over the ladder so they could scramble to freedom? Or would she and Peter be stranded, stuck on the killing fields in the full glare of the spotlights and rifle sights? What if they couldn't get through the wire? What if this section of the Wall had already been mined? What if there was no ladder waiting for them? What if . . . ?

The silence of the early morning along the Wall wrapped itself around them and made her shiver once again. She looked at Peter's handsome young face twisted with tension, his ears straining for any give-away sound, his eyes focused like magnets on the barbed wire. Neither of them was yet twenty years old but suddenly she felt like an old hag with fingers she could no longer feel and limbs which weighed like lead. She could sense the numbing effect of the panic which was beginning to rise within her. She knew she wasn't going to make it. And there was the baby – surely he must be smothering in the tight wrapping of blankets? She desperately wanted to hold her son just once more, but after the endless hours of waiting she had run out

11

of time. Peter was already nodding that the moment had come. She knew she was beginning to lose control, that her chance was beginning to slip away, but it didn't seem to matter any more so long as Peter and the baby got through.

'Peter . . .', she began, shaking her head, but he cut her short and squeezed her hand, and somehow just the very touch forced a little hope back into her. He bent low to whisper close to her face, all the time looking deep into her frightened eyes. 'Remember. Go for the hole in the wire. Don't stop for anything. And whatever happens, don't look back.'

The moment had come and, like a fox sniffing the morning air, Peter took one last look along the Wall and checked his watch. She felt his arms around her. One last embrace, she said, but there was no more time! Those arms which had always held her so lovingly and had always made her feel secure now thrust her out of the protective shadows and into the glare of the killing fields.

She could feel her legs running as if they were a million miles apart from the rest of her body, hitting the hard ground and weaving between the piles of rubble as if they were part of a machine operating in another time zone. It took her a couple of seconds to realize that it had all begun, that now there could be no turning back, and by that time she was already halfway towards the wire. She could see almost nothing, blinded by the brilliant lights which glared around her. She wanted to give in to her fears and turn around to see if Peter were following, but his sharp command not to look back echoed in her ears. Her heart was pounding and her lungs gasped at the cold night air with such violence that she must surely have alerted every border guard for miles.

Then she was at the wire. 'Take it carefully,' he had

instructed, but she threw herself at it; there was no time left for care, her responses were entirely automatic. She was crawling on the ground through the little tunnel of teeth, scrabbling to find a handhold on the assortment of broken bricks and rubble protruding through the snow, when she felt a searing pain across her back. She knew she had been shot! But where was the rifle fire, the sound of the bullet ripping through her clothes and scoring along her back? She froze, biting deep into her lip to stifle the cry of pain and trying to focus her scrambled senses. The wire! She had caught herself on the bloody wire. 'Don't rush it,' he had warned, 'the teeth are like razors. Once you get tangled up it will never let you go.'

But thank God it had let her free again. She shouted at her arms and legs to keep pulling her along, crawling low with her face almost in the dirt to avoid any more brushes with the wire. And then she was through. She was now only fifty yards from the Wall. She started to run across a tangle of rubble bleached white by the floodlights and looking like a charnel-house of bones and skulls. Every step made her feel as if she were walking on the graves of those who had gone before, and who hadn't made it.

Yet still there was no sound. No warning shout. No shots. And now she was approaching the Wall itself. God, it was a mountain! They had practised climbing twelve-foot walls, but this seemed far, far higher than she had expected and was growing with every pace she took towards it. And where was the ladder? As panic began to grip her again, a panic which she knew would leave her stranded and helpless at the foot of the floodlit Wall, she saw the heads of three men appearing over its top, waving at her as if to brush her fear away. She was almost there! Just a few more paces to go!

Then the dog barked. A mournful howl like a hound let loose from hell came drifting across no-man's-land, letting even the sleepiest guard know that havoc was afoot. Peter had heard it, too, and was now rushing through the wire heedless of the noise he made. In an instant the ladder was over the Wall and in front of her. But where were Peter and the baby? She stopped, but the voices above her were taking control, shouting the commands to her petrified limbs which she was no longer capable of giving.

'Don't look back! Up! Up!'

She was more than halfway up when the automatic rifle fire began splattering the Wall around her. She was almost to the top when a burst gouged out angry chips of mortar just six inches from her face, and in her terror her fingers lost their grip on the ladder. With a cry of despair she began to tumble backwards, but the hands of her unknown saviours were there to catch her and drag her the last couple of feet across the top of the Wall. She was almost over!

Behind her the gun fire was continuing, the original automatic rifle being joined by several others as shots peppered around the base of the Wall. The dogs had been let out now, and their evil barking was getting closer by the second. She was bent double across the Wall, being dragged head-first, heedless of the shards and sharp edges which tore at her clothes and scoured the flesh on her legs. Yet there was no cry of triumph, only fear. Peter and the baby! She struggled to turn around, but firm hands held her. 'Don't look back. Don't look back.'

Then a prolonged blast of sub-machine-gun fire hit the Wall just below its summit, forcing the helpers to duck down behind for protection, dragging her the last few inches to safety, into freedom. They heard the bullets spatter once more against the Wall, and the sickening crash as the ladder was blown away from its moorings and spun to the ground below.

'Peter! Peter!'

They tried to restrain her but she was almost free of their clutches when another sustained round of staccato gun fire burst through the night air.

Then there was silence.

Her head was now above the Wall again, peering down into the graveyard of no-man's-land. Just twenty feet from the Wall lay a bundle of clothing, with red blotches already beginning to spread across its back.

'Peter!'

The bundle twitched, and Peter began slowly to raise his face from the ground. It was grey with pain, already almost a death mask and beginning to melt invisibly into the charnel of the killing field. One arm still clutched protectively a tiny swathe of blankets which lay motionless at his side, his other hand reached out towards her and for the safety they had both prayed for, his lips struggling to find words from within his shattered body.

'Kather-i-i-ine . . .'

Then another volley of shots smashed through his body, shaking it like a rag doll before throwing it back lifeless on to the ground. It was over.

'Whatever happens, never look back,' he had told her. But as they pulled her down to the safety of the other side of the Wall, she knew she would spend the rest of her life looking back.

ONE

The White House, Washington D.C., Nearly Twenty Years Later

He didn't recognize the feeling at first, but slowly it came back to him. He was nervous. It had been many years since he had felt like this about anything, for nervousness is a characteristic which general secretaries of the Soviet Communist Party rapidly grow out of. You don't get to command all those megatons and personify the dictatorship of the great Soviet proletariat by whimpering. But there it was. A distinct fluttering of nerves in his stomach and a wrenching at his bowels which made him feel exceedingly uncomfortable.

'*Pizdets!*' Aleksandr Mikhailovich Andreyev swore to himself, softly enough so that none of the 800 or more journalists crammed into the Columned Room of the White House could hear him. Only his sour-faced interpreter who hovered just inches behind his right shoulder sensed his annoyance, but he had survived for too long to allow any surprise to register. In any event, the audience was intent on listening to the American President deliver the carefully crafted words of his speechwriters, and failed to catch the slightest sign of the Soviet leader's displeasure.

'. . . to mark a new era of peace in East–West relations; an historic turning point for all mankind . . .' droned the interpreter into his ear, squeezing all the relish out of the words and making them sound as dry as the technical-school lectures which Andreyev had

17

attended as a young man in post-war Kharkov. Still, it didn't matter. Words were tools, to be picked up or thrown aside as events required. Who would remember what either man had said in a few weeks' time, let alone a hundred years hence? Would their words be read and studied by future generations of schoolchildren? He doubted it. What mattered was what men achieved, and he had grown up learning to watch what was in a man's hands rather than trusting in his smile. As he watched the US leader reaching for the words from his autocue script and acting them out to a worldwide television audience of nearly two billion, hoping that every theatrical wave of the arm was worth another full point in the opinion polls, Andreyev struggled to maintain the look of interest which had frozen on his face while his thoughts fluttered elsewhere. After all, he had read and approved every line of the President's remarks the night before.

Andreyev's gaze wandered around the room. After five days of summit diplomacy in Washington he was finding it hard to keep up the permanent smile of sincerity required of him by the Western media. They were jackals, running mindlessly in packs after their prey. But the Russians had centuries of experience with jackal packs, and he'd had this lot practically eating out of his hand ever since he arrived. Of course they offered the occasional snarl, like *The Boston Globe* that morning. 'Can't they make clothes in Moscow?' it had quipped crudely as it identified his Parisian suits, mockingly admired his handmade shirts from London's Jermyn Street and speculated about which retailer on Milan's Della Spiga had provided his expensive silk ties. But that was standard dress uniform nowadays for all senior members of the Kremlin, particularly when in front of foreign television cameras. It wasn't his fault if it looked incongruous and even comical on his squat Slavic frame.

He tried not to let his irritation show as he blinked in the glare of the television lights and glanced around this great showpiece room of the White House, refurbished at unfathomable expense under the personal direction of the First Lady who had insisted that she be allowed to 'leave her mark' on at least one room in the House – and who in the timeless tradition of the bored and bounteous had buried a perfectly respectable reception room under a deluge of mock imperial trappings. Now it was having its first public airing and had been transformed into a stage on which to test the acting abilities of the two great leaders. Andreyev felt passionately, bombastically Russian as he noticed that there was not a single major feature of the room which could be identified as genuinely American, from the fake Corinthian plaster columns which towered above the reproduction Louis XIV furniture to the original but entirely European oil paintings adorning the primrose-clad walls. The crystal chandeliers were French, the television equipment was Japanese and even the carpet on which he stood was clearly oriental.

Give me the Kremlin any time, he murmured, for all its Tsarist baubles it was unmistakably, originally, authentically Russian. Behind its vast walls and even in its darkest corners you could smell the steppes which lay beyond the Urals and if you closed your eyes on a quiet night you might even hear the echoing cries of millions of serfs, whose bones had been the foundations on which the vast Soviet empire was built.

But these Americans, he thought, they have no culture, no roots. Everything American is borrowed or stolen, even their diplomacy. A quarter of a century earlier, when he had been a rising Moscow *apparatchik*, the Americans had covered their retreat from Vietnam with a fashionable foreign label – 'détente' they had called it. The more accurate term, 'defeat', would have been too brutal, too Anglo-Saxon. Now they had gone even further and adopted *'glasnost'*, a Russian word which they only partly understood yet which served to hide the confusion and imprecision in their thinking. The Yankees were once again in retreat but this time from an enemy even more difficult to identify and combat than the Viet Cong. Economic recession was undermining the capitalist West and destroying its sense of purpose, even while the President was attempting to distract his electorate's attention with a new superpower understanding all dressed up in ringing moral and humanitarian tones.

'. . . the world will be a safer, more peaceful place tonight. In place of pain, we can give the hungry hope. Instead of disease, we can give the poor a more secure future. And instead of bitterness, we can extend to each other the hand of friendship . . .' the President intoned in his sincerest, much-practised voice, redolent of hours of rehearsal. It might for a time confuse the public, but deep down the American leader recognized the fundamental weakness of his position. The United States could no longer afford to play policeman to the world. Recession was hitting his popularity ratings. And he would soon have a re-election campaign to fight.

'. . . Our agreement will dramatically reduce the number of troops carrying arms, dismantle the weapons systems, destroy the fears . . .' And relieve us both of the hideous cost, the General Secretary thought. Andreyev had his own battles to fight. Not that he was facing re-election, but that wouldn't save him if it all went wrong. And things inside Russia had a habit of going wrong recently. The long, empty years of the Living Dead, when the brain-defunct Brezhnev had tottered through the Kremlin stifling everything that moved, had left a dreadful legacy. Everyone agreed that they couldn't go on, not as they were, with confusion mounting throughout the empire and leaving a trail of riots and protest marches from Prague all the way to Red Square and the Moslem Republics beyond. They all knew there had to be change but getting agreement to change was something else entirely, and the years since Brezhnev's doctors had at last allowed his body to catch up with his brain had been a time of turmoil and indecision as the old guard had done bitter battle with the young reformers. In the end they had fought themselves to a temporary standstill and, faced with the prospect of burning separately or collectively on the nationalist bonfire, had reluctantly agreed to compromise. So they had passed the poisoned chalice to Andreyev, someone to piss on the flames. He was a man approaching seventy with a chronically weak stomach and no obvious angle to his politics apart from bureaucratic loyalty to the machine, a figurehead with bushy eyebrows and big ears and a crumpled face so full of wrinkles it made him resemble a bloodhound, a small stubby man with a quiet and occasionally ponderous manner which meant that he was often overlooked and underestimated. They all thought they could control him, or replace him at will once he had been thoroughly scorched on the flames. Yet he had surprised them. He may have been a bureaucrat and a loyalist, but he wasn't blind. History wasn't going to stop while they sorted themselves out. And it was because he knew the machine so well that he had been able to keep his colleagues and rivals off balance and at

21

bay, to push them forward step by patient step, even to push them into this arms agreement.

There were risks, of course, huge risks. Some of his colleagues argued that the only way to put out the fire was with the boot, but that couldn't work, not any more. The days had gone when you could use the Red Army as one huge assassination squad. After all, rivers of blood wouldn't stop the food queues. Yet it was an uneasy balancing act and they were waiting for him to stumble. Just before he had left for the summit had come the news that some poor sod of a Russian tax collector had wound up with a knife in his guts down some Armenian backstreet, and all hell had broken loose. The hardliners had said it showed he was too soft, the reformers that he was too slow; the only thing they had agreed upon was that Andreyev was to blame. And the US President thought he had problems.

He struggled to find a measure of consolation. At least the American's own troubles made it easier for Andreyev to rebuild fences, to compromise, to play for time and reach a deal without being taken advantage of. He desperately needed time. So he would wave at the Western cameras and sign the treaty, pray for a breathing space, take the huge foreign credits on offer and concentrate on getting rid of the queues which were so much part of every Soviet houswife's world. *Peace with pork bellies!* he shouted to himself, his smile growing more genuine with the thought.

His quiet celebration was brought to a halt by another sickening groan from the pit of his stomach. At this rate he would never make it through another party congress with its interminable speeches. He realized he was beginning to sweat. Damn! It would ruin the carefully applied makeup and his balding forehead would start glowing in the TV lights. Why on earth did he feel so nervous? Not because of the man who stood at the podium in front of him, nor because of the parchment documents which lay to one side on the baize-covered table where shortly they would sit for the signing ceremony. No, it was what lay behind him, back in Moscow, that really mattered.

He glanced to one side at his wife, Nadia. She was his second wife, nearly fifteen years younger than him, and Latvian rather than Russian, which had saved her from the thick-waisted plight of so many Muscovite women. It was an advantage she was not slow to exploit, and she stood with the American First Lady, each vying with the other for the accolades of the fashion critics. And then, a little farther behind, the plain and dumpy wife of Bykov, the chairman of his security service, the awesome KGB. He flinched. She ate too much garlic, had unsightly facial hair and was built to replace the oxen pulling the plough if the need arose. She was a Russian survivor like the millions of other *babky* who swept the roads and drove the trains and enabled the Soviet economy to creak through yet another winter. Andreyev needed women like that, even more than he found them personally disgusting. But he would rather her husband had come. He had asked Bykov to accompany him to Washington to show his tangible support for the accord, but Bykov had refused, claiming that someone must 'stay at home to look after the back yard' as he chose to refer to the nine million square miles of the Union of Soviet Socialist Republics. 'You can never be too careful,' the old dog had warned. 'My wife will go instead.'

Bykov's wife was now eyeing Nadia with a mixture of intense jealousy and quiet satisfaction. Jealousy because of her slim looks, her fashionable Western clothes and simple but expensive jewellery which only the wife of the General Secretary dare be seen wearing in public. And jealous most of all because she was the wife of the General Secretary. All this he understood and could cope with, but he did not care for the look of satisfaction which she cast over Nadia, like an old hag beside the guillotine who had just heard the sound of the approaching tumbril. Perhaps Bykov had told her something, had led her to believe she might soon be the wife of a new general secretary. His guts rumbled violently once more, forcing him to clench his buttocks for safety. What were they trying to tell him? Yes, he would have to be very careful when he got back to Moscow.

Berlin

Harold F. Benjamin Jr had the feeling it wasn't going to be his day. The flight from Eilat had been delayed when the young woman next to him had decided shortly before take-off that she couldn't bear to leave her new Israeli boyfriend, and with growing hysteria had insisted on leaving the aircraft. Pan Am's strict anti-terrorist rules had required that her baggage be taken off the plane with her. She had only one small suitcase, but it had taken an hour to find it in the Boeing's cargo holds. Sitting in the blazing Red Sea sun on the tarmac at over 120 degrees had quite overwhelmed the aircraft's air-conditioning and the crew's ability to cope. The new suit he had put on to mark the transition from brief Israeli holiday to official arrival in Berlin now both looked and felt as if he had been using it to clean cars.

Berlin was Harry's first posting abroad. He was still inside Tegel airport and already he was lost. He hadn't exactly expected a Marine guard of honour, but he thought that they might at least have sent a car. As he piled his luggage into the back of a battered taxi, he suspected that the views of Personnel had arrived ahead of him.

'You're smart, Benjamin, but not so damned smart as you think. You need the sharp edges kicked off you, and we know just the place for it. We're posting you to Berlin.'

Berlin: a tremor of foreboding had gone through him. It was punishment, of course, for making the life of his superiors a little too uncomfortable. They interpreted his lack of deference to established procedures as lack of respect, and Harry was always in too much of a hurry to bother lying to them. So they had given him Berlin, the tiny relic of a world war fought half a century ago stuck somewhere in the middle of the map of Europe, and so small they could have dropped it in the middle of Chesapeake Bay and the ripple wouldn't even have rocked the fishing boats. It had been years since anything of significance had happened in Berlin, a generation since John Kennedy had flown to the encircled former capital of the German Reich to proclaim *'Ich bin ein Berliner'*, with the American public rushing to applaud. They were years in which time seemed to have stood still for Berliners as their hopes of tomorrow, of fulfilling the heady promises of *détente* and *glasnost*, of being again one city, had somehow failed to arrive. Now it was all but forgotten, a fading relic of a faded era surrounded by rusting barbed wire and buried in its own paranoia. It was a memorial park for the dead and a burial ground for the ambitious, and that was why they had sent Harry here.

As he sat in the back of the taxi trying to ignore the attack being mounted on his suit by the freezing afternoon air, his thoughts once again went back to his father. Harold Senior had been born in Berlin. In 1935, at the age of ten, after a lifetime of taunts and bullying, he had been sent away to a distant American uncle, leaving behind both his fearsome but much respected father and his adored mother. Neither had survived the concentration camps, and with them had perished any chance Harold Senior had of finding pleasure or happiness in life.

Harry Junior had been an accident. His father had not wanted to risk inflicting on any other human being the nightmares of his childhood, or being responsible for yet another generation of suffering. But one day he found he had no choice, and Harry Junior had grown up in Columbus, Georgia, surrounded by the dark memories of a world far away which haunted his father until the old man's last hour. And they had all centred on Berlin.

During the flight, as for many weeks beforehand, Harry had wondered how it would feel to be 'home'. His father had always refused to talk about his childhood, unable to face the pain which would have come from ploughing up fields in his mind which had remained fallow and barren for all those years. He had been a remote and tormented man, unable to show his son the love and affection normally due to an only child but instead using him all too frequently as a target for his bitterness and anger.

Harry had tried hard to understand, but he couldn't. Yet now he had come to Berlin, and if he could actually see and touch his father's birthplace, then he might be able to understand, to forgive, and to stop secretly hating the man he so much wanted to love. If only he could blame the city instead . . .

He was supposed to have reported to his new boss

more than two hours ago, but the flight had already made him late. Harry always seemed to be late. Anyway, there seemed to be no problem, they would all be busy watching the televised signing ceremony in Washington. As the taxi drove out of the airport, an impulse made him decide to go looking for his father instead.

'Adalbertstrasse,' he instructed, and settled back into the seat of the car. The CIA's station chief in Berlin could do without him for another hour.

Lake Seliger, outside Moscow

The enormous log fire coughed and spat as Bykov rearranged the glowing embers with a huge leather boot before piling on more sweet-smelling chunks of spruce.

'Get me a drink,' he barked, 'and I suppose you'd better turn on the fucking television.'

Georgi Vassilievich Bykov, Hero of the Soviet Union and recipient of the Order of Lenin, chairman of the KGB, member of the Politburo of the Communist Party of the Soviet Union and veteran of the battles for Stalingrad, Warsaw and Berlin, was not in good humour. The female chauffeur rushed to pacify him. He had been silent since they had driven some three hours earlier out of the massive black iron gates of the KGB headquarters which stand, almost contemptuously, just beyond reach of the political overlords in the nearby Kremlin. The driver had taken him north-west into the Moscow hills, past the anti-ballistic-missile batteries which were hidden behind the industrial complexes of Kalinin and through the snowdrifts tracking the Osuga River, until they had reached his huge wooden *dacha* overlooking Lake Seliger. Only once had he spoken, briefly, to complain about the ventilation in his Mercedes, which was either too stuffy or let in the freezing, dank March air from the dark pine forests outside. Some idiot mechanic had shorted out the micro-sensor in the air-conditioning unit, and it was taking forever to get a replacement.

They had both arrived cold, and now he was intent on warming his ageing bones. It was her first trip with him, and she didn't know how to read his mood. But she had been well briefed. 'When in doubt, pour,' they had told her. It was sound advice. Within seconds of his barked instruction he was sipping at a large tumbler filled with *cha-cha*, his favourite brandy whose aroma took him back to lush green valleys as they carved their way through the mountains of his native Georgia. It was the memories of his childhood rather than its wicked alcoholic kick which normally brought out his more avuncular side, but tonight it seemed to make little difference as he watched the images of Andreyev and the US President acting out the signing ceremony half a world away. The open contempt with which Bykov curled his pencil-thin lips at the sight of the American head of state changed to a quieter but no less perceptible hostility as Andreyev took his cue cards from his pocket and began his response.

Bykov sat in his huge leather chair, not seeming to hear the words but gazing with a fixed, bitter stare at the face of his leader and rival. Even at sixty-three years of age Bykov displayed tremendous energy, with the muscle tone still evident beneath his general's uniform. The skin was stretched over his weathered face, his head was bald and bullet-shaped with a short neck which gave him the impression of a charging bull. They said he had grown his moustache to remind people of Stalin, to whom he bore a strong resemblance when wearing his officer's cap. He was not a man to be trifled with, in or out of uniform.

She stood nervously to one side, unsure what to do as mechanically he sipped the brandy from his glass until he had emptied it completely. Yet he did not put it down; he seemed not to notice, sitting there immobile, his thoughts captured by the flickering screen, drinking from an empty glass. Finally she could stand her uncertainty no longer. She rushed to put the entire bottle on the coffee table beside him, banging it down hard and nearly tipping it over in her haste. He started at the sound, his concentration broken just as Andreyev finished his speech to the applause of his audience and the ringing praise of the Soviet TV commentator. She stepped back in fear at what she saw. His gaze burned through her. His eyes had lost their normal bright, rather disrespectful light and were as cold as the darkest Siberian night, showing not a measure of compassion or pity. They were like the open gates to hell and she stood before him, trembling.

'I . . . I'm sorry, Comrade General,' she stammered.

Somewhere inside him a switch was thrown and in an instant his face came back to life. 'Sorry? Sorry for what? This is a night to celebrate, not to be sorry,' he exclaimed.

He poured himself another full measure of brandy and threw it back with a violent toss of his head before uttering a mighty roar and dashing the glass into the fireplace, where the flames soared as the remnants of the spirit exploded together with the glass.

'Bring us two fresh glasses,' he ordered, 'and turn that crap off. I don't need to watch them signing their names. I know they can bloody write; I've been forging both

29

their signatures for years!' He was laughing now, released from whatever spell had gripped him before.

In an instant the glasses were on the table, and she stood before him at rigid attention.

'Tell me, Comrade Lieutenant, how do you pack away those almighty tits of yours inside such a tight uniform?'

'I . . . I am proud to wear a KGB uniform, Comrade General,' she blushed.

'Well, it can't be good for you. Take it off. Pour us both a fresh drink. And stop being so damned military.'

'Do I take it that the Comrade General will not require driving back to Moscow this evening?' she enquired.

'*Nu pobljadushka*, that's the last thing I shall want tonight. Relax. That's an order!'

They had told her what would be required before they had assigned her to Bykov. Fifteen months of hard work in the driver's seat and on her back, with plenty of perks such as access to the exclusive GUM department store off Red Square and a posting of her choice at the end of the assignment – so long as she kept her mouth shut. In any event, she had thought, it couldn't be any worse than serving in the Outer Mongolian capital of Ulan Bator, a cold concrete mausoleum to socialism which seemed a million miles from Moscow, where she had spent ten awful, hungry months and had to screw the stores quartermaster just to get make-up and fresh food.

She was still standing to attention as he raised his barrel-like frame from the chair and began to unbutton her tunic, fumbling slightly as his huge labourer's hands tried to grasp the small, shiny metal buttons. The tunic fell to the floor and he started on her rough cotton blouse, finding even more difficulty with the tiny plastic buttons until, with a quiet curse of impatience, he had ripped it off her.

'Sorry,' he said. 'I'll get you a new one.'

Silk, she thought, as he unclipped her bra with more practised ease, and her breasts fell into his eagerly waiting hands.

'Shoulders back, chest out. Mustn't let our standards slip,' he chuckled.

'I think it's time to celebrate the new era of world peace, Comrade General,' she said.

He roared with delight, and led her towards the bedroom.

Washington D.C.

President William B. Michelle gazed through the thick green glass of the Oval Office window towards the Washington Monument and felt very happy with his day's work. The applause of the White House audience was still ringing in his ears and he knew it was being repeated across the nation. He had already instructed his advisers to rush through the opinion research to see how many points his rating had improved. Who knows, he mused, perhaps in a few years' time they would be erecting a monument to him – nothing elaborate, just something simple and tall, with a short inscription – 'Peace Maker'. He wondered whether they had signed the agreement in time to qualify for this year's Nobel Peace Prize, and turned to his companion for counsel.

He was perturbed to see that the other man did not appear to be joining in the general festivities.

'Leo, why the mournful face?'

Leo Grossman, the President's national security adviser, began to fiddle with the signet ring on his little finger, a habit which had followed him from the lecture hall at Harvard's Kennedy School of Government where he had been one of the more eminent members of the political science faculty. He often thought there was little difference between Harvard and Washington. In both places he spent his time controlling his impatience and lecturing to half-interested individuals with half-formed minds about the realities of modern international politics. Except at Harvard he had never had to deal with a student quite so distracted as William Michelle, whose mind was not only half-formed but seemed constantly to be fixed on matters other than those being discussed. Grossman had been trying for six months to concentrate the President's attention on the potential dangers of the East—West summit he had insisted on convening, but Michelle never seemed able to get his eyes above the level of opinion polls. Even in a year when he was coming up for re-election that was unforgivable. Grossman swallowed his impatience, and began his lecture once again.

'Mr President, you know I want this treaty as much as you do . . .' That had always been clear. After a controversial career spent reinterpreting history books, this was his chance to have them written according to his own script, and to take revenge for the years of condescension he had been forced to tolerate from the clans which inhabited the ivory towers clustered around Harvard Square, '. . . but it's vital that we get the details right. What you signed this morning was virtually a blank sheet of paper, an agreement to agree. Nothing more.'

'But we've agreed the principle of huge troop reductions in Europe. Damned historic, I'd say. Soviet troops being withdrawn behind their own borders, American boys coming back home. An end to super-power confrontation. So it will cost us a bit in foreign aid and credits to bale them out. What's wrong with that?'

'Plenty – if we don't get the details right. We haven't agreed what type of arms, or the precise number of arms to be cut, or the conditions for verification and a host of other major issues, let alone how much it's going to cost us . . .' Grossman's arms were waving in the air as they did at campus lectures to give added emphasis to his guttural, unattractive voice with its heavy middle-European tones which came from somewhere deep be-hind his tonsils. 'It was virtually a blank sheet of paper. All you have committed yourself to is negotiating and agreeing those details within six months.'

'But, Leo, think of the billions we'll save on military expenditure. We can afford to give them generous lines of credit and still have plenty left in the bank.'

'It's more than money, Mr President, much more. Europe is where all the great decisions are being made right now. Once we withdraw troops they'll be stuck in base camp on the other side of the Atlantic Ocean, yet at the first sign of trouble the Red Army could be there within a couple of hours. Just at the moment when Soviet colonies like Poland and Czechoslovakia seem bent on gaining a greater degree of independence, we could be handing them back to Moscow on a plate trussed up like Thanksgiving turkies – if we get the details wrong. Without proper safeguards we could dis-cover that all our financial aid has gone on nothing but strengthening the Red Army's grip on Eastern Europe. We cannot simply rely on handshakes and ex-pressions of goodwill. We must keep a strong foothold there!'

There was uncharacteristic passion in the academic's dry voice, and he visibly had to rein back before becoming more personal. 'And what's more, you're committed to coming up with an agreement just weeks before the presidential elections. It makes me very nervous. I'm not sure it's wise.'

'Why on earth not?' snapped Michelle. He had considerable regard for Grossman. The man was clever, indeed brilliant, and had a good record of spotting the flaws in some of the more harebrained proposals put to him by both State and the CIA. But why did the bloody man want to spoil today of all days, the President's special day of triumph?

'To negotiate the details of an agreement in the immediate run-up to an election takes all negotiating flexibility away from you. They will know you have to come up with an agreement before polling day, and they will squeeze you dry on the details. They'll have you over a barrel.'

'It's precisely because it's in the run-up to the election that makes the whole thing so damned perfect, Leo!' These bloody intellectual middle-Europeans never had any understanding for democratic politics. 'The best thing for this country's security is continued stability. That means my re-election. Let's face it, with the way the Fed and Treasury are screwing around with the recession I'm not going to get tumultuous public support for our handling of the economy. So we need this agreement.'

'General Secretary Andreyev is not facing elections, Mr President. He won't be the one to blink first.'

'Oh, don't you worry about Andreyev. He's got problems of his own. His economists have messed up even worse than ours, and some of those hardline sons-of-bitches in the Politburo are none too happy about the way he's carrying on with *glasnost*. He needs a major international agreement as much as we do.'

'But the details are crucial . . .'

'I pay you to fix the details, Leo.'

'In this case, it might be easier to fix the election.'

Lake Seliger

Bykov lay back on his pillow, smoking one of his disgusting peasant cigarettes which were handrolled in Baku. She still didn't know whether he really enjoyed the simple fruits of life or did it purely for effect, to emphasize the difference between his proletarian origins and the affected sophistication of the Andreyevs. But she had been warned not to underestimate him.

Idly she ran her fingers through the thick hair on his chest but she could already sense that his mind was elsewhere, no longer between the sheets. 'Did I . . . displease you, Comrade General?' she asked in trepidation. The earth hadn't exactly moved for either of them.

'You'll be fine,' he assured her, 'just as soon as you stop that comrade-general crap while we're in bed. It's difficult to screw you while you're standing to attention.'

'I . . . I'm sorry,' she said.

He took a swig of brandy and lit another cigarette. 'What do you think of the treaty?' he asked in a tone which made it sound as if he were asking the time. She shivered, she was now completely on her guard. High politics was a dangerous game to discuss with the head of the KGB, either in or out of bed.

'My father died in Afghanistan,' she responded carefully, trying to sense his mood and wanting to avoid a direct response. 'He was a helicopter pilot. Shot down by an American ground-to-air missile fired by the *mujahideen* terrorists. I find it very difficult to think of the Americans — all of a sudden — becoming our friends and allies . . .'

Bykov drew fiercely on his cigarette, expelling the smoke with a sigh which came from deep within. 'They are not our friends,' he said softly.

'But then, why . . . ?'

'Because our beloved General Secretary is a man of peace. Because he believes that great problems can be solved by talk. Because he never served at Stalingrad, or froze in Leningrad, or liberated the concentration camp at Treblinka. Because he is a fool . . .'

She was filled with terror. He was pulling her into outright condemnation of the General Secretary which at best could get her posted on guard duty to one of the *gulags* of the frozen Kamchatka Peninsula, and at worst could get her locked inside as one of the Forgotten Ones. She dared not contradict him, yet it was dangerous and disloyal to remain silent. And even if she were foolish enough to try, where could she complain about him — except to the KGB? Now she knew why his chauffeurs always kept their mouths shut.

'But then, why . . . ?' she repeated in a low whisper.

'Ha! All that today, you mean? The expressions of goodwill?' He took another deep lungful of tobacco. 'Because fortunately the Americans are even more naïve than he is.' He chuckled fiercely, but it held no humour. 'The struggle has not finished. It goes on. It's just that our deeply respected General Secretary and the American President don't realize it.'

'*Glasnost?*' she asked.

'*Glasnost!*' he roared. He was sitting up in bed now, punching the air with his thick forearms.

'*Glasnost* is the best fucking weapon we've ever invented. Remember Khrushchev? Of course you don't – before your time. That old bastard promised to bury the West in wheat. But instead our peasants starved. Then Brezhnev threatened to bury them in warheads, but they manufactured more.' He swallowed another mouthful of brandy. 'Now we are burying them in love, and already they're falling over themselves to lay down their arms and welcome our embrace. The fools!'

He gave an excited gesture as if strangling a chicken.

'So it's not all over?'

'Maybe for the General Secretary and for the Americans. But not for us!' he exclaimed. 'The struggle goes on. Talking of which . . .'

He ran a coarse palm over her breasts and down towards her navel. The humour had returned to his eyes. She nestled back among the bedclothes, preparing herself for the next onslaught with a sigh of resignation worthy of any survivor of a Siberian winter.

Berlin

'You sure you want Adalbertstrasse? In Kreuzberg?' the taxi driver asked Harry sceptically.

'Why? What's wrong?'

'Well, it's just . . . Kreuzberg's not the greatest part of town, if you know what I mean. You sure you haven't made a mistake?'

'No. No mistake. It's where my family used to live,'

he responded in a tone which told the driver to mind his own business.

As the taxi traced its path across Berlin, the driver studied his passenger carefully in the mirror. He was slightly under medium height – not short enough to be Napoleonic or even out of place in Middle Europe, but his slender frame seemed to be bursting with an energy which somehow overflowed and disrupted everything around him. The crumpled suit was out of place on a young man who looked as if he preferred jeans and running shoes to a collar and tie, and the tussles in his thick black hair stubbornly refused Harry's careless attempts to straighten them. From his mother he had inherited an easy smile full of strong white teeth, and from her father a square jaw which had a hint of stubbornness. Only his eyes bore the mark of his own father. They were deep set and dark, suggesting a sharp intelligence and a strength of passion which had captivated many young women and several of their mothers. When he stopped smiling, though, there was restlessness and fire in them, too. They made the taxi driver feel uneasy.

'You're the boss,' the cabbie replied, making his reluctance plain, and in silence they began the drive around the highway which circled the city centre.

It took only twenty minutes before they came off the ring road and had passed by the huge, curving Luftbrücke memorial to the Allied airlift which had saved the city in the days when world war had turned to cold war, and a Soviet blockade had tried to throttle the life out of West Berlin.

'They were terrible times,' the taxi driver said encouragingly. 'The Americans saved us.'

'Adalbertstrasse,' Harry repeated coldly, wondering if the ageing taxi driver could have been one of those who had made his father's schooldays such a misery, and suspecting that he was taking the long way round.

The driver drew back into his shell until five minutes later they hit the traffic intersection at Kotbusser Tor. As they passed the U-Bahn station, the Berliner announced, 'That's it.' He pointed ahead at a wide road running off the intersection, the entrance to which was guarded by a mountainous concrete warren of apartments, cafés and untidy shops, all of which bore the scars of a war which had been fought with aerosols between a multitude of competing protest groups.

'Drive slowly,' Harry ordered, and the car crawled its way along the kerb.

It was not what he had expected. His father's family had been doctors and, although they had remained among their patients in the blue-collar district of Kreuzberg, their home had been a substantial one. The buildings which crowded alongside the pavement had indeed once been grand affairs, proud statements of the confidence which the architects of the Prussian capital had felt in the days of the last century when it had been one of the greatest cities of Europe. But now the paint peeled and the masonry crumbled, covered in blisters and lurid graffiti which completely overwhelmed any trace of the street's former pride.

Women who were dressed in sombre, unfamiliar clothing and headscarves watched idly from the doorways and street corners; the shopfronts bore undecipherable names and sold unGermanic goods, and even behind the closed windows of the car he could detect the discordant, stringy sounds of music of the bazaar echoing across the street.

'The Turkish quarter,' the driver explained, 'I did warn you.'

Harry tried hard to imagine what it must have been

like in his father's time, but failed. He had strong preconceptions about Berlin, but none of them matched the strange and exotic reality which now confronted him. This was not the tinselly Berlin of the guide books.

They were proceeding up the street now, towards the section where his father had lived. They passed dusty electrical repair shops with windows full of old appliances and supermarkets piled high with crates of vegetables and brightly coloured fruit which spilled on to the street. As he looked from side to side, Harry saw the washing laid out on the window sills to dry, the overcrowded courtyards which appeared fleetingly off the alleyways between the houses, and dark-eyed urchins who played inside battered old cars which had been stripped for spare parts and left abandoned at the roadside. He could not find his father here. Perhaps it will change as we drive on, he was thinking, when the driver drew the taxi to a halt and firmly engaged the brake.

'What's the matter? Why aren't you going on?' Harry asked in annoyance.

'Where to go?'

Harry took his eyes off the houses and their inhabitants and looked once again down the street. Their path was blocked by a shabby, ugly construction, covered in garish murals and even more graffiti, which slashed right across the street and brought it to a complete and illogical halt. The row of houses came to an abrupt end as if their neighbours had fallen over the edge of a cliff, and the split had been roughly cemented over to prevent the others following. It was like a sandcastle whose childish builder had suddenly become bored and, so that no one else might enjoy it, had taken a spade and with a huge sweep had battered half of it back into the sand. Harry was getting his first glimpse of the Wall.

'It's not how I expected . . .'

Harry clambered out of the taxi to get a closer look. He approached nervously, like a small boy at the fence of a forbidden orchard. Tentatively, with more than a trace of apprehension, he reached out and touched. This was it? The Wall was shambolic, with handfuls of mortar thrown at and around it, and cracks of daylight peering through the joints where the mortar had missed. It seemed to have been created with all the precision of a farmyard chicken coop. It had been so easy to believe that the Wall had been consigned to the history books. But this wasn't history. History wasn't covered in graffiti.

From the top of a pile of rubble which children used as a playground, Harry could gain a full view into the East. The buildings there seemed to be so close, not much more than a hundred yards away. He could even see people walking in the streets – his father's streets – arguing and gesticulating with each other, and an old housewife dressed in black who was washing up at an apartment window – his grandmother, perhaps? But his grandmother was dead, like so many others who had lived here.

On the other side of the Wall there were many signs of construction. Harry had heard back in Langley of this perverse twist to *glasnost*. The border was being sanitised. Not removed, but hidden and obscured, to help impress the tourists and foreign businessmen with their wallets full of hard currency. The ugly and ancient barbed wire and concrete barriers which ran parallel to the Wall on the Eastern side were being taken down and replaced with high technology and infra-red scanners, much less visible, yet far, far more effective at alerting the border guards and dog patrols to any disturbance.

No-man's-land, where so many had died, was now a broad stretch of sand, white and inoffensive. The anti-personnel mines which had ripped apart so many would-be escapers and blasted them all over the front pages of Western newspapers had been removed and the whole area was waiting to be landscaped with plants and low-lying shrubs. Soon from the East the disguise of the frontier barriers would be complete.

The contrast with the shabbiness of the Wall on the Western side was overwhelming. Away to his left a young woman in a bright yellow boiler suit and an oversized anorak was standing a yard from it, staring, pensive, concentrating hard – like a devotion in front of the Wailing Wall, Harry thought – until from her satchel she produced a spray can and began painting a new creation to cover the many layers of Wall-art which had gone before. 'God Doesn't Live Here' she scrawled in huge, misshapen letters. Here, in front of the Wall, Harry could believe it.

The girl gave a nod of self-approval, pocketed the spray can and began wandering in his direction. As she approached she smiled, but he didn't respond. He felt numb.

'You OK?' she enquired. She was in her early twenties, with bleached white hair cropped close to her skull. The anorak looked as though it had shared at least two previous owners.

'I . . . I'm looking for my father,' he muttered, still in another world.

She glanced up and down the Wall and shrugged her shoulders.

'Your first time?' she asked.

'I somehow never imagined it like this,' he said softly. 'I suppose you get used to it . . .'

'Not if you live here, you don't. Never,' she contradicted. She looked at him curiously from under a huge amount of eyeshadow, with her every word accompanied by the rattling of several oversized bangles on her wrists. 'You want a go?' she suggested, proffering the spray can.

Harry shook his head slowly, still gripped in the spell cast by the Wall.

'What's it like on the other side?' asked Harry, thinking of his father once more.

'Don't really know. Haven't been over for ages. Why should I? Got no friends there. Food's awful and I hate the opera.' She stopped to roll herself a cigarette from a small leather pouch she carried around her neck, moistening her lips to shape and fix the thin paper tube and carefully retrieving every loose strand of tobacco for later use. 'But that's not really the point. It's more a matter of principle. Why should I pay good money for a stinking visa to visit my own country? It's no better than being a serf in the Middle Ages. You go through a checkpoint, bow and scrape to the border guards, pay for your visa, convince them you're not trying to smuggle out every piece of subsidised sausage they produce or smuggle in heroin or AIDS, and even when you've done all that they can still turn you away if they don't like the look of your face. Or give you a body search if they feel like a cheap thrill.' She shook her shoulders as if trying to shake off a distasteful memory. 'It's still a frontier, even if they let you cross it. Kick it and you'll break your bloody foot. They all call themselves Germans, but it still marks where one politician's turf finishes and another's starts. Bastards. East, West, they're all the same, the stupid bastards.'

'Isn't that a little cynical?' he asked.

'Is it?' she responded quietly. 'Then you tell me why it's still here.'

There was a long silence. Harry felt out of his depth

43

and the numbness began to descend on him again, but she responded with an encouraging smile.

'Here, do you want to go for a drink or something?'

'Sorry, I can't,' he muttered, waving in the direction of his taxi.

'Suit yourself.' She started on her way once more before glancing back over her shoulder. 'Hope you find your father.'

Harry watched as she disappeared into the distance, the sound of her jangling bracelets marking her way. Her parting words left him feeling empty and alone. Find his father? As a child, particularly after his mother had died, Harry had longed to be taken into his father's arms and to be read stories, to be held like other children and told he was loved. Yet even though his father might be in the same room, his mind and his heart were constantly elsewhere. In another world. In Berlin.

Getting to know the place would change all that, he had told himself. A chance to learn, to understand, to go back to his father's world and to bury the resentment. At last he would be able to forgive. Yet as Harry gazed around him, he knew this was not his father's world, just a city with two lives and a troubled soul, divided by an expanse of dirty concrete against which scruffy kids played football and over which they scrawled rude tales about each other. For the children of new Berlin the Wall was a playground; for their parents a constant reminder of just how insignificant and inconsequential their lives were in the hands of the superpowers. It was not what Harry had expected. This was not a place of heroics and intrigue; he would find no explanations here. He felt cheated. He wasn't going to be able to see and touch his father's hidden memories after all.

Suddenly he felt very American and knew he was a long way from home.

'The American Mission,' Harry ordered, and slumped back into his seat in a foul mood. It really wasn't his day. His mind wandered back to Angie.

It seemed like a lifetime ago in another world but it had been only hours since they had said goodbye at Eilat airport. They had shared a great physical relationship which had started seven months before when they met at a barbecue in Virginia and he invited her back for coffee. Once through the front door they hadn't even made it as far as the kitchen, and many nights and every weekend since then they had shared the simple pleasures of being young and free. But that's all it was. Neither had said so, but both knew that their trip to the Red Sea would be the end of it. Harry would have at least three years in Europe, Angie would go back to law school in Georgetown, and there was no point in promising to wait. Neither would. She had decided to stay on an extra week after Harry left, and even now he imagined she was probably taking free lessons from the scuba instructor whose trunks had tightened every time he saw her.

A dark mood of self-pity settled over Harry long enough to distract him from the fact that the taxi had slowed to a crawl as it meandered its way through a throng of people who were spilling on to the street. The old bastard of a driver was clearly giving him the expensive, scenic route and the taxi was now skirting the Tiergarten, the patchy remnants of an old hunting park which had once bordered the Kaiser's palace and which now provided a green lung in the heart of modern West Berlin. The crowds grew steadily thicker until the taxi had been brought to a near-halt as people from all

45

sides seemed to be converging on one spot within the Tiergarten. There were old men wrapped up against the cold and leaning on walking sticks, young children with bright pink faces grasping the hands of their parents; there were *Hausfrauen*, mechanics in their overalls and office workers. All the inhabitants of Berlin seemed to be descending on this one place. Many held torches which were beginning to shine brightly as the winter dusk gathered.

'What's going on?' Harry demanded. He was now four hours late for his appointment with his new boss, and if he didn't make it within the next twenty minutes the office would be closed for the night.

'A little Berlin miracle,' the driver said in a soft voice. 'You wouldn't understand.'

'Try me.'

The taxi had come to a complete halt against the human tide, and the driver lowered the window to smile and wave at a group of young schoolchildren before replying.

'Your President signed an agreement today which he said brought an end to confrontation. If we have no confrontation, we don't need the Wall. So we don't need East and West any longer or foreign troops in our backyard – just Berlin. One city. The people of Berlin are gathering to say thank you, like a long nightmare coming to an end.'

'But the agreement said nothing about the Wall.'

'The agreement didn't say much about anything,' commented the driver with a hint of sarcasm. 'But if it means anything at all it's got to mean an end to that damned frontier – very soon.'

Harry was perplexed. There was nothing about this in the briefing he had received back in Langley and he was certain the dismantling of the Wall hadn't even

46

been discussed. Yet he found the simple logic of the taxi driver irritatingly compelling. 'So who organized this demonstration?'

'Organized? No one. When you've been locked in a cage for nearly fifty years and some bastard comes and rattles the keys, d'you really think we Berliners need to be given instructions before we get off our asses to give thanks? No. We've waited a long time for this moment. No one needed to organize a celebration. It's just happening.'

'But there was no mention at the summit of pulling down the Berlin Wall,' Harry persisted in some confusion.

'Precisely,' said the driver with a hint of anger in his voice. 'Peace to all mankind, so long as it doesn't include Berliners, eh? No, mister. We've been dumped on the scrapheap too often in the past, and we're not going to let you forget it now. If your Michelle and that shit Andreyev can kiss and hug each other, I want the right to do the same thing with my brother without getting permission from the Kremlin or the White House first. And that's what all of Berlin's saying tonight.'

'You have a brother over in the East?' Harry asked in a more subdued voice.

'And two sisters. And almost every native Berliner has a brother or sister or aunt or mother on the other side. It's time to finish with all these sides. No more border, no more Wall. If we want to be one family again, that's our business, no one else's. The rest of the world may have other ideas, but Texas will freeze before we let you forget!'

There was a defiant mood in the driver's voice which made a deep impression on Harry. As more people swarmed around the taxi before disappearing into the Tiergarten, Harry took another look at his watch and shrugged his shoulders. There was no chance of getting to the office now before it closed. Anyway, this seemed a good chance to learn something about Berlin which he couldn't get out of a dossier. He took several notes from his wallet and thrust them at the driver.

'Here. Take my luggage to the Hotel Schweizerhof. I'm getting out here. And thanks for the ride.' The driver took the money without a word.

Harry began to mingle with the steady stream of people who were disappearing into the Tiergarten along the pathways of the ancient park. It was a few minutes before he saw where they were all headed. Rising out of the trees ahead of him, like a beacon shining in the dark Berlin sky, the Victory Tower drew them all forward. The tall, cylindrical monument had been erected to mark some ancient Prussian military success and atop it, bathed in floodlights, stood the winged goddess of victory: Golden Ilse, as she was known and loved by Berliners. Beneath her flared and gilded skirts they gathered, thousands of them, as if drawn by a command which only native Berliners could hear.

The traditional street lights adorning the Tiergarten shone warmly on the gathering, brightened still further by the lamps and candles held in the gloved hands of almost everyone there. Happy faces radiated a quiet excitement. Small groups of people were singing traditional folk songs, everyone seemed to know his neighbour, and a quiet celebration was under way without anyone being in charge. As Harry watched, more people came out of the trees and crowded into the traffic intersection beneath the Tower until it seemed possible that the crush might get out of hand. Suddenly, as if someone had pulled a lever and without any word being uttered, the crowd began to flow in orderly fashion down the broad boulevard which led away from the foot of the monument. They linked arms and smiled at one another, their candles and torches thrust out in front of them to light the way.

Harry was swept along in their midst. Beside him an elderly couple held the hands of their granddaughters who sang and skipped and laughed so much that their candles nearly blew out. To the other side shuffled an ancient veteran, his long, thick moustaches drooping beneath his chin, almost touching the row of medals which he wore proudly on his overcoat and which sparkled in the light. In front of Harry, chatting like old friends, walked a park-keeper still wearing his working clothes and a businessman whose immaculate mohair coat looked as if it would have cost the other at least a month's wages. All of Berlin seemed to be here. There was an old *Oma* wrapped up in her dark shawl against the growing chill of the winter night, supported by a teenage girl with more ear-studs than teeth and a shock of spiky green hair. Tears were running down the old woman's cheeks, and for a moment Harry thought that the cold bite of the evening air was too much for her. But they were tears of happiness and excitement, an excitement which had brought Berliners together, touching all ages and classes and making them one. There was a tremor of magic running through the crowd which Harry found difficult to understand yet impossible to mistake.

As the great body of people moved slowly forward, away to his left Harry saw the dark, forbidding outline of a war memorial and behind it loomed the infamous Reichstag, the old parliament building where Hitler had screamed and ranted and proclaimed his thousand-year Reich, and where just a few winters later Russian soldiers had scrambled over the rubble to plant their flags of victory. And before him, looming out of the sky, glowered the Brandenburg Gate, the triumphal arch which stood at the very heart of old Berlin in the days when it had been one of Europe's proudest capital cities. It was the symbolic centre of Germany, through which incessant victory parades had once passed and foreign emissaries had scurried. That was why the Russians had chosen to lay the first bricks of the Wall directly in front of the Gate, so that it now stood just yards inside the Eastern sector, mocking West Berliners with its alien flags, a monument to a dismembered nation.

The head of the procession had reached the area of the Wall in the shadow of the Gate, and marchers began to spread out along its length. The two West Berlin policemen on patrol did not intervene. A wooden crate appeared from somewhere and, as Harry watched, a man climbed on it to place his candle on top of the Wall. It was soon joined by other candles and torches passed up from the crowd. A flickering glow began to spread along the top of the Wall, growing brighter with each passing minute. Small stepladders, park benches and other crates began to appear from all around, anything which might be used for people to reach up. The Wall seemed like a battered rock as the tide of Berliners swept defiantly against it, leaving their lights to shine into the East before retreating to make way for the next wave.

From somewhere within the crowd Harry heard the soft voice of a woman reaching for the words of the national anthem – the same defiant chords to which his father must have listened even though they carried a modern, less menacing refrain. The singing swelled as others joined in, and Harry wondered how long it had been since the German anthem had been sung with such passion on this spot.

On the other side of the Wall the *Volkspolizei*, uncertain of what was happening, quickly dispersed the handful of youths who had begun to shout their encouragement. But Harry heard later that the light from the candles and torches which were left that night on the Wall could be seen for almost a mile down Unter den Linden, right into the very heart of East Berlin. Thousands of East Berliners saw this gesture of unity and many hundreds of thousands more had heard of it before dawn broke.

He watched as the punk with the green hair reached out to place the old lady's candle alongside the others on top of the Wall, before turning to smile at her elderly companion and hug her. They walked away hand in hand. Harry noticed that the old lady wasn't crying any more.

The White House

The light burned bright in the basement office housing the President's National Security Adviser. As happened on many long nights, Grossman was alone with his thoughts, trying to make order out of a chaotic and unruly world. He sat in front of a large laminated map of Europe. He had been there several hours, scarcely moving as he concentrated, a dark furrow chiseled deep into his brow, his unfashionable three-piece suit reduced to a crumple. A cup of coffee stood cold and untouched on the table beside him. The only indication of the energy with which he was attacking the problem was the rapid blinking of his eyelids and his short, shallow breathing. He needed no papers, no briefing material, no computer terminal to help him; all the evidence he needed was on the map before him, and in the generations of experience locked deep away within him.

Midnight had long since passed when he took one deep, trembling breath and exhaled slowly. Perhaps there was a way, after all. Keeping a foothold, a strong American presence, some way of preventing Central Europe crumbling to dust and turning the last fifty years on their head. Yes, perhaps there was a way.

He pulled himself out of his chair and straightened his back before moving to the map and drawing a circle, so small and insignificant that it was almost lost in the vast stretches from the Atlantic to the Urals. A special case. An exception. An anomaly left over from the war which might yet hold the key to the future, and prevent another war. A place belonging to no one, and yet to everyone.

Berlin.

As long as they held on to Berlin, they could continue to cling on to the reins in Europe.

He smiled in satisfaction before picking up his overcoat and switching out the light.

TWO

Lake Seliger

As dawn broke over the Moscow hills, Georgi Bykov had already been awake for several hours. He knew he needed to make two important decisions. The first was pleasurable and had been confirmed several times in the comfort of his bed since the previous evening. His new chauffeur would do very nicely.

He was still anguishing over the second, and time was running out. Andreyev would shortly finish his sightseeing tour of the United States which had followed the signing ceremony – 'getting to know our new friends', as he told the Western press – and would be back in Moscow very soon. It would not wait.

He had forsaken the warmth of his *dacha* and had set out along the track which ran beside the shore of Lake Seliger with his handpicked bodyguards trailing a respectful twenty yards behind. The lake was still solid ice as he crunched through the crisp snow, but already his trained eyes could see the signs of life returning to the woodlands as the bark of the birch trees began to regain its silvery lustre and the copses echoed once more to the chorus of newly arrived birds. The sun would soon begin to regain its heat, the water would flow again, spring would be here. Life in Russia is never quite what it seems, he mused, yet somehow remains the same no matter which Tsar rules. In his native Georgia, the peasants still reaped the harvest and smuggled the contraband over the mountains to Turkey and Iran, just as they had been doing for hundreds of years. Except now they used tractors and diesel trucks instead of donkeys.

Andreyev wanted change. Not uncontrollable chaos like some of the younger hotheads, but change nonetheless. The first sign of unrest amongst the cadres in Kiev or nationalist riots in Uzbekistan and there he was, blaming the old guard, criticising their ways as being harsh and inefficient, mouthing stern words about lawbreakers and threatening to clamp down on agitators, yet at the same time promising still further reforms. And the more he promised, the more they demanded. They'd already had the shirt off his back; now they wanted his trousers. And they would get them, too.

Andreyev was weak. Instead of trying to halt the rush into anarchy he was content simply to slow it down, using a smile and a soft glove instead of the iron fist which all great states occasionally needed. He was like an early spring, bringing the promise of summer while the ground beneath was still frozen solid, encouraging the blossom to break and the new plants to burst forth, only to discover they had been betrayed and were back once more in the destructive vice of a Russian winter, deceived and destroyed. He would destroy Russia, or at least the Russia which Bykov had fought for and his comrades had died for throughout those long, dreadful campaigns of the Great Patriotic War. That's why Bykov had built his *dacha* up here in the hills, much farther out of Moscow than most of his Politburo colleagues, because up here nothing changed. And Bykov didn't want change.

He thought once more about the report he had received on last night's scenes at the Wall, and made up his mind. He would call them together – tomorrow, before Andreyev came home waving his scrappy bit of paper.

54

Harry was late. He wasn't sure how late because he didn't know precisely when the staff of the US Mission on Clayallee normally got to work. He guessed nine o'clock and had tried to get in at a quarter to, but the jet lag and excitement of the night before had put him out. It was gone nine-thirty before he arrived breathless and ruffled in the entrance hall asking for the special assistant to the US Commandant, the title given to the CIA's chief of station in what acted as the American embassy for a city still technically under Allied military occupation and supervision. It didn't help when he discovered from the guard on duty that most people had already been in the office for more than an hour and a half.

The guard escorted him to the second floor and propelled him into an outer office where a middle-aged woman sat at a secretarial desk browsing through a file. She looked pinched and serious, and Harry decided to bring a little glamour into her life by flashing one of his most reassuring smiles.

'Hi, I'm Harry Benjamin. I guess I'm a little late,' he said, his southern drawl becoming more pronounced as it often did when he met women for the first time.

The woman studied her watch intently. 'Nearly eighteen hours late to be precise, Mr Benjamin.'

Harry's smile remained fixed and bright, but this old bird was clearly going to be a tough one to crack.

'Another six hours and we would have had a serious alert,' she continued. 'We don't like it when an agency officer goes missing in Berlin.' She eyed his unruly collar-length hair with disfavour. There was a parting hiding in there somewhere over which Harry had taken great trouble only an hour earlier, but by now his hair had reverted to its normal imitation of a wild hedgerow. 'I trust you have an explanation?'

'Well, there was this rather pretty girl sitting next to me on the plane . . .' he began with what he hoped would be winning informality, before realizing that there was little point in continuing. He gave a guilty shrug of the shoulders. 'Not the best start, I'm afraid. And I understand the chief can be a bit of an old dragon . . .'

At that moment the outer door opened and a young woman came in bearing a tray of coffee. 'Would you like this in your office, Miss Pickerstaff?' she asked. The older woman nodded and the tray was taken into the inner room. Harry knew this was not going to be his day.

'You are . . . ? he enquired, already knowing the uncomfortable answer.

'Mary Pickerstaff,' the woman responded drily. 'Special assistant to the Commandant, otherwise known as chief of station. And your boss.'

Harry followed meekly as she led the way into a large office which had very little furniture and even less character. Everything was functional and antiseptic without even a photograph or newspaper to give a clue to the character of the occupant.

'Sit down,' she instructed and Harry did so, hoping that someone would pull a handle and propel him through a hole in the floor. Miss Pickerstaff, mid-forties, unmarried, shrewish, and immensely proud of the efficiency which had brought her through the ranks to a position of considerable responsibility, started punching away at the computer terminal which stood on her desk, and which clearly contained reference to Harry.

'Benjamin, Harold. Twenty-eight. Born in Columbus, Georgia. PhD in security studies from the Fletcher School in Boston. Joined the agency two and a half years ago. Your first posting abroad. Not a good start to be late on your first – or rather second day, is it?' She turned her grey eyes from the screen towards Harry. 'Do you know why they sent you here, Benjamin?' she demanded.

Harry realized that his smile was frozen into a useless, lopsided grin which had become entirely redundant. He put it away, and tried to think how on earth he could correct the damage he had inflicted on his career during the last five minutes.

'No, ma'am.'

'You got sent here because I run a tight ship. There's no room on my team for cocky young graduates who think they've learned it all from behind a desk in Langley and who aren't either able or willing to realize that intelligence work is a matter of patience, organization and hard work. And of taking orders. I know Berlin, you don't. I know intelligence work, you don't. If you do as I say you will learn something which might make a good career officer out of you. If you don't you will be out. Is that clear?'

'Yes, Miss Pickerstaff.'

'Your status will be that of commercial analyst. That's the lowest of the low so don't get any grand ideas. We're a small section here in Berlin, what with all the cutbacks, so there's a lot of ground to cover and a lot of work to be done. You will be responsible for looking after economic intelligence on West Berlin. Make a success of that and in nine months or so you can take on similar responsibilities for the Eastern sector. In the meantime, you will keep your nose clean and out of East Berlin. Is that clear?'

'I was hoping to make a visit . . .'

'No chance. No trips to the Eastern sector for at least six months, and then only under strictest supervision. This is not the 1950s with its pulp fiction of clandestine trips into the East to smuggle out blueprints and atomic scientists. This is *glasnost*, which means we step very carefully on each other's turf. If they had thought you were suited for hazardous field duty they would have sent you to Syria or Angola. But they didn't. So no bright ideas. Understood?'

Harry was on the point of explaining about his father, but decided that if she didn't know already it would certainly not help his precarious situation, so he kept quiet. He would try to be patient.

'West Berlin should provide more than enough excitement for me, Miss Pickerstaff. After last night . . .'

'What have you read about last night?'

'Read? Nothing. I was there.'

'You saw the demonstration?'

'I practically took part in it. I saw it all,' said Harry with some measure of pride. He wouldn't need to get this intelligence from a dusty file.

'You participated in that mob? Before reporting here? Without authorization?'

Shit, Harry muttered to himself. He'd done it again.

'Benjamin, for Chrissake you're not an undercover agent. I thought I'd just made that abundantly clear. Walking about with a quarrelsome crowd of agitators is not going to teach you what Berlin is all about.' She buried her head in her hand in a sign of genuine despair, and Harry decided it was not the best moment to contradict her description of what he had seen.

'We want chaos in Berlin about as much as we need another cut in our appropriations. I don't like mobs, and I don't like my officers encouraging them. We trade in certainty, not confusion. As soon as there's a crisis or another screaming headline which we've failed to predict, do you know where our paymasters back on Capitol Hill lay the blame? On us. The intelligence services. You and me. So I like stability. Which means I won't tolerate guerrilla warfare on my patch!'

He tried his best to look contrite.

'Benjamin, I'm going to try, very hard, to forget this morning ever happened. Frankly I would prefer not to see you for at least another week, but unfortunately I was unwise enough to get you invited to a small dinner party this evening being given by Edward Schumacher. He's a senior Berlin businessman and *Vorsitzender* or chairman of the city's governing party. He also happens to be a rather good friend of ours in this Mission. Over the years he has used his trading contacts with the East to provide us with a good deal of useful information, and he's extremely well connected on this side of the border. He'll have a small group of influential people around the table tonight and I thought it would be a useful introduction for you. You will accompany me, keep your mouth buttoned and your ears open. So smarten yourself up. And don't make me regret it!'

Harry departed feeling distinctly rattled. He suddenly felt out of his depth. He'd been in Berlin less than twenty-four hours, and already the confidence and certainties he had brought with him were being assailed from all sides. What was worse, he was no longer even certain who the enemy was.

The West Berlin carved out of the Soviet zone of occupation after the war was a tiny oasis scarcely a dozen miles wide with a prevailing air of uncertainty about what tomorrow might bring. Berliners lived for today, and especially for tonight, like panthers prowling restlessly inside a great urban cage, never seeming to rest. The night life was renowned for its variety and indulgence, and amongst the most indulgent of Berlin's nightspots was Kempinski's, where the city's rich and famous took their cares and credit cards in an attempt to lose them both amidst the sparkle of fine German crystal and the enticing bouquets of the restaurant's huge wine list.

Harry's determination to be on time had almost worked, but he had cut himself shaving and at the last moment was forced to change his shirt. When he arrived five minutes after the appointed time in a grey suit which showed all the signs of having spent two weeks in a much-travelled suitcase, he was disconcerted to find his fellow diners already seated and one empty seat beckoning accusingly in their midst. What was worse, they were all wearing formal evening dress.

The smile on Miss Pickerstaff's lips looked as if it had been carved with an ice chisel as she introduced him to their host.

'Herr Schumacher, may I introduce one of my new assistants. Henry Benjamin. He's . . . new to Berlin,' she added, as if by way of apology.

'I can see that,' commented Schumacher as he took a long, cool look at Harry's floral tie before tardily extending a stiff hand. Harry could smell the whiff of alcohol on his host's breath as he spoke; Schumacher had obviously not wasted his time while waiting for Harry to arrive. 'Welcome, Mr Benjamin. Allow me to introduce my other guests.'

He went around the table making the formal introductions. There was Otto Strelitz, a prominent local businessman, accompanied by a young blonde whose smile got lost in her cleavage and who most clearly was not his wife; two couples whose names Harry didn't

60

catch as he tried to take his mind off Strelitz's companion; 'And, finally, as a new friend, you have the place of honour: next to my wife.'

Harry sat down, hugely conscious of his improper dress and feeling like a pilchard in a bowl of caviar. He turned to mutter further apologies to his neighbour, Frau Schumacher. She was a few years younger than her husband, perhaps about forty Harry reckoned, and a woman who had matured with stunning elegance. She was graceful, like a bird – a pink flamingo, Harry thought, which knows no way of doing things other than supremely gracefully. She held her head high, her voice was full of melody and her reddish copper hair glinted with fire in the candlelight, like a flamingo at sunset. She was bright, altogether unlike the ponderous and heavy character of the typical Berliner. She didn't fit; she was different. And instinctively Harry decided that he liked her. She was laughing now, the end of her nose twitching in merriment as Harry struggled to suggest that the luggage with his dinner jacket had yet to arrive.

'Don't worry, Mr Benjamin. As we say in Berlin, worse things have happened on the walk to Canossa. Germans have a tradition through the centuries of getting the important things wrong and having to eat humble pie. You must forgive us if we occasionally enjoy a little amusement at others' expense.'

Harry tried to retain a semblance of dignity, but her smile was infectious and soon they were both laughing together. At the far end of the table, other diners at Kempinski's were stopping to exchange noisy words and handshakes with Schumacher, who was clearly well known. Miss Pickerstaff, seated next to him, appeared to be basking in the reflected attention.

'Berlin is like one great family,' Harry's companion

explained. 'There are less than two million people here, it's smaller than your own Manhattan Island, and everybody seems to know everyone else. There are few strangers in a town like ours.'

Harry noticed that Frau Schumacher was looking with a mischievous gleam at Strelitz's blonde companion, who somehow felt the need to adjust her dress straps and reveal even more of her ample cleavage every time a new man approached the table. He realized that he was staring just a little too hard at the performance, and looked back to find Frau Schumacher no longer able to control her laughter. Once again he could not prevent himself joining in the merriment at his expense, and the rest of the table turned to discover what they found so amusing. He had known this woman for less than five minutes, yet already he knew they shared a sense of humour and a well-developed touch of irreverence which would be enough to get them through the most boring of diplomatic evenings. Harry was delighted to discover that not all of Berlin was frost and formality.

He glanced around from the laughing face of Frau Schumacher to notice her husband looking at them both from the other end of the table. The host flashed a short smile, but Harry felt no warmth in it. Schumacher was scarcely taller than his wife, with a squat and rather corpulent figure which betrayed his middle-European origins and the excesses of years of living at the top. His mouth had a downward cast and a thick lower lip which protruded just a little too far from his fleshy face, suggesting petulance, and when he spoke in a deep, rough voice he revealed a small gap between his front teeth which Harry thought made him look predatory. After all, this was a man who had succeeded both in business and in politics, a man used to getting his own way. Yet as Harry examined him carefully, he thought he noted signs at odds with this image of solid security. Schumacher had a quick, darting expression which never seemed to come to rest, and fingers which toyed constantly with the signet ring he wore on one of the thick fingers of his left hand. He seemed full of inner tension, Harry decided, like a man always in the public spotlight who is never able to relax. Schumacher had ordered himself yet another drink, and his ruddy features were beginning to glow as he continued to stoke the alcoholic fire within him. Harry was glad he had been paired with the wife.

No one asked Harry what he wanted to eat; the meal had obviously been chosen beforehand, and a team of well-regimented waiters began fussing around the table. The wine steward arrived with a bottle already opened and began pouring a sweet German hock into the glasses. Harry covered his glass with his hand; he found most German wines tasted like melted lollipops, and asked for a beer instead.

'Not trying the wine, Mr Benjamin?' growled Schumacher from the other end of the table. He had a resonant voice which came from deep within his chest, and even his quietly spoken words carried clearly across the noisy room.

'I prefer beer.'

'But I insist,' responded Schumacher, paying no attention to his guest. 'It's an excellent hock. Pour him a glass,' he instructed the wine steward.

Harry's hand went out once again to cover his glass, but the wine steward was clearly more in awe of Schumacher than some dishevelled-looking foreigner, and the result was a glassful of wine poured over the back of Harry's hand and on to the immaculate table setting around him. The blonde twittered in amusement at the chaos while Harry and Schumacher glowered at each other. A waiter mopped up the mess as best he could, and the wine steward returned with a fresh glass which he had taken care to ensure was brimming with more wine. As he placed it in front of Harry, Schumacher gave another cold smile.

'I hope you enjoy your wine, Mr Benjamin.' The German was clearly claiming victory in their private battle of wills.

'I'm sure I shall,' replied Harry, defiantly picking up a glass of mineral water instead. But he was not to get off so easily. Strelitz had been matching Schumacher drink for drink, and decided he wanted to join the hunt.

'A toast,' he said, raising his glass. 'To the treaty.' He was clearly intent on forcing Harry to drink.

'Even though it made no mention of Berlin?' prompted Harry quickly.

It was a deliberately provocative comment couched in impertinent terms, and he could feel the *frisson* of hostility around the table aimed at him. Miss Pickerstaff's withering look he had expected, yet the frigid stares he was receiving from the other end of the table were more of a surprise. Still, they had started throwing stones in the pond; they had to expect some ripples.

There was no trace of affability in Schumacher's voice when he replied: 'If you decide to stay a little longer than one day in Berlin and get to know us better, then I believe you will discover that living in a divided city crammed with foreign soldiers is not a matter we joke about, Mr . . . Benjamin.'

The emphasis he placed on the pronunciation of the name succeeded in its intention of conveying condescension and ill will: 'You snivelling little foreign creep in your disgusting floral tie,' he seemed to be saying, and most of the others around the table seemed to share his view.

Harry knew they were all examining him, looking closely at his straight nose and ear lobes, wondering about the dark hair and tanned complexion, trying to find the signs that would confirm his semitic blood. Harry felt as if they were stripping him in public; unlike Strelitz's companion, he did not enjoy the experience.

'I'm sure Mr Benjamin didn't mean it quite like that,' interjected Schumacher's wife in an attempt to dissipate the sudden sharp atmosphere.

'Sorry,' added Harry, his dark eyes smouldering defiance. 'Clumsy use of words.' But no one smiled.

'Benjamin – is that an American name?' enquired Strelitz in a tone which took pains to indicate he already knew the answer.

'There hasn't been a truly American name since Cochise and Geronimo,' said Harry with a forced chuckle. The game had gone far enough for tonight, and it was time to call for a respite. The other players took their cue and went back to their food and chatter, but Harry noticed that the twinkle had gone out of Frau Schumacher's eye. Her mood had changed; he could see there was vulnerability and sadness lurking behind the laughter.

'I'm sorry if I upset your husband,' he offered, without any real sincerity.

'It's I who owe the apology,' she said quietly. 'There was no need for my husband to be rude.'

'It seems that being an American in Berlin is not one of life's most predictable experiences,' he observed, trying to divert the conversation away from her husband.

'Who were Cochise and Geronimo?' she asked.

'Two murderous American Indian warriors who between them killed thousand of settlers.'

'What happened to them?'

Harry gave a wry laugh. 'They both lived to a ripe old age and died in their wigwams. Which I suspect is not quite what Miss Pickerstaff has in mind for me,' he continued, looking down the table to where the other American was once again in animated conversation with Schumacher.

'I'm afraid Miss Pickerstaff believes that Berlin can be viewed in black and white, when in reality there are only shades of grey. I get the impression that everything has to fit into neat little boxes for her which she can tie up and file. She's stopped asking questions. Perhaps she's been here too long.'

Harry wondered whether it was possible for this beautiful woman to be jealous of the pinched Miss Pickerstaff, who was monopolizing her husband at the other end of the table. Was this what left the edge of sadness in her eyes? As if reading his mind Frau Schumacher shook her head, and Harry was captivated as he watched the burnished copper highlights in her hair glowing in the candlelight.

'No, Mr Benjamin. Jealousy is not part of my life. And Miss Pickerstaff is not part of his.'

'Any more than I am,' he thought he heard her whisper. There was an emptiness in the way she talked about her husband. Her voice had no hostility or animosity, no sign of a woman scorned, but neither did it hold any affection or warmth. They may be one of Berlin's most elegant couples, Harry thought, but here, close up, he could find no trace of what bound them together.

'You don't like Berliners, do you?' she asked simply.

'Why do you say that?' he asked, not bothering to contradict her.

'I think you knew what you were doing back there, reminding us that Berlin was not our city, that we'd been forgotten. You were testing us.'

Just like you're testing me now. He chased a piece of venison around his plate, treating it with unnecessary reverence, giving himself time while he tried to figure out this direct and unusually perceptive woman.

'I've been in Berlin scarcely a day. I'm finding it confusing, not what I expected,' he admitted. 'It's like an onion. You peel off one layer only to find several others hidden beneath. I guess I was biting back just a bit too hard a moment ago.'

'Here a day and already so cynical?'

'Let's just say I'm having a few adjustment problems. I got into a taxi at the airport yesterday and upset the taxi driver. I got to the office and upset our Miss Pickerstaff before I'd even been introduced. Now I come to Berlin's finest restaurant and upset a room full of complete strangers. And I'm supposed to be a diplomat!'

'Looks like I'm the only friend you've got, Mr Benjamin.'

'Then please call me Harry,' he smiled.

'I'm very pleased to meet you, Harry,' she said softly, and meant it.

'And you . . . ?'

'Katherine. My name is Katherine.'

Schumacher couldn't sleep. He sat and watched the cigarette smoke rise slowly towards the high ceiling and then hang motionless in a shaft of moonlight. His eyes wandered restlessly around the room, trying to find comfort in its expensive furnishings. Not bad for a boy raised in the back streets of a town on the German –Polish border whose father had worked in a sawmill.

67

He had long since brushed aside the thick accent which betrayed his impoverished origins, but he had never forgotten.

Often on these long nights when he couldn't sleep his thoughts went back to his father. Schumacher had to struggle hard to hang on to the memories of a man who had died when he was only eight. His parents had brought him to West Berlin in the days after the end of the war when it was still easy to walk from one zone to another and tens of thousands had done so in search of 'the better life', before the barbed wire and barriers had soared into the sky. But they had discovered that the queues were just as long, the piles of rubble were just as high and the swarms of soldiers who occupied the city were just as foreign as on the other side. Refugees with their families crowded into every corner of the city which was habitable and many which weren't, fighting for jobs and food amid the ruins which still made up most of West Berlin.

He had grown to hate the foreign soldiers most, particularly the American GIs with their thick wallets and copious supplies of cigarettes and nylons, who thought everything was for sale, including his mother. She had refused where so many Berlin women had weakened and sacrificed themselves in order to feed their children. Schumacher could remember only his mother's tears of despair, his own cries of hunger, and a sick father forced to work out of doors on murderously cold winter days in one of the gangs trying to glue the city back together. His father had been such a giant of a man, a godlike figure who had fought so hard and who had spent the last year of his life dying a little every day from the ravages of tuberculosis while he struggled to keep working and his family fed. Schumacher had lain awake through many long nights then, listening to the terrible sound of the cough which had slowly torn apart his father's lungs and the rest of his once-proud body. They had robbed him of the only person he had ever truly loved, and in the days when life in post-war Berlin had been an unremitting struggle for survival, there was no one to help.

They buried his father late. For a full ten days the ground had been frozen too hard to hack out a grave. And there had been no time to mourn in Berlin. His boyish tears had scarcely dried before he discovered that his mother, desperate and alone, had at last weakened and succumbed to the blandishments of the American soldiers and their conquerors' appetites for instant gratification. One evening, through a living-room door left ajar when he was supposed to be soundly asleep in bed, he had discovered the secret of how she was managing to pay for his food and clothing. He had resolved never to trust any woman ever again, and his hatred of all things American was total. The lingering memory had driven him on, to climb out of the ruins, to make his money and to ensure that neither he nor anyone for whom he was responsible ever went without again.

And if it meant selling out to the Russians and becoming one of their most important agents in West Berlin, it was a small price to pay for getting his own back on the Americans.

Even now they were swarming over Eastern Europe, wallets stuffed with dollars and mouths filled with promises of a better life while they plundered the natural resources and raped the local industries, stirring up discontent as they went. Foreign investment they called it. But Schumacher remembered the GI. The Americans hadn't changed. And neither would he.

He glanced across at the form of his sleeping wife. If

he had any regrets they were reserved for her. She had literally fallen into his arms as he pulled her across the Wall that night, and he had been more than happy to provide a comforting shoulder on which she could lean as she tried to readjust to the challenges of life in the West and the horror of life without Peter and the baby. She had been an ideal companion, an attractive hostess to help with his political and social life, someone who could at least understand some of the suffering which still tormented him. But she had wanted children, desperately needing to replace the family she had lost at the Wall, and he had always known that he would never agree. Not after seeing what the GI had done to his mother. 'Not yet, soon,' he had told her. First it had been his business which kept him travelling so much throughout West Germany and to the East, then he had implied that he was unwell and only finally had he admitted that he was unwilling, until eventually their marriage was no longer like that. A gulf opened between them which had grown wider with every new excuse, until the sharing had stopped completely.

Except for the escape ring; they had shared that. It had been a way of giving Katherine something to hold on to as she became increasingly oppressed by the guilt she felt for surviving while Peter had perished. 'I spend so much time looking back,' she had explained. 'At least with the ring I have something to look forward to, helping others get out.' And it had been such marvellous camouflage. He had used his 'business' contacts in the East to find those who were willing to risk the Wall, while she arranged the details of the escape. He had insisted that they keep the two halves of the operation separate; if security were breached, he had explained, there was no point in the whole operation going under.

It meant that Katherine knew little or nothing of

what he did in the East, and was unable to understand how complete the deception was. The Russians helped him build up his trading business, and encouraged him to supply the Western authorities with low-grade intelligence picked up on his travels behind the Iron Curtain. The business also allowed him to run the escape ring, which in turn enabled his KGB masters to penetrate the refugee movement, to keep tabs on dissidents, to infiltrate their own agents through the ring into the West and to decide who managed to escape, and who didn't. Meanwhile, Schumacher gathered the wealth and the impeccable social credentials which provided a wonderful platform to build a political career and at the same time affording perfect impenetrable cover for a Soviet spy.

He hadn't needed Soviet help once they had suggested it was time for him to turn from business to politics; there were already enough friendly and influential voices in West Berlin who thought he was an ideal candidate and who were willing to give him that vital push up the ladder. And he hadn't needed the ring any more, which was fortunate, since by the time they had buried Brezhnev and the first glimmerings of *glasnost* had begun to infect the political climate, fewer people were willing to risk it across the Wall. It had been almost a year since anyone had tried – why risk it, let's wait, they thought, just in case *glasnost* really works, just in case they are about to throw open the checkpoints and we can walk across. Of course it hadn't happened, but it had robbed Katherine of what she needed most, the chance to make amends for Peter every time she succeeded in getting one more person across.

And as her nights grew longer and lonelier, so the last thread which held their marriage together had snapped. Pity. But the marriage, like all the other falsehoods in his life, had served its purpose well. It all seemed so perfect – from the outside. He exhaled gently and let the cigarette smoke play silent games in the moonlight.

It was only in the early hours before dawn when he sat alone with his insecurity that the confidence began to seep away. The endless hours of fatigue, the drained resources of nervous energy, the constant self-doubt and the unremitting fear of exposure which gnawed away inside him had all taken their toll. Surely at some time they would realize it was all a front? Sometimes he marvelled at how long his good fortune had lasted. He had taught himself to hide the strain and to block out any sign of real emotion, as Katherine knew all too well. He had even ingratiated himself with the Americans. Only occasionally did the telltale redness around his eyes betray the stiff drink or three he had to take to drown his nagging fears. And it was becoming more difficult. He shouldn't have had a go at that ridiculous young American who was late for dinner – there had been no point – but the drink had urged him on and, like every young American, Harry had reminded him of that damned GI. They could all burn in hell, and he didn't particularly care whether he pushed them or dragged them down after him.

He knew the signs of strain were beginning to show. The expensive suits no longer fitted him so well as his figure began to bulge into middle age and the lines on his face deepened and sagged. He hoped that the streaks of grey which were now splattered through his once-dark hair succeeded in persuading the party faithful of his maturity, while every morning they shouted at him that he was growing older and more vulnerable.

Yet it was the thick hands which gave the game away, with the almost imperceptible tremble in their fingers which signalled the warfare deep within him. He needed a good night's rest to silence the screaming nerves, except he couldn't remember when he last had a good night. So he drank. Not constantly but increasingly and, occasionally, excessively. And he knew he was smoking too much, trying to get himself through the times when he wanted to pack it all in. But then he would remember his father, and his mother, and knew he must not give up. Maybe soon, but not yet. His control had told him much the same earlier yesterday as he had described to Schumacher 'the task for which we have been preparing you all these years, the one which will make all the difference'. God, he had needed a drink after that, and he knew he would need many more before this was all over.

The first faint lines of day were beginning to trickle through the sky – 'the dawn of a new age' the American President had called it in his cliché-riddled address – and Schumacher knew he would get no more sleep. The world was about to be engulfed in a new wave of history, and Schumacher had a terrible feeling that he might be its first victim.

Lake Seliger

The black Chaikas and Zils were drawing up outside the *dacha* and disgorging their cargoes of powerful occupants. As his driver opened the door, Malinin glanced enviously at Bykov's Mercedes. The road out of Moscow had been long and unrelenting, and while they had the expertise to put a cosmonaut on Mars they were still unable to master the simple technology of the mass-produced shock absorber and hydraulic suspension system. He glanced even more enviously when he saw Bykov's chauffeur. The old dog hadn't lost his touch. But then Malinin knew that already. Why else had three of the most influential men in the Soviet Union dropped everything at his summons and hurried through the freezing early morning fog to his *dacha*?

Power. The exercise of naked power. And Bykov understood more about that particular game than anyone this side of Vladivostok.

Malinin grew concerned as he recognized Bykov's other guests, who all arrived within ten minutes of each other. There was Semyonov, the ageing leader of the Party in Moscow who had his finger into everything. The most eminent men in the country lived on his patch, so he could study them relaxing out of the office, with their guard and often their trousers down. He made sure he knew who was doing what to whom, and made sure they knew it, too. Political fashions come and go, but men's follies are perpetual and Semyonov's knowledge of them had enabled him to survive every twist and turn of the screw since Brezhnev's time. Until now. Rumours had been circulating that Andreyev wanted him retired, and didn't give a damn what the old man felt about it.

Then there was Marshal Palin, the diminutive Commander-in-Chief of Soviet ground forces. He was almost dwarfishly small but no one ever laughed at him. Over the years he had succeeded in ducking too many of the bullets which had caught his colleagues ever to be underestimated. Yet even he had been forced into impotent rage as, with mounting disgust, he had watched Andreyev's diplomatic forays steadily eating away at his military establishment and cutting back on both his budgets and his power base. He had led the opposition to the summit inside the meetings of the

Politburo, in the belief that he was too well entrenched within the military for even Andreyev to remove him. But what power had a commander with nothing to command?

Malinin did not care to be associated with dissidents, no matter how powerful. Like Semyonov and Palin he had his own deep doubts about *glasnost*, although he preferred to keep them to himself. He was the chairman of the Ukrainian Federated Soviet Socialist Republic, the second most important of the fifteen supposedly autonomous republics comprising the Soviet Union, with a population of some fifty million. He also knew his place in the pecking order, and in spite of enjoying such a power base he knew it did not do to be openly opposed to the General Secretary. Yet even he had not been able to contain himself when Andreyev succumbed to the demands for greater autonomy from the Armenian malcontents who lived within the borders of the Moslem republic of Azerbaijan. The feuding nationalities within the Soviet empire were a Pandora's box of chaos; Andreyev should have slammed the lid shut, but instead he had vacillated and allowed loose a problem which threatened to infect every one of the Soviet republics. A few harsh words of exasperation from Malinin had been enough for Bykov to overhear, and to understand.

Now, in the greatest secrecy, he had gathered them all together: the man who controlled Moscow, the head of the armed forces, the political opponent and, of course, the KGB.

'Bollocks,' Malinin muttered, 'he hasn't invited us here just to admire his new chauffeur.'

Throughout breakfast Bykov had led the conversation: the state of traffic in Moscow, how best to catch a river pike, the brewery manager who had been shot

75

for watering down the beer, as if they were old friends with not a care among them. It was only after the steaming cups of sweet black tea had arrived and been drunk that Bykov suggested a walk around the lake. A walk. A simple enough invitation, but one which for older generations throughout Eastern Europe carried the connotation of secrecy and intrigue. For in a world where sons had spied on fathers and all men had lived under the constant threat of being overheard and betrayed, it was only under clear skies that they could feel at ease and free to share their secrets.

As a child living in the mountains of Georgia, a thousand miles from the civilization and conspiracies of Moscow and in a village which lacked either electricity or running water, Bykov's father would still insist on taking him into the orchard before attempting to answer his many questions. 'Out here, there's only God to listen to us — until they learn how to put bugs up rabbits' asses!' he had explained. Of course, it hadn't saved him. They had arrived one day in the middle of yet another of Stalin's purges, and Bykov had never seen his father again. Some might have sworn revenge; Bykov had sworn to control and master those forces which made ordinary men like his father run in fear. And he had never forgotten that of all the powerful men he knew, only Stalin had died in command and in bed.

Even today, with all his terrifying power as chairman of the KGB, Bykov preferred to trust his instincts rather than the aides who regularly swept his *dacha* and Moscow flat for listening devices. You could never be too careful. So they would walk.

The invitation had set off nervous banter amongst his guests. Semyonov, Muscovite to the last, had forgotten his boots and had to borrow a pair. The weather

76

was still well below freezing, and ground mist swirled through the forest.

'I wonder whether at my age it is more dangerous to join you or to stay behind,' Semyonov quipped cryptically.

'Depends whether you prefer to die of pneumonia or get shot,' growled Bykov. After that, they had remained silent until they were well away from the house.

They had traipsed slowly and in single file for ten minutes or more behind Bykov, treading in the footsteps which he had carved in the thick, crusty snow, not knowing whether they were walking across road, frozen stream or meadow but certain that Bykov did. The KGB guards had been left behind and they had only one startled snow rabbit for company until they came to the top of a low hillock which rose just high enough to pierce through the ground mists, and where they could rest in the weak March sun and gaze through the trees to the lake beyond. Bykov stopped, clapped his gloved hands to revive his circulation and produced a bottle of vodka from his pocket.

'Drink,' he ordered, and they did so willingly, each feeling the pure spirit burning its way through his chest and welcoming its warm, familiar embrace, until Bykov's next words cut through them like Arctic frost.

'You're all dead men,' he muttered.

The silence of the snow-covered forests wrapped itself around them like a white shroud. He let them suffer for what seemed an age before continuing.

'You have been fools,' he snapped. 'Andreyev returns from his imperial wanderings tomorrow and I'm told the first thing he intends to do will be to get rid of any member of the Politburo who opposes the treaty. That means you three – yes, including you, Malinin, because if you've been so loose-tongued about your feelings that

I've heard then you can bet your pension he's picked it up, too.'

The Ukrainian looked suitably embarrassed and tried to hide inside the folds of his thick fur coat.

'You three bastards have come up the hard way. You've left behind plenty of political corpses and quite a few real ones over the years, and once Andreyev boots your hides out of the Politburo there will be a pack of vengeful wolves just waiting to tear you apart. Believe me, you're dead men.'

'Georgi Vassilievich,' said Semyonov, who appeared to be less perturbed than the others at the prospect of imminent dismemberment, 'I think you exaggerate.'

'What?' growled Bykov. 'You think I'm playing games?'

'Not at all,' responded the Muscovite. 'Andreyev's desire to get rid of me has been hinted at in every edition of *Pravda* for months and undoubtedly the seeming success of his trip to Washington will temporarily strengthen his hand. It simply occurs to me that you show no apparent pleasure in the thought of our demise, and you are bothering to take the quite unnecessary and potentially dangerous trouble of warning us. You would not do so unless you had an alternative to offer.'

Bykov's brown eyes sparkled and he began to chuckle. 'You cunning old fox, Sergei Ivanovich. Now I see why you've survived as long as you have. Yes, there is another way,' he said slowly. 'None of you has ever heard me whisper any criticism of the treaty, and I shall raise my paw in support along with all the other kowtowing bastards on the Central Committee. But you'd better believe that I am as bitterly opposed as any of you. For seventy years we've been able to fend off all the vices and ambitions which infect the West, yet now, when we've got miners' strikes and dockers' protests and every sort of nationalist flea scratching away at our backsides, he wants to throw away our armed forces for a few pieces of yankee gold and bring the plague right up to our doorstep. We can take on every division in the American Army and give as good as we get, yet what on earth do we do when every peasant this side of Budapest wants to become a fucking Coca-Cola salesman? No,' he shook his head in defiance. 'The General Secretary has got himself hopelessly confused, like a choirboy in a whore-house.'

As he spoke his condensing breath settled and froze on his bushy moustache, flecking it with snow and ageing him in front of their eyes. Suddenly he looked vulnerable.

'The treaty should be the means to build our strength and undermine the Americans while they're in an economic mess,' Bykov continued. 'Instead, for Andreyev it's become an end in itself, his entire stinking strategy. He's convinced himself he can trust the Americans, and he's selling out to them just when for the first time since Lenin we've got the upper hand and should be screwing them like Manchurian tarts.'

'It's not exactly peace and prosperity inside the Soviet Union,' muttered Malinin. 'Or hadn't you noticed?'

'We're used to a little hunger. The Americans aren't,' snarled Bykov. 'This is our chance to win back everything that's been thrown away in the last few years, while the American President has his head in his underpants worrying about how he'll be able to bribe his way to re-election. If only our beloved leader would seize the opportunity . . .'

There was no mistaking the bitterness in Bykov's voice, and he paused for a moment. 'He must be stopped.'

The words sent a chill through them all. It was

Semyonov, more used to treason than the others, who recovered first. 'How do you propose we stop the conquering hero?' he prodded.

'It won't be easy. He will ride the crest of the wave for a while.' Bykov looked directly into the eyes of each of them in turn. 'He will get rid of you, one by one.'

'Surely there's something we can do?' interjected Palin, his voice lacking its usual conviction. He seemed to have shrunk even further as he sheltered from the biting cold beneath his oversized uniform cap.

'Not immediately. But there is a way through. When you offer your resignations, as he will demand, you must all make it clear that you are going because of your opposition to the treaty. Let no one doubt that is the cause. I can protect you from the wolves for a while, and we only need a few months – hell, we only *have* a few months. The details of the treaty have to be agreed and come into force by the end of the year, when he starts withdrawing the troops. That must not happen. And if it doesn't, it will be Andreyev who is torn apart by the wolves and you who'll be warming your boots by the fire inside the Kremlin.'

'But how do we overturn the treaty?'

'We don't overturn the treaty. The West does – but that's as much as you're getting.'

Semyonov smiled, a sharp, sarcastic, untrusting smile. 'Georgi Vassilievich, it's very good of you to worry about our welfare and to take us into your confidence, but forgive me if I am left wondering why. What do you want us to do?'

'Do? Apart from resigning, absolutely nothing. That's the whole damned point. We have only a little time in which to succeed. Once the treaty is in force, it will take a war to smash it. We must succeed by the end of the year or not at all and I want nothing to happen, nothing which you may be planning, no plot or opposition, to get in my way. If our little tsar hears that anything is going on, he'll become suspicious and my plan could fall to pieces. So I don't want any of you to start pulling surprises. When the time comes, resign, blame the treaty, and then keep quiet. We're all in the same bed together, and I don't want any of you bastards farting under the covers.'

'And if we decide instead to reveal your plan to Andreyev . . .?' As always, Semyonov was not one to miss an opportunity.

'You have nothing to reveal. Publicly I shall remain a loyal chairman of the KGB and join in denouncing you along with the General Secretary. I shall particularly enjoy that, Sergei Ivanovich.' Bykov's laugh was cold and menacing. 'And if anything were to happen to me, if they retire me or shoot me or you hear I've gone swimming with concrete boots – remember. You will be left to the mercy of the wolves.'

Malinin turned to Semyonov. 'What do you think?'

The old man considered for a moment before replying, his breath leaving a trail of frozen vapour in the sharp morning air. 'I think that for the next few months I shall be breaking wind with the greatest of care.'

Washington D.C.

It was still the middle of the night on the other side of the world, and deep within the confines of the Soviet embassy a bedside light went on in the presidential suite. Andreyev's wife, disturbed by the activity, lifted her eye pads and rolled over.

'What's the matter, Aleks?'

'Nothing. Go back to sleep. It's just indigestion. Too much of that disgusting American coffee at the reception.'

'You're getting far too many stomach upsets. You're going to a doctor when we get back to Moscow.'

'Stop nagging, woman! It's just a touch of indigestion I tell you. A glass of decent vodka and I'll be fine.'

He ought to see a doctor, of course, but he no longer knew if he could trust them. He kept getting that feeling that he couldn't trust anyone any more. Ridiculous paranoia! He would be glad to get back to Moscow; he'd been away too long. He threw down a couple of antacid tablets, only to hear his guts give a further sickening roar. This was going to be another sleepless night.

THREE

Washington D.C.

President Michelle was in excellent spirits. The opinion polls he had commissioned following the signing ceremony had shown a sharp increase in his popularity rating, and for the first time in the last eighteen months more people agreed he was doing a good job than thought he was an incompetent cretin. The couple of days since then had been spent showing Andreyev around some of the best examples of American prowess, from Manhattan Island to Disneyland and several other places where the electoral college vote later in the year would be crucial to his re-election. It had been a complete media triumph, and scarcely a minute of prime-time news coverage went by without more shots of Michelle in his pose as the father of the nation, towering over the substantially shorter Russian and symbolizing all that was great and good in the United States. He didn't need more opinion polls to tell him that his star was rising once again.

It was a clear, crisp day at Andrews Air Force Base as he waved a formal goodbye to the Ilyushin 62Y disappearing into the blue sky. The General Secretary's departing words from the tarmac had been particularly generous about Michelle's personal contribution to 'the new era of peace and freedom which will reach into the farthest corners of the globe', and he in turn had praised Andreyev warmly. After all, if it must be, he didn't mind too much sharing the Nobel Prize.

The media men were in equally felicitous mood at the

airport press conference which followed the departure ceremonies. Squashed into an undersized reception room, the gathering had a much more informal and intimate feeling than those in the White House, and Michelle was enjoying it. The questions they threw at him were soft and slow and he was able to hit them back over the perimeter fence with little trouble. It was also an opportunity to make amends to some of the foreign press. They had complained bitterly at the way they had been squeezed out by the American and Soviet media throughout the summit, and Michelle had asked his press secretary to ensure that a couple of the foreign representatives had a chance to ask questions at this final conference. Now that the polls were turning in his favour, he could afford to indulge them.

Yes, he responded, he believed that the agreement to reduce spending on defence would enable him to restore some of the cuts in the foreign aid programme which had been forced on the United States by the economic recession. And he was delighted to say that although the summit hadn't discussed South Africa directly, he was sure the new East–West relationship would put decisive pressure on the Pretoria government to hasten the pace of reform. This truly was an agreement with worldwide implications.

It was at that point he acknowledged a correspondent of enormous girth with a bright pink face which during the week had grown steadily more bucolic from chasing breathlessly after the presidential cavalcade. The journalist's size made him less than fleet of foot in the pursuit of a story, but it certainly helped him stand out from the crowd in this tightly packed room. At last his patience had been rewarded, and his full jowls quivered in satisfaction as he pushed himself up from his chair.

'Hans Prost from the *B.Z.* newspaper in Berlin. Mr

President, you mentioned that this agreement has worldwide implications.' He referred briefly to his notebook. 'I think Mr Andreyev said something to the effect that it would reach to the farthest corners of the globe. What are the implications for the divided city of Berlin?'

Michelle smiled broadly at the questioner, and took the opportunity to take a sip of water. What the hell sort of question was that? Berlin hadn't been on the agenda, hadn't even been mentioned, and frankly he hadn't any thoughts about it. Technically Berlin was still a city divided into the four military zones left after the war and governed by the Allied Powers. In a way, it wasn't strictly foreign soil at all, was it? Maybe this was an exception. Tricky one . . . As he sipped his water, he glanced across at Grossman who was standing to one side, carefully positioned to be out of view of the cameras but clearly in line of sight for his President in case he was required to offer some immediate guidance. The national security adviser gave the slightest shake of his head, and Michelle's eyes returned immediately to his audience.

'Mr Prost, we did not discuss Berlin,' he responded. Make it short, he told himself. No bullshit to cover up the void in his mind, no expansive *ad hoc* statements which might offer up hostages to fortune. 'Berlin is not part of the deal, for obvious reasons which I'm sure you'll understand.'

Prost tried to struggle back to his feet to insist that he certainly didn't understand and would the President be somewhat more helpful in explaining his reasons, but the pressure of bodies around him got in his way. By the time he had regained his feet and was properly balanced, a different question was being asked from the other side of the room, and all his waving of notebooks was to no avail. Foreign correspondents don't get a second bite at the cherry.

The Berlin journalist was still sitting in his chair, mopping his brow from the exertion and the intense heat of the packed room, several minutes after the President had left congratulating himself on another successful media event. But Hans Prost didn't mind. Michelle had tried to give him the brush-off; a week's effort and scarcely a dozen words to show for it. But that was all an old press hack like him needed. Berlin was not to be part of this superpower peace package. He had his headline. And he was sure his readers would be able to provide their own explanation in place of the one the President had so woefully failed to give.

Vnukovo Airport, Moscow

It was still snowing heavily as the Ilyushin taxied to a halt amid the slush. The airport commandant had called in troops to try to keep the reception area clear for the return of the General Secretary, but it had been a never-ending battle as the grey skies deposited wet snow as fast as they could remove it. The guard of honour felt miserable, for the snow had brought with it not the sharp frosty bite which their bodies had been trained and toughened to resist but an insidious, creeping dampness which found its way through the seams of their boots and made itself at home in the woollen undervests which were supposed to keep them warm. It was one of those dark Moscow days which insists that spring will never arrive and which brings with it a peculiar type of depression that few Muscovites have the ability to shrug off – least of all General Palin, who watched the preparations for disembarkation, conscious that his highly polished boots had long since given up the unequal battle with the elements and now looked as if he had been playing football in them.

As the door of the aircraft swung open, the band struck up a rather laggardly version of the national anthem, while the guard of honour came damply to attention. At the foot of the aircraft steps a small forest of black umbrellas bobbed in the wind, like mourners gathered around a grave. The entire Politburo, including candidate members, had turned out to welcome the arrival of the General Secretary, and some twenty elderly men were trying to rekindle the fire in their frozen faces and warm up their smiles so that their leader could be greeted as a returning hero for the benefit of the cameras and everyone could get back to the warmth of their waiting limousines. At this moment Palin would have given almost anything to exchange his job for that of a chauffeur. As he watched the figure of Andreyev appear in the aircraft doorway, he considered he would be lucky to get even a chauffeur's job if half of what Bykov had predicted were true.

The most powerful man in the entire Union of Soviet Socialist Republics came stiffly and cautiously down the stairs, as befitted one who had spent the entire ten-hour flight either in or close to the airplane's toilet. His stomach was in turmoil. His mood matched that of the skies as he accepted the bouquet of flowers thrust at him from somewhere and methodically began to embrace his Politburo colleagues in strict order of precedence.

There were no speeches – no one was in the mood

for them – and Andreyev began to squelch along what an hour before had been a red carpet towards the airport terminal, where a small, subdued crowd of party members and airport workers had been gathered to provide evidence of popular support. As had been meticulously planned, this would take the General Secretary past Palin and the guard of honour which it was the army commander's duty to present. As his leader approached, Palin offered an immaculate salute of welcome.

'Would the comrade General Secretary care to inspect the guard of honour?' asked Palin formally.

'No!' snarled Andreyev and stomped past without stopping.

Palin was left frozen to attention as the rest of the Politburo marched after their retreating leader. Several muttered in astonishment both at Andreyev's extraordinary breach of protocol in ignoring the assembled guard and at the public insult he had thrust on Palin. None of them wanted to look directly at the diminutive general, whose grey complexion resembled a man who had just seen his executioner testing the trapdoor. Only Bykov turned his head, staring deeply into Palin's shocked eyes before passing on.

Palin was left standing on the concrete apron, a lonely and shrunken figure in the half-light, buffeted by the elements and the misfortunes of Kremlin politics. He braced his shoulders defiantly as another squall of wet snow slashed across his face and began to trickle down inside his collar. It would have to be tomorrow, he reasoned; he had no alternative. He must resign before Andreyev had the chance to force him out and humiliate him further. He would go with honour, protesting his loyalty to the party and his opposition to the treaty – and praying that Bykov would be in time to save him from the wolves.

Berlin

It was Schumacher who as party chairman had made the suggestion to the chief *Bürgermeister* – the head of West Berlin's civilian government – and the proposal was grasped eagerly. The old man was little more than a figurehead, and very open to the ideas of his younger colleagues for anything which would give him another public platform to play out his role as Berlin's most eminent grandfather.

So the announcement was made. A rally was to be held outside the Schöneberg town hall on the Saturday following the summit 'to mark the occasion' of the new East–West accord. The original draft had used the words 'to celebrate the occasion', but Schumacher had strongly suggested that the alternative wording would be more appropriate and the old man, uncomprehending, conceded the point – as he usually did with his colleagues.

Miss Pickerstaff was in her element. It was to be a gala occasion – the US Ambassador was flying in specially from Bonn – and she set about her tasks of preparation with remarkable ferocity for a woman who looked as if she never ate a proper meal. Her staff were instructed, her hairdressing appointment arranged, and Harry was told to prepare a comprehensive briefing document for the Ambassador on Berlin's economic situation and prospects. He recognized it as an instruction to get lost in a roomful of dusty folders and dry statistics and to keep out of the way while everyone else carried on with the real work. They were too busy to brief new hands.

After a day of wandering mindlessly through the data, Harry made his first executive decision since arriving in Berlin. He grabbed a copy of his predecessor's most recent report and in three hours had rewritten it. Harry's prose was stylish and bore little resemblance to the report he had hijacked. Anyway, there was little chance of anyone actually reading it – except possibly his successor. It would do.

At least, that's what he thought until he arrived in Miss Pickerstaff's lair. Her desk was covered in neat little mountains of paper which she was organizing into a voluminous briefing for the Ambassador. She was determined that it would be sufficiently comprehensive to cover any contingency short of World War Three; nothing in Miss Pickerstaff's efficient world was going to be left to chance. Least of all a rookie straight from Langley.

'Thank you,' she said primly as Harry handed the report across her desk. She laid it to one side, separating it carefully from the other material.

'Would you like to go through it now?' Harry volunteered.

'Not now, Benjamin, I'm rather busy. We'll do it some time next week.'

So he was right. She wasn't going to risk incorporating it into the briefing after all. It had been a complete waste of his time.

'What will you want me to do tomorrow?' he asked. He knew that the rest of her staff had been put on call for the arrival of the Ambassador, just in case . . .

'Nothing. I'd like to get to know your work better before putting you into the front line.'

Meeting their own Ambassador? The front line? He was beginning to see why Miss Pickerstaff had risen so quickly. He also realized with depressing clarity why Langley had sent him to Berlin. Miss Pickerstaff was going to squeeze him dry, like a crushed orange, until there was nothing left inside him but mangled flesh and dried pulp. They wanted him to be a replica of her.

'That's all,' she said, dismissing him. Harry turned to leave, feeling as if the desiccation process had already begun. He foresaw three years of working in the desert of Berlin with only Miss Pickerstaff for company. He desperately needed a drink.

It wasn't until after his fourth or fifth bourbon that he began to feel better, and not until a couple more that he began to feel depressed again. Visions of Miss Pickerstaff came back to haunt him, and he realized that he hadn't met a single friendly face since he'd arrived. Except Katherine. She at least had a sense of humour and a presence which made men turn their heads. Pity she was so much older. And married . . .

It took another drink before he phoned her.

'Katherine?' His tongue felt thick and seemed to be getting in the way of his teeth, slowing his speech and emphasizing his southern drawl. 'It's Harry Benjamin, ma'am.'

'Is everything all right, Harry?' Her voice sounded concerned, as if she detected that something were wrong.

'I believe I'm drunk,' he replied, with all the dignity he could muster.

There was a peal of laughter down the phone, which Harry found infectious. He began laughing, too.

'Sorry. I think I've had one too many, and I needed to hear a friendly voice.'

There was more laughter. 'Where are you?'

'Damned if I know, ma'am. Some bar on the Ku'damm. "Reinicker's" it says above the telephone. I suppose you'd find me rude if I asked you to join me?'

'I don't want a drink, Harry. But you sound as if you need rescuing. In your state, anything could happen to

91

you on the streets of Berlin.' She chuckled once again. 'I'll be there in twenty minutes.'

And she was. As she walked through the door of the bar, Harry's blurred eyes thought they saw a halo of light shining behind her golden hair.

'My guardian angel,' he said sheepishly.

'Come on, Harry, it's time to go home,' she said.

He was too drunk to protest, and with as much co-ordination as his clumsy limbs could manage he allowed himself to be guided to her car outside.

'Feeling homesick?' she enquired as they set off on the short distance to his hotel.

'No. Just disappointed. Berlin's not what I expected.'

'It's a wonderful city, really. I'll show it to you if you want, when you're – feeling better.'

'I'd like that, really I would. How about . . . how about coffee tomorrow? I wouldn't want you to think I get drunk all the time.'

They were both laughing as the car drew up outside his hotel.

'I may be about to say the wrong thing, Katherine. But you're beautiful as well as kind. I think so when I'm drunk, and I'll think that in the morning, too, when I'm sober. I like you.'

Katherine was silent. Her smile had gone and she looked straight ahead, seeing nothing. Harry suddenly felt guilty.

'Hell, the only friend I've found in Berlin and I make a mess of that, too. I'm truly sorry,' he said, full of remorse. 'Goodbye, Katherine,' and he made to get out of the car.

As he did so, he felt her hand pulling him back. She didn't want him to leave like this. So much about Harry reminded her of Peter: the irreverent twinkle in his eye, his disrespect for authority, his sense of fun even when drunk, the sinewy arm she was now touching. And as much as she found the comparison captivating, the memories hurt.

'Don't be sorry, Harry. It's all right. I suppose I'm just not used to getting many compliments nowadays.' The laughter had gone out of her voice. There was that hint of vulnerability again.

'I didn't mean to offend you,' he apologized.

'You didn't. I'll see you tomorrow for that coffee you promised. Call for me at four.'

She squeezed his hand as Harry found himself on the pavement, fumbling for the right words to use and finding none. As he watched Katherine pull away, he decided that Berlin might not be such a bad place after all.

Miss Pickerstaff's preparations for the peace rally later that day were proceeding characteristically smoothly, until the morning's edition of *B. Z.* landed on her desk.

'Berlin In The Cold', it announced in huge black letters.

She cared even less for the copy.

'While the two superpower leaders this week declared a new era of peace which would affect "every corner of the globe", US President Michelle admitted yesterday that the divided city of Berlin is not to be included. "It's not part of the deal," he said at a press conference.

'Although he has announced his intention of withdrawing large numbers of US troops from defending Europe, it appears that no new guarantees of Berlin's future have been gained or even sought. Foreign troops will continue to occupy the city. The President refused to answer further questions on the subject.

'However, Michelle made clear that the summit accord had been accompanied by considerable discussion of other sensitive international problems. He announced that the new US–Soviet agreement would be accompanied by increased aid to Third World countries and a stepping up of pressure on South Africa to reform *apartheid*.

'No one in the US administration was available to explain why Berlin was to be left out in the cold from these developments . . .'

Miss Pickerstaff felt annoyed, but was having trouble deciding why. She disliked any criticism of her President but inevitably had grown used to that, particularly with this incumbent. She debated with herself whether it made any difference to her careful preparations for the rally later that day and the arrival of the Ambassador. Probably not, she concluded. What was really making her annoyed, she finally told herself, was the incompetence of those idle bastards in the State Department who were supposed to brief her on any diplomatic developments affecting her responsibilities. Nothing had come across from Foggy Bottom in that day's news digest, no mention of any important presidential statement about Berlin. She read the story once again, and concluded that it was another example of media exaggeration and hype. She would check back with State anyway, but it seemed she could probably ignore it.

After all, *B.Z.* was a sensationalist rag. No one took it seriously . . .

The house in Charlottenburg was large and impressive, right in the heart of Berlin's old aristocratic quarter where the avenues are broad and filled with linden trees which provide shade from the heat of summer and keep out the bustle and noise as the rest of the city rushes about its daily life. Unlike so much of Berlin, the wealth in Charlottenburg is displayed discreetly, except early in the mornings when the chauffeurs double-park their BMWs and Mercedes station wagons as they wait to take the children to school.

Harry knocked on the great oak door shortly after four. He had tried to be prompt and had almost succeeded, but he'd been told that it was the custom in Berlin to take a bunch of flowers whenever visiting a family home, and no florists were marked on any of his maps. He was surprised when Schumacher opened the door. Unable to find a suitable way of dealing with the problem of Katherine's husband, Harry had been trying to put him out of his mind. Now he felt like a complete fool standing on the doorstep with a bunch of flowers in his hand, waiting like a small boy for permission to enter.

'Good afternoon, Mr Benjamin,' Schumacher said formally.

As Harry walked into the hallway, he received another shock. He had been expecting something light and modern – like Katherine – but the decorations were sombre and the furniture dark and heavy. This was Schumacher's house, and Harry didn't like it.

'My wife will be only a minute,' Schumacher said, and stood awkwardly with his hands clasped in front of him, as if standing guard and making sure that Harry didn't run off with the carpets. A silence descended between them, matching the oppressive mood of the house. Although they had met only once before, Harry already knew they were natural rivals. They both had a competitive and uncompromising approach to life which insisted they had to win. And instinctively they both knew that, if they were ever in the same race, they would without hesitation or remorse cripple the other before allowing him to win.

They stood without speaking on opposite sides of the

hallway. Harry had great difficulty figuring out what Schumacher was thinking. When he blinked, the German's somewhat bulbous eyes closed forcefully and deliberately, as if he were having trouble with contact lenses. It had the effect of wiping out his expression, leaving his eyes empty and impossible to read. Only the constantly tapping fingers seemed to show any animation. The silence became oppressive, and both men turned in relief as Katherine came down the stairs. It was the first real chance Harry had been given to notice her legs, which were long with elegantly shaped ankles. He liked ankles. He had to struggle with himself in order not to stare.

'If you'll excuse me, I shall be off,' Schumacher said. 'I've been invited to meet with the American Ambassador before he addresses this evening's rally.' With that, he was gone.

Harry was glad when Katherine suggested they did not stay in the house but had coffee in one of the local *Kücherei*, the excellent cake shops which flourish on the corner of almost every street in the towns and villages of Germany. As soon as the front door had closed behind them, their spirits seemed to lift and their conversation tumbled over itself as they joked and drank coffee and filled themselves with rich chocolate cake. It was not until much later that Harry raised the question which had been nagging away at the back of his brain.

'Aren't you going to the rally with your husband?'

'No,' she said firmly. 'Politics is part of Edward's life, not mine. I only accompany him when it's absolutely necessary, and there will be more than enough people there tonight. I won't be missed,' she added as an afterthought, as if not to sound disloyal.

'I was hoping to persuade you to take me, if you're

free. After the march on the Wall earlier in the week, I need to learn a little more about these strange creatures caller Berliners. Come with me?'

'As your self-appointed teacher I suppose I feel under some obligation to help you with your education,' she reflected. 'But, please, not with Edward and the official party. Berlin officialdom is enough to squeeze the pleasure out of any occasion. Let's go on our own. After all,' she added with a grin, 'I have to be careful where I'm seen with a young man like you, Harry . . .'

So they left the cake shop and made their way south to the nearby district of Schöneberg, mingling with the crowd which was gathering in the square outside its famous town hall. The *Wurst* salesmen were busy, selling rich-smelling sausages from their barrows and vans, and a band was playing to whip up the atmosphere. But in spite of the thousands who were beginning to squash together in front of the town hall, Harry couldn't find the mood of celebration and unity he had discovered that night in the march on the Wall. There was no spectacular display of warmth here. Berliners were not sharing with one another, but keeping to their own little family circles, subdued and restless. Perhaps it was the cold of the approaching dusk, Harry told himself.

Floodlights had been erected to throw a glow along the length of the brown stone building, which Harry was surprised to see was of relatively modern construction. But then most of Berlin was of relatively modern construction; so much had been raised from the rubble and painstakingly rebuilt in the original pre-war style. Somehow this city was never quite what it seemed.

The town hall in Schöneberg was special to Berliners as the place where John F. Kennedy had come at the height of the Cold War to tell Berliners of his country's commitment to the city and to proclaim proudly in front of the cameras of the world that he, too, was a Berliner. You could always guarantee a large crowd here in the square renamed after the assassinated President, and American and German politicians made regular pilgrimage in an attempt to capture some of the excitement and adoration which Kennedy had left behind.

Tonight was no exception. As the principal guests filed out on to the balcony, accompanied by a fanfare from the band, even the subdued and frozen crowd around Harry came to life and offered polite applause. The *Bürgermeister* acknowledged the welcome, and entered into another of his rambling speeches without notes which he regarded as an informal, grandfatherly chat to his large family, but which Berliners had long regarded as the verbal wanderings of a whiskery old man who should be sent off to grow cabbages as soon as the squabbling politicians could agree on a successor. When at last he came to a conclusion, the listeners stamped their feet and beat their hands together before settling back in what he thought to be the warm glow of their approbation, while they tried to get their circulation going once again.

Then it was the turn of the American Ambassador. Armed with a sheaf of notes which Miss Pickerstaff had helped prepare, he began his own personal battle for the veneration of the Berlin crowd. From a balcony bedecked with flags, he began a long peroration about freedom, about commitment and support, about the summit, and about the hopes for a freer and more secure future.

'There is in the tower above our heads a Liberty Bell, subscribed by over seventeen million Americans as a token of our esteem for the people of Free Berlin, which you Berliners ring on special occasions. It is a symbol of our mutual commitment to freedom. Let that bell be rung tonight, to mark this new era of peace. Let its sound carry around the world and into the hearts of every free man and woman. And let it tell those who still are born in chains that help is at hand.'

But the fine words which had been crafted in a warm office failed to carry the chilled crowd. The Ambassador, fresh off the plane from Bonn, seemed to be reading them for the first time. His delivery was stilted and occasionally stumbling, his flat mid-west accent delivering a monotone which even the running translation could do nothing to lift. As his words drifted across the square in a cloud of condensation, they seemed to freeze and die.

Harry turned to wrinkle his nose at Katherine. She smiled and linked her arm through his for warmth. As she drew closer, Harry could smell her perfume and his senses exaggerated every tender nudge of her body. He was glad it was dark now; they could nestle together like good friends without worrying about being observed and misunderstood by those around them.

Then the lights went out. The glow which had dressed the town hall all evening suddenly disappeared, as if the fuses had blown. A restlessness had overtaken the crowd as they watched the ambassador's rhetoric disappear over their heads, and the rustling grew more pronounced as the lights disappeared and the organization seemed to be falling into disorder. The watchers grumbled impatiently as yet another figure strode through the gloom towards the microphone to delay their return to the warm bars and restaurants which now beckoned.

That was when the twin spotlights came back on, trained above the heads of the crowd to where the official party stood on the balcony. In a moment the scene was a single pool of brilliant light, making the atmosphere instantly intense and filling the night with expectation. And at the front of the balcony stood Schumacher.

As reward for suggesting and arranging the rally, the *Bürgermeister* had agreed to let Schumacher offer the vote of thanks to the visiting Ambassador. Now he stood there alone in the spotlights, with his arms folded, for seconds which seemed endless. He said nothing. As the crowd continued to rustle, he stared back at them, swinging his body from side to side, seeming to stare back at each and every one of them, demanding their attention. Those around Schumacher began to draw back from him, embarrassed and uneasy, leaving him alone on the brilliantly lit balcony. Schumacher appeared not to notice, standing proud and erect, ignoring his companions and defying the restless crowd.

Soon the shuffling dropped to a murmur as the crowd sensed that something unusual was taking place. If the speaker were insisting on silence, he must have something important to say. For a full minute and more the solitary figure on the balcony said nothing, his arms wrapped around himself like an impatient school-master as he gazed down at the people gathered below, his silence almost threatening in its intensity until the discipline drummed into generations of Prussian schoolchildren asserted itself and complete quiet settled upon the assembly. The dark square with its single pool of light had been turned into a cauldron of anticipation. Then, and only then, did Schumacher begin to speak.

'Dear friends, Berliners,' he began in a pronounced local accent. 'There will be no ringing of the Liberty Bell tonight.'

A gasp went up from the arena. A gauntlet had been thrown down, although they were not yet sure at whom the challenge was aimed.

'It says in the Pledge of Allegiance, sworn by every American, that freedom is indivisible: One nation, under God, with liberty and justice for all. Yet Berlin is divided. And while Berlin remains divided, so Germany is divided. It has neither liberty nor justice.'

He paused for a long while, refolding his arms and staring back at the crowd. No one uttered a word.

'For decades our city has been a pawn in the power games of others. While they argued about communism, about capitalism, about Cuba and Vietnam and the Middle East, it's always the people of Berlin who have had to pay the price for their disagreements. Cut in two. Surrounded. A killing field for foreign troops. How many Berliners have been shot in the back simply for wanting to embrace those they loved?'

Harry felt Katherine stiffen as the words hit her, and he knew those around them were reacting, too. Schumacher's forefinger was jabbing the night air, emphasizing the words which now began rattling out like machine-gun fire.

'How can *we* celebrate liberty? All we ever asked for was to be left alone, to decide for ourselves. Yet Berlin remains nothing more than a doormat on which foreign troops and politicians wipe their boots. And why? Not because of the *Hitlerzeit*. Not because of the Second World War.' He shook his head theatrically, his straight hair falling across his forehead as he did so. 'How many of us were even alive in 1945, let alone old enough to be responsible for the follies of our grandfathers and our great-grandfathers?'

A murmur of agreement ran through the crowd. Beside Harry three young mothers with their children were nodding in assent. Shouts of approval began to echo around the square.

'The Soviets and Americans have announced peace throughout the world. Yet they ignore Berlin. They hand over billions of Deutschmarks to the warring tribes of Africa which are butchering each other and forcing their children into slavery and starvation. Yet Berlin remains forgotten. They bless and support the religious zealots of the Middle East who are trying to exterminate each other in the name of their competing prophets. Yet the peace-loving people of Berlin are condemned. As the American President has said in faraway Washington, you – are – not – part – of – their – deal!'

With every emotive sentence, the ripples of applause and support began to swell and grow. All eyes were trained on Schumacher now; he had hypnotized them.

'You are not responsible. You should not be blamed for the errors of your grandfathers. You bear no guilt for the disputes of the superpowers which they insist on fighting around the streets of Berlin. You are being punished for the sins of others. So when they ask you what you feel about this new era of peace, say to them simply "When?". When will Berlin share in their peace? When will our city be reunited? When shall *we* be set free? When will they give us back Berlin?'

Chants of 'When? When? When?' began to ring around the square, through which Schumacher battled with rising voice to make himself heard.

'So there will be no ringing of the Liberty Bell tonight. Without *one* Berlin, *our* Berlin – we have nothing to celebrate.'

A roar of approval erupted from the crowd. Katherine remained stiff and silent, while Harry looked around at the cheering citizens, both young and old, rich man and worker, who shouted their support of Schumacher.

They were the same people he had watched a few nights before place candles along the Wall; now they looked as if they would be willing to tear it down brick by brick with their bare hands if Schumacher told them to. A cold river of fear ran down his backbone.

'You must leave here tonight with your heads held high. There is no need to bow your head in submission or bend your knee in gratitude. Remember we are not part of their deal. Remember that others have never solved the problems of Germany. Be proud to be Berliners. Give thanks that you were born German. And never forget – you are not responsible.'

A tidal wave of emotion which Harry felt to be a strange mixture of relief and joy swept over the crowd. This was not like any political speech he had ever heard before, it was more like an individual absolution for every single Berliner packed into the square, delivered by a spiritual messenger who had told them to cast aside the false gods and return to the true faith which had been burning inside them all the time. As the wave of noise and enthusiasm hit the front of the town hall, Schumacher gave one last look at his audience and turned sharply, disappearing back into the shadows. The balcony was empty. The people refused to accept that they had been denied their ovation and redoubled their shouts, demanding his return. They wanted more, more, more! But Schumacher had gone.

After several minutes of confusion the elderly *Bürgermeister* walked to the microphone and tried to calm them, but was greeted with shouts of derision. The crowd stamped and clapped to drown his spluttering, until somewhere a switch was pulled and the lights went on all around the square. In an instant the atmosphere was gone and the tension released. People laughed as they began to drift away to resume their evening's pleasure, the passion of previous moments put aside as they resumed their ordinary lives. But Harry noticed that they went with their heads held high.

On the balcony, the *Bürgermeister* introduced yet another speaker, the leader of the local Turkish community, but most of the crowd had already turned their backs and were wandering home. A small group of youths stayed behind to heckle and shout abuse, and after a few faltering phrases the microphones went dead as if the technical gremlins had struck again, so the speaker gave up. The *Bürgermeister* had sent an aide to the bell tower to ensure that the Liberty Bell was rung as ordered, but he arrived to discover the bell room securely locked and the janitor nowhere to be found. The bell would not be rung that night.

As the crowd dispersed, Harry and Katherine began to walk silently through the streets of Berlin, he not knowing where they were going, she not seeming to care. His mind was tumbling with the images of what he had just seen and he could only guess what was going on in hers. But in the cold glare cast by the street lamps he thought she looked older and drawn. They passed a wine bar and Harry decided they both needed a drink. Without asking he took Katherine's hand and pulled her in after him. She made no protest, but sat silently as the glasses were laid out on the wooden table and filled. She drained the wine in a single draught.

Harry had refilled their glasses and she had taken another stiff gulp before she spoke. 'You know, Harry, they say that the wine in Berlin is ferocious. The vines used to grow on the hill in Kreuzberg, not far from here. The wine they produced was so strong that it took three men to drink it: one to swallow and two to hold him down.' She laughed, but there was no pleasure in her voice. Harry began to sense that the humour she so

104

often displayed was little other than a well-developed cover for a deep inner distress which was now showing through. 'That was pretty strong stuff Edward was serving up tonight, eh?'

Harry scarcely knew how to respond. He felt as his grandfather must have done, perhaps sitting in this same bar having witnessed another rally, only partly comprehending the terrible consequences which would flow from it, fearing them enough to send his son away to America yet praying that it would never, could never get *that* bad, and remaining behind with the rest of the family. Until it was too late.

'It was like . . . some old black and white film footage I remember seeing as a child,' he whispered.

'You wanted to know what Berlin was like. Your education just started,' she said drily.

'Are all Berliners . . . ?' he began before remembering that Katherine, too, was a Berliner, and recalling how she had stiffened and reacted under the hammer blows of Schumacher's words.

They stared at each other. A huge gulf had opened up between them which they knew would never be bridged, unless they did it quickly, now.

'Harry, listen to me. There are very few foreigners who truly understand Berlin, rather than just accepting the manure they serve up in guide books. You may not care for what I'm going to say but if you want to find out about us, listen to me.' She took another drink of wine and a deep breath.

'I am a Berliner, and I'm proud to be a Berliner. And I share something deep and fundamental with almost every German in this city. Every day I wake up and I'm surrounded by that obscenity of a Wall. I can't escape it. I go shopping and it's always there in the background. I go for a meal and queue for a table behind foreign troops who guard it. I go for a walk in the countryside and there it is, the barbed wire and watchtowers blocking my way, forcing me back. There's a claustrophobia in Berlin which affects everyone who lives here and who isn't just passing through.'

Like you and your American colleagues, she meant.

'You can't escape the Wall. You can't get away from the reminders that your life has been shattered by that bloody thing.' In spite of her efforts, the emotion was beginning to seep through. 'Every Berliner has relatives and loved ones on the other side. Every German government and American president has promised that one day we will be reunited. But how much longer do we have to wait?'

'But . . . isn't it easier now? Don't you simply have to show your ID?' Harry realized he only had a vague impression of how the Wall worked.

'Identity cards! To visit your dying mother! Scurrying like rats through holes in the wall! Is that what you call freedom? Is that what Americans would tolerate?'

The gulf between them yawned wider than ever, and Katherine took another sip from her glass to calm herself.

'Harry, so long as the Wall is there, it will turn every Berliner into a revolutionary. Berliners want to be part of *one* city. We are brought up with it. It's part of our soul. And you could see tonight how deeply it affects us. The crowd outside the town hall wasn't full of fanatics and political activists; they were simple, ordinary Berliners who have one honest demand: unity. It's what your presidents have promised them ever since they can remember. Do you know, the balcony from where Edward made his speech tonight was the same one Kennedy used to proclaim, *Ich bin ein Berliner*? Every German member of the crowd tonight remembers that promise. But it's ancient history. Today your President tells us that we are not part of his deal. He's saying that Berlin has been thrown on the scrap heap, that we will never be brought together again.'

Harry looked into her eyes. They were smudged with emotion, vulnerable, wanting support. He poured out the last of their bottle of wine.

'You have people over there?'

'Almost everyone in Berlin does.'

'But you, Katherine?'

She answered slowly, the words clearly hurting as she spoke.

'My family lived just a hundred metres across the other side of the Wall. That's where I was born.'

Just like my father, thought Harry.

'When they divided the city they couldn't build the Wall quickly enough; for a while there was just barbed wire and guards. From the Russian sector you could see the people in the West going about their lives, chatting, laughing, waving at us. If we waved back there was usually a *Vopo* to chase us away. Every Sunday morning we used to go as close as we could to the wire and shout across at my grandparents before the *Vopos* caught us and moved us on.'

Harry caught his breath. It reminded him of the stories his father had told him about the ghetto. He wanted to feel no sympathy for Berliners, who had surely brought their fate upon themselves. But this was Katherine, and what in God's name had she done to deserve this?

'Then one Sunday there was just my grandfather dressed in a black suit. My grandmother had died, and we didn't even know about it until after she'd been buried. The *Vopos* came and my mother pleaded with them to let her talk a little longer to Grandfather. She was hysterical so they just beat her. A couple of weeks later the Wall was finished, and after that it wasn't so much that we were divided, it was more like being in prison, peering at the outside world through bars and cracks. We could get only brief glimpses of Grandfather standing on one of those wooden observation towers overlooking the Wall. But we were kept even farther back and all we could do was wave. We couldn't hear what he was trying to say. It went on like that for months. Then one Sunday he didn't turn up, and we never saw him again.'

There was a silence. She didn't want to go on, but Harry insisted. The bridge between them had to be rebuilt tonight or not at all.

'How did you get over?'

'I was married. His name was Peter. We were both so young, so eager about life, so wanting to be free. Then our little baby was born. He nearly died because the apartment was so ferociously cold and damp, because we could never get coal for the stove or medicine for his cough. We knew then we had to come West. I had watched my grandparents die without being able to do anything to help them; I wasn't going to watch the same thing happen to my own baby. Peter was conscripted like every other young man, and he did his time guarding the Wall. He searched out the weak points, knew when the guards were at their laziest, where the wire had been laid carelessly. He was also able to contact a group in the American zone who would help. There were lots of people willing to risk it in those days.'

She bit her lip to stop the tremble. She tried to take a sip of wine, but her shaking hand wouldn't let her. 'So one night I came over the Wall,' she blurted out, struggling for control.

Harry felt like a complete bastard, knowing how much the next question was going to hurt. But he had to ask.

'And Peter and the baby?'

'They didn't make it, Harry. They didn't make it.'

The tears were rolling down her cheeks now as the pain of twenty years of misery flooded into her eyes. Harry found himself struggling with his own emotions. He imagined the scene at the Wall, the pointless sacrifice of innocent lives, the bullets and the brutality, the scars that would never heal. And he remembered his own father and the memories that had haunted him until his dying day. Berlin was a city of inhumanity, inflicted by Berliner upon Berliner. How could he feel pity for them, even for Katherine, without betraying his father and the relatives he had left behind in this damnable place? Yet he knew that Katherine was as innocent as he, and he couldn't hate her. As he looked at her he could find no words to express his torment.

He reached across the table and grasped her hand. She saw the tears in his eyes and squeezed his fingers tightly. They were both victims of evil worlds – they shared that, and something much more. The bridge between them had been rebuilt.

The White House

'What's all this shit in Bonn, Leo?' the President demanded.

'Berlin,' corrected Grossman.

Michelle put down the State Department telexes he

had been studying and turned to his national security adviser for enlightenment.

'Hell, the next batch of primaries are only days away and everything's looking good. I don't want a bunch of damn Germans jeering our ambassador and screwing everything up. Makes you wonder who the enemy is, for Chrissake!'

The President was in a particularly peppery mood this morning. The latest opinion polls had restored his natural bullishness and bluster, and he would go to hell before he would allow a group of distant foreigners to question his judgement, least of all on such electorally advantageous matters as the agreement with Moscow. 'So what do we do?'

'Nothing,' replied Grossman.

'Nothing? You mean let them get away with it?'

'Let them stew in it, Mr President,' he replied in that guttural accent which the television cameras so loved to capture and which made the White House press secretary wince. After all, Michelle had been elected on the promise of introducing an 'all-American presidency' – whatever that meant – and Grossman emphasized his foreign origins every time he opened his mouth. But Grossman was certain about the German question. His ancestors in Warsaw had spent generations both as Jews and as Poles dealing with it, and Germany had meant nothing but trouble. It had cost most of his own family their lives and had dragged America into two world wars; he had no doubt that it would drag the world into a third, given the chance. And withdrawing troops from Berlin would give them just that chance – to reunite, to dominate and desiccate Europe all over again. He had worked hard to deliver a new and more stable world order, and there was no way he was going to allow Germans to mess that up. So the American

110

and Soviet troops must stay, the exception to the rule.

'No one outside Germany wants reunification – not the British, the French, least of all the Russians. They're on their own, so just ignore them.'

'Do you think we can do that, Leo? With the primaries coming up?'

Grossman was at his most magisterial.

'Mr President, ask yourself. How many votes are there for you in Berlin?'

Berlin

Miss Pickerstaff was in a foul mood. What was supposed to have been a triumph of organization had turned into a fiasco on the balcony of the town hall. All her best preparations had been blown aside, the Ambassador had been furious with everyone and had made it clear he was most unlikely to come to Berlin again in the near future, so she would have no opportunity of regaining lost ground. What was worse the Minister, the head of the Mission in Berlin, had remembered that it was on her suggestion he had invited the Ambassador to attend the rally in the first place. It had seemed like a good idea at the time, but there wasn't a soul willing any longer to admit it and the Minister had spent the last half-hour kicking hell out of her, just as the Ambassador had earlier kicked hell out of him.

It was unfortunate that Harry's fresh enthusiasm led him to knock on her door while the other, more experienced hands in the Mission had given Miss Pickerstaff a wide berth that morning. He was her first visitor and walked right into the firing line.

'I've had some thoughts about last night,' he ventured as he walked into her office.

'Benjamin, I've had more than enough thoughts expressed to me on that matter,' she said tartly, not lifting her eyes from the papers she was shuffling on her desk. 'I don't need any more.'

Harry refused to heed the warning. He had been struggling all morning with the events of the previous night, trying to decide whether his coalescing views about Schumacher were being guided more by the interest he realized he was developing in Katherine than objective and dispassionate analysis. The fact that he had to ask himself the question made him suspicious of his own conclusions, but on the other hand he couldn't bury his doubts about the husband just because he fancied the wife. To hell with it. There was only one way to find out.

'I think it was a set-up.'

'What on earth do you mean?' demanded Miss Pickerstaff, dragging her attention away from the papers for the first time. Harry noted that her eyes were blazing with anger. Not at him, of course. What had he done?

'Wasn't it all a little too convenient? Like some unseen hand was switching things on and off to ensure that Schumacher became a star, without any distractions or competition? So this morning I started asking around. I found out that it was Schumacher who suggested the idea of the rally in the first place. He was responsible for much of the organization. If he arranged for the lights to be turned on, I guess it was just as easy for him to arrange for them to be turned off as he was preparing to speak. And for the microphone plug to fall out while the Turk was speaking.'

Harry was warming to his theme, and didn't notice the growing fire in Miss Pickerstaff's face. A wisp of her usually tightly secured greying hair had fallen into her eyes, and she was struggling impatiently to put it back in place. The hair-grip clenched between her teeth prevented her from responding as Harry ploughed on.

'In one night he's managed to get himself elected the unofficial leader of the Berlin crowd and at the same time do a lot of damage to relations with the United States.'

'You cannot be serious . . .' Miss Pickerstaff instructed through clenched teeth, but it was too late. Harry was already on to his next furrow.

'Why, it wouldn't surprise me if he turned out to be the one who invited the Ambassador here in the first place and I guess . . .'

She could take no more. The hair-grip clattered off the desk top and the hair flopped forward once again, giving her a dishevelled and faintly demented look as she banged her fists in frustration.

'Benjamin, I'm going to stop your guessing and fill you in on some of the real facts of life rather than the fanciful ones you're dreaming about,' she spat. 'I'll say this only once. I don't want to hear your half-assed ideas about Schumacher. Frankly I don't want to hear your ideas about anything. You are employed to do as you are told, by me. Which for the next nine months means being a commercial analyst and not chasing around Berlin like some deranged version of J. Edgar Hoover!'

'But I thought I might have a closer look at Schumacher and see who some of his friends . . .'

'I don't know whether you are stupid or just slow. You will do nothing about Schumacher and particularly his friends. You will present me with a daily digest of what you are doing, who you are seeing, and where you are going in Berlin.' She had thrown a lasso around him, and was just about to hang him from the highest branch she could find. 'And I shall personally scrutinize all your expenses!' she exclaimed.

Harry shook his head in disbelief. He was being lashed to his desk, without even a credit card for comfort. But the bad dream continued.

'You're an arrogant imbecile who appears incapable of taking orders, and I suspect your time in the agency will be short and not particularly sweet. It is my misfortune you were posted here. I intend to make sure you cause as little trouble as possible.'

'But Miss Pickerstaff . . .'

'Get out!' she screamed, and Harry at last resolved that retreat was his best course before another flush hit her.

As he closed the door behind him, he caught sight of Miss Pickerstaff on her hands and knees, scrabbling on the floor for her lost hair-grip. He left wondering whether the KGB made hormone boosts compulsory for their middle-aged female officers.

Moscow

The telephone rang several times before a sleepy voice answered it. Bykov had forgotten that Malinin was something of a puritan who took to his bed early and only for sleep.

'Malinin. My apologies for waking you so late. But I thought you would like to know that an extraordinary meeting of the Politburo has been called for tomorrow afternoon. You will not hear about it officially until the morning. He is expecting your resignation then.'

'And if I don't?'

'You will be expelled by a unanimous vote and an immediate enquiry ordered into the means by which over the years you have amassed the largest private collection of foreign art treasures in the Soviet Union.'

'Doubtless the results of that enquiry have already been determined. Even in the era of *glasnost* the admiration of French Impressionism is enough to get one branded a capitalist roader,' said Malinin, the sleep having disappeared entirely from his voice. 'And if I resign?'

'The enquiry might be delayed for several months – so long as you remember to make the reason for your resignation clear.'

'And break wind gently. Yes, I have not forgotten. First Palin. Then me. How long does Semyonov have?'

'How long do any of us have . . . ?'

'I trust the wolves are not too hungry at this time of year, Comrade General.'

'They have fed well this spring. You have nothing to fear until the snows return next winter.'

'For that I am grateful.'

'Goodnight, Malinin.'

FOUR

Berlin

Harry didn't put much store in faith. The son of a bitter Jewish father and a non-practising Christian mother, he had taken a very caustic view about any form of zealotry. It had left him with an open, questioning mind, but it had also left him with nowhere to go when he needed reassurance and support. After his session with Miss Pickerstaff he had wandered around the streets of central Berlin, getting lost in the crowds of shoppers, taking a cup of hot, dark coffee at one of the kerbside stalls, trying to ignore the rain which was gusting down in sheets.

He had inherited some of his father's pessimism, and as the rain trickled down his neck he found it difficult to argue with. Miss Pickerstaff might have been out of sorts, but she meant every word she said. He could already envisage his annual performance evaluation from her: 'Severe attitude problem. Uncooperative. Not a team player and poor at accepting orders. Has achieved little in his first twelve months.' How could he, stuck in the basement of Clayallee sifting old volumes of *Die Berliner Wirtschaft*? 'Not recommended for promotion.' Normally they would give people a second chance, another position to see if there were any saving talents to be found. But not in his case. He had nobody back in Langley who would be willing to fight his corner. He would be out.

He found it easy to hate Berlin, for what it had done to his father and for what it was now doing to him.

Except for Katherine. They had only just met but she had worked her way into his waking hours, into his dreams, and into his desires. He remembered that first time, at Kempinski's, as the silk of her evening dress had clung to her body, suggesting so much more than it displayed. She moved with such natural elegance, with the grace of a model and the hips of a woman meant to be loved . . .

Another gust of cold rain hit him from behind and began to creep down the back of his neck, waking him from his dream.

'She's married, dick-head,' he muttered to himself and decided he must try to stop thinking of Katherine like that.

The rain was falling heavily and Harry looked for somewhere to shelter. He couldn't take any more coffee and he had no desire to squelch round any of the fashionable jewellery and clothes shops he found close at hand. He looked up, uncertain where he was, and found himself staring at an extraordinary architectural confection of old and new. In the middle of the square formed by the intersection of several major streets stood the tower of an old church, battered and gnarled with a broken steeple pointing up to the sky like a fractured tooth. Clearly it had been part of a great Prussian cathedral at the heart of pre-war Berlin but now it stood alone and isolated, mimicking the smile of an old hag with one last molar clinging to her jaw. Beside it, like a dentist's desperate attempt to buttress the sole remaining tooth, stood the separated components of a modern church, all sharp rectangles and glass, a complete contrast to the old tower which had defied the ravages of time and twentieth-century warfare and proudly bore the scars to prove it.

Old and new Berlin stood side by side, begging for

comparison, and Harry found he had no doubts. It was the new Berlin which fascinated him. Not the old city of half-ruined Prussian monuments kept as memorials to an era long dead and hopefully buried, but the new which had risen from the rubble and expressed a different kind of ambition. Like Katherine; not like his father. As Harry wandered inside the modern construction, he found himself entering a womb. The noise of the traffic was reduced to a distant rumble and the thousands of tiny stained-glass windows set in the high church walls flooded the interior with a rich, deep blue glow.

Harry sat quietly in one of the simple seats, his damp clothes forgotten, trying to feel the spirit of this new Berlin. Many people would have found the atmosphere calm and reassuring, a place for troubled souls to settle and come to terms with their lot in an unhappy world. But for him it brought back the turmoil which had been part of him ever since he was born. Above his head, suspended by some invisible force in mid-air, towered an impressionistic bronze sculpture of Christ, fashioned in the form of a cross from twisted and tortured metal. 'The Christian symbol of suffering,' his father would have reminded him, 'and whenever you find one of those, remember the pain and suffering they have inflicted on your people.'

Yet Harry wasn't like his father. He couldn't spend his life wrapped in cynicism, brooding about the past. And he had never been very good at doing what he was told. As he sat listening to his father's insistent voice, his stubbornness returned. He felt neither Jew nor Gentile. He couldn't bring himself to acknowledge that he was bound by any fate. He bore no inherited guilt nor reproach for others. This was *his* life, and he would screw it up in his own way.

He remembered Miss Pickerstaff. He knew there was no chance of rehabilitation with her. If he were going to make anything out of his time in Berlin, it must be on his terms not hers. It would put his career at risk, but that was already in jeopardy, so what had he to lose? It wasn't in his nature to follow blindly. He was simply too determined and single-minded – or was it pig-headed? He would never find out for sure, unless he gave himself the chance.

So he would chase his instincts about Schumacher. And Katherine, too. And trust to luck that whichever of the gods claimed him as of right would be in a forgiving mood.

The following morning's edition of *B.Z.* landed like a lash across the back of Berlin.

'BETRAYAL!' it roared.

The helter-skelter ride of emotion which had hypnotized Berliners in the last few days was about to continue.

'Berlin is to lose its special status and its lifeline of economic subsidies as soon as the new East–West treaty is signed, it was revealed last night.

'Documents leaked from the Interior Ministry in Bonn reveal that plans are being laid to save much and possibly all of the eight billion Deutschmarks paid every year by the federal government to support the economy of Berlin. "The pressures of recession force us to look at some difficult and unpalatable measures," the official report says. "In light of the new international situation and with the prospect of Soviet troop withdrawals in the East, we can no longer justify the present level of subsidies. If we are to avoid Berlin becoming a permanent and growing economic burden while releasing resources for pressing needs in the rest of Germany,

119

substantial cuts in taxpayers' support for Berlin must be achieved."

'Contacted late last night, *Vorsitzender* Edward Schumacher responded to the report with "a mixture of intense anger and disbelief. Berlin cannot survive without the support of other freedom-loving Germans," he said. "We are a small island in dangerous seas many miles away from the rest of West Germany. How do they expect us to survive on our own?"

'Schumacher predicted that the savage cuts in economic subsidies would force the closure of many Berlin factories and the loss of tens of thousands of jobs.

'"Berlin's industrial heartland in Siemenstadt will become a desert," he predicted. "Unemployment will soar, schools and hospitals will close. We will be slowly strangled to death. Bureaucrats and spineless politicians in Bonn will do what Stalin failed to achieve – the destruction of Free Berlin."

'"We have been betrayed," he added.

'Senior representatives of both Siemens and AEG, the two largest manufacturers in Berlin, both indicated that their present operations in the city would become uneconomic and unsustainable without the continuation of the subsidy from the federal government in Bonn. "It's the only reason we came to Berlin in the first place," said another industrialist. "Without it, who would bother sending trains full of raw material to Berlin, only to send the trains loaded with finished goods back again?"

'The *Bürgermeister*'s office refused to comment on the report last night, and no spokesman was available from the Interior Ministry in Bonn.'

B. Z. sold out that morning. Berliners had been taken to the top of the mountain by their initial enthusiasm for the summit agreement, and shown a future brimming with peace and prosperity. Now they were to be denied, and shoved from behind into the pit.

It was not until several hours after the story had spread from the news-stands across the breadth of Berlin that any official comment became available – the unofficial comment varied from the confused to the profane as questions bombarded the Interior Ministry's press office – but by early afternoon a terse statement put out to assembled newsmen denied that any such document existed. When asked why it had taken so many hours to make this announcement, the perplexed spokesman tried to explain that it always took longer to establish that a document didn't exist than to confirm that one did.

Unfortunately, this served only to make matters worse when, several hours later, someone in the Ministry discovered that there was after all such a document. The spokesman returned in a state of even greater perplexity to confront the television cameras and assembled press corps. A document containing some of the quoted references did exist, he acknowledged, prepared by a lowly civil servant looking at a number of purely hypothetical options which might be considered. No, it certainly didn't represent official policy, and in any event the quotations used had been taken out of context. Yes, it was an embarrassment that he hadn't known about this document earlier, but it was one of simply thousands of documents prepared and filed away in the labyrinths of official Bonn. Perhaps he had slightly misled them, but it was quite unintentional, and in any event the document did not represent the views of the government and he was sure they would understand.

Which, of course, they didn't. Particularly when it was discovered that the document had been written only days previously by an official who was not available for comment since he had left somewhat unexpectedly for a distant holiday in the Indian Ocean. In the view of the media, the whole thing stank of incompetence, or worse.

As far as Berliners were concerned, the worst was everything they had ever feared in the moments of insecurity which lingered beneath the surface of their extravagant lifestyle. They could feel the Wall slowly closing in around them.

The audience for the early evening news show on Television Free Berlin was always good, and that night was the highest for years. The face of the flustered official spokesman in Bonn came and went with its contradictions and corrections, succeeding only in emphasizing that nothing he said could be taken on trust.

'To comment on the somewhat confused events of today we invited to our studio this evening both the US Minister to Berlin and also the chief *Bürgermeister*. Unfortunately, neither was able to accept our invitation . . .' That was a cheap shot, of course. Every Berliner knew that in spite of having been in the post for more than three years the US Minister could still speak no more than a dozen words of German, and it had been an equally long time since the ageing *Bürgermeister* had risked his dulled wits on a substantive political debate. 'So we have instead the Minister's senior information director along with the chairman of the governing party, Edward Schumacher.'

The American was at his best. His tone was moderate, his nodding head not too condescending, his words full of understanding for the anxieties of the people of Berlin. He was doing well, very well, until Schumacher hijacked the programme and took over the questioning.

'I'm sorry to interrupt,' said Schumacher without the

slightest hint of apology in his voice, 'but the American President stated that there was to be no change in the status of Berlin as a result of the treaty. No change,' he repeated, stabbing his finger across the studio to emphasize the words. 'Yet now we learn that plans are being discussed which will impose immense change. What are the American government doing about it?'

'I'm . . . sure we shall be in contact with the West German government to discuss the matter,' the American responded with a trace of uncertainty.

'I can't believe I'm hearing that. Either the President lied, or he's been appallingly misled. If he wasn't lying, why hasn't he already been in touch to demand an explanation?'

'Let me reassure you that there is nothing sinister in this,' smiled the American. 'It all seems to have been a misunderstanding.'

'So that there is no further misunderstanding, tell Berliners out there when the US government will be starting talks to dismantle the Wall and hand back Berlin to its people.'

'That's scarcely the point,' blustered the American. 'We're talking about the East—West treaty, not reunification.'

They were clumsy words from a man under pressure. He could have bitten his tongue off the moment he said them, but it was already too late. Schumacher had come prepared, and knew exactly where he wanted to lead the discussion. His jaw jutted stubbornly forward; he would not be denied.

'Let me ask you again. When will you begin discussions to bring down the Wall and reunite Berlin?'

It was an impossibly specific question to answer. He didn't know – no one knew. So the American reverted to generalities.

123

'I scarcely need to remind you that the Americans have always been the closest friends and allies of West Berlin. We have helped support and defend this city for decades. Surely you haven't forgotten that, Herr Schumacher?'

Schumacher's tone was quiet, full of controlled anger. The words were spoken slowly and picked out one by one, building steadily in their passion like a musical score which had been well rehearsed – as indeed Schumacher's script had, earlier that afternoon: 'I'll tell you what I haven't forgotten. I haven't forgotten it was the Americans who agreed to the original division of Berlin, at the Potsdam Conference in 1945. I haven't forgotten it was the Americans who refused to help when the people of East Berlin rose up and pleaded for freedom in 1953. You left them with nothing more than stones to throw at Russian tanks before they were finally crushed. I haven't forgotten it was the Americans who in 1961 watched as the barbed wire was stretched across Berlin and who assisted the Russians to build their cursed Wall . . .'

The American was shaking his head in disbelief and rebuttal.

'Oh, shake your head, but it was your soldiers who held back the crowds of Berliners who wanted to tear down the foundations with their bare hands!'

'That's a gross exaggeration,' protested the American but it was too late.

'I was there! At the Brandenburg Gate on the thirteenth of August 1961. With hundreds of other Berliners. We shouted protests. We could see the Russians ripping out the heart of our city. We wanted to pull the Wall down before the mortar had dried. We wanted to tear it down brick by brick. And who stopped us? Who held us back? American soldiers with loaded rifles!

124

Pushed us back a hundred yards so the Russians could get on with their building, while we could only watch from behind American rifle butts. *You* divided the city. *You* helped them build the Wall. So I ask you once again. When-will-it-come-down?'

Schumacher had been pounding the table as his anger flowed, but now he stopped. There was complete silence, leaving the question to hang in the air across the studio, as it was doing in living rooms across Berlin.

The American hadn't been briefed for this. He hadn't even been trained for this. He was an information officer, not a gunslinger versed in controlling the tension of a shoot-out. He had nothing to say, and the TV lights suddenly seemed intensely hot. He flushed and made no comment.

Schumacher's voice was quiet again, full of dignified control and sadness as he twisted the knife, not as a butcher but as an executioner. 'Your silence speaks louder than all the words we have heard over the years from American dignitaries as they swept through Berlin to tell us how much they identified with us before catching the next plane home. The United States and the Soviet Union are carving up the world. "Peace across all the world", you proclaim, but it's *your* peace, an American and a Russian peace, not peace for us Berliners. You don't want us united, disturbing your cosy control. The two of you have been playing with us for years, but now you're bored and have decided to declare your game a draw. You've thrown Berlin away. Haven't you?'

There was no reply from the stunned American, terrified that anything he might say could only make matters worse. The silence spread as he battled to unscramble his thoughts and find the right thing to say, until the interviewer spoke for the first time in several moments.

'I'm afraid that's all we have time for tonight. Goodnight, Berlin.'

Moscow

The remote control switched off the television which stood at the end of the bed, and the scenes of battle from Television Free Berlin picked up by the satellite dish on Bykov's roof faded to a small dot in the dark room. His wife rolled over, disturbed by the sudden silence, and the mattress bent sharply. God, thought Bykov, how can she snore like thunder yet sleep so lightly?

'Anything wrong, Georgi?' she asked, rubbing the sleep from her eyes with the back of her hand.

'No, nothing's wrong. In fact everything is going just fine. Sleep.'

She did as she was told, and was soon snoring again, leaving Bykov to muse in the dark. Things were developing extremely well, just as he had planned. And tomorrow his wife was off to spend the week at her sister's in Odessa. Which meant he should get a good night's rest, because there was little chance of his getting much sleep tomorrow, what with the encouragingly rapid way his chauffeur was learning the ropes. Yes, things were working out very well indeed.

He slipped deeper under the bedclothes, wishing it were tomorrow already.

Harry was glad he had taken the trouble to consult the computer file on Schumacher the night before. They were backing up for it the morning after the interview, led by the Minister's assistant, his senior information director and Miss Pickerstaff. But they wouldn't find anything. The files were like obituaries; they had little to say about the living, and by the time they had anything worthwhile on anyone it was usually too late. So it was with Schumacher who, according to IBM, had been a model politician and businessman until a week ago.

But for the moment Harry had other things on his mind. The Mission's General Services Officer had come up with the addresses of two apartments for him to look at, and he was keen to begin living somewhere other than in his suitcase. Until the previous year Mission personnel had lived relatively luxuriously in designated accommodation paid for by the Germans as part of the occupation costs, but that was yet another arrangement which was beginning to fall apart under the remorseless pressure of recession and financial constraint. At least it gave him greater freedom to choose where he might live. So he had given Katherine a call and asked if she would drive him to the addresses and offer her advice. It seemed a reasonably plausible excuse for inviting her to spend more time with him, but he didn't particularly mind whether she believed him or not. The important thing was she had agreed.

They had inspected the first apartment, but it was entirely unsuitable for Harry. It was part of a concrete and glass rabbit warren which had been built for young couples and was so abstract and anonymous that Harry felt he could have been in any city in the world. He wanted Berlin, not a universal cubicle decorated out of some overpriced designer's catalogue, and they were soon on their way to the second address, with Harry reflecting ruefully that the great American dollar didn't buy as much as it used to.

The second, as he had requested, was in Kreuzberg. Officers from the Mission didn't live in Kreuzberg, so the GSO had argued, but couldn't find a suitable explanation as to why. Such bureaucratic opposition only made Harry more insistent, so the GSO had sulked and muttered that he would regret it. Now Harry was passing the strange sights of the Turkish quarter once again, with its women in dark headscarves and brightly patterned shawls which he had glimpsed from the back of the taxi on his first day in the city. Yet there was more. A new wave of immigrants had established a foothold in some of the streets; they were the young – students and artists in the main with a fair smattering of social dropouts – who treated the wide streets of Kreuzberg as a theatre, a canvas, or a place simply to escape from the frenetic materialism of the rest of West Berlin. Vast modern frescoes adorned the walls of old buildings, and everywhere seemed to be filled with activity and colour. A street market offered a host of stalls selling paints, books and bric-à-brac which was thronged with young Germans holding hands and pushing cycles. The mixture of cultures and styles presented a kaleidoscope of patterns which seemed to change with every street corner, never conforming or agreeing with the last.

As Katherine drew her Mercedes to a halt outside the address, a crowd of Turkish children began to gather around and make faces at themselves in the brightly polished coachwork, and above the doorway on a small portico a young black man braved the cold to serenade the street on his saxophone.

Inside, the hallway was dark and traditional. As they clambered up the creaking staircase, they could smell the coats of varnish which seemed to have trapped the atmosphere of old Berlin, cutting through the tang of *Sauerkraut* bubbling away on some stove in the back of the building. They were both panting slightly by the time they reached the heavy oak door on the third floor. Harry had taken her hand to help her up the last flight and they were both laughing like schoolchildren on an adventure. He produced a bunch of old-fashioned brass keys and the door swung open slowly but easily on large hinges.

They walked into one huge, towering room. In the days before the building had been converted into apartments the room had obviously served as a library or music room. Along one wall were two large, curtained windows which threw streams of light on to the corniced ceiling, where a large if grubby chandelier still hung. The wallpaper was rich and faded above the wooden half-panelling, and there was only one piece of furniture in the entire place – a brass bed with a bare mattress, jammed up against a fireplace which was blackened with soot and clearly hadn't been used for many years. The GSO had got his revenge.

Katherine walked slowly around the room, her footsteps clicking across the wooden floor, checking the dust on the marble mantel above the fireplace, shaking the curtains, looking through the two doors which led into the tiny kitchen and an oversized, draughty bathroom, giving the bed the most cursory of glances before looking at Harry and bursting into laughter.

'It's a tart's emporium. No one's spent more than a

129

couple of hours in here at any one time since the place was converted.'

Her laughter echoed around the enormous room, but Harry appeared not to notice. He had gone to one of the windows which stretched all the way to the ceiling and pulled back the lace curtain covering the unwashed panes of glass. He stood looking out, his attention no longer in the room.

'Harry, what is it?' she asked, putting a hand on his shoulder. She followed his stare. Less than fifty yards away, across a strip of scrubby grass still covered in the last of the winter snow, was the Wall, and beyond it the empty streets of the East. A young man stood in front of the concrete barrier, carelessly spraying it with graffiti. 'Fuck the Treaty', he inscribed, a comment which had been appearing at many places over the city in the last few days.

'I'm taking it,' Harry said in a low voice.

'You can't. It's so . . . impractical.'

'Nevertheless, I'm taking it.'

'But why? Why Kreuzberg? Why here?'

'Because I want to be among the real Berliners, the people who are the heart of the city, not stuck amongst the socialites and diplomatic cocktail circuit in Dahlem or Schöneberg,' he replied in a moody voice, still staring out of the window. He didn't mean it to be, but it sounded like a rebuke.

'But how can you spend your weekends looking at . . . this?' she asked, gesturing at the dismal view, her voice full of the pain which any reminder of Peter gave her.

When he turned around to face her his dark eyes were smouldering. 'Because my father was born over there,' he said.

'He was a Berliner?' she asked in astonishment.

130

'He was Jewish, Katherine.'

She froze as she comprehended what history must lie behind any Jew of his father's age who had lived in Berlin, and what emotion was now reflected in Harry's eyes.

'I was brought up to hate Berlin and everything that was left in it,' he continued. 'And I know I shall hate it even more. Because of you.'

'What do you mean?'

'I'm not sure. All I know is that you're the only thing I've found in this city which hasn't confirmed my father's worst views. Yet . . .' He found himself impossibly tongue-tied, his cheeks coloured and he cursed himself for acting like a teenager.

'Yet I'm married, considerably older than you, and German. You're young, a diplomat. And a Jew. Is that about it?'

'How much more do you want?' His voice rose in frustration. 'There's a damned great wall running straight between the two of us, and it's got me so confused.' He wanted to sit down, but there was only the bed and the thought of that made him feel more nervous. He couldn't look straight at her for fear she might be laughing at him.

'You don't need to be young and a foreigner to be confused about this city, Harry. The older I get, the less certain I seem to be about anything. There are things we can do nothing about, no matter how hard we try – like that,' she said, pointing through the window. 'But there are some walls in our lives we can knock down. I want you to come with me.'

She took his hand in a way they had never touched before, leading him down the stairs and out once more into the street. They drove in silence for more than twenty minutes, all the while Katherine holding on to

131

Harry with one hand as if afraid that the world would rush between and separate them if given the slightest chance. They were on the other side of Berlin and Harry was hopelessly lost before she slowed the car and began driving up a narrow road which wound through dense woodlands. She drew to a stop in a little courtyard laid out among the trees, at one end of which, leading through a high wall, stood a pair of wrought-iron gates.

'Harry, what I'm about to show you could ruin many lives. I must trust you.'

She swung open the gates which creaked in protest, and led Harry into a neat, crowded cemetery. It was an old graveyard, protected by the high walls from the bustle and intrusion of the outside world. The gravestones and memorial tablets were squashed tightly together and the ivy and evergreen shrubs tumbled over each other as they fought for space. Yet everything was in its place, cared for, a garden of peace where the memories could linger in the rose bushes, reminding the visitor that whatever peril had swept over the city, the generations of man somehow still managed to continue. You felt welcome here.

It was only then that Harry noticed the Star of David on the tombstones.

'The Jewish cemetery,' Katherine explained, leading him past family memorials in distinctive Hebrew script named for Isaac and Ruth and Rosa and Aron, and a simple tablet dedicated to those 'whose names are not written, yet who are not forgotten'.

In the far corner away from the gates she led him towards a family plot where stood a brightly polished stone, not weathered by the passage of many years. It was a memorial to a baker, his wife and their son, all of whom had died within the last ten years. Etched in the black marble beneath their personal details was

132

carved the inscription: 'Born in Brandenburg. Died in freedom. We give thanks to God.'

'The Jakobsohn family,' Katherine explained.

'You knew them?'

'I got them over the Wall,' she said simply.

'You?'

'Me. And Edward. And a handful of others. The Jakobsohns were just three of many we helped. Before the gates were opened. And it didn't matter to us if they were Jewish or German or gypsies or bank robbers. All that mattered was that they wanted to be free.'

'I would never have thought . . .'

'What do you think I am, Harry? Just a bored Berlin housewife? You forget I have my own debts to pay.'

'I'm sorry. Tell me about it.'

She took his hand and they walked slowly along the path which meandered between the gravestones and monuments to the dead, while they talked about the unquenchable desire to live.

'There's no great mystery, really. I couldn't accept life without Peter and the baby. The first few months in West Berlin were so desperately lonely I often felt like . . . well, I wished I hadn't made it. It would have been simpler if all three of us had finished together, just as we had started. Peter is the only man I have ever really loved.'

Harry would never have believed he could feel jealous of a man dead more than twenty years, but he felt a dryness in his throat as she spoke.

'I needed something to fill the gap or I would simply have fallen apart. Yet everything I thought or dreamed about always centred around the Wall. It was like a magnet; I couldn't get away from it, I was always drawn back there no matter how hard I tried to get away. So I decided to use it. Edward had been one of those who helped drag me across the Wall, and I asked him if I could help with others coming over. Soon we were running a successful escape ring. Edward used contacts through his trading company to find people who wanted to come across, and I organized the escape details from this side of the Wall. He would tell me when someone wanted to run and delivered him or her to a prearranged spot; I would take care of the details from there. Nobody knew the whole plan, even today no more than a handful know what I've just told you.'

'How often did it happen?'

'Whenever someone was desperate enough to risk it. We disguised them as freight or bribed an African diplomat to smuggle them through in the boot of their car, or occasionally we'd bring them directly over the Wall if we discovered a weak spot.'

'Is it still going on?'

'Not really. Maybe once or twice in the last three years, nothing for a long while.' She seemed saddened by it, as if she had lost something which was important to her. 'People are waiting. They're not sure for what. All the changes in Moscow have given them a glimmer of hope, a little more patience.'

'Why the secrecy?'

'Because it was a dangerous business, Harry. And not just in the East. Some people made a lot of money smuggling refugees, and they were pretty ruthless with anyone they regarded as competition.' She saw the astonished look on his face. 'Why should that surprise you? There was a huge amount of money involved for some, and unlike drug smuggling it was all perfectly legal – at least once you got to this side of the border.'

She stopped and took both of his hands, looking directly into his eyes.

'And there's always the gnawing fear, deep down

134

inside, that one day the ring will be needed again. No one can be sure, not until the Wall comes down for good . . . That's why I must trust you to keep this secret.'

'Then why tell me? I don't understand . . .'

'Because your father was wrong. Because you are wrong to build unnecessary walls around yourself. So you're Jewish and I'm German. So what? Must we always look back a thousand years and be afraid to take a single step forward? I've spent my whole life looking back. Don't waste your life as I've had to waste mine.'

'But you seem to have everything . . .'

'And yet I have almost nothing. I left too much behind on the other side.'

'I want you.' God knows why he said it, but there it was.

'I know you do,' she whispered.

She was close to him, confiding secrets which were only for him to hear. He could feel her breath and smell her hair, and he no longer knew what to do. He leaned forward to kiss her.

'No, Harry,' she said, turning her face away. He felt a complete idiot for having misjudged the moment so badly. She sensed his embarrassment and tried to make him understand.

'Edward pulled me over the Wall. He was there to help me get through those first few awful months. We started the escape ring together and he has supported me ever since. I owe him.'

'Forgive me, but that doesn't sound like love.'

'It's not. Perhaps it never was. But he deserves my respect.'

'Looking back still?'

'That's cruel, Harry. But perhaps you're right. Maybe I have so little to look forward to.'

'I still want you. And I'm taking the room.'

She laughed lightly to break the tension. The lesson was now over.

'Thanks for kicking away a few bricks,' he said, and meant it.

Just behind her head, in the part of the cemetery which caught the afternoon sun, a climbing rose clambered up the bricks of the old boundary wall. New shoots were beginning to sprout from its many stems; in a few weeks it would help lighten the soul of the saddest mourners. One solitary blood-red bloom was early, defying the calendar and bursting into life ahead of itself. It would never survive, of course; the slightest hint of a late frost and it would wither and drop. But for now it stood alone, alive, and very beautiful. Harry reached around her and carefully, even tenderly, plucked the bloom, savouring its fragrance before handing it to Katherine.

'For you. I don't normally go round raiding cemeteries, but I have a feeling today is very special, meant for the living.'

She thought for a moment before nodding and accepting the rose, and smiled. 'Take me for a cup of coffee, Harry Benjamin. It's not good for young people like us to spend all our time in cold graveyards.'

They walked off hand in hand back towards the gates. Harry was silent. It had been a moment of enlightenment for him, but one which also caused him considerable consternation. He was beginning to realize how very little he understood about either Edward or Katherine Schumacher.

The White House

Grossman walked into the Oval Office without knocking and found the President helping himself to a stiff tumbler of bourbon.

'CBS is just about to publish its first exit poll,' he announced, crossing to the television and switching it on.

Michelle had been waiting nervously all week for a major batch of primaries to be held in the mid-west. He had fared reasonably well in the handful of ballots over the previous weeks, but they had mostly been in east-coast states where as a New Yorker he was expected to do well. The mid-west was different. The recession had hit there hardest, both in the industrial cities and in the wheat belt, where land prices had tumbled and the banks had started calling in their loans.

'What can I do with *glasnost*?' one farmer had said the night before to the nation's best-known television correspondent. 'My cattle can't eat it. I can't use it to pay my debts. I'm real glad that the rest of the world is sleeping peaceful tonight, but tomorrow they're coming to auction off my farm. If the President had spent more time sorting out my problems than sucking up to the Soviets, then maybe I'd vote for him. But he'll have to excuse me. Tomorrow I've got other things to do, like trying to find somewhere for my wife and kids to live.'

Men didn't normally cry in Missouri, explained the TV correspondent as the farmer unashamedly wiped away a tear from his face, but when your farm had been in the family for over a hundred years, even grown men get emotional.

Grossman had checked with the White House pollster just a few minutes earlier. Their latest poll was two days old. Michelle's vote seemed to be holding up, he reported, but there was no great enthusiasm for the President. All this news about the anti-American demonstrations which had begun to appear in Berlin and other parts of Germany in the fortnight since the summit hadn't exactly helped sell what was supposed to be Michelle's greatest success. Although what did the mid-west care about Berlin . . . ?

They would soon know. The TV monitor still showed lines of voters trudging through the falling snow to the polling stations as Michelle settled silently into one of the easy chairs and hugged his drink. The TV scene shifted to the controlled chaos of an election-night news room and the profile of one of the nation's best-known political pundits.

'There are still three hours left before the last vote is cast,' he intoned, 'but already we have some exit poll figures. They show that President Michelle is likely to win a clear majority of the votes in both Arkansas and Oklahoma, while in the crucial electoral states of Texas, Florida and Missouri the local favourite sons are putting in a surprisingly strong showing. In all three states the results at this stage are too close to call. It seems that many of his traditionally loyal supporters are firing a warning shot across the President's bows.'

'Goddamn those bastards!' shouted Michelle, pushing himself out of his chair in frustration and striding across the room to refill his glass. 'Christ, Leo. What's going on? Could they be bum exit polls?'

'They could be, Mr President,' Grossman's flat voice began as if embarking on another Harvard lecture, 'but I think not in this case.'

'For fuck's sake, why?'

'Recession breeds cynicism. That's why we gave them the summit and the troops agreement, to fill the gap which our economic policies have left. But for the last couple of weeks we've been hearing nothing but criticism about the deal, particularly from Germany. It's rocked the boat. You must have noticed that your personal rating has begun to decline for the first time since the summit.'

Grossman had an academic habit of giving his views straight, including the bad stuff, unlike so many other presidential advisers. It was what made him so valuable – and so bloody irritating.

'So what do we do, Leo? Promise that we'll start talks on German reunification?'

'That would be a disaster,' Grossman chided as if he were scolding a confused undergraduate. 'It would make the troop negotiations almost impossible and would fatally damage your image as a strong leader. You must *never* give in to pressure like that!'

'But I can't just sit here on my fanny watching my support in the primaries shot to hell.'

'Precisely,' said Grossman, wondering how on earth a man both so crude and so stupid as Michelle had ever become President. Was television style really all that counted? 'So I would suggest that you ensure the negotiations on the details of the treaty are concluded as quickly as possible. Don't let us wait until the end of the year, let's push them through now.'

'Won't the Russians see that as a sign of weakness?'

'In normal circumstances there might be some risk of that, but these aren't normal times in Moscow. Several leading members of the Politburo and central committee have resigned in protest at the summit agreement, so it would appear that Andreyev is having problems of his own. And I've just had a report in from our embassy that there are rumours flooding Moscow about Andreyev's stomach disorder being so bad he may

139

even have to go into hospital. You'll remember that the Secret Service reported they had somehow managed to obtain urine samples from the General Secretary while he was here in Washington – God knows how, I've never dared ask . . .'

'Didn't I ever tell you, Leo? Those madmen from the Service had a team stationed in the sewers beneath the White House while he was here, just waiting for him to unzip his flies.'

Grossman did not try to hide his distaste. 'In any event, their analysis disclosed that Andreyev probably has a serious intestinal complaint on top of possible diabetes, and now he's in his sick bed. If he's in the middle of a purge or power battle then bed is the last place he will want to be. He's under pressure. It seems to me he'll want the treaty concluded just as much as you.'

'Okay, that sounds right. So let's get these idle bastards in Geneva moving on the talks. I want you to instruct them that they've got three months instead of six to get the details sorted out. I want to sign the final treaty in Moscow . . . when? About July?'

'As an adviser on diplomatic matters I'm an insensitive fool when it comes to party politics. You would only have my incompetence to blame if the treaty signing were to coincide with the nominating convention of your opponent and bury all his news coverage, Mr President. My only excuse would be that I couldn't possibly allow partisan considerations to get in the way of important affairs of state and delay the signing of a vital arms treaty.' Grossman allowed himself a rare smile of approval.

'Why, you cunning Hungarian bastard!' The elderly Pole winced, while Michelle nodded vigorously, knowing that however loud the farmers in the mid-west squealed this would all but tie up the election for him. 'This calls for another drink.'

Grossman hadn't yet been offered a drink, but this time Michelle poured him a huge tumbler of bourbon, failing to remember that his national security adviser never touched anything stronger than a glass of wine. Under duress, Grossman raised the glass to his lips to take a mandatory sip.

'A toast, Mr President. To the treaty.'

Michelle raised his own tumbler. 'Yeah. Screw the Democrats. And the devil take Berlin!'

Berlin

The pretty young undergraduate felt elated. She had spent the entire afternoon on the campus of Berlin's Free University joining in the protest meetings and shouting her approval at the endless stream of speakers who had grabbed the microphone and berated the student crowd. It was her first year at university, and discussing the important things of life seemed so much more involving and relevant than anything her sociology lectures had to offer. Her parents had kept her on a tight rein with their narrow and inflexible views, and she was having to work hard to make up for lost time. Mind you, it had been a little confusing at times trying to unravel what was truly important, because every meeting she attended seemed to have its own distinct angle. As the demonstrations had meandered through the week and across the campus, their purpose seemed to change.

At the start there had been a discernible focus, attacking the Wall and demanding reunification, but after a few days this had been diluted by typically kaleidoscopic protests at everything from student loans to Third World famine, and the energy and numbers of the crowd had begun to sag. In the last few days, however, a new focus had brought greater clarity and a renewed sense of purpose to the activity. Shortly after the leak of the policy document from Bonn, Schumacher himself had visited the university to address the biggest meeting of the week, and the demonstrations had once again become single-minded. Except now they were attacking the Americans. 'Foreign Troops Go Home', 'Give Berlin Back' and 'USAsshole' the banners cried, and the oratorical protests were even fiercer.

A Turk had addressed the crowd for several minutes, a mature student like so many foreigners who seemed to find ways of staying around campus until they were at least thirty, living off the subsidies and patience of the university authorities and finding constant excuses to delay the return home to relative poverty and conscription in the military. Haluk had a strange, almost musical way of speaking German, getting his grammar hopelessly confused but always managing to be very clear about what he was saying.

The crowd had been under no illusion about his passionate commitment to peace, to pulling down the Wall, to a Germany which was neutral between East and West, to the harmony of nations and races. It had been an excellent harangue, well received by the massed students who always respond to a foreigner who could crack jokes and swear in German. They even applauded when he demanded that the Turkish *Gastarbeiter* in Berlin should, as part of the new order of freedom they all wanted, be given full civil rights and equality with native Berliners: 'Turks Too!' It was a demand which had begun to surface in the Turkish press and on the doorsteps and graffiti-covered walls of Kreuzberg. There had been some torrid complaints among the right-wing press that this was typical of the immigrant Turks, 'climbing on the bandwagon, trying to use the protests against the Wall to squeeze still further social security and unemployment benefits out of the rest of us', but generally this had been little more than a sideshow. And the audience was spurred on by his attacks on 'The System'.

'They treat us like slave labour,' he cried. 'But many Turks were born in Berlin. We live in Berlin. We are committed to Berlin. And many of us will die in Berlin. For too long the fat and decadent rich have lived off the backs of the working-class Berliners, both Germans and Turks. We must stretch out our hands to each other across the Wall and across the classes. Unite in brotherhood and sisterhood, I love you all, and fuck America!' He finished with a wave to the crowd before clambering down from the platform and being congratulated by those around him.

She had scarcely finished clapping enthusiastically when she found him next to her, smiling and flashing his pearl-white teeth. She had needed no encouragement to accept his invitation to a cup of coffee, and she had spent an hour listening with rapt attention as he delved into his stock of reminiscences about Turkey which he kept for such occasions – the smell of the crowded markets; the summer evenings spent picking olives; the snappers and red mullet which seemed to compete with each other to jump into the boat if you cast your net just as dawn was rising; the British nurses who wanted nothing more than to spend their week's holiday getting laid on the sandy beaches under an enormous yellow moon. He laughed and she listened and was fascinated to learn about this strange land at the edge of Europe. After all, she had never been much farther than Cologne and had never heard of Kemal Ataturk.

She was delighted when he asked her to come back to his apartment in Kreuzberg to listen to some Turkish music and drink Anatolian wine. Leaving home and her parents for the first time to come to university had opened the door on so many different worlds, and she was determined to make the most of the opportunities which thrust themselves at her.

They had taken the U-Bahn and walked along the streets of the Turkish community, smelling the aroma of the coffee shops and restaurants which crowded the pavements, returning the open smiles of the shop-keepers who stood in their doorways greeting the passers-by. She was hungry by the time they reached his apartment – it seemed a long time since she had rushed down the green salad at lunchtime – and she wondered whether he might invite her to explore one of the strange and alluring eating places they had passed.

The apartment was spacious and well furnished. It was unlike any student's place she had ever seen. There were plenty of books and magazines scattered around, but none seemed to relate to any academic studies she could identify. Indeed, he had been very vague about his student activities, describing himself as a mature student in marketing studies. The walls were clad with rich Kilim rugs which looked expensive, and the stereo equipment and television were much better than the ones her far-from-impoverished parents had bought her for Christmas. Student life seemed to be treating him well.

She perched on a huge, overstuffed cushion as he put a compact disc on the player and soon the strange, stringy harmonies of a *bouzouki* were bouncing off the walls, while he told her more fascinating tales of the bazaar. The wine he poured was thick and sweet, tasting heavily of anis, and he rolled a cigarette which gave off a smell and taste of a type she had never experienced before. He told her it was special Turkish tobacco, but she began to feel light-headed. Her mouth felt dry from the unaccustomed smoke so she drank more wine — 'raki' he called it — which only made things worse. Soon she was having trouble focusing on the delicate seams of colour which were woven into the rugs around her, and she wished desperately she had something to eat to fill the cavern in her empty stomach.

When he moved behind her and began to massage her shoulders she found it impossible to protest, even if she had wanted to, which she didn't. His strong hands helped her to relax as they manipulated her tight muscles, and the music and *raki* and the strange tobacco seemed to lift her to a different plane where she was outside her own body, a free spirit, floating.

It was several moments before she realized that his hands had gone from her shoulders and were now inside her blouse, massaging her breasts. It felt good, her nipples responded eagerly to his touch, so that when she protested and muttered 'no' her objection lacked conviction. This was all new to her, part of life's rich tapestry which she had discussed with her girlfriends through endless long nights, and her thirst for experience overcame her innocence. Soon her blouse was off and his tongue was exploring her nipples, her neck and her lips and many places she had not realized could give her so much pleasure.

It was only when he tried to get his hand down the front of her trousers that she knew she had to draw the line. Experience was one thing, but she wasn't ready for this. Yet he continued undoing her fastenings, ignoring the protests which she hoped were firm and decisive but which she knew weren't. He handled her in a far more experienced way than any boy she had fooled around with before, and she found her body telling her things which her befuddled mind didn't want to hear. She was still struggling with her inner feelings when her trousers came off. Only at the point when he was tugging at her underwear did she make up her mind.

'No, please. No. I don't want this! Leave me alone!'

'What's the matter?' he asked. 'I thought you were enjoying it?'

'I . . . I . . .' She found it impossible to deny it or to explain what she felt, and her confusion came tumbling forth.

'Have you ever done it before?'

'Yes,' she lied. Well, she had almost, never quite going all the way with her boyfriend back home in Westfalen, but she had promised faithfully to wait for him.

'You were enjoying it, I know. So what's wrong?'

'Nothing,' she protested.

'It's because I'm a Turk, isn't it?'

'What do you mean?'

'You're just like all the rest – a racist!' he accused.

'No, no,' she pleaded. She wasn't, no matter what her parents were, and the last thing she wanted was to be identified with them. 'I'm not prejudiced. I like you.'

'You're a racist. You can't deny it!' He appeared angry now, his complexion dark with hurt pride. 'You go to great rallies and claim you believe in equality, but underneath you're just like everyone else. It's good for your conscience to demonstrate – just so long as no one asks you to do anything about it. You're no better than your father's generation.'

She could feel his contempt. She prided herself on her sincerity, and she couldn't bear to have it assaulted. For anyone to claim she was no better than her father and his warped prejudices was more than she could stand, and she began to sob. Her mind was swimming in confusion. She wanted to be sick.

'I'm no racist. I'm really not,' she pleaded.

'Then prove it to me,' he demanded and pulled her towards him.

She could find no further arguments or resistance. She lay back, crying softly, as he penetrated her. Her body had lied to her, suggesting that this moment should have been one of the greatest physical pleasure, but it gave her only cruel pain. And her mind had lied to her, too, persuading her that she thought of all people equally when she knew that she would hate this man and all his compatriots for ever.

When he was finished and had rolled off her, she lay back for a few moments contemplating the ruins of her idealism and her innocence. Without a word he got up and busied himself rolling another joint. She knew life was never going to be the same for her now. Perhaps her father had been right after all. Quickly she dressed, trying to stifle her sobbing and inexpressible anger.

'What's the matter, little girl?' he sneered. 'Is a Turkish prick too much for you to take?' His mood had changed with victory, and he seemed intent on belittling her.

She thrust her blouse hurriedly back into her trousers and gathered up her shoulder bag, taking one last look at him. He was laughing at her. As she fled out the door, he smiled coldly to himself. Almost invariably they fell for it. Call them racist and they would do anything to prove you wrong. And equally invariably

147

they hated you for it afterwards. But that's what he was paid for. It was all part of the job.

He hadn't thought he would end up with a number like this when he had arrived in Berlin nearly four years before, fleeing from Turkey and the prison sentence he knew awaited him there. When he arrived on campus he had pretended to be a political refugee; no one had discovered that he was charged with pushing drugs. Then they had approached him. He didn't know who 'they' were, but he could guess – from the East. 'They' had known all about him, and within hours could get him deported back to a stinking jail in Istanbul. But keep his nose clean and take their money, and he could have a marvellous life in Berlin. All he had to do was help them out: keep an eye on the Turkish community, distribute leaflets, scrawl graffiti, break a few windows and the occasional nose, a little rabble-rousing on campus and in the cafés and drinking places where the Turkish workers gathered, sowing the seed of dissent wherever and whenever he could. He didn't give a damn about the disruption; it was what he would have done for entertainment, and they paid him for it!

And if he could stir up trouble between the Turks and the native Berliners, so much the better. With Turks he was always seditious; with Berliners always arrogant and grasping, representing the type of immigrant which most got under their skin. And into their knickers, too, leaving them bitter and disenchanted. It was a wonderful excuse to screw away a few years in great comfort. He lay back on his thick pile of cushions and chuckled. By the time he had finished doing his masters' bidding, there wouldn't be a happy Turk or a single German virgin left in Berlin . . .

FIVE

Berlin

The American was beginning to hate his job. He was a diplomat; he liked negotiation and conclusions, not shouting matches in smoke-filled rooms which went nowhere. He wasn't used to people saying 'no' and meaning it, particularly when they were supposed to be allies. And the smoke from the German's cigar was getting up his nose.

The regular meeting of the Public Safety Committee responsible for public order matters in Berlin had been going nearly an hour and the lack of air-conditioning coupled with the growing acrimony made the atmosphere fetid. Normally the representatives from the American, British and French military powers and the Berlin civil authorities were able to thrash through the agenda with relative ease and today there was only one item, but they seemed to be going backwards.

'Let me run through this one more time,' insisted the American, who gloried in the official title of US Adviser for Public Safety yet who felt like throwing a chair at the fat, impassive German. 'Schumacher has called a protest march for this weekend which is designed to congregate on one of the checkpoints in the Wall, probably Charlie or Potsdamer Platz. God knows how many thousands of people will be joining him, but it looks like a big one. And nobody yet knows what they are planning to do, but it seems possible they may just try to walk right through the goddamn Wall, right through the checkpoint and into the Soviet zone, and make pigs' backsides out of all of us.'

An air of ponderousness came over the American before he began his next sentence, and he licked his lips to moisten his parched mouth. 'I have been instructed by the White House, on the personal orders of the President, to ensure that Schumacher's plans are foiled. We cannot afford to have a confrontation along the Wall at this time. The negotiations with the Soviets are at a crucial stage, and nothing must be allowed to threaten those talks. So the Berlin police must stop or divert the march. It must not be allowed to reach the Wall.'

He glared at the German, daring him to disagree with the US President. All he got in return was a blank stare and a cloud of fresh cigar smoke. The other man was clearly determined not to be harried.

'I'll spell out the problem once again,' the German said slowly, his deliberation contrasting with the American's rising tide of wrath. 'I understand your concerns, but you must also understand my position. The march is perfectly legal. Our constitution in Berlin is perhaps the most liberal in the world, and we pride ourselves on that. I don't know whether your constitution allows you to break up peaceable crowds outside the White House . . .' – they all knew perfectly well it didn't – '. . . but in Berlin we encourage and protect freedom of expression. Unless you can prove that Herr Schumacher has illegal intent, which you cannot, you give us no grounds for banning this march.'

'But the negotiations . . . !'

There was just a trace of a smile at the corners of the German's mouth as with meticulous care he ground his cigar stub into the ashtray.

'Ah, yes. The negotiations. You will forgive me, but I didn't think Berlin was part of that deal.'

The American choked at having the President's words thrown back in his face. His voice rose in anger.

'Don't quote your constitution to me. We Americans damn near forced it down your throats after the war, and I don't need any lessons in democracy from . . .' – he wanted to say 'from any son-of-a-Kraut-bitch', but after three years of tedious committee work in Berlin even he knew that there were limits – '. . . you!' he exclaimed in frustration, throwing the word like a gauntlet across the table.

'Steady on,' intervened the British representative, who had been trying to referee the discussion and guide it towards some form of compromise. 'I don't think aggravation will get us anywhere.'

'Neither will ten thousand bloody Berliners trying to walk through Charlie on Saturday!' exploded the American. 'Do you want to kick their asses, or wait and watch the men from Moscow do your dirty work for you?'

'I'm sure it won't come to that,' said the flustered Englishman.

'It will if you guys don't lift a finger to stop it!' The American battled to regain control of himself before turning once again to the German. 'Be in no doubt as to the seriousness with which my government view this demonstration, and our firm request and expectation that the Berlin civil authorities move to defuse it. For the last time, can we rely on your assistance?'

The reply was equally slow, and equally firm. 'I would be exceeding my powers if I ordered the march to be halted. But that isn't really the point. I consulted with several senior officers of the police force before I came to this meeting. Not one of them believes their men

151

will obey any order to turn out on Saturday and stop the march.'

'A strike?' frothed the incredulous American. 'But it's not allowed . . .'

'A strike, a stoppage, an extra holiday – what you call it is not important. What is vital is that you understand the depth of feelings involved here. Far from preventing it, I'm told we can expect large numbers of Berlin policemen to participate in the march,' he replied calmly. 'In civilian dress, of course,' he added as an afterthought.

'Jesus H. Christ,' mumbled the American. He had failed, and he realized he would have to report back on the depth of his failure. The march would go on. He knew the President would not be happy.

The White House

'Stop the march, Leo. Stop the march!'

'But Mr President . . .' Grossman was beginning to feel distinctly uneasy about Berlin. Things were getting out of hand.

'No "buts", Leo. They're making a monkey out of me. The march must not reach the Wall. If it does I can kiss goodbye to New Jersey and California, and half a dozen others, too. There are some things which are more important to the world than the civil rights of a couple of hundred Berliners.'

'The Berlin authorities will not co-operate.'

'Hell, who runs Berlin? It's under our military occupation, let the army do the job. Defend the peace – that's what the Allies are there for.'

'The French and British will not agree to provide any of their troops.'

'All support short of actual help, eh? To hell with them and their marching bands, who needs them? We've got 10,000 American troops stationed there.'

'Six thousand,' corrected Grossman.

'That's enough. Get them out on the streets on Saturday. And keep those bastards off the Wall . . .'

Berlin

Harry was miserable. He had been looking forward to the weekend and his opportunity to spend time with Katherine. They had planned to take a picnic to the shores of Lake Havel, stretching along the western extremity of the city limits and surrounded by woodlands which were just coming into springtime bloom. In his imagination he had conjured scenes of a lakeside seduction, when at last she would put aside her reserve and succumb to his charms, in spite of the fact that the wind whipping across the water would still be cold enough to give them both frostbite. The prospect had got him through several tedious days of shuffling economic reports at the Mission. Then she had called to say it was off.

Edward's march, she explained, had made the picnic impossible. Edward had not asked her to participate but, whatever else happened on Saturday afternoon, it was clear that she could not risk being seen with a young American sipping soup on a picnic for two while her husband and several thousand other Berliners were confronting US troops on the streets. Even Harry had to acknowledge the impossible circumstances. But it didn't make him feel any better.

Instead of a picnic they had agreed to meet in the morning at Café Kranzler, Berlin's most famous coffee shop, and in his eagerness he had arrived uncharacteristically early. The weather was surprisingly warm and sunny — perfect for a picnic, he told himself — but the thought did nothing to cheer him. A pair of ancient *Hausfrauen* at the adjoining table delayed their attack on two large slices of cake in order to inspect him, one pulling up the half-moon spectacles which dangled on a piece of ribbon around her neck in order to get a better view. He glared back ferociously so they reverted to the cakes, muttering darkly.

Harry passed the time watching the waitresses as they glided discreetly around the tables serving caffeine and cake dressed with liberal amounts of whipped cream and judicious gossip for the regulars. They ignored the solitary Harry. He was sulking and pretending to read the menu when Katherine arrived. He rose reluctantly to greet her, wondering if he would always have to make do with a formal handshake rather than taking her in his arms and devouring her. The old biddies were muttering in his direction again as they stared at the new arrival.

'What's the matter, Harry? You look as if Miss Pickerstaff caught you with your hand in the cookie jar.' She flashed a perfect smile, teasing him as she often did about his comparative youth. It offended him today, largely because he knew he was reacting like a lovelorn teenager, but knowing this did nothing to improve his mood.

'If only I'd got as far as getting my hands on the cookies,' he muttered irritably.

A waitress in black dress and immaculately starched

pink apron came to take Katherine's fur coat and an order for coffee, while Harry looked sullenly out of the window from their first-floor table across the Ku'damm, where the morning sun had enticed the shoppers out and the bright colours of spring were again reappearing on the streets.

'Lovely day for a riot,' was all he could manage by way of conversation.

'Harry, what is the matter?' She wrinkled her brow inquisitively, but couldn't manage to lose her slightly mocking smile, like a mother with a petulant child.

'Nothing.'

'I see,' she replied, her soft green eyes seeing everything.

Outside on the street Harry watched two young lovers running to embrace, whirling each other around in joy before sharing a deep, thirsty kiss. The display of public affection changed his mood to one of anger at his own furtive and unfulfilled relationship, and he decided it was time to raise the stakes.

'You know, Katherine, I was really looking forward to this weekend. Yet all I've got for the days and nights of thinking about you is endless cups of coffee and small talk.'

He knew it was unfair, but so what? He had gained nothing by patience and seemed to have so little to lose.

'What are you saying, Harry?'

He was about to offer another snide comment when the waitress appeared with refills, and the interruption allowed him to get a hold on his wayward feelings. When the cups had been replenished, he leaned across the table and looked straight into Katherine's eyes. She could see that his were turbulent and moody.

'You're the most enticing woman I have ever met.

155

When I'm with you I feel as if my feet never touch the floor, and when we're apart I think about you constantly. Yet my feelings can't survive on a formal handshake and a chaste kiss of your cheek. It's making me miserable.'

He was having to whisper in order to avoid being overheard by their nosy neighbours who were straining to eavesdrop, and it made him furious. He paused to throw another fierce glance in their direction. They made him feel as if he were on stage. He had always been emotionally dramatic, perhaps in rebellion at his father's stonelike qualities, and having an audience was not helping him to remain cool.

'I want more. And if I can't have it – I don't know. Perhaps we should stop meeting.'

They were only words, as if from a play, but having uttered them he found they caused him great pain. From the expression on Katherine's face, it was clear she was suffering, too.

'Harry, I'm married . . .'

'We've been through all that before. You don't love him, he doesn't love you. You can't pretend you're happy as you are.'

'No, I'm not,' she acknowledged quietly. The conversation was beginning to hurt and she hid the moistness in her eyes with a quick sip of coffee. 'But where would it all lead?'

'I don't know. There are risks involved in anything which is important. You understand that better than I do. But it's a risk we would share. Together.'

'I'm not sure I was ever meant to be happy,' she said. Harry could see she wasn't joking. He reached across the table and took her hand, ignoring the clucking which this caused from the next table.

'I want you, Katherine. There has to be more.'

156

She withdrew her hand to raise her cup of coffee once more to her lips. She did not drink. She needed the time and the distance from Harry to think, to decide what she felt. But she already knew what she felt. She wanted him, too. And not just as some passing affair which could be discarded with yesterday's newspaper, but as something much deeper. She was at a crossroads in her life and she knew that, whatever direction she took, there would be no turning back. Yet he was nearly fifteen years younger! Her head kept battling with her emotions, telling her that any road she might travel with Harry would inevitably be a very short one. Confusion tumbled through her thoughts.

'Harry, I . . . can't. Not . . .' She couldn't finish. She had no idea what she was trying to say. But Harry forced her.

'Not when? Not now? Not ever?'

'Not . . . this morning?' She gave a little laugh, trying to fall back on her sense of humour, but it didn't work. Harry could see the tears beginning to form and trickle down her cheeks, even as the lips went in desperate search of a smile. 'I don't know. I just don't know. I need time.'

Harry picked up his own cup for reassurance, to give himself a moment to form his thoughts, anxious not to rush his response. But he found the cup trembling in his hand and he returned it quickly to the saucer. He cursed his lack of self-control; he knew that the old biddies had seen it and he felt humiliated. He pushed his chair back from the table as if trying to escape. He felt offended that she couldn't say yes and impatient with her hesitation, blaming Katherine for his own confusion. He was searching for another argument to overwhelm her and put the old ladies in their place when he saw the waitress advancing once again and

157

felt pressured into responding. He had no idea what he was going to say as the words began to form.

'Katherine, we can't go on, not as we are. We can't just sit back and watch all our pleasure turning into pain and frustration. It's up to you,' he heard himself saying. 'If you decide you want me, you know where I am. But remember . . . in Berlin, time is on no one's side.' With that he rose from the table and without a glance backwards walked out of the restaurant. He wondered if his action looked manly and decisive, but he knew he was running from his own uncertainty and the emotion which was welling up inside him and about to break through. He was acting like a complete jerk.

He hated not being in control. That's why he had joined the agency in the first place, responding enthusiastically to the induction lecture during his training course at Camp Peary which had emphasized how knowledge and understanding gave control, and how the agency and the intelligence it gathered provided the United States with a more effective grip than any hardware in the hands of the Pentagon. But as he stepped out on to the pavement and into the sunshine of Berlin, he realized he hadn't been in control ever since he had set foot in this god-forsaken city.

Katherine watched him go with a mixture of horror and relief. She tried hard to deny the tears which were falling from her cheeks in one of the most public places in Berlin, but she couldn't. It hurt. The mad, impetuous, youthful, lovable, selfish fool! Damn Harry! How could she be so stupid? Some of her closest friends and contemporaries were already grandmothers, approaching middle age with contentment and elasticated support stockings, yet here she was burning up inside about a man young enough . . . Oh, damn. Damn. Damn you, Harry Benjamin!

She wiped away her tears and glanced around cautiously to see if anyone were staring at her. At least there was no one in the restaurant she recognized. The coffee had gone cold but she sipped it nevertheless. Her dignity wouldn't allow her to leave now and seem as if she were rushing after him, even though her emotions were fluttering like a teenager's. It was at least ten minutes before she had composed herself, repaired her makeup in the ladies' room, paid the bill which Harry had forgotten and followed in his footsteps on to the street.

She was hoping she would find him loitering in some nearby doorway, waiting to apologize, to laugh and make up and explain that it was all a silly flash of temper. But he wasn't. She wandered aimlessly up and down the Ku'damm, window shopping, not buying, trying to find some message hidden in the ridiculous price-tags about what she really valued in her life. She knew that she didn't love Edward, that she wanted Harry with his fun and his vigour – and his body – more desperately than she had wanted anything for years. But something was holding her back. Loyalty for the years she and Edward had shared? Uncertainty as to what would lie ahead with Harry? Fear of the unknown? Perhaps a little of everything. She had no idea what to do, her confusion was beginning to bring back the puffy redness to her eyes, and her feet were screaming from the continued pounding of the hard pavement.

The cinema beckoned invitingly. She took no notice of what was playing, it didn't matter. All that mattered was that it would get her off the street and into a dark, private atmosphere where she could be alone to sort out her heart and make repairs to her running mascara.

*

The Public Safety Adviser and the Brigade Commander, US Forces, Berlin, stood in front of a vast map of the city. Neither spoke while they pondered their new role. Their mutual distaste for the task of filling the vacuum left by the local police and keeping order on the streets was matched only by their complete lack of experience in doing so and their anger at their French and British allies for leaving them to it. The British and French had declined to become involved in what they regarded as an entirely civilian affair. The Americans were on their own, and were having to build their plans from scratch.

The General stubbed a thick finger at the map.

'That's where they're gathering, in the Grünewald by the goddamn university. That's where they're headed, to the Wall just about here and one of the nearby checkpoints. Once they make it to the open spaces of the Tiergarten in front of the Wall there's not a hope in hell of containing them. So this . . .' – he banged his forefinger like an arrow into the heart of the display – '. . . is where we've got to stop the bastards.' His finger rested on the Ku'damm, just where it ran into a tangle of streets around Olivaer Platz.

The General was a veteran of many campaigns, all of them waged on paper from headquarters and most of them against inquisitive local congressmen and senators, which left him feeling rather bitter that his first taste of street action embroiled him with punk students rather than a professional opponent. Success in such a battle would scarcely provide him with a ringing commendation from his superiors in the Pentagon, and was unlikely to hasten his departure to greater things from this dull city in the middle of Europe where the biggest challenges his troops had to face were clap and terminal boredom. He wanted action, and if that's what

160

this rag-tag mob of students, anti-Americans and other ungrateful backsliding German bastards were after, that's precisely what they would get.

The Public Safety Adviser looked on dubiously. The latest reports suggested that tens of thousands of people would be taking part in the march, and he doubted the General's ability to bring them to a halt in the middle of the Ku'damm. But he didn't say so. The one time he had offered a counter-suggestion to the General he had been swiftly reminded that, had he done his job with the Public Safety Committee properly, none of this would have been necessary. And a civilian doesn't argue over military matters with a general, even a one-star version like this.

So the plans were laid. All leave for American army personnel had been cancelled, the battle plans drawn up, and the orders given. It was then the problems began. The Berlin police authorities refused to co-operate, which meant that all their civilian crowd control equipment remained under lock and key and out of American hands. There were no plastic riot shields, no riot sticks or helmets, no water cannon and no mobile command posts available. Nothing which the US Army had previously faced in Berlin had required them to stock any of this equipment.

The General improvised. His men would carry their standard-issue M16 rifles, although on mature reflection he decided that they should not be loaded. And he hijacked firefighting equipment from the military airport at Tempelhof, which would replace the water cannon and provide him with enough liquid firepower to wash away the resistance of the most determined of demonstrators.

He was concerned that his troops and officers had no experience of crowd control and realized that

161

his intelligence and command capability would be stretched to breaking-point if the crowd were allowed to disperse around the streets. So he decided that he would use the intersection between the Ku'damm and the streets converging on Olivaer Platz to contain the demonstration. His men, backed by their makeshift water cannon, would block off the intersection like a cork in a bottle neck, allowing the marchers nowhere to go but backwards into their own advancing supporters. The organizers of the demonstration would become uncertain and lose control. The body would lose its head, and the mob would break up in confusion and chaos. It would not reach the Wall, he concluded with evident satisfaction, not when faced with the immovable resolution of the US Army.

And that is precisely what Schumacher saw as he strode up the Ku'damm with his fellow demonstrators at the head of the march. They had already walked a couple of miles or more from their starting point in the open spaces of Grünewald. The day was set fair, with the spring sun shining down benevolently on a good-humoured demonstration which carried its banners high and was greeted with the waves and cheers of many ordinary Berliners as it proceeded up the city's major thoroughfare. Several thousand demonstrators were already on the march, with many thousands more waiting to join as the organizers guided them in orderly fashion out of the assembly point and on to the street. It was a good march, a splendid march which grew in numbers and confidence with every step along the way.

Until it saw the soldiers. As Schumacher and his supporters approached the intersection, it was difficult at first to make out what was in their way. The drab camouflage uniforms blended one into the other so that from a distance it looked no more than a smudge across

162

the street. But as the demonstrators approached, the harsh reality of what awaited them gradually became clear: American soldiers in combat fatigues, anonymous fighting men with helmets clamped firmly to their heads, standing shoulder to shoulder and four rows deep to form an impenetrable barrier with their M16s grasped in front of them like clubs. When those at the head of the procession saw the rifles, there was a momentary hesitancy in their stride. They weren't to know that the rifles were unloaded and intended only to replace police riot sticks. But as the doubts of those at the head of the column grew, they weren't allowed to show it. The pressure of numbers behind them, from the thousands who were still being guided on to the street to fuel the demonstration far to the rear, forced them on. There was to be no turning back.

As he strode – or rather was pushed – closer to the barrier of foreign troops spread across the street, Schumacher looked around. The Ku'damm was blocked. The minor streets which also joined the intersection around Olivaer Platz were similarly plugged by soldiers, and behind them he could see the angry red paintwork of the General's commandeered fire tenders, which from Schumacher's level had all the menace of tanks. There was nowhere to go. The last side street which could have provided any escape route for the marchers was by now several hundred yards behind them. As the General had so clearly foreseen, there was no way out.

What the General had so tragically misunderstood, however, was that crowds have a life of their own which overwhelms the wishes and desires of the individuals within them. Everyone at the front of the procession was now feeling deeply uncertain. But the march pressed on. Even had Schumacher issued the command

163

to stop, it would have been futile. He would not have been heard more than a few yards away, let alone by the thousands who were marching behind, oblivious of the confrontation developing ahead of them, pressing irresistibly forward. As those at the head of the column slowed their pace and linked their arms for security, the pressure from behind quickly built up and carried them forward. They were now only some ten yards from the cordon. The grim and nervous faces of the soldiers could be clearly seen above the rifles which were gripped in white-knuckled hands and thrust out across the soldiers' bodies to block the way. No one in the crowd had time to notice that none of the M16s had magazines clipped to them; all that the marchers could see was cold, grey, American steel.

With one final effort the first row of marchers dug in their heels and came to a halt. There were women and priests among them, and a battle with armed soldiers was not what any of them had planned. But they no longer had any choice. With explosive force, the pressure of the crowd behind hurled them forward the last few yards directly on to the rifles and clenched fists of the GIs, as if they were mounting a deliberate assault on the line. The last thing Schumacher saw before being enveloped in the maelstrom of screaming bodies and flailing rifle butts was the television cameras at the first-floor windows above them. The soldier who hit him had only a moment to wonder why he was smiling.

Two hundred yards away in a side street, the General sat with a handful of officers and his communications team confidently waiting to accept the surrender of the protestors. He was disconcerted to hear the screams and pandemonium which reached into his command post even before the radio started crackling and informing him that he had a fight on his hands. God, he

164

hadn't really expected this. When he heard that the mob was still pressing forward and that his immovable line of men was in fact buckling, he had no hesitation in ordering the fire tenders to douse the passions and drown the protest. Within seconds four fire tenders had emerged through the barrier of GIs and forced their way on to the Ku'damm.

That was another mistake. The tenders should have stayed behind the cordon of soldiers and doused the crowd from there. But once into the chaos they were quickly forced to a halt. No driver wanted to plough heedlessly into a crowd of unarmed civilians. Once stopped, however, the fire tenders themselves became targets. The tender which had forced its way furthest into the crowd was immediately surrounded by protestors banging on its sides. The alarm showed on the faces of the young GIs inside, which turned to fear as a brick came hurtling through one of the side windows. The tenders were designed for fighting fires, not protestors, and no one had thought to reinforce or protect them. As the glass shattered around the driver's cab, eager fingers reached inside to unlock the doors and moments later the four-man crew had been grabbed and bundled out on to the street. Then the battle of the water cannon began. New young hands manned the controls, turning the tender around until it faced the GIs and spraying them with their own high-pressure water hoses. Chaos ruled as the scene turned into one of total confusion, hoses spraying everywhere, the orderly cordon of soldiers breaking up in disarray, and a hundred individual battles taking place as soldiers with rifles were taken on by protest banners, placards and bare hands.

Ultimately it was an uneven contest. The protestors had numbers on their sides, but the US Army had fitness, relative discipline and many more fire tenders. Eventually the crowd was forced back and into retreat, leaving behind it soggy placards, many tears and a not inconsiderable amount of its blood. As reports of pending victory filtered back into the command post, the General made his final mistake. He had been caught by the thrill of battle; ever since boot camp he had been trained to press home his advantage, and now he thought he saw his opportunity.

'Go after them,' he barked. 'Don't let them re-form. Sweep the bastards from the streets!'

'General, I think they've had enough,' one of his officers responded over the radio, feeling sick to the stomach as he watched his trained troops reduced to beating up innocent men and women. He had certainly had enough, even if his commanding officer hadn't.

'Punk! I said get after them. Now!'

So the troops and the fire tenders moved forward, forcing the crowd back down the Ku'damm and increasing the waterlogged chaos and confusion. But the battlefield had not been prepared. The Ku'damm was Berlin's major shopping area on a Saturday afternoon. No one had expected anything more than a passing peaceful demonstration. The shops and cafés were still open. Women and children were still on the street, going about their weekend chores, ignorant of what was now about to hit many of them. As the demonstrators retreated, they were pursued by fire tenders which doused everything in sight. Demonstrators, little old ladies and tiny children in pushchairs cowered for protection in shop doorways, and the high-pressure hoses hit them without regard, knocking them off their feet and soaking them in freezing water as the tenders made their indiscriminate way down the Ku'damm.

The plate-glass of shop windows was buckled and

smashed and parked cars were battered as the assault continued and people fled blindly in panic. Bones were broken and faces cut by flying glass, families enjoying an afternoon snack in the quiet security of fashionable restaurants were bowled over as windows shattered and the water cannon reached deep inside, knocking over tables and chairs. A pot of hot coffee went flying, only to land in a baby's cot and give the screaming infant hideous first-degree burns. The baby had become the youngest casualty of what was to be known by the time the morning newspapers had been printed as the 'Massacre on Ku'damm'.

In a nearby shop doorway an eighty-two-year-old pensioner had been hurled against a door frame, knocking her unconscious. A young demonstrator ran towards the fire tender, pleading with it to stop the carnage, but through the cracked and water-smeared windows the young soldiers could see only another protestor running at them, so she too was met by the direct blast of a water jet and thrown back into the same doorway, to lie senseless alongside the old woman.

As Katherine emerged from the cinema, blinking in the sunlight, she could not comprehend the scene in front of her. At first she imagined she must still be inside, watching the film. A second and then a third fire tender passed by, leaving sodden wreckage in its wake and turmoil in her mind. What on earth . . . ? Then she remembered Edward's march and the awful truth began to dawn.

She stood rooted in the doorway of the cinema, unable to move as a fourth tender came into view, dousing everything and everyone that moved. The water jet swung from side to side, like the tongue of an angry lizard, swatting the ants scurrying around it. As slowly it turned to face Katherine, a young woman clutching a small bundle threw herself on to the steps of the cinema. She was already drenched, with a cut on her forehead where she had been thrown down on the pavement. Her efforts to resist the water cannon had clearly exhausted her, and she no longer had the strength even to make it up the short flight of steps to the cinema entrance where Katherine stood. She raised her head, her hair matted against her skull from the water and blood, and with the last of her strength held out the bundle towards Katherine.

'My baby! Please take my baby!'

Katherine was frozen in horror. The baby was about the same age as her own had been. As the woman lay on the steps, just feet from the relative safety of the cinema entrance, the memories flooded back of that night at the Wall and the last time she had seen Peter. And the jet of water, like the volley of bullets she could never forget, was slowly working its way towards them.

As she had done that night, she hurled herself forward, and this time there were no hands to hold her back. The water jet seemed to hesitate before launching itself at the mother and child, and Katherine threw herself protectively across them, using her own body as a shield. The pounding of the water pressure across her back was irresistible, but there was nowhere for her to be flung. She was already on the ground and the concrete steps would not give. She was trapped. She could not breathe, she thought her back was breaking and knew her clothes were ripping. But she could feel the mother and the child beneath her, safe.

In less than five seconds the tender had moved on to seek fresh prey. Slowly it dawned on the women that their ordeal was at an end. The pain in their bodies was gradually receding into a dull ache of release, and they sucked in deep lungfuls of air, grateful to be able to

168

breathe once again. The two women hugged each other and let the tears of emotion and release flood out without inhibition. Then the baby cried, and the women's tears of anguish turned to relief and joy as they fussed over their bundle, damp but undamaged.

It was only later, when she had got home and soaked herself in a hot bath and let the tension slowly ease out of her, that Katherine remembered her own bundle once again, and this time the tears would not stop.

It was early evening when Edward got home. He was ruffled and unkempt, but somehow had managed to escape the worst of the battering and injuries which had befallen those around him in the march. He had spent the last few hours being photographed with the wounded and giving endless interviews. He should have been exhausted, but the adrenalin was coursing through his system and the front door closed with a crash behind him as he raced up the stairs.

Katherine was on the bed, where she had cried herself to sleep. As she heard the noise of the front door slamming she awoke with a feeling of relief. Edward was home, and she desperately needed some company. Suddenly she realized she had not given him a single moment's thought since the march, although she had no idea what might have happened to him. Her guilt made her particularly effusive as he walked into the bedroom.

'I'm so glad you're home!' she said as she rose to greet him. But as her arms stretched out, he strode past, ripping off his tie and jacket.

'I'm in a rush. Got to be at the television studio in forty minutes and I need a change of clothes.'

He prepared to take a shower, flinging his clothes carelessly into a corner.

'Edward, the demonstration was awful. I got caught

in the middle of it. There was this mother with her baby . . . please listen!' she implored as he dashed into the bathroom.

'Katherine, I don't have time. I'm needed at the studio,' he shouted over his shoulder.

'I need you, too. What about me?'

'Oh, come on! You haven't needed me for years. In any case, I'll be back later.'

'But I need you now, Edward!'

It was pointless. She was talking to a closed bathroom door.

There were no further tears or pleas for attention. She was dressed and repairing her makeup when Edward came out of the bathroom, and they exchanged scarcely another word as he threw on fresh clothes and knotted his tie. Katherine walked out of the house barely five minutes after her husband, knowing as she left that she was also closing the door on what was left of her marriage.

Harry was sitting at his recently acquired table, reading and attempting single-handedly to demolish a six-pack of beer, when he heard the knock. He had still not mastered the antiquated central heating system, which was going full blast on a warm spring evening, and he was stripped to the waist, wearing only a pair of jeans when he opened the door.

'Katherine! What on earth . . . ?'

She looked studiously at him and his sinewy, youthful body, as if she were some regimental sergeant-major inspecting a guard detail. He was slim, without an ounce of extra flesh. Just like Peter. And when she touched him, she could feel the firm muscles and count his ribs. It was unlike any body she had been that close to. Since Peter. And when their lips met, his tongue

170

explored her mouth in a way which no one had ever kissed her. Except Peter.

As she led him to the big brass bed, still stuck up against the fireplace, she whispered in his ear. 'Don't rush it. It's been one hell of a day.'

Edward Schumacher sat in the television studio as the lights dimmed and the credits of the late-night news programme rolled. It had been a suave and competent performance as he calmly relayed the story of the day, how a peaceful march of ordinary Berliners had been turned into a bloodbath by the hasty action of untrained American soldiers. He didn't have to drive the point home. The videotape had done that, and would continue to do so for many days to come.

As he fiddled with his signet ring, he noticed his fingers were trembling again, more noticeably over the last few days than ever before. He was glad of the low lights and the silence which now hung over the studio. God, it had been such a helter-skelter ride, and he still couldn't believe how things had fallen into place so superbly. He knew he couldn't carry it off for ever, but at the pace which events were moving he wouldn't have to. Berlin was coming to the boil.

He thought of Katherine. He'd been short and uncivil with her, but it was difficult enough coping with his own problems at the moment, let alone hers. What had she said? She needed him? Strange. She seemed to have been crying, too; something had obviously upset her. He would find out what when he got home. Katherine was no longer part of his plans – there were too many other demands on his loyalty now – but there was no need for him to be unnecessarily cruel. She had been part of his life for almost twenty years and had served her purpose gracefully and well, and he owed her something. But he had neither the time nor the energy to be unduly sentimental. There were going to be many innocent victims if his masters' plans succeeded, and the moral vacuum with which he had surrounded himself left little room in his life for anyone, including his wife.

As the credits ended the atmosphere in the studio relaxed, and the producer came out of his control booth and sat in the vacant chair opposite Schumacher. It had been reserved for a spokesman from the US Mission, but they had declined to provide anyone. The chair had been left unoccupied as a symbolic reminder that no one from the American side was willing or able to justify their actions that day, as if they had run away.

'That was some programme, Herr Schumacher.'

'I'm glad you liked it.'

'No, I didn't like it. It frightened me to death if you want to know. In all my years as a producer I've never seen such scenes on the streets of Berlin. What happened today caused the sort of damage which I doubt will ever be properly repaired. What does it all mean?'

'It means that Berlin is growing up, that it's no longer willing to bend its knee to foreign powers, least of all those who claim to be our friends. It's time we were treated as equals, not like naughty children in kindergarten.'

'But the cost . . . ?'

A bleeding heart in a pink silk shirt, Schumacher muttered to himself disdainfully. Why do faggots always end up controlling the media? 'There were more than a hundred Berliners taken to hospital today as a result of what the Americans did. There's no report of a single US casualty. How much longer can we afford the cost of that type of protection?'

'But without the Americans, who else have we got?'

'We have ourselves. We don't need anyone else. We certainly don't need their rifle butts in our bellies.'

'We started down a new road today. Heaven knows where it will lead.' There was genuine sorrow in the producer's voice.

'What alternative would you suggest?' challenged Schumacher.

'I have none, sir. Frankly, I don't know what the answer is, and I envy you and the other politicians who seem so certain all the time. I'm left only with nagging doubts. Perhaps that's why I'm the producer and you're the politician.'

Schumacher fiddled energetically with his signet ring, and offered no further conversation beyond a snort of ridicule. Theirs was a dialogue of the deaf, the producer voicing his intellectual doubts, the politician offering nothing but dogmatic certainties. Both mistrusted the motives of the other, but it hadn't stopped the producer presenting a programme which had given Schumacher more than enough scope to express his certainties. *Which makes who the bigger fool?* thought Schumacher.

The producer sensed the other man's contempt and rose to wrap up his work, relieved that he didn't have to deal with types like this every night. No sooner had he gone than one of the cameramen approached. He shook Schumacher's hand and gave a formal nod of respect.

'Herr Schumacher, I'm not very good with words but what you did this afternoon was brave. Berlin thanks you.'

'Your producer doesn't seem to agree.'

'That creep? What does he know? He takes loving his fellow man a little too literally, if you know what I mean. It's time we Berliners stopped allowing ourselves to be pushed around. I tell you, if ever you want to mount another march on that damned Wall and want a few of the guys to help you pull the friggin' thing down, just come round to my local club. You'd be welcome there, any time. And every single man there would volunteer.' He glanced at his watch. 'Frankly it's about the only thing in this town I would volunteer for. And I'm glad to say for the last three hours I've been on double-overtime, thanks to your march. Lots of luck to you.' And with another respectful nod, he had gone.

Schumacher sank back in his seat and downed the tumbler of whisky which had appeared at his side. The adrenalin had stopped now, and he felt exhausted as the nervous strength which had sustained him all day collapsed within him. He wanted to go home and sleep for a hundred years. But that was out of the question. He still had much more work to do.

SIX

Air Force One, above Nevada

Michelle was going over the draft of yet another campaign speech when the press secretary tugged his sleeve. They were some five miles above the deserts of Nevada on their way to an evening campaign rally in Los Angeles, and Michelle had been hoping to get a couple of undisturbed hours to work on the draft. His last few speeches had been awful, written by computer and read like an automaton, and he knew he needed to put more work into them. He was not best pleased at the interruption.

'Can't it wait, Fred?' he grumbled.

'No, Mr President. The CBS lunchtime news is going to lead on a new story, sir. You'll need to see it.'

Michelle picked up his papers with a bicker of protest and moved reluctantly to a seat where he could watch the TV monitor. Reception was never great at 26,000 feet as the 747's directional antenna struggled to stay locked on to the satellite, and there was a short delay as the press secretary set up the equipment.

'What is it now, Fred? You want to watch your basketball team or something?'

Fred ignored the sarcasm. He was used to it.

'Give me a clue. Are we winning or losing?' the President badgered.

Fred preferred not to reply, and concentrated his attention on the screen. The snowstorm produced by the poor reception was particularly bad today, but the words of the newscaster came over loud and clear.

'At the top of the news at this hour, tragedy as a peaceful demonstration turns into a riot after US troops use guns, clubs and water cannon on civilians. Hundreds are injured as the streets of Berlin become a battlefield. The American general in charge admits: "We got it wrong".'

None of the other occupants of the cabin made a sound as they took in the pictures which flickered in front of them. The anoraks, clerical collars and sweatshirts of the marchers could be clearly seen, as could their smiles as they set out for what looked to all intents like a weekend stroll in the sun. The President started swearing silently as soon as he saw the troops in camouflage uniforms with rifles at the ready. His silent swearing changed to loud and repetitive cursing as he watched the carnage which followed. By the time the shots of the scalded baby being rushed into the casualty department flickered on the screen, words had failed him. A grim-faced nurse gave a cautious prognosis while the father, struggling to control his emotions, was asked to explain how the accident had occurred in the middle of a family outing. 'Accident? How can you call that an accident?' he choked, and unreservedly blamed the Americans. The footage left nothing to the imagination.

The press secretary punched the remote-control button as soon as the item finished. 'We'll have to say something to the press when we reach California. What do you want to do?'

Michelle was breathing in short, sharp bursts as the tension and his exasperation gained the upper hand. 'Number One, I want the State Department to undertake an immediate enquiry.' His face was quivering with anger. 'Number Two, I want General Fucking Whatsisname ordered back home for immediate consultations. And for Number Three, by Monday I want his balls nailed to the highest ceiling in the Pentagon. And you can quote me!'

His anger gave way to frustration as he realized how much damage the pictures would do to him. Already he imagined the Democrats arranging picket lines of protestors to greet him in California, to dog his every move around the state with shouts of shame and hurriedly scrawled placards: 'Butcher of Berlin'. They would blame him, of course, and so would many of his supporters. He slumped in his chair, bereft of inspiration. The pages of the draft speech lay beside him, unattended, unimproved, and now completely irrelevant.

Fred was trying to move away, discomfited by the President's embarrassment, when Michelle reached over and grabbed his arm.

'I only asked him to keep them away from the Wall. I didn't order a bloody massacre,' he pleaded. Someone had to know.

'Of course, Mr President. I'm sure it will be fine.'

They both knew Fred was lying.

Kreuzberg, Berlin

She held him tightly in her arms, wanting this never to end. Katherine felt young again, eighteen years young, as if she were with Peter once more. Harry was impetuous, vital, and made love to her with an energy she had quite forgotten men possessed. When she closed her eyes and let her mind and her feelings run free, the years of silent mourning were stripped away. She was back in Peter's arms, in their bed, in love.

She had never felt such release as this in all the time she had spent in the West. A door into her past had been opened and she was able to embrace the feelings and emotions she had thought were long since dead. Harry's lips were Peter's lips, his body was Peter's body, she was his once again. For a moment she felt guilty, as if she were using Harry. But he wasn't complaining.

She opened her eyes and saw the chandelier providing a lurid backdrop to his sweating head. It wasn't the same, of course, but she knew that she was at this moment as happy as she could ever be again. She remembered the first time Peter had made love to her. She was only sixteen and she had never been with a man before. He was scarcely a year older than her, but proud like a fully grown man and immensely considerate. They had decided some time before that they would become lovers, with all the earnestness that only the young possess. But he had refused to sneak away with her like so many of their friends to find a disused cellar in some bomb-damaged building, or to grab ten minutes during the day in one or other of their families' cramped homes where they would run the constant risk of being disturbed and discovered. Although he was too embarrassed to admit it to her, it was his first time, too, and he wanted to make it very, very special.

So they had waited until June had brought with it the first of the summer warmth, when the blustery winds of spring had dropped to a gentle breeze, and one evening they had borrowed a motorbike and travelled to the forests of Müggelheim outside Berlin, where their bed was the sweet smell of warm pine cones and their bridesmaid a full orange moon shining above the calm waters of the Müggelsee. And that had been the start of it.

It was not the same with Harry – it could never be the same, not with the moon replaced by a grubby chandelier in a former bordello – but it would do. It would have to. Harry was now looking down at her with the quizzical look of all men who want to know if it was as good for the woman, but are afraid to ask. Like Peter had done that first time. She took Harry's head in her hands, smiled at his concern and kissed him warmly on the lips. 'Thank you. You're a wonderful man.'

Harry grinned in relief and buried his head in the pillow to wipe off the sweat trickling from his brow.

'Damn the central heating. I want to make love, not chicken broth.'

He rolled off her gently and went to open one of the tall windows, which creaked and rattled in protest at being disturbed abruptly after a winter's hibernation. Then he returned to her, and for the next two hours Katherine talked to him and stroked him and made love to him in a way which left him breathless with wonder and physical exhaustion, and to hell with the heat.

Afterwards they lay back in each other's arms, laughing and sipping beer, and both hating the thought that the evening would ever have to come to an end. Then a distant noise began to intrude into their private world. They ignored it at first but it was insistent and growing louder. The sounds of shouting, of breaking glass, of sirens and of disturbance came into the night and through the open window. Something was up on the streets of Kreuzberg.

'Harry . . . ?'

'I don't know, Katherine. Sounds like one hell of a fight.'

They continued to listen as the noise of disturbance grew, resenting the intrusion but no longer able to resist it. She turned towards him with a look of concern.

'I left my car right out in the street. Not a great job of parking – I was in a bit of a hurry.'

'That's not an excuse to leave, is it?'

'No,' she smiled. 'I'm not looking for excuses. But I would like to make sure I've still got a car when you throw me out.'

'Okay,' he said. 'I'll go check on it, and find out what on earth is going on.'

He jumped into his jeans and a sweatshirt while Katherine fumbled in her bag for the keys. 'I won't be long,' he shouted as the door closed.

But he was gone more than an hour, and when he returned his face was sombre and dark.

'It's a nightmare,' he said quietly, going straight for his bottle of bourbon. He sat on the edge of the bed holding his glass in both hands while Katherine pulled the bedclothes around her as if a chill had suddenly entered the room. Harry seemed to have trouble looking at her, and stared off into some imaginary distance as he recounted his tale.

'Apparently there was a rally earlier this evening in some local park. Turks copying the demonstration this afternoon, demanding civil rights, permanent residence, the vote and God knows what else for all foreign guest workers in Berlin.'

Katherine remembered the fresh graffiti which had been springing up on walls in various parts of the city in the last few days, demanding new rights for Turks, Yugoslavs and the rest of the sizeable immigrant groups based in Berlin. Some had even appeared on the stretch of Wall outside Harry's window.

'It got out of hand. A group of young Berliners

muscled in on the act. They'd been drinking. Seems they didn't like what happened on the Ku'damm this afternoon, and were looking for some way to get their own back. Didn't matter against whom. The rally broke up in fist fights and violence, and the whole thing spread on to the streets. I've been all around Kreuzberg. Turkish shops have had their windows smashed. Some have been set alight. Anybody who tried to intervene was beaten up. Even the firemen were stoned as they tried to put out the fires.'

There was a long silence. He was clearly having trouble coming to the next part.

'I found a policeman just watching as a group of young Berliners smashed the window of a Turkish grocery store and threw everything out into the street. I asked him – why don't you stop it? Do you know what he said? "Because there are many more of them than there are of us. If I tried to stop it, they'd throw me through the window, too." He was really scared . . .'

Harry took a long sip of bourbon and seemed to get a grip on himself. He was calm when he looked at Katherine once again, his eyes full of sorrow.

'I walked down the streets. They're quiet now. They're covered in broken glass. Everywhere you look, little shards of glass glistening in the lamplight. Then I came across a sign which someone had scrawled on a wall. The paint was still wet and dripping down. It said: *Kristallnacht*.'

He couldn't say any more. As he looked at Katherine, great sorrow clouded his eyes. She knew immediately what he was feeling. *Kristallnacht* was what they had called that hour of darkness when the Nazis had declared open war on the Jews and had looted and closed down every Jewish shop in Berlin and burnt the synagogues, when the gutters had shone bright with the

181

crystal-like glint of shattered windows. It had been the beginning of the end for his father's family, like most other Jews left in Berlin. Now it was the Turks' turn.

Harry's father was back again, nagging in his ear, reminding his son that she was just another German. Katherine could feel his anguish, and for the second time that day the tears slid down her cheeks. In shame at the plight of innocent Turks. In sorrow at Harry's pain. And in self-pity that the ugly reality of Berlin had once again destroyed her fleeting moment of happiness.

The morning was well advanced by the time Schumacher awoke. The emotional and physical strain of the previous day had left his body aching and lethargic, and he lay still for several minutes, trying to discover whether his head still belonged to the same body and wondering what crisis or opportunity the new day would bring. He had been immensely fortunate in the way events had developed, but he knew his luck couldn't last. The greater his success, the greater the chance that someone would begin to question and suspect. And he knew his frayed nerves couldn't take too much of that. It had taken him nearly half a bottle of whisky to get himself to sleep and, while half of him knew that the drink was getting too firm a hold on him, his other, weaker half couldn't stop it. He was beginning to take a calming shot of whisky earlier and earlier in the day, and he knew the strain would soon begin to show publicly. After that, it was a race against time: success or exposure. He prayed he would have enough time to get away, before they knocked on his door.

The sound of the front door closing filled him with alarm, and it was some seconds before he untangled reality from his private nightmares and remembered that, if ever they came for him, they were unlikely to use a latch-key. Only then did it dawn on him that Katherine hadn't been in the room and hadn't shared his bed. She said nothing when she came into the bedroom, offering him only a look of disregard as she grabbed a brush and put it through her hair.

'Where have you been?' he demanded.

'It astonishes me that you were even aware I was gone.' There was a note of quiet sadness in her voice which cut him far more deeply than any shouted words of anger.

'I have a right to know where you've been, dammit!' he snapped. 'You can't just walk off without a word.'

'It was you who walked off, remember?'

This was a very different Katherine from the previous evening. He recalled her words: she had needed him, she said, and it had been a long time since either of them had felt the need to use words like that. He had walked out on her; he hadn't even had time to find out what was bothering her. Now she had spent the night elsewhere. It wasn't too difficult to imagine why.

'Is there another man?'

She stopped the mechanical brushing of her hair and turned to look at him. There was no love left, but after twenty years she had no desire for deceit and bitter recriminations. She had too much self-respect for that.

'Yes,' she said softly.

A surge of male vanity and hurt pride swept over him. It had been years since they had shared any meaningful form of physical relationship, and he had always assumed that she would find comfort elsewhere, just as he had done. But his acceptance of a hypothetical possibility hadn't prepared him for the shock of contact with cold reality, and for her brazen admission that she was cheating, deceiving him.

No sooner had his wrath risen than he knew he

must suppress it. He shouted at himself not to be so shortsighted. It wasn't her fidelity which was important: it was the fact that she knew so much – too much – about him. The last thing he needed right now was an angry and errant wife wandering around Berlin. He mustn't lose control! His hands were trembling so much he was forced to hide them under the sheets. Christ, he wished he had a drink. There was no pretence in his distress when he spoke.

'Katherine, I know I haven't been the most attentive of husbands . . . heaven knows, at times I've been intolerable. I know that. You needed me last night, but I was too much involved with my own problems to give you the time you needed. I'm sorry.'

His contrition amazed her. She hadn't thought he was capable of it.

'You've never been interested in politics but you must understand that right now, this very moment, is the most important point of my career. I can't just drop everything. If it were only me I'd say let's go away somewhere, have a little time to ourselves, try to patch things up. I want to fight for what we have, really I do.'

Katherine's astonishment grew. This was an entirely unexpected, indeed unrecognizable Edward.

'But there are many other people depending on me. What's going on in Berlin at the moment will affect millions of people for years to come and, for better or worse, I'm right in the middle of it. Be patient with me, for just a little longer. Please?'

All the resolution Katherine had drummed into herself during her car ride home was torn to shreds. She had imagined many different types of verbal duel with Edward and had practised her ripostes, but not this one.

'Edward, it's too late . . .' But he could detect the note of uncertainty which had crept into her voice.

'Don't say it's all over, not after all this time. We've shared so much. Not physically, perhaps, ours has never been the greatest romance. But those nights we've spent by the Wall have been more than enough for me. How many couples can look back on something as powerful and say "that's us; that's what we made together"?'

He was pulling none of his punches now, knowing just where the most vulnerable parts of her emotional system were and how to hit them with precision. It left her breathless.

'It's not enough any longer . . .'

'But must we throw it all away?'

'There are too many other people standing between us. The whole of Berlin – what did you say? "For better or worse." It's them you love, Edward, not me.'

He knew he couldn't persuade her of something which they both knew didn't exist. But there were other ways to hold her. 'Katherine, if we no longer love each other, at least let's keep our respect. We still have the escape ring. We built it; let's not bury what we achieved. Don't throw everything away.'

He could see in her eyes that he had found some spot to touch, a feeling they still shared. He moved over to clasp her hands, something he hadn't done in many years. He had to play for time.

'Don't rush any decision. I need your help. The next few weeks will be critical to me and everything I've worked for over all these years. If there's any public scandal about our marriage it will destroy me and all my work. You know how much it means to me. Give me just a little more time, a few more weeks.' There was a slight pause. 'I need you, Katherine.'

The unexpected rush of reason and affection began to overwhelm the defences she had prepared against him. He needed her. After all these years, how could she say no? She tried to think of Harry, but there were too many other thoughts trying to crowd into her head.

'I make no demands on you,' he continued. 'All I ask is for your patience. And your discretion. Just a few more weeks – after all this time, is that really too much to ask?'

She drew a deep breath: 'Very well, Edward.'

He had done it. He had bought himself a little more time. Time enough to finish his task, he hoped. And time enough to deal with whichever bastard was making a fool of him with his own wife.

The Kremlin

The two soldiers on guard beside the high doors snapped precisely to attention, presenting their Kalashnikovs to each man as he passed the oversized black marble bust of Lenin and entered the inner sanctum. Bykov occasionally wondered whether the guard was there to keep intruders out or the members of the Politburo in. If he had his way, today's discussion was going to be tricky, and at least one member of the group would be leaving prematurely.

Andreyev was the last to arrive, through a separate entrance in the rear of the room, and was heralded by a fanfare of grumbling from the plumbing system in the nearby bathroom; he had obviously been caught short yet again. He looked grey; his cheeks were sunken. The drugs prescribed for his stomach pains were strong, and he ought to have been in bed. But he knew he couldn't afford to give in to his physical disability, not with the rumblings of dissent which could be heard around the

186

corridors of the Kremlin. If he took to his bed now, he might as well stay there – permanently.

The General Secretary opened his red leather folder, shuffled the papers within, and called the meeting to order.

'Comrades, there are only a few items on the agenda. We all have heavy burdens on our time; I suggest we dispense with the business as quickly as possible.'

But the discussions did not flow smoothly. The Foreign Minister decided that now was the time to inform his colleagues that Nigeria was threatening to renege on its debt repayments to Comecon countries, who in turn were beginning to bicker about the loans they had been forced to make against their better judgement to bolster Moscow's diplomatic objectives. That led to griping from some members about the renewed consumer agitation in the Baltic republics and the strange priorities which caused the Politburo to approve huge loans to indigent and ungrateful African nations while Soviet citizens formed endless queues in the cold at home. Andreyev needed to get a grip on the discussion but lacked the energy; it was going to be one of those days, and he turned in relief to his colleagues when the last agenda item had been dealt with. He snapped his folder shut and consulted his watch.

'Comrades, I am grateful for your diligence in discussion, but I believe that draws our business to an end.'

He was easing his chair away from the huge mahogany table when a voice interrupted him.

'Comrade General Secretary, I believe it would be a grave dereliction of duty if we finished our meeting without discussing events in Berlin.'

It was Semyonov. As the others turned their heads towards him, the old man sat erect, his eyes flickering with fire and his mouth set in a deliberate and determined manner. Andreyev gave him a withering look from the head of the table.

'If you wish to discuss Berlin, Comrade, I suggest we ask the Foreign and Defence Ministers to prepare a report for our next meeting.' Andreyev continued his preparations to leave.

'That will be too late. I insist we discuss it now,' said Semyonov slowly.

The rest of the room's occupants froze. This was an extraordinary challenge to Andreyev's authority, which in previous eras would have meant blood on the floor before the day was out. Even in the days of *perestroika* it left most members of the Politburo feeling that Semyonov was about to become as popular as a nuclear accident and left them uncertain how widespread the fallout from his challenge would be.

Had Andreyev had his wits about him he might have decided to ignore the matter and simply walk out, closing the meeting and making Semyonov look a fool. But the drugs had dulled his wits, and he was still struggling to think of his best move when the old man began talking once again, starting the discussion which now had to be dealt with.

'In previous days we might have looked on the disturbances in West Berlin with some equanimity: the capitalist world reaping the evil of what they have for so long sown. But that approach is no longer feasible. These are no simple squabbles between workers and employers, or between civilians and state police. We should not fool ourselves that this is a great working-class uprising as a prelude to socialist revolution.'

'Nobody was naïve enough to suggest it was, Comrade,' interjected Andreyev with undisguised tetchiness. 'We are all agreed that Berlin is not to be seen as part of anyone's great Marxist dialectic. So perhaps you would be good enough to tell us what you *do* make of it, before we all go about what little is left of our busy morning schedules.'

'This is reborn German nationalism, pure and un-adulterated. The desire to reunite Germany, to rebuild its place in the centre of Europe, and to kick the back-side of any foreign power which opposes it. For the moment it's the Americans who are handy and who are the target of their aggression, but be under no illusion that they will soon turn their bitterness towards us. We are the ones who stand in their way.'

'But these are West Germans, not our Germans,' someone said.

'There are no East Germans or West Germans, you fool. Just Germans! Scratch any member of the govern-ment in our beloved German Democratic Republic and you will find a nationalist who is enjoying every minute of what he sees on the other side of the Wall. Ask him if he would prefer to remain a satellite of the Warsaw Pact or take his ideological chances as part of a reunited Greater Germany and he'd regard you as a cretin for even bothering to pose the question. This is Germany, remember? Or have you already forgotten the twenty million Russians who died on the end of their bayonets during the last war?'

Andreyev smirked at the old man's passion. He felt he knew how to handle this one.

'So we are all agreed. A united Germany poses a threat to world peace. Which is why we are not proposing that Germany be reunited. I fail to see what your problem is.'

'You are the problem, Comrade General Secretary. Or rather your treaty is.'

The non-participating spectators at this duel were

189

now sure that blood was going to be shed. But whose? The old man gave no impression of volunteering to be an easy sacrifice.

'Unless it is stopped, the disease of nationalism will spread from the German heart of Berlin. The Americans will not stamp it out. So we must, before it infects East Berlin and the rest of East Germany and sweeps into Georgia, the Ukraine, Armenia, the Baltics and who knows where else. In the last few years there have been outpourings of nationalist discontent from almost every non-Russian republic within the Soviet Union. Food, religion, land disputes – they'll grab any excuse, but underneath it all is a continuing and growing desire to rid themselves of the great Russian yoke. And just at the time when we shall need our armed forces most to keep the lid on this cauldron, what do you do? Trade them away in deals with the Americans!'

'So, you oppose the treaty!' Andreyev accused.

'I do not believe the Americans are our friends. They wouldn't wish to do deals of this sort unless they saw it as giving them some sort of advantage, which by definition must mean our disadvantage. Do you think it's a coincidence that German nationalism should be rekindled at the very time we're about to reduce our troop levels? Are we so blind as to miss what may lie in store for us? And once the Russian steppes are ablaze, do you think the Americans will be there to help us piss on the flames?'

'You have no understanding of American politics, Semyonov,' barked Andreyev. 'Their President is no mastermind. He is weak. He can't even outsmart his own electorate, let alone us. We have nothing to fear. America is feeble, with a failing economy and a pathetic excuse for a President.'

'Then why in Lenin's name do a deal with them?'

Semyonov exploded, banging his hand on the table. 'If they are so desperate, don't negotiate. Humiliate. Squeeze them. Destroy them. At the very least let them destroy themselves. Why throw them a lifeline? You are missing the greatest opportunity we've ever had to undermine the American system and all it stands for.'

The heads of the rest of the Politburo turned towards Andreyev, looking for his answer. No one said anything, but he could see in many of their expressions that they agreed with too much of what Semyonov had said. He had to go for the kill. A compromise would not be enough. He had to make an example of the old man's insubordination, and make others fear to follow in his footsteps. But it also went wider than that. He knew that there was no longer any chance of his failing to reach agreement on the treaty, for failure would prove Semyonov right. The old man had cut away all his negotiating flexibility. Andreyev now needed the treaty more than Michelle, because the price of political failure in the Kremlin was still far, far heavier than anything facing the American President.

He drew in his breath, gathering his strength for the delivery of what would be a long and dreary condemnation which would culminate in the dismissal and disgrace of Semyonov. It had been the prerogative of general secretaries throughout the ages to dismiss their colleagues, only nowadays they had to work harder at providing at least the semblance of a political justification. But he was still drawing breath when Semyonov spoke again.

'So there we have it. I cannot agree with the General Secretary over a matter of cardinal importance. But if we are under such threat, as I believe we are, then equally firmly I believe that now is not the time for damaging wrangles within the highest councils of the party which our enemies might use against us. It is time for me to retire. I shall blame my great age and thank you all fulsomely for the opportunity of having served the State and my beloved Moscow for so many years, and I shall not make a public fuss. I ask only one thing of you. That you *remember* what I have said.'

With that the old man rose and with a firm stride and straight back marched out of the room. No one spoke. Remember? How could they forget a scene like that? They all watched as the guards saluted him for the last time before the doors closed again and he was gone. Without a word, Andreyev gathered up the papers in front of him and strode after his former colleague. But he was short and dumpy, and no matter how hard he tried he couldn't manage the dignity displayed by Semyonov.

Slowly and silently the rest of the Politburo filed out after them, each afraid to share with another just how much he had agreed with Semyonov's cautions, until only Bykov was left.

'Masterful, you old stoat,' he muttered under his breath. Semyonov had been even better than he had expected, betraying none of the nervousness of the day before when he and Bykov had agreed on the plan. And his exit line had been sheer brilliance, laying down his office for the good of the State in such a noble and selfless fashion that Andreyev would find it impossible to move against him now; it would look like the action of a weak and desperate leader. Semyonov had guaranteed himself a peaceful retirement, just as he had made certain that Andreyev would live under a cloud of suspicion until the treaty had been finally signed.

Bykov exulted. He had Andreyev by the balls. Now was the time to put on the real pressure.

SEVEN

Wannsee, Berlin

Nearly a million years ago great sheets of ice crept irresistibly down from the polar region and gouged their way across the north German plain, leaving a flattened landscape and a series of trenches which filled with water when the ice retreated. Around what was to become Berlin, these water-filled trenches provided a series of beautiful winding lakes, fringed by beaches of yellow sand. After the building of the Wall, these beaches became valued more highly than gold, providing the encircled city dwellers with the illusion of escape and a reminder of the free, open spaces of earlier times. It was on one of the sightseeing boats which ply the largest of these lakes, the Greater Wannsee, that Harry and Katherine had agreed to meet.

Harry had been waiting anxiously some while before Katherine turned up. He had tried to call her during the week, but she had insisted that he not call her at home and there was no other number he could try. He had been forced to control his impatience, muttering many incantations and swearing that he would not be late for fear of missing her. Instead it was she who was late and Harry had spent twenty frustrating minutes pacing up and down the dockside, two tickets in hand, fearful that she might miss the boat which would take them away from the city streets and allow them to mingle anonymously with the tourists.

The ticket collector was beginning to close the gate and Harry had all but run out of time when he saw

Katherine running down the steps from the car park to the landing stage. He persuaded the ticket collector to delay a moment longer, and his day brightened as she drew closer. Some way behind her two men were also running for the gate. Harry hoped that the boat wouldn't be too crowded – he wanted to be alone with her – and felt a twinge of relief when the men stopped in indecision, realizing that they would not be able to board without a ticket and looking in despair at the long line in front of the booking office. They weren't going to make it.

Katherine approached him with a smile and he threw open his arms to welcome her, but to his confusion she offered only a handshake.

'Harry, when we're in public we're just good friends, and as far as the rest of Berlin is concerned the only sights I'm showing you are in the guide book. Got it?'

'Sorry,' he mumbled. His inexperience was showing.

'Don't look so put out,' she grinned. 'It doesn't hurt me to see that you've never had an affair with a married woman before. It makes me feel . . . rather special.'

'You *are* special, dummy.'

'I'm glad.'

There was a scrum developing as the other passengers congregated around the bar, and they walked towards the bow to find themselves a seat where they could be alone. The boat cast off, and they relaxed in the first warm wind of an early summer. Another week and the boats and banks of the Wannsee would be crowded with Berliners seeking a few hours of escape. There were many sailing dinghies taking advantage of the breeze and several water skiers battling against the slight swell. The trees of the surrounding woodland nudged each other as they competed to get close to the water's edge and, beneath their branches, lovers could be seen

194

strolling hand in hand along the many secluded pathways. The thumping cadence of the engines and the gentle swaying of the boat took them past a tapestry of rural scenes, all brushed with sunlight. A brass band was playing Strauss waltzes at a lakeside restaurant, with the sound of the *glockenspiel* mingling with the chatter of guests and wafting across the water. Harry's anxieties began to drift away. He closed his eyes and let the sun soak into his skin, imagining they were on a desert island, completely alone, with only the rustle of palm leaves and the rippling of blue water to disturb their privacy, and nothing more to worry about than which side they tanned first. Katherine's body would tan beautifully, he told himself; her skin glowed, he remembered, even those parts which rarely saw the sun. Almost instinctively his hand reached out to touch her.

Without ceremony, she placed his hand firmly back in his own lap.

'Not in public, Harry. Remember? There are some simple rules, and we just have to obey them.' She sounded like a schoolmistress giving him his first lesson in elementary mathematics, and her tone was deliberate.

'My head tells me you're right, but certain other parts of my anatomy are in open rebellion.'

She threw her head back and laughed, the breeze blew through her hair, and Harry's eyes travelled from the ski slope of her nose, around her lips, down past her long and elegant neck to the other curves on her body, mentally ravishing her as he did so. But he knew it wasn't just lust; she made him feel very special, too. For the moment, it was enough that they were together.

'What would you like to do for dinner tonight?' he asked, trying to take his mind off sex. It didn't quite work. He hoped she would choose a hamburger or fried chicken, anything which would be fast and convenient. He didn't fancy spending several vital hours surrounded by hovering waiters when they could be alone, in private, in bed. Time enough later for romance. But he watched with dismay as her face lost its laughter lines, and somehow the sun seemed to slip away and the breeze picked up a sudden chill.

'Harry, no. I can't. Edward has a dinner party tonight which I must attend. I'm sorry.'

'That's great, absolutely perfect,' he muttered. He felt the same dark mood coming over him as had taken control at the Café Kranzler. He felt only slightly relieved that this time he couldn't be petulant and walk out on her – not until they had docked, at least. 'After the other night there's got to be more than day trips around the Wannsee admiring the scenery, hasn't there?' he asked grimly.

'Listen to me.' This time she took his hand, as if the stolen moment of intimacy would strengthen the force of what she was about to say. 'Edward knows I'm having an affair.'

'How on earth . . . ?'

'Because I told him. I've done nothing I feel ashamed of and I'm not going to get caught in an endless round of lies and deceit.'

'Does he know it's me?'

'No. And I don't want him or anyone else to know. You have to understand that after all this time I can't just kick him like an old car I'm bored with. We owe each other. And I can't suddenly let him down by deserting him when he needs me. This is a small town, as I've told you. People gossip. And if I suddenly started failing to appear at my own dinner parties, the whole of Berlin would know before the cognac was served. It

196

would destroy him if there were any hint of a scandal right now.' There was a slight pause. 'Particularly one involving an American diplomat.'

There it was, politics again. You couldn't get laid in this city without showing your party card first. But he knew she was right. In the last few days he had begun – most reluctantly – to focus on how the news would be received by Miss Pickerstaff that, within days of arriving on station, one of her agents had begun an affair with a foreigner who just happened to be married to the local political firebrand. He didn't care for any of the conceivable scenarios, all of which ended in great pain for him, and gratification for Miss Pickerstaff.

'So what does Edward want?' Harry enquired.

'He wants a little time, a few weeks,' she responded calmly, trying to ignore the wisps of fire which were beginning to burn around his brow. It was when he was so impatient and angry that she realized just how much younger he was, and how much she was sounding like the older woman. 'In its present mood, public opinion in Berlin is like a tiger with a sore head which has been abruptly woken by somebody stepping on its tail. Edward seems to think that the next few weeks will decide whether he ends up riding it or being torn to pieces.'

'Let me get this straight,' said Harry. 'Your husband knows you are having an affair, but doesn't mind. He knows you are sleeping with another man, but is perfectly happy so long as you are there to host his dinner parties. Anything goes, as long as it doesn't interfere with his politics?'

'You make him sound very callous, Harry. It's just that his political career has changed so dramatically. A few weeks ago he was enjoying a relatively quiet life as anonymously as most politicians, with no one really minding whether he turned up to meetings or not. All of a sudden he's on television every night, addressing great rallies, being courted by newspaper editors and stopped in the street by ordinary men and women . . . It's taken him by surprise as well as everyone else. He's just asked for a few weeks to sort it all out, to see where it's all going.'

'And after that?'

'I don't love him, and I shan't love him in a few weeks' time, either. You must be patient.'

'You sound like my mother.'

'It's not easy for me, either,' she chided. She had spent the last couple of days trying to be sensible and mature about their situation, but she found it so difficult when they were together. She had stopped holding Harry's hand and was looking into her lap to avoid those dark, lustrous eyes which seemed to dig right inside her and make her feel as nervous as a schoolgirl. She was fiddling self-consciously with her wedding ring, twisting it around below her knuckle. Harry noticed that it was a tight fit, as if it had grown into place and hadn't been removed for many years.

'Do you think I can lightly give up any of our time together?' she asked. She was clearly upset. 'You'll be in Berlin for – what – two or three years before getting another posting? How many weeks do I have to look forward to before you leave? Or do you think the other night was just a one-night stand, adding to my collection of trophies?' The strain was showing in her voice.

'Hell, no, Katherine,' he acknowledged morosely. He hadn't thought this through at all. All the previous women with whom he had been to bed had been nothing more than that – women with whom he had been to bed. He was having trouble adjusting to something deeper, having to think it through as well as simply feeling it.

'Then we must both be patient.'

At that moment the boat's skipper saw a sailing dinghy sliding out of control beneath his bows and spun the helm, jolting the passengers to one side and throwing Katherine into Harry's arms. He was close enough to feel the softness of her body and to touch the parts other men could only admire, and they both knew it hurt. She made up her mind.

'Harry, we're going to make ourselves miserable beyond measure if we go on like this. Let me show you Berlin. Let's be good friends and have fun. And leave it at that for the next few weeks. But just for the next few weeks.'

'Why does being sensible always make me bloody miserable?' he complained.

They spent the rest of the boat trip in silence, Harry now despising the sight of the young couples on the shore and Katherine wondering how it was she had managed to convince herself even for only a few weeks to be loyal to a man she no longer loved and to stay out of the arms of the man who made her feel eighteen once again. Neither of them enjoyed the scenery. When the boat had finished its circular tour and had returned to its landing stage, they decided they'd had enough of the frustrations the day had brought. The sun was already dipping behind the evening clouds and the colours and fun had disappeared. 'I'll take you home,' she said.

As they climbed into her Mercedes, Harry noticed the two men who had missed the boat, and who were now sitting in a green Opel in the car park idly reading newspapers and sipping from polystyrene cups propped up on the dashboard. They were having a long wait for someone, but he wasn't in the mood to feel sympathetic.

On their way back into town, Katherine seemed to cheer up a little and Harry recovered his sense of humour. As the street lights went on and the anonymity of the Berlin night began to close around them, they could afford the luxury of holding hands and the surge of physical energy which flowed between them made them both feel better. They knew they had much to look forward to – even if they had to wait. She promised to call regularly; they arranged to take a trip the following weekend to the secluded and ancient village of Lübars, tucked away to the north-west of the city at a point where the border curled around and the land dipped to form a tiny rural pocket. In the Middle Ages the peasants had hidden there from marauding armies, and now it might hide Katherine and Harry from the prying eyes of others. As they planned ahead, the next few weeks no longer seemed to stretch endlessly in front of them, and their sense of anticipation returned.

'And door-to-door chauffeur service, too,' she smiled as they approached the neighbourhood which was now his home.

'Not if we are to remain discreet! Drop me here, I have some shopping to do,' he requested as he remembered he didn't have any bourbon left, and he felt like doing considerable damage to a fresh bottle to fill the gap in his unexpectedly vacant evening.

She drew the car sharply to a halt. 'No difficult goodbyes, Harry Benjamin. Just get out, and I'll see you next weekend. And remember. Nothing but cold showers and press-ups!'

He managed a laugh, waving at her as the car sped off into the evening lights and towards her wretched dinner party, leaving him alone on the pavement. He waited for a gap in the busy traffic and crossed the road to a Turkish delicatessen, wondering if the Turks were

200

heavily into bourbon. If not, he would have trouble finding a bottle in Kreuzberg.

As he was entering the shop he noticed the green Opel, parked some thirty yards down the street with its lights out and the two men still inside. They seemed to be slow readers, for they were still glued to the same newspapers they had been studying in the car park at Wannsee. It was only when he had found his bottle of bourbon and had time to think of anything other than getting drunk that he remembered he didn't believe in coincidences. But if not coincidence, then what was the car doing outside? As he piled bread rolls and fresh milk into a wire shopping basket, he knew it didn't take a trained intelligence agent to figure that one out. They had followed Katherine to the lake, but were not following her now. They were waiting outside. For him.

Shit. Her husband must be trying to track down the mystery lover.

As he stuck a sceptical thumb into a tub of rock-hard Camembert, he knew he was facing a first-class mess. An outraged husband was never good news within the agency, particularly when he probably had your boss's direct line number. As he paid for his purchases Harry tried to persuade himself that he did, after all, believe in coincidences and he would discover that the car and its occupants had gone by the time he left the store.

But they hadn't. They were still parked, lights off, reading the newspapers. As Harry walked down the road away from them, he heard the car engine start and could sense the headlamps shining on the back of his neck. What the hell did he do now? He was acutely aware that, contrary to what he had pretended to several young and impressionable women in Washington, life in the CIA consisted mostly of shuffling papers and writing reports, not racing round the streets of some foreign city trying to lose a tail. That's why they recruited graduates with PhDs rather than house-breakers.

Harry stopped under a street lamp and ostentatiously began inspecting the contents of his shopping bag to ensure he had got everything, before walking briskly back towards the deli as if to pick up some forgotten item. The Opel was still hovering at the kerbside, lights glaring, waiting to pounce. Once back inside the store he made immediately for the rear, where he had noticed two large swing doors beside the dairy produce which presumably led to the storage area. Once through them, he found himself in a large and tatty room piled high with boxes of detergents and racks of bread and veg-etables, illuminated with a solitary, unshaded bulb dangling from a long flex. The flex had a loop in it to raise the light well above the piles of boxes; to Harry it looked more like a noose waiting for him.

He watched the store through the gap between the swing doors, and found he had stopped breathing as he saw one of the men enter and begin to look around the shelves in search of something. Harry was under no doubt as to what the man was looking for, and it would be only a matter of seconds before he discovered that Harry had flown and figured out how. As a child Harry used to wet himself when he got excited; he wasn't feeling too great right now, either.

It was only then it dawned on him that there must be another exit from the storeroom. He kicked himself when he discovered it behind two large metal waste bins full of rubbish and old cardboard. In a moment he had squeezed through and found himself in a long and dimly lit service street of cobblestones and high walls which stretched in front of him, bare and empty. There was no hiding place here; he would have to run for it

202

and make more than a hundred yards to the safety of the next corner, and he only had the few seconds it would take for his pursuer to discover the hidden exit.

Harry took off, wondering why there were so few Jewish Olympic medal winners. He was halfway down the street when it dawned on him that he was still carrying his shopping, clutched protectively to his chest. He was in danger of making a real cock-up of this. As he threw the bag to the floor, it landed with a sound of shattering glass which left him feeling sick. There would be no point in bothering to reclaim the bourbon. But he was almost at the corner, and still there was no sign of the other man. Only when he had dragged himself round into the protective shadows of an alleyway did he stop to gulp down huge mouthfuls of air and try to clear the pounding in his ears so that he could listen for the sound of pursuit. He had only a moment to wait before he heard the distant door bang, shoes scraping on the cobbles in indecision, and then the door bang again as his pursuer admitted defeat and returned the way he had come. Harry had escaped!

Then he began to feel a complete idiot. What the hell was he running for? He hadn't murdered anyone. Why was he shaking and breathless on the corner of some disgusting back street? Get a grip on yourself, Benjamin! Stop running and start thinking! Why were these bastards chasing him? If they had nearly caught up with him once, they were bound to succeed eventually. He couldn't just duck out. He had to find out who they were and what they were up to.

He continued up the alley and was now back in the main street, some way up from the delicatessen. Outside its entrance the two men were arguing, one waving his hands around as if to describe how the catch had got away, the other gesticulating at his watch. It was clearly the end of their useful night's work and they clambered back into their car, oblivious of being watched. But now the tables were turned. Harry was the hunter, and his quarry was preparing to escape.

The two students driving an ancient Volkswagen Beetle through Kreuzberg were puzzled to find a rumpled-looking foreigner knocking at their window as they waited for the lights to turn green, but who were they to turn down the hundred Deutschmarks he offered for providing him with an instant lift, particularly as the money came up front in the form of a handful of crumpled notes? Within seconds Harry was sitting in the rear seat, searching for his next words. He bit his tongue as he found himself on the point of saying 'follow that car', and settled instead for a vague wave of the hand and the instruction, 'Drive. I'll tell you when to turn.'

He was in charge again, guiding the VW as it swung in and out of the evening traffic, following the lead car as it proceeded into the darkness along Gitschiner Strasse in the direction of the Anhalter S-Bahn station. The occupants appeared to be in no hurry, relaxing after a fruitless few hours' work, perhaps contemplating what they might do with the rest of the evening.

There was a large number of cars on the road as Berlin geared up for another Saturday night, and progress was slow. Yet it was less than five minutes before the car ahead turned off and pulled into a small car-hire depot just down from the S-Bahn station. The two men handed in their keys and within moments were on their way again on foot.

Harry clambered out of the VW's narrow back seat and instructed the students to wait. He had only gone a few paces when he heard shouts of derision and the rattlesnake whine of the Beetle's engine as it revved up and raced off into the night. Balls. A hundred Deutschmarks and they'd driven scarcely a mile. He was on his own again.

He had expected his quarry to turn left towards the railway terminus but instead they branched right into the narrow streets leading away from it. Then a left, right, left and another right in quick succession, before the men turned left one final time. They seemed very familiar with the back streets of Berlin. Harry hurried to catch up as they disappeared once again, eager not to lose them yet anxious that, if they bothered to look behind them just once, they would discover that their missing fish had jumped straight back into their arms. He rounded the last corner cautiously, heart in mouth, before almost gagging in surprise. Less than two hundred yards ahead, brilliantly lit and crawling with military personnel, rose the Wall and Charlie, its best-known checkpoint. The two men were approaching it casually, as if they had done it a hundred times before.

They did not stop at the American sentry. Without pause they were past the signs warning them that they were leaving the American sector, and walking nonchalantly into the checkpoint. They disappeared from Harry's view as they entered the squat concrete transit building where travellers have to report, show their passports or identity cards, fill out customs forms, pay for their tourist visas and exchange hard Western currency for inflated East German marks. The bureaucratic checks are usually unhurried and occasionally cumbersome, but remarkably the men re-emerged as if no one had bothered to interrupt their casual stroll and within moments they were waiting for the final metal gate to be opened to give them access to the streets of East Berlin. On the night shift there was only one border guard operating the two traffic barriers as well as the pedestrian gate, but as soon as he saw the pair approaching he scurried across to allow them through, giving a quick, nervous salute as he did so. Christ, he seemed to know them! And no sooner had they stepped through the gate than a car drew up and they clambered into the back seat before being whisked away into the East Berlin night. The chase had come to an abrupt end.

Harry tried to grapple with what he had seen, and went on staring for several minutes just to make sure he hadn't mixed up his men in the half-light. But there was no mistake. The cage door had been opened in five-star style and his birds had flown.

He approached one of the US duty sentries and flashed his Mission ID, explaining that he was new to Berlin. The GI offered a smile of welcome as he smacked his way through a mouthful of gum.

'Tell me, who uses the checkpoint?' enquired Harry.

'Charlie? Tourists mainly, plus a few diplomats and the like. It's OK if you wanna use it. Never been to the East before? Go right ahead, buddy. Be my guest.'

Harry looked at the black lance-corporal who stood well over six-three in his boots, but decided he would be no match for Miss Pickerstaff and reluctantly declined the invitation.

'What about Germans?'

'Hell, no, not West Germans. This one's for foreigners, always has been. The home crowd use other crossing points. Not Charlie.' He could see Harry's puzzlement. 'Unless you mean East Germans. They can cross here, but not many of them do . . .'

Harry felt the colour drain from his face. They were East Germans, and they looked damned official. His brain was burning. Whoever needed to know his identity must have some pretty strong reason and quite

206

astonishing contacts if officials from the East were doing the dirty work. Who could possibly want to know about him that much, let alone have that sort of influence? He thought about it for several hours and over many beers. At the end of the long night, he could still only guess at one name.

Edward Schumacher.

EIGHT

Berlin

Harry woke with a heavy head. It wasn't the beer but the confusion and questions which had been buzzing restlessly around his head, even while he was asleep. He had dreamt he was running down an endless, dark alley, pursued by unknown adversaries and searching in vain for a door or some other means of escape. He could hear the pursuers getting closer. They were almost upon him, reaching out for him, the pounding of their boots ringing in his ears, yet try as hard as he might his legs would not respond. Then up ahead, in a pool of light cast by a solitary street lamp, stood Katherine, calling to him, her arms outstretched, ready to rescue him. She was his salvation. Even as he could feel the breath of his pursuers on his neck he had thrown himself forward into the safety of her arms – only to discover that it was not after all Katherine, but Edward, wearing the uniform of a KGB officer, a wicked snarl on his face, with his hands held out to strangle him.

Harry decided he had no wish to go back to sleep for round two. Instead he took a cold shower and a huge mug of coffee, and tried to sort out his thoughts. How could he suspect Schumacher? The only link was through Katherine, and he realized that this made him far from objective. Wasn't he allowing his personal interests and prejudices to cloud his judgement? Schumacher was a pillar of West Berlin society. A successful businessman. And leading politician. Someone who had provided the Western authorities with considerable intelligence material from his travels in the East. Who had run an escape ring. They seemed perfect credentials for a man beyond suspicion.

Perfect credentials. And perfect cover for ... for what? Harry didn't know. But he was going to find out.

The Mission was quiet and empty, as was normal on a Sunday, when Harry signed in. The guards on duty seemed to resent his intrusion since his presence would require them to put away the magazines, turn off the portable TVs and spend a mind-numbing morning staring at the ceiling.

It was even more frustrating for Harry. He stared in disgust at his computer terminal, praying for enlightenment which refused to come. The Mission's archives had been computerized on the powerful IBM 3090 which toiled away in a bomb-proofed concrete basement specially set into the light, sandy soil which underlay Berlin. But computers, no matter how powerful, give out only what has been put into them, and the computerization of the Mission's records had been completed less than six years before. Schumacher's details were there in front of him, but there was no flesh on the bones, particularly no early flesh. As far as IBM was concerned he was just another, albeit particularly hardworking, local politician climbing assiduously up the greasy pole, sitting on worthy committees and expressing even worthier views. Harry noted wryly that the file hadn't been updated to include any record of his town hall speech.

There was a cross-reference to another computer file, GDR-ECONINT/DOC, doubtless covering the intelligence-gathering which Schumacher had undertaken on his business trips, but the directory was classified and only available through the computer-coded permission of the head of the East German desk, and he didn't work Sundays. Harry played around with the keyboard, trying the files relating to East–West trade, the Berlin Senate and the political parties, but none had individual reference to Schumacher. It was useless.

The sun was streaming in through the window, yet it did nothing to lighten his mood. In desperation he tried the various paper-bound almanacs, annuals and gazettes which were held in the library, but quickly discovered that they were kept for only a couple of years before being thrown out or sent to the roomier archives of the embassy in Bonn. It was as if a veil had been drawn over Schumacher's earlier activities.

Harry knew none of the other Mission staff well; he had been in Berlin such a short time and his reputation for being something of a maverick hadn't helped, particularly with the old guard. So the chief librarian was surprised and not particularly overjoyed to be dragged down from his rooftop sun terrace by Harry's telephone call. He was one of the oldest members of the Mission's staff, due to retire in less than two years, and he liked being disturbed on a Sunday even less than he liked Harry.

'Benjamin? It's the weekend,' the old man complained in a querulous voice as he tried to prevent his sunglasses falling down his nose.

'Sorry, Paul . . . Mr Potts,' Harry apologized, deciding that undue familiarity would probably not help his cause. 'I need some advice, and I couldn't think of anyone else who might have the experience to help me.'

The old man sounded mollified by the flattery, and Harry continued. 'Miss Pickerstaff has asked me to put together an analysis of the development of cross-border trade going back some time, yet a lot of the earlier

210

records aren't available at the Mission. Is there anywhere apart from the archives in Bonn I can get at that sort of information?'

Potts snorted. Miss Pickerstaff had obviously decided that Benjamin was fit only for the most menial of tasks and should be loaded down with irrelevant nonsense to keep him quiet and out of the way. He had heard as much on the grapevine around the office. He was irritated to be disturbed by such a trivial request, but if Miss Pickerstaff had given the instructions . . .

'How far back?' he barked.

'Perhaps even the sixties,' Harry improvised.

'That's ancient history, Benjamin. Can't imagine what use anyone will be able to make of it. Still, if you want to bury yourself in economic and industrial archaeology, you might try the Free Economic Institute in Mariendorf. Full of old records and outdated nonsense. Just right for what you've got to do.'

Harry heard a cackle of desiccated laughter down the phone before it went dead.

Having spent an empty and unfulfilled Sunday, early the following morning he arrived outside the door of the Free Economic Institute. It was located in a small row of old houses which had survived the war but had little else to say for themselves, being architecturally dull and pressed in on all sides by towering new office blocks and shopping developments. The paint was peeling on the window frames and the city dust and cobwebs seemed to have collected in every corner. The doorstep was bowed and chipped by the passage of years and many feet, the railings bent and broken, and angry scars were splattered across the façade bearing witness to the savagery of the Allied bombing which had so narrowly missed yet which had destroyed almost everything else around. The building had the decaying air of an elderly

211

maiden aunt whom the world had long since passed by and who waited in a quiet corner for her final release. Harry struggled around a battered bicycle propped in the hallway and toiled up the stairs, past dull brass plates which announced the presence of an accountant, several indistinguishable trading companies and a radical news-sheet which was long since defunct, until he got to the top floor. There was only one door, with no obvious markings, and he walked in.

He entered a long room which he guessed had been knocked through into the next house, and seemingly built solely of shelves on which were piled books, manuscripts, boxes and small mountains of loose paper spilling over on to the bare wooden floor. In the middle of the room, squeezed with difficulty between the encroaching piles of reading material, was a long table covered in a green baize cloth, at the far end of which stood a vase of fresh daffodils and behind the flowers, looking expectantly at him, sat a woman. She stood up and advanced towards him. She had cropped grey hair and lively eyes set in a masculine face, and he noticed that beneath her flowing floral skirt she was wearing short white socks and tennis shoes.

'Fräulein West,' she introduced herself with a handshake. 'Welcome. We don't get too many visitors nowadays, do we, Gretchen?'

Harry looked over his shoulder to see she was addressing a large tabby cat, who had her paw stuck in a saucer of milk.

'How can I help you?' she asked with an unusual degree of eagerness.

Looking around the room, Harry wondered if Potts had deliberately sent him on a wild goose chase. It seemed impossible that there could be anything of interest to him in this firetrap of dried papers and cardboard. Everything seemed old and untouched, like relics of an ancient time.

'I wanted to consult some early records on East–West trade and the companies and people who were involved in it. Do you have anything which might help me?'

'My dear young man,' she said, taking Harry's arm as if he were an old friend, 'up to ten years ago we had the most comprehensive set of records anywhere in Berlin. Better even than the Free University or the *Statistisches Landesamt*. Then the endowment money ran out, so I'm afraid we've been a bit sparse since then. We've had to sublet most of the rest of the building and I've been looking after the shop on a sort of care and maintenance basis. Along with Gretchen, of course.' She tried to stroke the cat, but it seemed more interested in the milk.

'The lease is up next year, and they'll want to try to evict us and develop this into another of those hideous concrete shopping precincts. I don't know what we'll do then,' she muttered absentmindedly, lost in a faraway thought. 'You're not from the landlords, are you?' she snapped suspiciously.

'No. From the university,' he replied.

'Oh, good. A student. You don't play table tennis, do you? It's the only sport I can manage at my age.'

Harry apologized and explained that he had always been on the clumsy side, never athletic. She cast a curious eye over him and seemed to satisfy herself with his explanation.

'So, Herr Doktor. It's cross-border business, is it?' she said.

'A paper I have to give to a university seminar,' he explained. 'I want to trace the development of trade between East and West Berlin by following the fortunes of a selection of individual companies.'

'Interesting,' she mused, polishing her glasses vigorously while she pondered the task. 'Yes, I suspect we can help you. Which companies in particular?'

'I thought I'd look at both ends of the spectrum – one of the big public trading companies, perhaps, and then a couple of the smaller private companies. Any ideas?'

'That's a pretty murky area. Not too many records kept on those matters in the early days. The early traders didn't go in much for paperwork. Or telling the authorities what they were doing. They shifted around a lot, too, as the city was rebuilt. Helped keep them one step ahead of the tax man and the customs . . . What exactly do you want to know?'

'When they started, where they were based, what they did – that sort of thing.'

'Well, start with the simple stuff. They may not have cared much for filling in tax returns, but no matter how fast they ran they almost all had telephones. You might start there. We've got a complete set of post-war *Branchenfernsprechbücher* – commercial telephone directories – for up to, well, ten years ago.'

She led him briskly down to the other end of the room and began handing over thick books bound in battered red cardboard covers from one of the lower shelves, blowing a thick layer of dust from them as she did so. Gretchen, whose curiosity had drawn her to watch the activity from the end of the table, quickly retreated in disgust to the safety of one of the taller bookshelves where she continued to view the proceedings with considerable disdain.

They soon had a large pile of directories on the table, and Harry began to browse through them while Fräulein West busied herself collecting other materials. It didn't take him long to realize that he was getting nowhere. While the entries were broken down into various broad

214

commercial categories from tobacconists to banks and engineering firms, he didn't know where to start and there was no sign of anything connected with Schumacher. His troubled face told its own story.

'No luck?' enquired Fräulein West.

Harry shook his head. 'I'm looking for a particular name, but I can't seem to find it anywhere. Any clues?'

'A small business you say? Difficult. Bit of a needle in a haystack. Still, it used to be a pretty threadbare haystack in the old days after all that bombing. Office space was scarce and a lot of small businesses were run from home. If you have a home address, you might be able to find the business that way. Look, the domestic directories are on the shelf above.'

Harry grabbed the 1964 directory, ignoring the grubby marks which the accumulated dust and grime left on his shirt sleeves as he shuffled through its pages. Sure enough, there it was. Edward Schumacher, aged just about twenty-two and beginning to make his way in life, was listed at an address not far from the main railway station. Harry went back to the 'Import/Export' section of the commercial directory, but still he could find no match. No business working out of the same address or anywhere near it.

'Fräulein, I can't seem to trace the importer I want from this,' he said as she approached him with yet another pile of dusty folders.

'But of course you won't. Not if you're looking for trade between the East and West Berlin. For years direct trading was almost impossible, particularly after the Wall was built.' She stopped to give her glasses another vigorous polish and smooth down the sleeves of her cardigan. 'It could take months to climb the mountain of paperwork which was necessary to trade between the zones of Berlin. It was supposed to be permissible, of course, but then Berlin was also supposed to be one city. Trouble is, nobody told the bureaucrats, all of whom jealously guarded their own little empires and defended them with red tape. The West Berlin officials were even worse than those in the East – afraid that every paperclip going East would somehow be used to build another Soviet tank or missile. They were supposed to acknowledge the right of Berliners to trade with each other, but our rights have never counted for much in practice.' She wrinkled her nose in disapproval.

'So they simply made it impossible,' she continued. 'To shift a bargeload of goods one mile across the Wall you'd have to wait six months for all the paperwork to be completed and all the necessary permits to be granted, and even then some pedantic bureaucrat would find fault in it. By the time they were willing to let the goods through, there'd be nothing left but a pile of rusty junk.'

'But trade did go on?' asked Harry.

'Most certainly. The Russians wanted to sell us the machine tools and power drills or whatever, and buy their high-technology goods in return. But not through Berlin, not once the Wall had gone up. So everyone began sending the goods across to West Germany and trading with each other from there. The Russians could keep their political dogma intact and at the same time fill their warehouses with the best manufactured goods West Berlin could provide. That's why for any West Berlin trading business, the quickest way to send your goods a couple of miles east was to start by shipping them the 150 miles in the opposite direction to West Germany. And you see, young man, trading goods between West Berlin and West Germany doesn't count as either importing or exporting, which is why you can't find it where you're looking.'

She was warming to her lecture; her pupil was paying rapt attention. 'Try looking under some other category,' she suggested. 'Manufacturing. Investment. Wholesaling, perhaps.'

Harry raced back through the 1964 directory. Fräulein West viewed his eagerness, so uncharacteristic of most visiting researchers, with some concern and withdrew to join her cat. Harry pored over the list of manufacturers, but could not find a match for Schumacher's address. Nor did the list of investment houses bear fruit. But there, under the heading of wholesalers, he found it: 'ES Industrial Suppliers'. At the same address where Schumacher lived. It was so easy, so obvious. He found the same entry for 1965 and 1966 but the following year Schumacher had moved to a new, better address. ES Industrial Suppliers had also found a new home. Schumacher was no longer living above the shop, and he was clearly making strides in life. Harry continued to trace the business through the directories and various name changes – 'ESI Suppliers' and eventually just 'ESIS', a legally registered but totally anonymous company.

'Is there such a thing as a register of company owners?' he enquired.

'Of publicly owned companies, of course. But for privately owned companies you only get to look at the records if you can persuade the companies inspector that you are a taxman, police detective, health official or some other worthy. University academics don't count.'

She could see how disappointed he was. 'Don't give up hope. There may be another way – the *Handelsregister-Verzeichnis*. It's a register of most business concerns in Berlin with a small description of what they do and who runs them. It's like free advertising, so most companies co-operate. Here they are,' she said, catching a sense of Harry's growing excitement and blowing still more clouds of cobwebs across the room. 'Which year?'

'The last ten.'

And so he found it. Edward Schumacher, and one partner – Otto Strelitz, Schumacher's friend he had met at Kempinski's. Schumacher disappeared from the register in the same year he entered politics – keeping everything neat and tidy – so in the latest register ESIS was listed with one sole proprietor: Otto Strelitz.

'You said that the early cross-border traders didn't have many records. Why was that?'

'Because in the West they were all bootleggers. Sanctions-busters. In the early days there were shortages of almost everything, and even those goods which weren't in short supply were piled high with quota restrictions and taxes, or were on the West's prohibited list for trade with communist countries. Most of the trading was done under the counter, through some form of black-market barter. The Eastern bloc desperately needed Western goods but had no hard currency to pay for them, even if they were available legitimately. So a vanload of Zeiss optical lenses or a truck full of Soviet oil would come West, and would return laden with everything from computer parts to surgical tape. No paperwork. No money changing hands. Everyone happy except the bureaucrats.'

'But how did they manage to get the goods across the border?'

'Because everyone was in on it. On every trip East you added a commission – a ten-dollar bill inside your passport, a box of cigarettes for this border guard, a radio for the local police chief. Whatever they wanted. As you passed through they'd let you know what they wanted next time: spare parts for the motor-bike,

218

perhaps even a television. And the same thing happened on the return trip West. The officer in charge of a border check-point wasn't going to argue where the new refrigerator came from, so long as his beer and schnapps were cold.' Her bright eyes twinkled behind her spectacles; she was enjoying herself.

'Was it really so widespread?'

'*Everybody* did it. Right up the scale. The "Impex" trading agencies in the East didn't give a damn how their factory managers got the goods, so long as they got them. The less they knew about the details, the less paperwork there was for them. And if a little "gift" or "sample" found its way into their desk drawer, so much the better. Only the Western authorities took a tight view over what was traded, and even they knew they couldn't control it because all their officials were in on the act, too. Remember, for some time after the war cigarettes were used instead of money and a bar of chocolate or silk stockings could buy you . . .' – she flushed when she remembered what they had often been used to purchase – '. . . well, almost anything. So minor officials on both sides of Berlin were well used to cooperating with traders. It's what kept the city alive for many years. And if you didn't play the game, you didn't survive. You wouldn't get your border guards suddenly to become shortsighted, you wouldn't get your goods across, you wouldn't get paid. You disappeared. You show me a trading company which lasted longer than six months in those days, and I'll show you a company which had its hands in everybody's pocket from the Brandenburg Gate to the Polish border.'

The light of understanding began to glow and illuminate some of the darker thoughts tumbling in Harry's mind. Schumacher's business had almost certainly been crooked, buying off the authorities in the East with straightforward bribes and in the West with titbits of intelligence he picked up on the way. So that's why he had such good friends everywhere!

'You ought to be doing my job,' he told his instructress appreciatively.

'In a university? No,' she said coyly, 'they wouldn't let me take my cat.'

When Harry left a few minutes later, she was still sitting in her chair, stroking the cat and remembering the good old days.

Schumacher sat blinking before the bright lights. A large crowd of journalists had gathered in the Steigenbergerhof for the press conference; none of them knew what was afoot, but Schumacher had become far too strong a political personality for his summons to be ignored. The buzz of expectation grew as yet more TV cameramen squeezed their equipment into the back of the room while at the front the stills photographers climbed over one another in the attempt to get their lenses closest to the subject.

When had there last been a press conference like this? Schumacher asked himself. Just one Berlin politician, not even the *Bürgermeister*, and without any supporting foreign dignitary to pull the crowd. He grabbed the arms of his chair, suddenly afraid that the bandwagon could not forever continue hurtling forward, knowing that at some point it had to tip over and crush him underneath. The faster he drove, the more certain it was that someone would begin to dig, to ask the impossible questions, to catch him out attempting to explain the inexplicable and burying the inconsistencies with another invention or lie. But not today, he told himself.

His mouth was parched with expectation and from

the whisky of the night before. He very much wanted to sip the water which stood beside him on the table, but his hands were shaking too much and the water would have spilled. Not the way to begin. He had even tried to write down the name of a journalist to whom he wanted to give additional briefing, but the pen just made indecipherable scrawls. Mercifully he had all the words he needed typed out and well rehearsed.

He fiddled with his signet ring, twirling it around, trying to dissipate the nervous energy which was building into a sea of burning acid somewhere between his bowels and his brain. He checked his watch. It was time. He lifted his head from his notes and put on his broadest, most confident smile.

'Good-day, ladies and gentlemen. Thank you for coming.'

The press conference came to attention and a score of camera shutters clicked simultaneously from just a few feet in front of him. They were like a firing squad with blanks. As he set off on his statement, he wondered how long it would be before he might be facing the real thing.

Washington D.C.

Grossman shifted the telephone uneasily from one hand to the other and wiped his sweaty palm, but the conversation was proving equally uncomfortable no matter which ear he listened with. The news had put Michelle in a foul mood, and he was taking it out on the messenger.

'It was at a press conference just an hour or so ago,

Mr President. He made the demand then. He insisted that the troop talks in Geneva be broadened to include negotiations for the dismantling of the entire Wall between East and West Germany. No, sir, not just Berlin, the entire country. It seems a shrewd political move on his part because the stand he's been taking in Berlin seems to have caught the imagination of many other West Germans . . . we'll have great difficulty in isolating him. It's becoming good politics in Germany to be anti-American.'

Grossman listened to another burst of profanity. He was glad to be in his basement office in the White House and some considerable distance away from Camp David, where the President was supposed to have been relaxing in the pine forests after another difficult bout of primaries. In order to compensate for his heavy mid-European accent the national security adviser had struggled hard as a young man to perfect his English grammar and he despised having to listen to the in-articulate outpourings of the President. He wondered whether Michelle had been drinking.

'What do we do about it? Well, we have very little choice, in my opinion. If we even so much as hint that we will broaden the negotiations to include the border question, the talks will fail immediately. Yet if we ignore the demand, we are likely to do considerable damage to our relations with West Germany, and poss-ibly other allies. There's altogether too much talk about American foreign policy being based on narrow US interests without any concern for our allies. They may be ungrateful' – he refused to repeat Michelle's full description – 'but the fact remains that many of them are beginning to feel uneasy about our commitment. The British and French fear we may be washing our hands of Europe; while the Italians and Belgians have at last woken up to the fact that they face huge potential losses if we run down our bases and cancel orders for European weapons systems.'

He looked once again at the map of Europe on his wall, and thought of the uncontrollable consequences if the garish purple frontier line which ran like a scar across its middle were ever to be erased. Who would gain? The reunited Germans, certainly, along with every other agitator in Europe who had a grievance. It would mean the effective dismantling of the old order. And he could see no profit for the increasingly dispirited Americans – not with this President, at least. Grossman hated uncertainty. The indecision being displayed on the end of the phone by the most powerful man in the Western world caused him as much anxiety as any new Soviet missile.

'What? Put it on the public agenda and privately agree to forget it once the troops deal had been concluded? No, I'm certain Andreyev wouldn't go for that. His colleagues would tear him to pieces.'

He listened a little longer before impatience overcame even his discretion. 'Mr President, please listen to me. You have only one choice – the choice you've always had. To deliver. To bring the negotiations to a successful conclusion, just as you have promised. You must show yourself to be a strong leader. Once you've done that, Europe will fall into line and the American people will applaud you. All the troubles of the recent primaries will be forgotten. Deliver on the agreement and you have your re-election in the bag. Hesitate – and it could be fatal.'

He hated having to reduce every discussion about the great affairs of state to the level of common opinion polls, but it was often the only way to save Michelle from himself.

'You must reject Schumacher's demand out of hand, and immediately. *You* are running American foreign policy, not him.'

In the circumstances it was something of a sick joke, but it worked.

'I'll draft something with the press secretary so we can issue it within the hour. Enjoy the rest of your afternoon, Mr President.'

Berlin

Few things are as universally oppressive as an urban thunderstorm in summer. The heavy air seems to squeeze a city, making the streets unbearable, dulling wits, crushing nerve ends and trying the patience of barmen and bishops. Dark clouds gather, yet all too often they produce neither rain nor relief, only a sense among those beneath of having been cheated. The noise of thunder rolls across the city, pressing down and leaving the man in the street angered and on edge.

Michelle's swift dismissal of the city's demands – for Schumacher was now generally seen as speaking for the majority of ordinary Berliners – had a similar nerve-tearing impact. The speed and curtness of the rejection made it clear that there was no room for flexibility or sympathy for what most of Berlin and the rest of West Germany felt to be their legitimate demands. There was not even a hint of compromise or consideration. The unity which had bound Berlin to the United States, and which had been expressed so eloquently by Kennedy, had been finally and savagely shattered. For many, Michelle's words were less like a thunderclap,

224

more like the sound of distant gun fire. And it was getting closer.

It did not require Schumacher to organize an outpouring of anger and protest. Editorial columns, TV commentaries, trade union leaders and even clerics jostled with a host of other politicians to lead the charge, but no one questioned Schumacher's right to be the commanding general. And deep within the trade unions, working men's clubs and employers' federations, Bykov's men were fanning the flames – not so that anyone would notice, because the general mood was so fraught that they had no trouble in finding an abundance of tinder.

Schumacher refrained from comment for a full twenty-four hours. He wanted to gauge the atmosphere, build up an air of expectation. And try to stop his hands shaking. When finally he chose to speak, it was from the back of a flat-bed truck outside the Osram plant in Siemensstadt, the heart of Berlin's industrial centre. When the day shift clocked off from the nearby factories, a crowd of many thousands quickly gathered as they recognized the visitor who waited for them outside the works gates. The posse of television trucks obscured the view for many, but Schumacher had been careful to ensure that his speaker system would at least enable them to hear if not to see.

'Dear friends. Berliners. Germans. Loyal allies . . .' – a slight pause – 'Idiots! You stand there after another hard day's work. What fools you are. You probably think your sweat is helping rebuild the might of Berlin. But you're burying it. Yes – burying it!' He paused to allow the accusation time to sink home. 'Our city is the biggest commercial centre in the country and its goods – *your* goods – are being used to keep alive the very system which oppresses us.'

The TV producer in one of the vans heaved a sigh of relief. His day's work wasn't going to be wasted. He knew already he had the top of the evening news.

'You are the industrial powerhouse of Germany, and much of what you made today will find its way east. To Poland. To Czechoslovakia. To Hungary. To the Soviet Union. And to the other half of Germany. The governments there will welcome the fruits of your labours because they cannot provide those fruits for themselves. And every time another shipment of your goods, your manufactures, your daily toil goes across the Wall, it reinforces their system and builds the Wall another brick higher. You're propping up oppression! And the more of your goods which go to the other half of Germany, the longer it will remain *the other half of Germany*!'

The crowd was still, not sure where Schumacher was leading them, but eager to know their destination.

'Think about that. What does their treaty mean for us? With one hand the Americans and the Russians reach out to each other across the Wall, while with the other they press down remorselessly on us Berliners. Freedom and unity, they cry, so long as it doesn't mean a free and united Berlin. Our tears, our sweat, our blood have all been shed at the Wall, and will continue to be shed – until it is torn down! Our backs should be bent to destroying the divisions in our city, not preserving them. Yet our work helps sustain the superpowers and their intolerable system of separation. It helps Andreyev to say *"niet"* and Michelle to say *"no"*. It helps keep Germany apart, when it should help bring us together.' His fist was smiting the air to work on their frustration. 'So how much longer are you going to accept it?'

Shouts of support began to be heard from among the onlookers.

'Which of you can be certain that your work today hasn't gone to supporting the Wall, to keeping us apart? Which of us can say, "I have clean hands"?'

The shouts from the crowd were growing louder and more angry. Schumacher had them.

'In years past we've all watched the rivers of Berlin flowing with blood as our loved ones were slaughtered on the barbed wire. And what was their offence? The unforgivable crime of wanting to be together with those they loved. They were willing to make any sacrifice! While we . . .' Schumacher appeared to succumb to his own emotion '. . . we seem to have forgotten them.'

Schumacher paused as if to collect himself, allowing the crowd to give voice to their frustrations and feelings. Someone began to chant 'Pull It Down' and the cry was taken up by those around him until it spread throughout the crowds. Chants of 'Pull It Down! – Pull It Down! – Pull It Down!' began to ring around Schumacher until he was standing in the middle of a sea of waving fists and protest. He let it build for a while, before waving his arms to quieten them.

'Don't waste your breath. We can't pull it down. We can't even demonstrate about it, thanks to our friends the Americans. We can't even get the Russians to talk about it. Thanks to our friends the Americans. We can't even hope that the Wall will come down some time in the future. And for that, we thank our friends – the Americans!'

In an instant he had focused the attack, his bitter sarcasm carving through the crowd like a razor, leaving in tatters any vestige of support for their allies. The chants of 'Pull It Down! – Pull It Down!' began to ring out again, but Schumacher quickly silenced them.

'Friends, I cannot encourage another peaceful march

by Berliners for fear it would turn into a bloodbath at the end of an American boot. Too much blood has been spilt on both sides of the Wall. But we cannot simply turn our backs or pretend that it doesn't exist. So I, for one, will be at the Wall next Saturday. At noon.' A wave of excitement ran through the workers around Schumacher, but he waved his hands as if to calm unnecessary excitement. His sarcasm bit deep. 'Our American friends need not be afraid. I'll not be there as part of a great march. I will be there on my own, as an individual making my own personal protest. I'm not telling anyone else to be there.' A sense of disappointment gripped the crowd, as if they were being deprived of their opportunity, until Schumacher threw them a bone. 'But if you are, I shall be proud to shake your hand. And if thousands of you are there, individual Berliners, I shall be even more proud. And if tens of thousands want to join me, making your own way to whatever part of the Wall you want, then no one can stop us. We can form a human chain of Berliners along the Wall which no one dare break, no matter how many soldiers they send. Will you be there?'

Roars of approval were shouted from all sides.

'The crafty bastard,' muttered the TV producer in appreciation. 'He's going to spread them like a flood-tide all the way along the Wall. There's no way anyone can stop that.'

'But that isn't enough,' Schumacher continued. 'No, my friends. Our shouts may reach as far as the Kremlin and the White House, but of what use are shouts amongst the deaf? We must do more. There are nearly two dozen crossing points from West to East Berlin. There are many more in other parts of Germany. The gaps in the Wall are the lifelines which sustain the régimes of the East and their ability to keep us divided.

228

I want those gaps plugged! Don't feed them – choke them. Let's squeeze them to death. If they want a Wall, let's give them a Wall! Are you with me?'

He was answered with pandemonium and a sea of waving fists, like ripe corn blowing in the wind to which someone had set fire.

'Christ Almighty!' gasped the producer to an assistant. 'He's going to mount a blockade like the Russians did in 1948. Except this time it's going to be the East on the receiving end.'

'Can it really work?' enquired his startled colleague.

'Damned if I know. But I think we're soon going to find out.'

Harry had been puzzling for days how to get inside the confidential computer files of the East German desk, but had come up with no answer. He couldn't afford to take any risks, for Miss Pickerstaff would be sure to find out and crucify him if he did. So if he couldn't get to the computer records, he would have to get to the man who controlled them.

Frank Rossi showed all the effects of having spent too long in Berlin. He was third generation out of Naples via Milwaukee, and both his nose and his stomach had grown more prominent with every passing year. He loved Berlin with its light professional demands and its multitude of playtime delights. *Glasnost* had taken the bite out of his job – there seemed to be few secrets worth keeping on either side now – but he knew he was never going to make director at Langley and he was eager to grasp the extra time which now became available to him. Keep the Virgin Mary – as he referred to Miss Pickerstaff – happy and his desk clean, and no one asked too many questions. They were all too busy with their own business to bother with his.

At forty-one he found himself liberated for the first time in his life. Class Three perks, a decent expenses limit and a new zest for life and learning that had come with the increasingly frequent absences of his wife to visit the kids at school in Milwaukee. 'They're going through a difficult phase,' she would explain, and they would commiserate with each other about their devotion to the children and the sacrifices of being apart. And like all good Catholic fathers he meant it. But no sooner had her taxi drawn away from the kerb in the direction of the airport than he would find himself in that sexual vacuum which surrounds men when they know their wives are thousands of miles away in a different time zone. And in Berlin, vacuums are not difficult to fill.

When Harry asked him out for a drink and made it obvious that he would appreciate some advice about Berlin, Rossi was happy to oblige. He didn't need excuses, not when the wife was away, but every little encouragement helped. It took only a couple of whiskeys in a bar a little way up from the Mission for him to decide that the new rookie was not another of Miss Pickerstaff's handpicked *Wunderkinder* who couldn't recognize a joke if it wriggled up his trouser leg, and only a couple more to realize that it was going to be a long night. His new colleague greeted every round of drinks like an old friend, and Rossi knew he would have to call on all his stamina.

Fresh air seemed to be the answer, and they started their bar-crawl through the hostelries of the old village of Dahlem, where the Mission was located, and up through Grünewald, with every round of drinks becoming more expensive as they moved towards the city centre, but neither seeming to notice or to care. Their conversation became more relaxed, drifting from their

230

backgrounds to their jobs to increasingly indiscreet gossip about their colleagues, as the alcohol turned them from new acquaintances into old and trusted friends. They had abandoned their taxi and walked as far as the Ku'damm — always the Ku'damm, thought Harry, as if Berlin had only one artery through which all life in the city must pass — before either of them dared exchange confidences about Miss Pickerstaff.

Rossi screwed up his face intently when Harry raised the subject of their superior, obviously considering his reply before letting forth a prolonged and violent belch which came from deep within his bulging stomach, followed by a hysterical giggle. Rossi was back in high school and Harry knew he had his man. If only he could keep his increasingly befuddled brain clear enough to squeeze out what he wanted. But, somehow, with every new drink, it didn't seem to matter quite so much . . .

'You know, Frank, that old dragon hates me.' Harry realized he didn't have to pretend in order to sound morose.

'Harry, baby, that old dragon hates everyone. But most of all she hates herself.'

'What do you mean?'

'When did they ever have a female director of the agency? The Pope'll get married first. She thinks she's the best in the business, but knows she's already pushed herself about as high as she's ever gonna go, and as far as Langley's concerned she can live and die in this rat hole. They know she'll take care of it and they can forget it.'

'So why does she hate herself?'

''Cos she's a friggin' woman. That's why she doesn't use make-up and starves herself so's she's got no tits at all. Half of her wants to be a fella, and the other half's a frustrated old maid. That's why she hates young bucks like you, Harry. She resents you because you're a man, at the same time as deep down she wants to get hold of your zipper.'

Harry stopped dead in his tracks as his mind conjured up lurid images of Miss Pickerstaff coming towards him, grey hair falling stiffly around her shoulders, smiling, and stark naked.

'I'd rather defect,' he muttered.

Rossi burst into another peal of giggles as he put a pudgy arm around Harry's shoulder. They were off the Ku'damm now and into one of the side streets where flashing neon lights indicated there were still many more bars left with which to experiment.

'Still, the old bat'll never be out of a job in Berlin,' Rossi laughed. 'Come on. I'll show you.'

Harry was pulled towards a door leading into what he assumed was another basement bar but which he realized was a club when he was asked for thirty Deutschmarks just to get in. As they squeezed down the narrow stairs he felt as if they were entering an alien, subterranean world where the familiar rules didn't apply, and he felt distinctly uncomfortable. Already he missed the comforting roar of the Ku'damm traffic. The place was crowded, the atmosphere smoky and dimly lit with the only bright light falling on a small stage which jutted away from the back wall. A three-piece band was crammed into one corner, and Harry and his companion settled down at a table barely large enough to get their knees under. It was all Liza Minnelli and cabaret *kitsch*. Without waiting to be asked, a bored young waitress with a face plastered in heavy make-up thumped a cheap bottle of sparkling white wine down in front of them, accompanied by two smeared glasses which certainly wouldn't have passed inspection had the lights been any brighter. Rossi seemed to know the place well and pounded the table in expectation as if it were a drum, spilling some of the sticky white wine across the table top.

'What is this place?'

'I call it Mother Mary's – in honour of Miss Pickerstaff,' Rossi exclaimed jovially.

'Why?'

'Wait, young man. You'll see!' he chuckled.

Perhaps it was time to dig, Harry thought. 'You know she won't let me blow my nose without getting her permission first. In writing.'

'Yeah. I heard you were having a tough time,' responded Rossi, without a shred of real interest as he concentrated hard on his glass.

'I met a Berliner the other day. This chap called Schumacher who's making all the headlines. I went to look at his file to find out more about him and got threatened with castration.'

'Schumacher? You don't have to worry about him. We know him well.'

'Provides us with some useful intelligence, I understand.'

'Been doing it for years. Usual sort of stuff, you know.'

Harry certainly did not know, but his attempt to get further information out of Rossi was cut short by a roll of drums as on to the stage slinked a tall woman in a long sequinned dress adorned with huge crimson feathers. Rossi joined in the enthusiastic applause which rippled around the tables. The woman began to gyrate to the music and sing a lewd song in a thick Berlin accent and husky voice about the *Bürgermeister*'s daughter. With every verse she took off part of her clothes and the feathers fell to the floor as if a

233

fox had found a chicken coop. Each new revelation was greeted with raucous shouts of impatience. Rossi was in his element. The singer had a curiously long body with narrow hips, as if she had been stretched as a young woman and her figure had never quite recovered. But her face was elegant and, as the layers were stripped away, Harry could see that her breasts were truly magnificent.

She was down to her undergarment now, a black lace one-piece chemise adorned with crimson frills and a multitude of tiny feathers. As she came to the final verse about the downfall of the *Bürgermeister*'s daughter, she grasped her breasts and thrust them out towards the audience, which howled with delight. The shoulder straps came off one by one, Rossi began to sweat and run his fingers through imaginary hair on the top of his bald head, spilling the last of the wine in his excitement.

With a roll of the kettledrum and a single quick wave of her arm, the chemise came off and was thrown to the crowd, leaving the dancer standing naked in a spotlight except for the tiniest of G-strings. Harry gasped in horror. The tits were falsies. She was a man. In the second or so during which the performer remained in the spotlight, he took in all the telltale signs which might have alerted him earlier. The sinewy neck and its prominent adam's apple, the all-too-heavy make-up, the pronounced muscles on the legs and arms. But even as he found himself revolted he had to acknowledge that the transvestite's deception was very, very good.

'Time to go on elsewhere, Frank?' he enquired as Rossi held up the empty bottle.

'Christ, no! The show's only just started. This is one of the best in Berlin, and this city's famous for 'em.' He waved to attract the attention of the waitress and Harry knew he was stuck.

'So tell me about Schumacher,' Harry persisted as the clamour subsided while the patrons waited for the next act.

'Usual sort of stuff, as I said. Reports of shortages. Rumours of discontent or an industrial accident which was stopping production. What materials they needed and which sanctions they were trying to get round. That sort of thing.'

'Doesn't sound . . .' began Harry, but he was interrupted as the waitress appeared to take the order. She sat on Rossi's knee as he whispered in her ear, while Harry stared rigidly at her for any sign of five o'clock shadow.

'But why should all that material get such a high security classification?' he started once again. 'Doesn't sound that earth-shattering to me.'

'It's not. But Schumacher insisted. If he was playing a double game on his business trips East, he didn't want the evidence left lying around on tables for the cleaners to see.'

'So he was playing a double game?'

'Isn't everyone in Berlin?'

'What was in it for him?'

'What was in it for him? Shit, Harry, where'd you come from? It made the mother-fucker rich. He came to us and said the Commies were asking him to do some pretty dubious trade. We told him, go ahead. Just let us know everything they're up to. Hell, they were gonna get it all from somewhere anyways. Seemed best we knew all about it.'

'We actually helped Schumacher break sanctions?'

'Within reason, sure. Helped us keep tabs on what those bastards across the Wall were up to.'

A howl of raucous laughter came from one side as

something distracted and amused the patrons. Harry had trouble hearing himself, let alone any of Rossi's answers.

'Was his information much use? Do you ever really learn anything new or important from someone like that?'

They could both now see what was causing the distraction. The dancer had reappeared. He had exchanged feathers for a leather tank-top which covered nothing below his waist, and he was now crawling along the floor on hands and knees between the tables with his backside in the air. As he passed by, the drinkers would force Deutschmark notes down between his false cleavage and slap his exposed flanks, before clutching their sides in laughter. It was like a pig-sticking festival. Rossi already had his wallet out and his notes grasped in his left hand.

'Did he ever provide anything significant?' insisted Harry.

'Confirmed what we already suspected,' bawled Rossi. 'Gave us a little flavour, you know.' He was on the edge of his chair now. The dancer approached, grinning stupidly as the blows rained down on his backside.

'Come on, Rossi,' Harry challenged. 'Sounds pretty amateurish stuff to me. Did he ever give you anything new?'

But it was too late. Rossi had already stood up to join in the sport. He launched himself at his target, left hand ready to thrust notes at the dancer while the right delivered several resounding thwacks on the bare flesh, before subsiding into a red-faced heap on his chair and downing a vast amount of fresh wine.

'Did he ever give you anything new?' Harry persisted, but his concentration was wrenched away. The

236

transvestite was now directly in front of him, and Harry found himself confronted by a painted face with a fixed, lopsided grin and greedy eyes. He froze, and the dancer's hand came up to rest on his knee, demanding attention like a whipped dog. Harry's flesh crawled. Every leering eye in the room was on him. He wanted to run, to hit out, to lash at this evil apparition. Instead he scrambled in his pocket for some notes and threw them on the floor. The dancer scampered off to collect them as the audience cheered and whistled, while Harry wiped away the sweat that was pouring down his face.

'Shit, Harry. Knew you'd enjoy it!' bawled Rossi, thumping him on the back in evident pleasure. 'And come to think of it, that old bastard Schumacher hasn't given us a damned thing we hadn't already guessed or couldn't have found out from elsewhere for years. But who does? And who cares?'

He gulped down more wine and turned to applaud as the next cabaret act came on stage. Harry slumped back in his chair. He remembered Katherine's admonition about Berlin being like a cage, and how animals often go crazy in captivity. But instant understanding still made him feel no better, and he thought he was going to be seriously sick.

'I've got to go,' he muttered and staggered up. Rossi scarcely noticed, his attention fixed on the three-man act which was beginning to do suggestive things with balloons.

Once back outside in the Berlin night, Harry gasped for air. His head was swimming and he felt dirty, as if no amount of scrubbing could get him clean again. As the alcohol bent his mind and allowed the pieces of the puzzle to fall in new and untried ways, he knew that Schumacher was false, and almost certainly a double agent. He couldn't prove it, perhaps — not yet. But he would.

He should have felt a sense of triumph, of elation at having spotted prey which for so long had eluded others, but instead he wanted to run away and hide from the world. He wished tonight had never happened, that he could still feel as clean and innocent as he had done a week earlier. Because he was in love with Schumacher's wife. And if Moscow were pulling his strings, whose side was she on?

NINE

Berlin

When Harry woke the following morning he felt appalling. The contamination of the night club still seemed to cling to his skin and he tried to wash it out of his pores with a steaming hot shower. That helped his hangover, too, but he couldn't so easily brush off the questions about Katherine. She was different from any other woman who had shared his bed. The others had been mere girls by comparison, shallow and simply convenient. Katherine was so much more. He had been gripped by the thrill of the chase and the chance to capture someone so very different from his previous conquests, but instead of his usual desire to move on to new pastures he had discovered a relationship of more depth and colour than anything he had previously known. This world was so new, yet already was beginning to look less certain. His doubts were beginning to shake the faith on which it had been built.

If Schumacher were deceiving the world, how far could he trust Katherine? Did she know that Schumacher's fortune had been built in the dark underworld of smuggling and contraband across the Wall? Yet if she were part of the deception, why did they need to follow her in order to find out who her lover was? And would she willingly help the very system that had murdered Peter?

Confusion washed over him. He desperately needed to see her again, to be reassured by the sparkle in her green eyes and to let her touch smooth away the doubts.

He threw himself back on his pillow and tried to imagine her there beside him.

He was lost in his dreams when the telephone on the bedside table rang with the sound of an alarm bell exploding inside his head. God, he needed more coffee.

'Harry?' It was Katherine. He tried to speak, but his throat was still strung out from the smoke and acid wine of the night before, and all he could manage was an unintelligible croak.

'Darling, are you all right? You sound terrible.'

Harry coughed to stretch his vocal cords and muttered something about a drink too many. He was confused. He didn't know what else to say.

'I sometimes think you need the guidance of an older woman,' she chided. 'But I'm afraid it can't be this weekend,' she said, suddenly more serious. 'I want to join Edward's walk to the Wall. Not for him, but for myself. Do you understand, Harry? I'm not interested in the politics, but it's a chance just to show how I feel. I just want to be there, with other ordinary Berliners, saying no. It seems so right somehow, as if it's my duty. You do understand, don't you?'

She was hesitant, a little nervous confronted with the mutually exclusive demands of Harry and her memories. Harry wanted to argue and say what about our bloody date and what about me and what about my doubts about you, Katherine Schumacher. But he was beginning to comprehend just how cleverly Schumacher was pitching his appeal to the emotions which lurked below the surface of the city, to feed the frustrations of tens of thousands of ordinary people, to give the helpless back their hope.

'I understand, Katherine. I don't like it, but I think I understand.'

'Thank you. I'll call you later.' There was a pause as Harry thought she was putting the phone down.

'Harry. Just a couple more weeks. I miss you.'

The phone went dead and Harry contemplated yet another empty weekend. He was beginning to understand Berlin a little better, but he still hated it.

He arrived at work to find a message stuck to his computer screen. 'See Miss Pickerstaff', it instructed. It was underlined three times. Moses Al-Bloody-Mighty, had she already heard about last night? He gave another vain dab at the tuft of hair that was standing defiantly askew on top of his scalp, and wondered whether he could save himself by dropping Rossi in it. He gave Rossi a call; at the very least they should co-ordinate their stories. But his secretary announced that Mr Rossi would not be in the office all morning – 'he has several important meetings in another part of town.'

'Starting with a liver specialist,' muttered Harry, but the sarcasm was lost. He was still debating how to handle the awkward questions when he arrived outside Miss Pickerstaff's office.

'Go straight in, Mr Benjamin,' the secretary said, lowering her eyes and blushing as if he were improperly dressed. She clearly knew what he had been up to last night, he thought.

As he knocked on the door, he still had no idea how he would handle it. This was one he would have to play by ear. So he was taken aback to find Miss Pickerstaff seated behind her desk, with a single sheet of paper in front of her, smiling.

'Come in, Benjamin,' she said in a voice which was sweeter and more generous than Harry had believed she possessed. It made him feel particularly wary as he sat down.

'As you know, I've had severe doubts about you and your sense of responsibility' – God, she did know about last night! – 'so I was surprised but greatly encouraged to discover from the weekend roster that you had been working on a Sunday.'

It wasn't last night at all. It was worse. She was still smiling.

'So impressed was I that I wanted to find out what had captured your enthusiasm. I don't know whether you are aware of it, but our computer system has an audit trail which records every request made of it, and as standard security procedure I receive a weekly report of all requests made out of normal working hours.' She held her hands together in front of her, as if giving thanks for some divine favour. 'I seem to remember giving you very precise instructions as to what the scope of your duties were. In particular, I believe I gave you specific orders that you were not to proceed with your ridiculous theories about Edward Schumacher.' The smile was now as broad as her pinched features would allow, her cheeks glowing with a savage satisfaction. 'It was therefore particularly stupid of you to sneak into the Mission on a Sunday and attempt to go behind my back. But, Benjamin, you can't. The audit trail shows that you attempted to access all our records on Schumacher, and even tried to break into a security file for which you are not authorized. How am I doing so far?'

Her hands spread wide as if casting a net. Harry said nothing. His vocal cords had congealed once again. He began to feel out of his depth, as if the chair beneath him were being lowered into a pool of boiling oil. He desperately wanted to touch something solid, but Miss Pickerstaff's smile seemed to dissolve his sense of reality.

242

Taking his silence as an admission of guilt, she moved on. 'None of that surprised me. Indeed, one might argue that you were simply getting used to our computer system, playing with it to see what it could do.' She offered Harry a way out, hoping that he might grasp it so that she could trap his fingers as she slammed the door shut. 'But you don't even have that excuse, do you? Because you then went to Potts with some cock-and-bull story about my instructing you to do some work on cross-border trade. Funny, I thought I had given you explicit orders to keep your nose out of the East. Remember?'

Harry could feel the boiling oil inching its way up his body, stripping his flesh away as Miss Pickerstaff lowered him into it with total precision. No wonder she was enjoying herself. She knew how painful it was, and how to eke out the torture.

'So, Benjamin, you will understand that it is with the greatest reluctance I feel forced to place this on your evaluation record.'

She slipped across the single sheet of paper which had been lying in front of her. The paralysis in his vocal cords seemed to have extended to his eyes, and he was able to take in only parts of the tightly typed note. But even in his present condition he couldn't miss many of the phrases: '. . . violation of explicit instructions . . . unauthorized attempts to access classified material . . . misrepresentation . . . disregard of security procedures . . . unfit by temperament or ability for his duties . . . formal and final warning'. No wonder the secretary had been blushing.

'As you will see, I am issuing you with what amounts to your last chance. If you so much as sneeze in the office, you will be out of Berlin. For good. If you wander even by chance upon the name of Schumacher in your work, I will know about it, and you will be dead. If you have anything to do with him, his friends, his business, if you even happen to be in the same football crowd as him, you will be on the plane back home within twenty-four hours, where you will be lucky to get a job looking after the car pool. Please tell me if I'm not making myself clear.'

Harry stared fixedly out of the window, as if it were the last daylight he would ever see before the oil rose above his eyes. He had to offer some resistance to her tirade; his self-esteem insisted on it, but his bewildered mind failed to find a suitable riposte.

'There is one thing I would like to know, Benjamin, before we finish this little chat. What is it about Schumacher that you find so . . . irresistible?'

'He's false – a phoney,' Harry muttered, surprising himself that he was able to say anything.

'A phoney what?' She seemed to be genuinely interested.

'A false friend,' he blurted out, not knowing how else to express it.

'I'm astonished, Benjamin,' she mocked. 'I thought over the last few weeks that Herr Schumacher had been making his political views so clear that even you could understand. Don't you yet realize that we have no friends in Berlin, only relationships of convenience? Schumacher is just like the rest of them – friendly so long as it suits him, a staunch Berliner when it doesn't.'

'But his business . . . it was almost certainly based on illegal trade. He was helping the East.'

'As was everyone else who was ever allowed to travel behind the Iron Curtain. The only thing we insisted on was ensuring that they help us as much as they helped the other side. After all, we took as many of

244

the Third Reich's rocket scientists to assist us with the space programme as we could lay our hands on. We don't expect them to be loyal, Benjamin, just useful.'

'But was Schumacher ever useful? I understand the intelligence he provided was low-grade material, rarely original.'

'You have been snooping, haven't you,' she snapped, and Harry realized he was digging his grave still deeper. 'But our knowledge of what was going on in the East was built up in the early days on fragments of information, none particularly important in its own right, but the pieces gradually forming a picture. Schumacher provided us with lots of little pieces at a time when we needed all the help we could get. And he was never proved wrong.'

'But wasn't that suspicious in itself? Couldn't he be a double?'

'How on earth do you conclude that because a man has given us useful information over many years he's a double agent?'

'He's not being very helpful now, is he?'

'Schumacher and about a million other Berliners! He's not alone in this trouble which is being stirred up. Do you think they're all KGB agents?' she spat out contemptuously. 'Surely with all your nosing around you must have found something more concrete than that!'

Harry wanted to tell her about the agents who had followed him and then disappeared back across the Wall. But he couldn't. He hadn't reported it then, and he couldn't do so now. They would find out about his relationship with Katherine. It was bad enough that he was playing loose with the rules about liaisons with foreign nationals, but to be doing so with the wife of someone he suspected of being a KGB agent would be all that Miss Pickerstaff needed. He might as well try to swim home.

'I tell you there's something wrong with Schumacher. Don't ask me to prove it. Call it instinct, if you like, but he's all wrong,' Harry said defiantly.

'Instinct! Instinct!' She was off the deep end now. 'You've been here two minutes, you're so wet you look as if you've been dragged out of the canal, yet you have the gall to sit there and talk to *me* about instinct!' She was taking this personally. 'This is the CIA, Benjamin, not some school for amateur astrologers. I will not have the likes of you dragging down my reputation. There's been trouble ever since you arrived. I had one of the best-run bureaus anywhere in the world, but we've had nothing but confusion and chaos from the moment you set your foot inside the door. You're a bad agent and you're worse luck. So you take your instincts, and you get out of my sight.'

'Does that mean you don't like my work, Miss Pickerstaff?' He couldn't resist it. After all, what had he got to lose?

'Get out! Get out!' she screamed.

Something had worked. Miss Pickerstaff was no longer smiling. In that respect, at least, he had levelled the score.

Katherine didn't know what to expect as she prepared to leave home and make her way to the Wall. Edward had left a short time before and had walked straight into a posse of newsmen and cameras which would follow him all day. Katherine had said she wouldn't travel with him; she wanted her own visit to the Wall to be a private affair with time to think of Peter and the baby, and not to get mixed up in a

246

political protest. For Edward it was enough that she was going; he would have at least one other person there, he joked.

But as she walked towards the Wall, aiming for the point where she had crossed all those years before, it was apparent that she and Edward would be far from alone. The whole of Berlin seemed to be on the move that day, spreading itself along the barrier like ivy. Edward had reckoned that 30,000 people would be needed to link hands and cover the entire border between East and West Berlin; there were more than ten times that number. In Kreuzberg, where Katherine stood, most of the others were young people, laughing and singing and joining in what was becoming a celebration as they had to queue just to get through the bustle to touch the concrete frontier. Overhead a military observation helicopter flew slowly along on the Wall Patrol, with nothing more sinister pointing through its open hatchways than camera lenses. There were a few policemen in evidence but they kept a respectful distance, except for two officers who pushed through the crowd to touch the forbidden Wall themselves before returning to their duty with the cheers of onlookers ringing in their ears. Of soldiers, particularly Americans, there was no sign.

As the minutes ticked away towards noon, the bustle subsided and a quietness settled across the gathering. A group of Christians knelt in prayer, the *Wurst* and ice-cream salesmen put away their wares and joined the throng, and people were left to their private sorrow. As the chimes of twelve rang out from the steeple at nearby St Michael's, hands were joined and a ripple of unity spread along the Wall. When the clock had finished chiming the church bells took up the protest, their sound mingling with the chorus from other belfries as

247

they rang out a message of defiance which could be heard for miles on either side of the frontier.

She knew she was within yards of where Peter had died. But it was all different now. The piles of rubble had gone, so had the barbed wire. The Wall itself looked as pathetic and pockmarked as an abandoned car. Behind it the frontier area with all its landscaping had lost its menace, yet still it remained obscene, if only because it was, still, a frontier. Nobody could hide from her what it stood for. She remembered.

As she stood in silent communion with her fellow Berliners, the sun appeared from behind a cloud to reinforce their hope, as if they were being given a signal that their long wait was nearly over. Electricity ran through the linked hands; like the others around her Katherine was taken with a new energy, as if their united strength could overwhelm and topple the concrete slabs. One concerted push, she felt, and they would all be down.

She thought of Harry. He was more like Peter than any man she had ever met. And he had helped prise open a door which had been slammed shut almost twenty years before. As she stood in the sunlight, she began to think that perhaps there was a future for her after all. She had no idea what it might bring but, after a lifetime of brooding in the past, any future was worth fighting for. She thought of Harry's body, of the fulfilment he had given her after all these barren years, and of the new life which even now might be growing inside her. She had been too impulsive to take precautions, but she didn't care. Tomorrow was exciting, worth taking risks for, simply because it was tomorrow. She had thought about it constantly since the night she had taken to Harry's bed, and she had even begun to welcome the prospect. She wanted one last chance. It might be dangerous if she were carrying a child at her age, but it seemed only right. Peter would have understood. And if Edward couldn't, that would be his problem. It was a challenge she was more than willing to accept and, as the sun warmed her body, she could almost feel fresh life and hope rising within her. She had been given one final chance of happiness; she was determined to grasp it with all her strength.

Less than a mile from where Katherine stood, the crowd swarmed even more thickly around the checkpoint at Prinzenstrasse, a major crossing point for goods traffic. The police guard had been ordered to intervene only if individual safety were threatened, and the mass of bodies which now spread across the broad approach road could hardly be described as doing that. It was some time before the sentries realized that the human barrier was not dispersing but was encamped and showed every sign of staying. A truck approached with the intention of carrying its load across the checkpoint and into the East, but after a short discussion the driver turned his vehicle around and headed back the way he had come, taking with him the applause of the pickets. The occasional car which drove up Prinzenstrasse during the afternoon received similar treatment, with identical results. Elsewhere it was the same. At Checkpoint Charlie the tourist coaches which normally would have taken their passengers through to the sights and souvenir shops of Unter den Linden came, saw, and retreated. Only military and diplomatic vehicles were allowed to pass, the human cordon parting as they approached, closing again as soon as the last soldier was through.

At crossing points all along the Wall, similar actions were taking place. Picket lines blocked access, no goods or civilian vehicles crossed, even the rare pedestrian with thoughts of visiting the East was dissuaded. Those who had thoughts of crossing from the other side were turned back by the border guards, uncertain of what was going on and unwilling to lend further numbers to the potential chaos. Along the Wall the steady stream of foot and vehicle traffic ground to a halt, and an uncertain quiet settled along its entire length. The S-Bahn, which carried more passengers to East Berlin than any other form of transport, rattled into Lehrter Bahnhof, the last station before East Berlin, and stopped. This was where the East Berlin driver was supposed to take over from his West Berlin counterpart, but the West Berliner removed the power control arm from the cab and took it with him. The train was stuck. When a supervisor came to see what was wrong, there was a row and the East Berliner demanded a new control arm. The supervisor didn't know whether he should use his initiative and intervene before all the traffic backed up behind, but it quickly proved to be an academic point. The West Berlin signalman refused to change the signals, leaving them stuck at red. By early evening hand-chalked signs informed passengers that the S-Bahn was terminating at Lehrter Bahnhof 'until further notice'.

More than a hundred miles from Berlin, it was the same at all the other road, rail and canal crossing points from West Germany to the East. The spirit of embattled Berlin had spread and nothing moved. All border crossings were blocked. Only the airports were still operating properly, but even they were heavily picketed and traffic was negligible. Every chink in the post-war curtain spread across Germany had once again been closed.

By Monday the authorities in East Berlin decided it was time to break the strike and began running convoys of lorries from East to West, but discovered that no one was willing to unload them. On Tuesday the convoys ran again, this time with additional men to help unload them. But they couldn't find anybody willing to sign for receipt of the goods, and no one was willing to dump the goods without a signature. After two days of TV cameras showing the trucks scurrying back across the Wall with their goods still piled high, the Eastern authorities decided to suspend the convoys. They were becoming an embarrassment.

The Wall was silent. It was like the deathly hush in the trenches which followed the artillery bombardments of the First World War, before the troops emerged from their dugouts to brave the murderous mud. Men waited, and wondered what was to come.

The White House

The President was smoking again. In spite of a much-publicized pledge of abstinence which he had taken on the spur of the moment during a campaign sweep through Massachusetts, he was back at it again behind the protective walls of the White House, smoking more than ever. He looked glumly through the windows of the Oval Office and across the lawn. In spite of the distorting effects of the rocket-proof glass, in the distance he could see the band of protestors parading up and down on the pavement, chanting and waving their placards.

'Dammit, Leo. I get attacked by the hardliners for negotiating troop reduction treaties with the Soviets, and screamed at by the liberals for not standing up to the Soviets over human rights and that bloody Wall. Which do they want me to do, declare war or surrender?'

251

'Unfortunately, Mr President, there's nothing in the Constitution requiring the electorate to be consistent or even reasonable.'

Such homespun Polish philosophy came as no comfort to Michelle, who needed more than philosophy to get over the latest batch of opinion polls.

'We were so damn close to agreeing the details of the treaty, and now the Kremlin's suspended negotiations. Why on earth they believe we control that rabble in West Berlin is beyond me. Don't they know it's embarrassing us as much as it is them?' he snapped through a haze of blue smoke.

'Perhaps it's a final attempt to turn the screw and squeeze a last concession out of us. They can read opinion polls, too. Or possibly they are simply unsure, and are biding their time.'

'Time is one thing neither of us has. I've got a nominating convention coming up in a couple of weeks' time. What the hell do I say then?'

Grossman said nothing, taking comfort in the fact that he was retained only to advise on foreign security matters, not to deal with the jackal pack at home.

'The treaty's too important for us to let a bunch of malcontents in Berlin ruin it,' continued Michelle. 'Should I send troops in and break the strike?'

'Not unless you want that crowd of protestors on your doorstep to multiply like cockroaches. In any event, I doubt if you could break the strike without considerable violence. The situation is already beginning to take an unpleasant turn. There are reports of growing agitation in Berlin about Turks supposedly taking German jobs and German money. The passengers on a plane arriving from Istanbul were set on by the pickets at Tegel airport yesterday. A lot of racist abuse and a few fists were thrown. Unfortunately, the

Turkish Ambassador was among them and collected a black eye, so Turkey's threatening to recall its ambassadors from both Germany and France.'

'Why France, for Chrissake?'

'Because Tegel airport is in the French sector and under French jurisdiction. They were technically responsible for the safety of the Turkish Ambassador.'

It was like talking to a child. The ensuing silence from Michelle indicated that he had no idea what all this meant, and Grossman was forced to continue.

'It means, Mr President, that the NATO alliance is in danger of falling apart around us. If it goes on like this, the Russians won't need a treaty to get rid of our troops, they'll be sent home anyway. We've had American troops fighting civilians in the streets of Berlin, the West German government becoming increasingly intransigent, and now the Turkish government threatening reprisals against fellow Western allies. It can't go on like this.'

'So what do I do, Leo?' Michelle banged his desk in fury, but his voice had a plaintive edge.

'You need the treaty, Mr President. If you don't get it, and quickly, it will be a race to see which falls apart more quickly – the Western alliance or your electoral support.'

'Thanks for the vote of confidence,' Michelle muttered, but did not argue, preferring instead to hide behind a fresh cigarette. 'So what do I do, Leo?' he repeated, more softly.

'Wait. Be patient just a little longer. The blockade of the Wall is an economic nonsense, and I'm willing to bet there will soon be squeals of anguish coming from those traders who are being hurt. Some factories are already warning about the need to lay off workers, and the blockade will soon become about as unpopular as the Turks. If Schumacher's got any sense he'll call it off this weekend. If not, it will begin to crumble anyway. In any event, as soon as the Russians get back to the negotiating table we tell our officials in Geneva to get on with the treaty as if they have a live grenade in their pockets.'

'And if the Russians don't play ball . . . ?'

'Announce that you've taken up smoking again and pray that you can still win in the tobacco belt.'

Moscow

From his position on the leather sofa which stood in the sitting room of his apartment in the heart of the Kremlin, Andreyev could gaze west across the rooftops of Moscow. It was a beautiful view, especially when the sun prepared to disappear and its dying rays set the sky on fire. He had often sat there marvelling at the sight, convincing himself that it heralded a new Soviet revolution in which he would lead the country out of feudalism and into the modern world. But tonight he saw the sky bathed red in his own blood.

'Aleks, what is it?' his wife asked in concern. The doctors had strictly forbidden him any alcohol, but he had been cradling a glass of Remy Martin all evening and taking careful but fragrant sips from it. He swirled the caramel liquor around in his cupped palm and savoured its bouquet before taking another small taste.

'Nothing,' he lied. 'Just a particularly bloody day.'

At its regular Thursday morning meeting the Politburo, in grim silence, had listened to a report of the five-day-old blockade in Berlin. East Germany was already beginning to hurt badly, not only from the delays and shortages of goods which were developing but more importantly from the drying up of the hard currency which was normally pumped through the border. Yet all this faded into insignificance when compared to the political turmoil it was causing. When the blockade began many of his colleagues in the Politburo – perhaps a majority – had feared it was an American plot to put pressure on the East during the final stages of the arms negotiations, and he had been forced against his better judgement to suspend the talks in Geneva to show that the Kremlin couldn't be pushed around. But he knew that suspension was only a halfway house towards complete termination. The spirit of Semyonov hung over their discussions, and he knew that several of them would be happy to see the negotiations – and his own political future – simply fade away.

He had to get the talks going again. And that morning he had used every ounce of political persuasion and outright muscle to twist his colleagues into agreement. It had cost him most of the political favours he was owed, and an additional petro-chemical refinery outside Minsk. The majority had come with him reluctantly, but some had not come with him at all. 'Be warned, Comrade General Secretary, that you are pushing us further than most of us want to go. The price of failure would be high,' warned the Minister for Culture. And he was supposed to be a friend.

Bykov, bloody Bykov, had sat silent, his thoughts impenetrable behind his broad, thick skull.

As the dusk gathered and the final red streaks turned to the dark clouds of night, Andreyev watched an Ilyushin gliding its way along the flight path to Seremetjevo, its navigation lights flashing a message of welcome to those waiting below. It was a sight he had watched many times, always with great pleasure, like a shepherd watching one of his flock return safely. Tonight he felt only apprehension.

'What is it?' his wife asked again, gently but insistently.

'Those are storm clouds gathering out there, Nadia. They could sweep us all away.'

'Is it going wrong, Aleks?'

'I don't know. If it weren't for that damned Wall we could have a treaty signed and sealed by now and be getting on with our lives. But somehow . . .' He shook his head in sorrow. 'I have to deliver the treaty, Nadia. If I don't, there's no telling what might happen.'

'But it's too ludicrous, Aleks. You told me that the treaty might bring a generation of peace, yet now you tell me it's all in danger – for Berlin?' Her voice was incredulous. Her father had died in Berlin, within sight of the *Führerbunker*, leading one of the final infantry assaults of the war. 'They caused it all, the Germans. Without them we would never have gone to war and the wretched Wall would never have been built in the first place. Now you tell me that the Germans are threatening to destroy the treaty?'

Andreyev nodded. 'And me and Michelle with it.'

'You must all be mad. To throw it all away because of the Germans. Let them rot in hell first! Why, Aleks? Why?'

Her logic had the clarity of the Urals sky at night, and gave as little comfort. He examined his cognac before responding. 'I'm not really sure why, *dushenyka*. Perhaps the Wall has become a virility symbol for us both; I can't deliver the treaty if the Wall comes down, and perhaps Michelle can't deliver if it stays up. Stalemate.'

'What can you do, Aleks? There must be something.'

'Get the treaty signed before there's time for any more chaos.'

'Or?'

'Or let them prepare for yet another funeral in Berlin. Mine.'

As the gates of the Lefortovo prison closed behind him, the crashing sound reached into Bykov's Mercedes like the closing of a coffin lid. It made even the chairman of the KGB feel cold to his bones. The smell of death and decay which infected every part of Moscow's main political prison still clung to his uniform, and he was impatient to reach the *dacha* and steam it all away. He was under no illusion; the turning point had been reached and, once he had made up his mind, there would be no going back. There would be bodies, that much was certain. The question was how many, and whose.

He had gone to the deepest, darkest parts of the old Lefortovo fortress, where the sights had scarcely changed in more than a hundred years. The stench of old air and fear still permeated every corner as in Tsarist times; only some of the new electrical equipment and the drugs revealed any sign of twentieth-century progress. It had been several years since Bykov had been to this part of the 'factory'; increasingly his task had been one of administration, looking after the paperwork, shuffling the numbers so they added up. The numbers, of course, were human beings – or at least had been human beings when they came in – but when reduced to statistics on an invoice it enabled him to become detached, dispassionate. Yet he felt the need to remind himself of what lay ahead as the price for failure – his failure, if he got it wrong.

There had been some changes, inevitably. It had been

a generation since as a young KGB captain he had been forced to stand in line and watch as the spy Penkovsky was paraded in front of them and abused before being pushed alive into a furnace. Amazingly, Penkovsky hadn't screamed, but many of those watching had screamed in their dreams every night for months afterwards. Methods of punishment had become less dramatic, but the principle of suffering remained constant. Not even *glasnost* and all its press conferences could change that. Nowadays they didn't throw you into a live furnace, they simply shut you in a room and threw away the key. Most of the rooms were cramped, dark and dank, but there was always a small amount of daylight which was allowed to pierce the gloom from a high, tantalizing, untouchable window. Take that away and you deprived them of hope and they went mad within months; keep that ray of hope shining into their lives, and it took long years of anguish and pain to squeeze their souls dry. Madness and death were too easy a route to escape from Lefortovo.

The price of failure was still high – he preferred the word 'failure' to 'treachery'; few things were constant in the Soviet Union, not even what constituted treachery, yet failure was always a sin sufficient to get a man condemned. And Bykov knew that if he failed there would be nothing owed to him which would save him from the consequences. Stalin's corpse hadn't even grown cold before they had taken Beria, the dead leader's chief henchman and the most powerful chairman the KGB had ever had, dragged him screaming out of a Politburo meeting and shot him. And he had been one of the lucky ones who got a quick exit card. Bykov would be fortunate, indeed, to be dealt with so considerately if all this fell apart.

Thoughts of failure preoccupied him on the drive out

to his *dacha*. Bykov did not expect failure, but he knew it should be considered. He was a brave man who understood the risks he was taking. The fruits of success were well known to him; he needed to remind himself of the cost of getting it wrong, to take a long, deliberate look into the abyss before deciding whether to jump.

As soon as they arrived at the *dacha* Bykov stripped off his uniform, hoping he would feel cleaner, but it didn't help. With scarcely a word he took his female driver and mounted her with as much sensitivity as a bull at work in the farmyard. It was not a success for either of them.

'Is it me?' she asked.

'No,' he responded frankly. He wasn't looking for excuses. 'Don't worry,' he smiled, one of those slightly puckered grins which she found so appealing. 'I'll be fine after some fresh air.'

He pulled on a favourite pair of shapeless trousers and a thick woollen sweater. The air outside was warm and fresh, heralding the approach of another scorching summer across the expanses of central Russia, but nowadays the sun took longer to heat his old bones and he was grateful for the protection of the heavy clothes. He was getting older – he knew it; his chauffeur knew it. As he walked along the sun-dappled trail which ran through the beech woods, now heavy with leaves of silver and grey, he conducted one of those conversations which men dare have only with themselves. He was still stunningly robust and energetic for his age, everyone acknowledged that, but with every passing year the emphasis was placed increasingly on his age rather than his energy. He had a few years left before any younger man could seriously challenge him, before his mind began to lose its grip on those little details which gave him true mastery of his task, before he spent his late nights snoring in bed rather than out-working and out-thinking his opponents. But the few years left were getting fewer, and he had to decide how to use them.

The easiest course would be to let Andreyev have his way, following reluctantly behind him, relishing the fruits of power which dropped from the General Secretary's table and turning on him savagely if he stumbled, just as the rest of them would do. But he was not as the rest of them. They were like pigs in the farmyard, scavenging and growing fat in the filth. And he remembered from his childhood what happened to fat pigs. After the apples had fallen from the trees and the pigs had eaten their fill of the rotting fruit, and as the cold nights of winter began to beckon in the Georgian mountains, the villagers would gather in front of a huge fire, pass around a bottle of rich Georgian wine and slaughter the fattest pigs. He recalled how as a five-year-old he had ridden on the back of a huge sow, beating it with a twig as the men stood around and laughed and the women sharpened the knives. Then they had taken him from the pig's back, and the burliest of the men had put his arm around the sow's neck, a sow which had served them faithfully and borne many valuable piglets, and plunged his knife deep beneath the thick hide.

At the last instant the pig had sensed that something was wrong. She had jerked her head as the butcher had lunged, and he had missed the jugular. With a sickening squeal of frenzy the wounded animal charged round, with the men throwing themselves on top of her to wrestle her down and slash her with their blades, trying to find a critical vein which would drain her. For several minutes the unequal struggle had continued until everyone lay in an exhausted pile with the dead pig underneath. The young Bykov couldn't believe the

260

amount of blood which had burst from the pig and which ran in rivulets over the ground and covered all the men. They gasped for air and jokcd like warriors after a famous victory, and his father had taken him and washed his hands in the blood so that he, too, could be part of the triumph. Then three of the women had dismembered the pig, singeing its hairy skin on the fire, while the men got drunk and chewed on the sweet crackling. During that winter they had eaten almost every part of the pig, until there was nothing left.

No, Bykov decided, he would not join the rest of the swine. He would end his days on his own terms, not as someone else's sacrifice. He would issue the orders, and take the consequences.

TEN

Berlin

The glare of the floodlights along the Wall distracted the eye and hid the movement among the long shadows on the Western side. In any case, there were few people around at 3 a.m. on a Monday to notice. Only an elderly insomniac out for a breath of night air bothered to stop and enquire what the four men in boiler suits were up to, and he retreated quickly when told they were from GASAG tracing a possible gas leak. 'Nothing to worry about,' he was assured, 'probably a leaky old valve in the lines which run along the Wall. But better to keep back – just in case.'

The four men worked quickly and expertly. From the back of their van they produced many yards of electrical wire, to which at one-foot intervals were connected small tubular containers no larger than a bottle of whisky, each weighing around one kilogram. These were spread out along an entire section of Wall and placed tight up against its base. 'Electronic gas sensors', if anyone had asked. But they didn't. No one even commented on the fact that the activity was taking place directly opposite the area where the East Germans were implementing their 'improvements' to the border and had taken down a long stretch of the barbed wire and concrete barriers which ran parallel to the main Wall.

Working in pairs, the men took no longer than twenty minutes; they clearly knew what they were about and proceeded without discussion, checking the wiring one final time before climbing back into their olive-green GASAG van and driving off. They seemed to show no interest in stretching the work for the overtime. An observer might have wondered why they left their equipment unmanned at the site of a potential gas leak, but he or she would have had only another couple of minutes to become curious. Less than a quarter of a mile away the three men changed in the back of their van out of their working clothes and into civilian garb before abandoning their vehicle for a nearby car. Once inside, they produced a small walkie-talkie device and a Sony Walkman. All they had left to do now was to start the tape and play four seconds of a pre-set coded signal. The car engine was running when they did so.

Harry woke with a start. The crashing noise dragged him out of a deep sleep and for an instant he was confused. It was as if he had driven his old Chevy Nova at suicidal speed into a lamp post and was listening to the parts fall off it one by one, but he soon realized it was the sound of his windows trying to rattle themselves out of their frames. He rose quickly to inspect them and check for breakage. When he looked through them, all he could see were three terrified dogs running along the Wall as if pursued by demons. He wondered what had disturbed them and was making so much bloody noise about it.

On the other side of the border lights, the duty Hauptmann of the Border Command Regiment also felt beset by demons. His senses were in turmoil. As he looked across no-man's-land, alerted by the sound of the explosion, a pall of smoke and dust hung in the air which, as it slowly cleared, revealed that an entire 200-yard section of the Wall had simply vanished. He grabbed for his binoculars, but they confirmed the impossible: the Wall was gone.

It took him three minutes before he dispatched his men to report, and another five before they did so. A long section of the Wall was lying in pieces on the ground, broken off from its foundations as if it had been made from a bar of chocolate. The Hauptmann immediately obeyed his standing instructions to inform all other duty officers along the Wall of an incident, but then he delayed for fifteen crucial minutes while making up his mind what else he should do. He was just preparing to order in a detachment of border guards to fill the gap with a human wall of steel when, on the other side of the strip, the first television crews arrived.

Within minutes the gap – 'the Gap' as it quickly became known – was ablaze with television lights, reporters and a growing crowd of spectators who had been dragged from their beds by the sound of the explosion. Plug the Gap, the Hauptmann told himself. But don't cause an international incident, not now, not in front of the world's cameras, he contradicted. So he called his Major for instructions. The Major called his regimental Oberst, who contacted the Major-General in charge of the Border Command Centre. Both as a matter of personal courtesy and professional concern the East German commander thought it prudent to discuss the matter with his colleague in command of the Soviet Brigade stationed in East Berlin, and a chain reaction set in which reached right up to the Defence and Foreign Ministries in Moscow. But the process had taken several hours of indecision and ass-covering, and another two hours went by before anyone was able to raise the matter with Andreyev, who was beginning a series of factory visits and walkabouts in the capital of the faraway Soviet republic of Kazakhstan, and therefore could not be brought quickly to a secure telephone line. Andreyev demanded more information and decided to fly back to Moscow immediately but, by that time, it was already too late.

No sooner had the TV cameras flashed pictures of the incident around the world than the commentators and pundits began their work. 'The greatest challenge to *glasnost*,' they unanimously concluded, 'the Big One which cannot be ducked . . .'

'Andreyev and Michelle are faced with the dilemma they always feared,' intoned the CBS network. 'Berlin was supposed to cooperate with their policy of reconciliation, to remain quiet and complacent while they negotiated. But now Berlin has shown it is no longer willing to wait, or to allow others to decide its fate. The Soviets dare not rebuild the Wall, for any such move would certainly destroy the arms negotiations and the era of *glasnost* with it. Yet without the Wall, the logic of German reunification would become irresistible, which in turn could cause chaos throughout Eastern Europe and inside the Kremlin. We don't know who blew up the Wall, although it is assumed the four men reported to have laid the explosive are part of the growing political discontent within West Berlin. We don't even know what to call them: terrorists? extremists? German patriots? freedom fighters? But whoever they are, they have thrown down a remarkable challenge to force both American and Soviet governments to show the world what they really meant at their recent summit with talk about "peace for all mankind". In Berlin, it is clear that the people have lost patience with the notion of peace behind bricks and barbed wire.'

As the day lengthened, a sense of uncertainty settled across the Wall. On the Eastern side no one would move without specific instructions from a superior officer, and none was forthcoming. In the West, the authorities waited, without knowing what they were waiting for. The police decided that something must be done to restore a little order to the situation and to prevent the crowd which was growing by the hour from getting out of hand, so a line of plastic no-parking cones was put across the entrance to the Gap, affording the cameramen a ludicrous view of the awesome Iron Curtain which they knew would appeal to their picture editors.

The wooden viewing platforms along the Wall were cluttered with bodies and equipment as camera crews struggled to get a panoramic view of the scene. But most members of the crowd simply stood quietly and stared, feeling they could almost reach out and touch their brothers and sisters, and believing that the barrier would never be rebuilt. For the first time in a generation they were able to look into East Berlin with a view unimpeded by the Wall. No-man's-land still stood in their way, but the rubble and barbed wire of earlier years had given way to a landscaped area of raked sand and grass which looked deceptively peaceful, as if crossing it would be as easy as taking a walk in the park.

Harry found Katherine there, as he suspected he would. He hadn't bothered going into the Mission, which was in a state of poorly concealed panic as they tried to analyse the new entrails and make sense of them in the reports back to Foggy Bottom and Langley. No one would either want or miss the most junior intelligence analyst with responsibility solely for commercial matters, least of all Miss Pickerstaff. So he had spent the morning hanging around the Gap, listening to the watchers, learning, and waiting for Katherine. He could guess at some of what she must be feeling and knew that she would not be able to keep away. When

266

he saw her she was standing silently like the others, staring. He said nothing, simply squeezing her hand to comfort her, knowing words would fail.

'This is where Peter died,' she said.

'I know, Katherine. I'm sorry.'

Now was not the time for suspicion. The woman next to him was the woman he had begun to fall in love with, not the one who had ignited his professional doubts, and she needed support and reassurance. There were no tears, just eyes which were filled with the pain of her memories and the rising glow of hope for the future. As they stared across, two East German workers waved at the crowd before being ushered on by the *Vopos*, and the people around Harry and Katherine threw their arms in the air and cheered. A dam of emotions had burst, flooding across the divide and submerging the barriers erected by others between Berliners.

Without the Wall, it was possible to imagine that East and West had never existed.

The Kremlin

Andreyev's clenched fists pounded the table with frustration. The hurriedly assembled session of the Politburo had spent two hours arguing around the subject but had been totally unable to reach agreement. The logic of words had failed and for the General Secretary, his patience and stamina exhausted, it was time for the intimidation of anger.

'No, no, no! How can you believe that the Wall was blown up deliberately by the Western authorities in order to browbeat us in the arms negotiations? There's no logic to it.'

He glared down the table at the Minister of Culture, but his colleague was not to be intimidated. He was just one of several who had been expressing serious doubts, and there was comfort in numbers.

'Comrade General Secretary, let me put it simply so you will understand.'

The impertinent, double-dealing little shit, fumed Andreyev. He had created this man, brought him up from obscurity and made him one of the best-known names in the Soviet Union, yet here he was siding with the motley collection of reactionaries and self-seekers who still clung to the Politburo. But behind his anger Andreyev could not fail to realize the danger for any General Secretary when his own placemen began to side openly with his opponents.

'Some of us have always had reservations about the West's attitude towards these arms talks,' the Minister continued. 'But we gave the benefit of the doubt to Michelle' – and, by implication, to you also, he was saying. 'No longer. Ever since the talks started there has been nothing but unrest and chaos on our borders. For decades we had no reason to look with concern at our frontiers with West Berlin and West Germany. Now the West wants to push us even further and cause still greater chaos across Eastern Europe. Have we learned nothing from our past mistakes? We must show that we will not tolerate such interference. We must crush this challenge now, before it has time to slip across the frontier and unites every malcontent in the Soviet Union.'

'And what do you suggest as a suitable display of force?' Andreyev enquired with as much sarcasm as he could muster. It failed to register.

'We must rebuild the Wall. Immediately.'

'That would ruin the talks! Michelle would be forced to break them off,' exclaimed Andreyev.

'Then some might say the talks are not worth the cost,' the Minister said, quietly but defiantly.

'Couldn't we at least move more troops into East Berlin to plug the hole,' interjected a colleague, anxious that the clash of opinions should not be allowed to solidify.

'Conduct troop withdrawal talks by reinforcing our units along the border?' exclaimed Andreyev. 'That would be madness. It would not only guarantee the talks would be called off, but also inflame opinion in Berlin still further. Can't you see this is precisely what they want? Whoever blew up the Wall wants the talks to fail. They want us to do something foolish. We'd be falling into the very trap they've set us. Riots in West Berlin. Unrest in East Berlin. A failed treaty and a new era of superpower hostility in which we both spend more on arms. It would be a nightmare. I can't believe we're even discussing the possibility. To suggest anything which would break off the talks now is no better than siding with terrorists.'

He glared around the table, but no one returned his stare. None yet seemed willing to make his defiance so open as to be accused of siding with terrorists. Then he heard a deep growl, like the sound of a wild bear which had spotted wounded prey. It came from the direction of Bykov.

'Comrade General Secretary,' Bykov began, 'there is another way.'

The clamp squeezing Andreyev's stomach tightened another turn. It was the first time in many weeks that Bykov had voiced any opinion on the matter, and his interventions in discussion were never casual.

'No one doubts that we are near to agreeing the final crucial details of the treaty,' the growling voice continued. 'And no one doubts the growing chaos which is making those negotiations more difficult and which is threatening our security. The only doubt we have is whether the Americans are behind that chaos in order to undermine our strength in negotiations. So we must put them to the test.'

Andreyev was having trouble in hearing. The foul-tasting bile was rising in his throat and his heart was pounding in his ears, making it difficult for him to concentrate, but everyone else around the table was deathly still, soaking up Bykov's every word.

'We give them until the end of this week – Sunday – to reach agreement, before the situation along the border gets out of hand. Time enough for the negotiators to sort out the details and to put a signature on a document – *if* the Americans are serious about the treaty.'

'Or else?' Andreyev heard himself say.

'Or else we are left with no alternative. We rebuild the Wall.'

Andreyev began to protest, but already many heads around the table were nodding in agreement. 'There's no choice,' chimed in the Minister of Culture, to a chorus of support from others. 'German reunification was never part of these negotiations,' a new voice remarked. 'The treaty was supposed to protect us, not land us in the shit,' said another.

Andreyev was in a cold sweat and the pain seared through his guts. His options were running out even as his physical strength began to fail him. He desperately needed a measure of luck and some support, but he knew he would get none from his sceptical colleagues.

His rhetoric and animal determination had bought him more time, but very little.

He had seven days left to save the treaty – and himself.

Berlin

They walked silently away from the Gap, hand in hand, overwhelmed by what they had just seen and neither caring any longer if others saw them. The world was changing, and they were part of those changes.

To Katherine, it was as if a heavy cloak of sorrow had slipped from her shoulders after many years. She had never been able to give Peter a burial, to mourn like other bereaved wives and to put aside the pain. She had been denied the opportunity to forget, to let go, but, with the destruction of that part of the Wall where Peter had died, had come release. The Wall was gone. She had her revenge, and could now honour her lost husband in peace.

With that peace had come a renewed optimism, a certainty that there was still something left to share in her life. And she wanted to share it with Harry. He was by her side. He would always be there when she needed him. The chance to breathe again in this cramped and claustrophobic city had come with his arrival. She no longer cared about the jangling logic of age and race and creed. She felt young again, she needed his body and she no longer cared what others said. So what if it couldn't last for ever. After years of yesterdays, just one tomorrow at a time would do. She would happily settle for that.

Beside her, Harry burrowed among his own thoughts. He didn't believe in fate, certainly not the fate that had sent a score of his own family shuffling in single file towards the mass burial pits without a word of protest or a raised fist of anger. But he knew something was happening to him which would irreversibly change the course of his life. He had been sent to Berlin to be buried, professionally and personally, but this was no longer the backwater in which he was meant to stifle. He was in the middle of a revolution – what type of revolution and led by whom he did not yet know, but as he had looked across the ruins of the Wall and into the East, he knew that life in this city was never going to be the same again. A door had opened into a new world. He didn't know what lay beyond it, opportunity or destruction, but he had to step through it. He had no choice; he couldn't stand still.

Yet could he walk through it with Katherine? They were drawn to each other like magnets of opposite poles. He had never been in love before and what he felt now was new and unknown to him, making him want to be with her even at the same time as he suspected her. He wanted so very much to trust her but he couldn't avoid the questions. There was still doubt.

They had walked along without exchanging a word, communicating only through intertwined fingers, ignoring the throng of people which streamed past them in the direction of the Gap. They found themselves in a park which overflowed with the strong yellows and fresh greens of early summer, mixed with the sweet smell of freshly cut grass. Ducks cavorted and splashed, disappearing with a neat bob below the surface of the lake only to reappear in a flurry of feathers many yards away, while the innocent laughter of children at play began slowly to wash away the dark suspicions brooding in Harry's mind. The June sun was shining in Katherine's hair, making it blaze like new fire. She had come alive and was bubbling with girlish enthusiasm. As they began to share the pleasures of the late afternoon, Harry's attention became fixed yet again on how gracefully her body moved beneath her light summer clothing, how the cotton clung so tenuously to her, like his doubts; how he wanted nothing more than to tear them all away. It had been only days since he had devoured her with inquisitive hands and greedy lips until he had lain back exhausted, but memories couldn't satisfy him for ever. He was so close he could feel her, smell her, almost taste her, and he knew he was becoming aroused.

He remembered, as a thirteen-year-old on a crowded bus travelling to school, how he had become fascinated by a woman with huge breasts and a tight sweater who had sat next to him. He had found himself in such difficulty that when the time had come to get off he couldn't rise from his seat, and had travelled three miles farther on before he could stand up without embarrassment. He hadn't been able to concentrate on his school books for a week afterwards, let alone the extra work given to him as punishment for being half an hour late yet again.

Now Harry felt like a teenager once more. He was losing control of himself, and he dragged Katherine towards the base of a huge chestnut tree where they could sit in the shade while he recovered his composure. She was laughing as he literally flung himself down; he suspected she had spotted his discomfort and was teasing him.

'Katherine, about our . . .' It was time for him to start protesting about their agreement, to make her understand that the weeks of self-denial could never go fast enough, but she interrupted by kissing him, biting his lower lip playfully before letting him go. She was in charge of her life once again, and she didn't care who noticed it.

'Harry, be quiet a minute. Let me try to say something. It isn't easy – I feel it more than I can express it, but I hope you will understand.' She was twirling her wedding ring once more as she concentrated on finding the right words. 'The Wall has always been a tombstone for me. Every time I've seen it, touched it, it's been like an unfinished grave for Peter and the baby – not a memorial where you can go and remember, be at peace with your thoughts, but a constant reminder of pain without end and an unfinished nightmare. Since then I don't think I've ever been truly happy. Until I met you, and until today.' She was looking directly into his eyes, searching for his reaction. 'Seeing the Wall blown up like that was like finishing off their memorial and closing the chapter. At last I feel their grave is properly marked. Now I can remember without mourning, and begin to look ahead. I've lived all my life in Berlin, most of it with the Wall looming over me as if it were about to fall and crush me. But now it has fallen, at last I'm out of its shadow, I feel free. Understand?'

Harry could. As Katherine talked, he was reminded of his father, of the dark moods and constant harking back to the memories which had haunted his life and which had been forced on Harry. *Never forget. Always remember. Look back*, he had said, trying to condemn the young Harry to share the burden of a life with no future and only a grim past. Harry had struggled, but had never been able to shake completely free of his inheritance. Some little remnant of his father's misery and suspicion always stuck to him, no matter how hard he tried to scrub it away. He was sure it caused him to doubt Katherine, as his father's ghost once again remonstrated with him – *A German tart! They were the worst of the guards in the camps. Never forget.* His father couldn't, so neither could he. He felt envious of Katherine and her new-found freedom.

'It's the start of something new for me,' she continued. 'I can't go on living a lie with Edward. I have to look forward to a life without him, while I've still got the chance. They'll never be able to rebuild the Wall, and I'll never be able to rebuild my relationship with him. As of today, it's finally over. I don't know what you're going to be doing tomorrow but, if you want me, I'll be there. I love you, Harry Benjamin.'

She's an anti-semitic German bitch! his father's voice screamed inside him. But he knew the voice was lying, blinded by prejudice and the blood of his family which had been so freely spilt. As his feelings ran through him like a burning fuse, every part of Harry was on fire, and he knew now he could trust her. She wasn't part of Edward's double life; she couldn't be part of it and still be willing to give him up, not for someone like Harry. Not now, when everything in Berlin was falling to pieces.

'When will you tell him?' Harry asked, insisting on putting her to one last test.

'Tonight,' she responded, noticing with surprise that the violent twisting had pulled her wedding ring from her finger. 'You know, this is the first time I've taken this ring off since we were married.'

'Does it make you feel sad?'

'No, not sad. Clean. Honest. Renewed. Not sad.'

'Will you tell him about us?' Harry asked, remembering the two men who had tailed them at their last outing. He looked around, wondering if they were watching now.

'No, I don't think so. In a way this isn't about you, Harry. It's about me and Edward and our life together which was empty and wrong long before you arrived. He knows that. He can still have my discretion, he even has my respect in many ways. But he can no longer have me.'

'Is there anything I can do to help?'

'Before tonight? Yes, Harry. Take me to bed.'

Edward had taken the call in his study shortly before lunch, as he was busily redrafting a speech for later in the week. The original had been left in shreds by the explosion at the Wall.

'Could I speak to Herr Brandt, please?' a voice had said.

Edward froze. He knew what to expect, but the knowledge didn't make it any easier. Normally when they wanted to brief him they would simply suggest a meeting somewhere in West Berlin with a disgruntled elector who wanted help sorting out a problem with the town hall. Only on rare occasions when it was necessary for the KGB to brief him in conditions of utmost security would they suggest a meeting in East Berlin, under the pretext of signing a trading contract. Yet that option was dead: he was the last person who could be seen crossing his own picket line. That's when Herr Brandt came to life. And that meant someone was panicking.

'There's no one here by that name,' responded Schumacher.

'I was dialling 439-8570,' insisted the voice. 'Have I got the right number?'

'Nothing like it,' said Schumacher, memorizing the grid reference and repeating the prearranged checklist. 'I should go through the operator.' He waited. If the voice said he would try again later, it meant a meeting in two hours . . .

'I'll do that right away. I'm sorry for the interruption.'

They wanted to get together immediately; no delay. And after consulting the street map which he kept locked in his desk drawer, he knew precisely where: the Berlin zoo, which would be crowded with so many visitors at a weekend that an entire motorized division could get lost in the scrum. He still took care not to be followed. A car drive to the U-Bahn, a quick dash into the station and out the other side before any pursuer had time even to buy his ticket, a taxi ride, a circuitous walk to check if he were being followed, a prayer to God that he wasn't. Then a meeting by the ape house where the orang-utans were entertaining a huge crowd of children with their antics at a tea party, and where adults could mingle safely in the crowd, with no distant microphone able to catch any hint of the conversation above the screeching of the apes and the squeals of their young audience.

It had been straightforward, with no problems. A verbal briefing from a KGB contact in shirtsleeves which had lasted scarcely two minutes while Schumacher threw peanuts through the bars, for all the world as if he were on a casual outing. They kept apart, close enough to hear each other but too far for any watcher to suspect they might have exchanged any package, yet even at that distance the contact could still see the uncontrollable shaking of Schumacher's hands and smell the alcohol on his breath. He had needed a huge tumbler of whisky before he could summon up the courage to leave home, and would need an even stiffer drink when he returned. One day he was going to get stopped by the police for drunk driving, and not even his town hall connections would save him from the consequences. That was the least of his worries. They were putting the pressure on him with a vengeance, and he knew he was wilting visibly.

He was slumped in his huge leather chair and nearing the bottom of the bottle when Katherine returned home late that night. She looked apprehensive. He looked awful.

'Edward, what's the matter?' she said with concern. Being out of love didn't mean that you automatically forgot the many years of caring.

'Where the hell have you been?' he demanded irritably, while not sounding as if he were interested in the answer.

'You're drunk.' *And you're old*, she thought. Suddenly he seemed to have aged many years. Or was it that she had long ago stopped looking, as well as loving?

'So what?' he snapped, taking another swig.

Was this the time? she asked herself. When he was drunk? Surely he deserved a better explanation than the one his befuddled mind would take in this evening? Yet she, too, deserved something. She had always been the one left waiting. It had to stop. Now.

'It's over, Edward. No more dinner parties, no more political meetings. I need my own life. I'm leaving.'

He stared at her with big, bloodshot eyes, his elbow propping him up unsteadily on the arm of the chair, trying to get her into focus and his mind into gear. Befuddled as he was, he knew this was a vital moment which, if he got it wrong, could bring everything crashing down around him.

'You . . . can't, Katherine.'

'What do you mean I can't? I can. I am!'

'We have one last job to do. Before you go.'

His voice was very deliberate as he concentrated hard on getting his thick tongue around the words. She was

278

surprised. There was no petulance, no temper, just a plodding insistence.

'The ring,' he continued.

Katherine was confused and clutched the finger where her wedding band had been, feeling instantly guilty and almost naked without it. No, you fool! she shouted at herself. He means the escape ring!

'One more job to do,' he repeated.

'What tasteless little game is this, Edward? We haven't had to bring anybody across for more than a year. Surely not now, when the Wall's been blown up and everywhere's in chaos.'

'It's precisely because the Wall's been blown up,' he said, shifting himself upright in his chair in an attempt to give his words more dignity. 'Katherine, this man is special to us. He was one of the ring's key organisers on the other side. Seems that in his time he's not only smuggled out refugees but also quite a few state secrets. Now the *Stasi* are breathing down his neck, and he's gone into hiding. He can't risk the crossing points because they're watching for him. And he can't hold out for ever. He's got to get across in the next seven days.'

'Why seven days?'

'There are rumours – strong rumours – that they're going to rebuild the Gap in a week's time. Once they do that it will put us back to the dark ages of confrontation and scalp hunting. They'll crack down at the crossing points and make escape next to impossible. So we've got to get him out. Now. Through the Gap.'

'Now I know you're drunk,' she gasped. 'They'll be watching the Gap even more closely. It would be like walking into their arms . . .'

'No, Katherine. We have the element of surprise. It

279

will all be over in seconds. The guards will be unsuspecting and confused. They're not going to do anything stupid in front of all those TV cameras.'

'You can't . . .' She started to argue, but he cut her short.

'Katherine, we have no choice! There's no time to organise anything else. We have this one opportunity – we have to take it.' Schumacher was fighting to keep his thoughts clear and to have his words carry sufficient authority. 'Besides, if they catch him they'll pull in everyone else who's been associated with the ring, and a lot of innocent people will suffer. Is that what you want? He knows what's at stake. Treason is still treason, and *glasnost* hasn't even peeped into the places where they want to throw him.'

'But we've always planned our escapes so meticulously,' she protested, 'down to the last detail. This is like some sick version of Russian roulette.'

'That's his choice, Katherine. He knows the risks of crossing – and of staying. It's his call.'

'When?'

'Night after tomorrow. Midnight Wednesday.'

'It's too soon! We must have more time to plan. To create a diversion, some distraction . . .'

'No time. He's already on the run. Left his home in Leipzig. Can't contact him. He's coming across at midnight on Wednesday whether we're there to help him or not.'

There was only one light on in the room, a table lamp beside Edward's chair so that he could see what he was pouring. The rest of the heavily panelled room was dark, and even had he been sober he probably wouldn't have seen the grief which began to grow within her before she turned to flee. But he knew he had won. There would be no more words about leaving, not until after Wednesday. And by then, who knew where they might both be?

She went to bed in the guest room, even though Edward had fallen asleep in his chair. She lay awake listening to the creaks and complaints of the darkened house, tormented by the thought that for a few hours during the afternoon she had been free of the Wall. Free! Yet once more it had dragged her, without pity, remorselessly, back into its shadow.

The White House

'I'm worried, Leo. I don't like getting shoved around, and I don't like ultimatums,' Michelle huffed as he struggled into his formal evening attire. The message from the Kremlin had arrived as he was about to accompany the First Lady to one of her favourite opera recitals. He hated opera, she hated his being late, and he was not at his most receptive. 'All this crap about the treaty agreement having to be reached by the end of next week or they'll regard the negotiations as failed. Who in hell do they think they are? Is this some kind of trick?'

Grossman sat and fumed as the President continued to act like a petulant child. The man wouldn't recognize a gift horse if it bit him in the testicles.

'They are offering you the treaty on a plate, Mr President. They clearly need the deal as much as we do, and I think they are simply suggesting – insisting – that we both get on with it. I suspect that the remaining details can be cleared very quickly.'

'First they suspend the talks, then they demand we

complete them inside a week. What on earth's got into Andreyev? I'll not be pushed around like that.'

Grossman's sigh was audible as he dug deep for a little extra patience. The President had the intellectual agility of a camel, and persuading him to jump through the constant succession of diplomatic hoops was beginning to exhaust both of them.

'I don't think he's trying to push you around, Mr President. Far from it. I think he's saying that whatever we want, so long as it's reasonable, we can have. He may be getting pressure from some of his own colleagues . . .'

'I still don't like it,' muttered Michelle, cursing as his carefully crafted bow-tie fell apart and he was forced to start again. 'Maybe we should play hard to get, put the squeeze on him a little. What do you think?'

'What would you get out of it?'

'A little fun, Leo! I'm sick to death of being on the receiving end all the time. Just for a change maybe it's my turn.'

'It will be your turn in ten days' time at your nominating convention. Get through that, kick hell out of the Democrats at the election. And do the same to the Berliners with the treaty. Once it's signed, no one outside of Germany will care too much what happens to the Wall.'

Grossman's bluntness, the result of his drained reserves of patience, was unusual. It was the turn of Michelle to adopt the statesman's role, which he rehearsed with dramatic gestures in front of the mirror. The two men had changed places.

'I can't help Berlin if I'm not re-elected, Leo. And Berlin would gain as much as anywhere from a reduction in international tension. Some would say it's my duty to see this treaty through,' he said, sounding as if he were already writing his memoirs. He relinquished the unequal struggle with his bow-tie and turned to Grossman.

'Do you think we could keep it quiet so I could announce it at the convention?' He smiled in anticipation of victory, before screaming for his valet to come and help him dress.

ELEVEN

Berlin

By Tuesday lunchtime, the Gap had taken on some of the atmosphere of a three-ring circus. Everywhere one looked along the 200-yard stretch there was the buzz of activity. Political activists and opportunists of all kind saw their chance to gather small groups of supporters and passers-by, delivering diatribes on everything from *glasnost* and *Gastarbeiter* rights to long and impassioned homilies on abortion or the Second Coming. A small group of Arab students from local universities and technical schools dressed themselves in the familiar chequered headgear of the Palestinians and marched repeatedly up and down the length of the Gap, waving assorted radical banners and shouting anti-Israeli slogans in the hope of interesting at least a couple of roving television reporters in their views about 'the other Iron Curtain'.

Street photographers offered instant portraits set against the backdrop of the ruins, an historic moment captured on film to take back home to girlfriends and relatives. Fast-food salesmen mingled with hawkers of flags and cheap plastic binoculars, while elsewhere young men sold fragments of debris in glass containers of every conceivable shape and size. 'Genuine pieces of Wall. Buy them here,' they appealed, adding to the steadily rising hubbub. Indeed, during the afternoon several people attempted to run to the fractured base of the Wall and struggle away with assorted chunks of concrete, often crossing into no-man's-land as they did so until someone gave orders to replace the ludicrous no-parking cones with proper steel barriers and move the crowds back several yards. Some complained but generally there was an air of excitement and good humour as the day lengthened and the Gap became firmly established as the city's newest and most popular tourist attraction.

It was only after dusk had settled that the trouble came. Young men who had spent a warm summer's evening sipping chilled beer in the bars of Kreuzberg began spilling out along the Gap. Alcohol and the excitement made a potent cocktail and several began testing their bravado by jumping over the barriers and running into no-man's-land, seeing how far they dare go before stopping to hurl abuse and fragments of debris at the hidden faces of the watchers in the East. Onlookers shouted warnings as they saw border guards moving about in the distant shadows, but the odds of beating the system seemed to improve with every drink. And the young men, intent on a public display of their courage, objected vigorously to having their moment in the spotlights cut short and being hustled back to safety by the West Berlin policemen. 'Who gave you the fucking right to stop a Berliner crossing the Wall, then? What are you, fucking Nazis? Or fucking *Vopos*? What law am I breaking? Show me? You're no better than the fucking Russians!' was the general line of argument, which became more heated and abusive with every passing hour. Then a group of youths decided to take umbrage at the Palestinian protest. Tempers flared, banners were pulled down and fist fights erupted. All along the Gap the excitement slowly turned to ill-feeling.

The situation was threatening to get out of hand

when Berlin's *Polizei Präsident* decided to telephone the US Public Safety Adviser.

'There's a problem,' he said without preamble. 'I'm afraid that if we can't keep people away from the Gap we shall soon get some very real trouble. It's only a matter of time before some alcoholic idiot goes too far and we have several broken skulls and an international incident on our hands.'

The American was not best pleased at having his evening disturbed. He had friends around watching a tape of the weekend's Red Sox–Baltimore baseball game, and Packowski was pitching. He went to great lengths to have the tapes flown in within hours of an important game finishing, and the roar of jubilation from the other room told him he had just missed yet another double-play.

'What are they doing in the East? Why aren't they grabbing the troublemakers?' he asked irritably.

'Border guards dragging off Western civilians – wouldn't look too good in Geneva, would it? No, they're under instructions to cool the situation and keep their hands off. This is one they're leaving to us.'

'Great,' muttered the American. 'So what are you doing? Why not put more men into the Gap?'

'Quite simply because I don't have the power to do it. Order along the Wall is the responsibility of the Allied *Kommandatura*, not the civil authorities. I have no power to stop people walking into the East, if they insist on it, and I certainly have no power at all once they have crossed the line of the Wall. We have to face it. This is one for the military.'

The American was fuming. The *Polizei Präsident* was trying to pass the buck, and he didn't like being pushed. There was another roar from the group in the

286

adjoining room. It was a tight game, and the ninth inning was coming up.

'Then arrest them for creating a public nuisance, for Chrissake.'

'I can't arrest several thousand people just for looking. And by the time any offence has been committed, it's already too late. It's on the other side of the Wall and beyond my jurisdiction.'

The bastard's got my pecker caught in a wringer, thought the American. He wanted to tell the German what he could do with his jurisdiction, but drew back. Orders had come from on high, from way on high, that extra vigilance and care were to be taken during this week to avoid any incident along the Wall. Something was up, and the chiefs in Washington wanted all quiet on the Eastern front. The instruction had been marked with all sorts of priority, and he would ignore it at his peril.

'So – we have a problem.'

'I think *you* have a problem, my friend,' corrected the policeman. 'And I would be grateful if you would let me know what you intend to do. My only advice is that whatever you do, do it quickly. It's attracting every freak and drunk in the city.'

Having delivered his bundle of trouble, neatly gift-wrapped and fully annotated for the record, the *Polizei Präsident* dropped the phone. He had covered his end.

The American, however, felt that his end was all too vulnerably stuck in the air. This was not the time to take risks; he knew he should play it by the rule book. He punched several numbers into his telephone and within seconds was through to the US Minister, who was in the middle of a dinner party to celebrate his wedding anniversary. In order to enable the senior diplomat to justify the intrusion to his wife, the Public Safety Adviser spared nothing in passing on the concerns of the *Polizei Präsident*. The Minister communicated those concerns to his Brigade Commander, who contacted the duty Colonel, who in turn instructed the Captain in charge of that night's Wall Patrol.

'Okay, Captain, we can't afford any flare-up along the damned Wall, so here's what you do,' the Colonel barked. 'You move as many men as necessary into the Gap so that it's completely sealed. I don't want any accidents or sleaze-bags getting their balls bitten off by guard dogs. Move the barriers back and keep the crowd as far away as possible. If any of them give you trouble, lock the bastards up. Play it safe and keep the Brigade Commander off our backs. Got it?'

'It won't get out of hand, sir. We'll squeeze it so tight it'll make their eyes water,' responded the enthusiastic Captain. 'Don't worry. You can rely on me . . .'

The convoy of trucks and jeeps rolled into the night from Andrews Barracks in the south of the city. The US Army was on the move.

'Say, Lieutenant,' shouted the driver of the lead jeep to his passenger above the noise of the diesel engine, 'what's this all about?'

The young officer, fired by the task given to him and under explicit instructions not to screw it up, stared ahead into the night. 'We're going to guard the Gap,' he replied with a determined edge in his voice.

'Jesus, what are those shitheads in East Berlin up to, sir?'

'Not the shitheads in East Berlin, soldier. The shitheads in West Berlin. We're going to plug the Gap and stop them taking advantage of the situation.'

'Hell, I thought we're gonna guard the Wall to stop the other side rebuilding it. But instead we're gonna guard it from the West?'

'Precisely.'

'Mother's milk, Lieutenant. Why?'

There was silence as the officer considered the GI's logic, but failed to reach any satisfactory conclusion. His response was automatic.

'Just keep your mouth shut and eyes open and drive, soldier!'

Twenty minutes later the detachment was strung out along the Gap, the 150 soldiers of the command moving the barriers as far back from the Wall as possible. It was the early hours of the morning but there was still a large crowd of students, drop-outs, late-night revellers and others with nowhere more interesting to go. They reacted slowly and with curiosity at the arrival of the troops. The police responded with much greater speed, their officers ordering them to relinquish their posts and leave the situation to the Army. In accordance with the *Polizei Präsident*'s explicit instruction, there was soon not a policeman to be seen.

At first the onlookers responded with enthusiasm as the soldiers moved the barriers as far away from the Gap as possible, pushing the crowd back with them. There was a buzz of excitement; something was up. But the excitement rapidly faded to dismay and irritation as it became clear what the purpose of the exercise was. The crowd became more resistant to the demands to move back, more force was needed to shift the mass of bodies, tempers flared and harsh words were exchanged. Yet the orders were clear, and within an hour the task was complete. The barriers had been re-erected in most places at least forty yards farther back from the Wall, and were reinforced by a solid line of grim-faced US soldiers restraining an increasingly disillusioned and angry crowd.

The Lieutenant's orders were to be fair but firm. So the first two students to vault over and run towards the Gap were politely restrained and asked to turn around. When they refused and tried to push forward, they were unceremoniously bundled back over the barrier, and when they tried it a second time they were picked up and thrown back. On their third attempt to defy the line, the Lieutenant gave the order to arrest them. As they were dragged away struggling and kicking, the hoots and jeers from the crowd started to erupt and empty beer cans began sailing through the air in the direction of the soldiers. They stood with their helmets clamped firmly on and rifles across their bodies, thrown into stark silhouette by the illuminations of the border area behind them. To the protesting Berliners they appeared as aliens from another world, anonymous and faceless shadows set against the harsh lights, little different from the Soviet-backed border guards, except much closer. These were not the peacekeepers and protectors of Berlin's freedoms. There no longer seemed to be any difference between the guards East or West; they were both there to oppress, to restrain, to keep Berliners apart.

It took four soldiers to drag each of the arrested vaulters off to the trucks, and in the continuing struggle the youths' heads bounced along the concrete pavement and their arms were twisted in their sockets. The GIs were more used to bar-room brawls and the touch-football team than pacifying belligerent protestors, and their lack of expertise showed. As the wriggling mass of arms and legs passed the Lieutenant, one of the youths let out a cry of genuine pain as his head cracked once more on to the pavement.

'Shit, Lieutenant, are you sure we've got this right?' asked the driver.

'We're controlling a disturbance.'

'You call this controlling a disturbance?' the driver demanded, waving at the line of soldiers which stood sullen and resentful as the onlookers hurled abuse at them. They were fighting men taught to act, not trained to stand mutely and take whatever was thrown or spat at them. It was clear that they were uneasy, many of them glancing at the Lieutenant in the hope of a change of instruction as the crowd pleaded, argued, pushed and swore. There was a further commotion as another group, three young women this time, tried to break the line, only to be dragged clumsily off towards the trucks, ripping their clothes and shouting for the benefit of the television cameras that they were being sexually molested. Nobody doubted there would be many more incidents before the night was out.

'Why are we arresting women, Lieutenant?' protested the driver.

'Orders, soldier. Clear and explicit,' said the agitated officer, trying to convince himself as much as the Private. 'We don't question orders, we obey them.'

'Now I know what it feels like to be a fucking Nazi,' mumbled the driver.

'What was that?'

The Private replied slowly, so that the officer wouldn't miss a single word: 'Now I know, Lieutenant, what it feels like to be a fucking Nazi. Sir.'

The officer thought of screaming at the soldier but he was flustered and confused. The situation was getting out of hand, particularly with all the TV crews around recording every incident. The young officer realized that he was on the point of becoming a national TV personality – all he had to do was to screw

291

this operation up. He decided to deal with the driver later. In the meantime, he chewed nervously on his lower lip and called for reinforcements.

Berlin is a battle front on many levels. High above its broken streets, the heavy continental air masses from Eastern Europe and the Russian heartland meet and fight it out with the lighter, more volatile air of the maritime West. The following night, Wednesday, the Russian weather gods had won and a thick layer of humid air sat atop the city, the same air which Berlin had breathed during the day and into which its factories and traffic jams had spewed their effluent. It was foul enough to taste, and there was no sign of the cool breezes which make any city night more tolerable.

Along the Gap, where the crowds still gathered from the previous day, it turned irritation into anger and made the tension a physical reality. The American soldiers still stood guard, their shirts stuck clammily to their backs, the sweat trickling from underneath their helmets and the doubts about their orders growing by the hour. Many of the protestors were young women, scantily clad in light cotton blouses or bikini tops. As they saw the soldiers' discomfort, several of them began to tease, undoing their blouses, slipping their tops, exposing themselves, enquiring whether the Americans were still men without their weapons. The young soldiers hated it; the girls knew it, and teased them all the more. At least it made the TV crews happy, giving the producers stuck in their fetid vans something to joke about while they waited for some disaster or other to occur.

Katherine knew there would be a disaster. From the moment Edward had told her of the escape attempt, she had been overtaken by a sense of impending doom.

There was no plan, no purpose for her. She couldn't even get close to the Wall. She now had to cope not only with the East German border guards, but also with a cordon of American troops and a swathe of demonstrators which impeded both view and access. She had no idea along which part of the Gap the escape attempt would be made, where to position herself, or even what she might do to help. She was working blind. And now, as she stood penned in by bodies at the front of the crowd, there were only minutes to wait . . .

She had pleaded with Edward to stop it. It was folly, no better than a public execution. But he was adamant; there was no means of contact. It was to be at midnight, no matter what the problems or the consequences. They had no choice.

A distant bell began striking twelve, as if summoning Katherine to a funeral. The crowd fell silent as they listened to the announcement of a new day and the Lieutenant instinctively checked his watch, quietly cursing that it would be another six hours before he was off duty and away from this mess.

The camera operator was the first to see it. The TV engineers had built raised camera platforms to give the crews a broader view of the scene, and the cameraman was conducting an idle sweep across the Gap when he found himself staring through his lens at a man running out of the shadows directly towards him. He shouted to alert the rest of his crew and his sense of urgency immediately communicated itself to the crowd. Within seconds they had all seen it. They watched dumbstruck.

He was already well past the piles of bricks and landscaping equipment at the edge of no-man's-land and into the brilliantly lit harshness of the border strip. The carefully raked sand was flying from the soles of his shoes as he ran, arms pumping to give him momentum. He was not a young man, perhaps in his early forties, and before he was halfway across he seemed to be wilting from the outpouring of energy. The crowd willed him on, silently reaching out to pull him home, wanting to scream and cheer encouragement but fearing that any noise would alert the border guards, praying instead that the guards would remain confused and incompetent.

Who was he? Why was he running? No one knew but it didn't matter. It was enough that he was a fellow German, one of their own, and he was coming home.

They could see his face now, ash-grey in the lights with eyes bulging from the effort. He was close enough for them to see the sweat on his forehead, the flecks of saliva which gathered around his lips as he gasped for oxygen, the look of triumph in his eyes. They imagined they heard the fevered pounding of his heart. He was nearly safe.

He was some sixty feet from the debris of the Wall when the solitary shot rang out. In the still of the night, they all heard it. The fugitive seemed to give a small hop, performing a small and graceless arc in the air, his arms thrown forward, his legs still cycling in a running motion even though they were no longer in contact with the ground. But once he had hit the sand with a thud, he gave only a small twitch before lying completely still.

His race was over. He would never reach home.

There was silence for several agonizing moments while the onlookers, as one, willed him to rise and stagger the few remaining yards to freedom. But it would never happen, could never be. In the silence a girl started to scream, setting in motion an explosive flow of rebuke and hatred which began pouring like molten lava across the divide. Some of the bitterness was directed towards the East and its hidden gunman, but much also engulfed the young American soldiers who held the angry crowd back. 'Why didn't you protect him? Give covering fire? What are you here for? What use are you? American pigs! Yankee bastards! Fucking Nazis!'

How were they to know that the GIs were under the strictest instructions to avoid any incident along the Wall? To give the authorities in the East the benefit of any doubt, and to keep the peace along the frontier at all costs? And how could the GIs explain that under standard procedure their ammunition was in their pouches, not in their magazines, and couldn't be used without explicit orders from brigade? *That this was not supposed to be a fire zone any longer?*

Katherine had watched the escape attempt in some sort of daze. Her worst fears had come to be. She was trapped in the crowd, unable to move in the crush, and anyway there was nothing for her to do. Except stand and watch. Now those around her began to come to life, recovering their voices as they spat taunts across the barriers. Katherine reached out and grabbed the sleeve of the nearest soldier.

'Let me through. Quickly. I must get to him.'

The American seemed uncertain, perturbed, and pulled her hand off his uniform. 'No one gets through, ma'am. Orders.'

'You must! Don't you see he needs help?'

'Can't do that. No one's to get across this line.'

'For God's sake I must get to him!' she shouted, her tone becoming shriller, less controlled, and she grabbed at him once again. It helped the soldier make up his mind. This was just another hysterical woman.

'Let go. Get back. Please!'

'Let me through! He needs help,' she screamed. He

took a step back to break her grip, but she clung to him tenaciously and was pulled across the barrier where she tried to slip past him. But it was to no avail. Sobbing with the effort, she was pinned firmly in his arms. She was going nowhere.

'Can't you see?' the soldier said softly. 'He's beyond anyone's help.'

And it was already too late. A detachment of border guards had emerged from the shadows of the East and was approaching the body, which lay like a dark, solitary pebble on a harsh beach. The guards trotted briskly forward, tracing the footsteps of the escapee across the sand, ignoring the storm of fury which engulfed them as they approached the crowd. Katherine watched limply in the soldier's arms as they straightened the body, laid it on a stretcher, threw a blanket over it and without delay or ceremony doubled back the way they had come, as if they had done this all a thousand times before.

She had failed. The man she was supposed to help, who had relied on her, was now spread across a stretcher and on his way to an East Berlin morgue and an unmarked grave. He had been as close to freedom as Peter; she had seen his face as clearly; it was as if she had been watching a re-enactment of that scene from all those years ago.

She knew the bullet had killed something inside her, too. A flickering light which had spluttered and survived for so long had at last been blown out. There would be no more idle dreams about the future, no more preposterous thoughts about tomorrow. Finally it was over.

'Go on home, sweetheart. Forget everything you've seen here,' the soldier said, trying to comfort her. But, as she turned away, she knew that she could never forget. She would never be able to escape from the shadow of the Wall.

Harry rubbed his eyes hard. He had slept very badly, and now it seemed he wasn't going to sleep at all. He'd gone to bed late, trying vainly to ignore the humidity which caused the sheets to tangle around him whichever way he turned. He was insecure and ill-at-ease; it wasn't just the clammy atmosphere. He still hadn't heard from Katherine, and he hated not knowing what was going on.

He had fallen asleep shortly before midnight, only to find himself cheated once more. His windows were wide open, like sails of a windmill trying to catch the faintest suggestion of any breeze, and the noise travelling across the rooftops shook him awake. He couldn't make out the sound. It was not quite like a football crowd, more like an angry drone of bees or the rumbling of a distant volcano, long thought extinct but now warning of its return to life. It was an unsettling sound, feeding on the sultry night. He thought it might come from the direction of the Gap. God, what a place this was! Full of surprise and hidden menace, the most heavily fortified and occupied city in the world, yet somehow still out of control. He had come here full of such confidence – about Berlin, about his career, about himself. And now he felt sure of nothing.

He was staring into the darkness, searching in the shadows for enlightenment, when he heard the light tapping on the door. He thought he must be mistaken and ignored it, but there it was again. He got up to investigate and found her standing there, trembling.

'I need you,' she said quietly.

She had needed him when they had returned from their first sight of the Gap. She had needed him then like no other woman ever had, ripping at him, clinging to him, unable to get enough of him, as if she were trying to cram a lifetime of love into a few short hours. It had left him exhausted with flesh wounds on his back from her excited fingernails and the hope that, when he was forty, he would have half as much enthusiasm and energy. It was a new beginning, she had explained, and she had so much lost time to make up for. They had made love and laughed and made love again until it was well after sunset and it was time for her to go and confront Edward. That was the last time he had heard from her. Now here she was, in the middle of the night, needing him again.

But he could see it wasn't the same, or anything like the same. This was a different woman from the one who had left him two nights before. The hair was bedraggled, the eyes which had brimmed with confidence were now ringed with tiredness and fear, the face sallow, the lips thinner and less feminine, the once-fine features now haggard. She seemed to have shrunk, become older, the laugh lines now deep cracks in a crumbling façade. The joy which had glowed within her when they were last together was no longer shining, and a dark shadow seemed to have fallen across her.

'I need you, Harry,' she repeated, and he felt foolish. She was still standing on his doorstep, he was practically naked and somehow it all felt wrong. She walked into his arms and held him tight. There was no passion there, just a need to be held in the arms of another human being who cared. Katherine clung to him as if he were the last piece of firm ground left in her life. He could feel the warm trickle of tears running down his chest, but she made no sound.

'I was afraid you were never coming back,' he said.

'I have nowhere else to go, nowhere in the world,'

she responded. It was a voice from a million miles away, a cry of great loneliness.

'What's happened?'

As if every movement were full of pain, she broke loose from his embrace and crossed to the window, staring into the night. She must have known how she looked and she had no desire for Harry to see her like this.

'We tried to bring someone across the Gap tonight. We failed, and he's dead.'

'In Heaven's name, Katherine, I thought you were all finished with that.'

'So did I. But there was . . . something unexpected and Edward insisted.'

'But now of all times?'

She offered no reply or excuse, but hung her head in dejection.

'Tell me about it?' Harry asked, more gently.

So she did – of her confrontation with Edward; of his insistence on using the Gap before it was rebuilt. Of the two endless days and nights spent searching for a way of helping, yet finding none. Of the breathless crowd, of the flying sand, of how he had got so close and how they had all watched him being cut down. Of how they watched him die. Her voice was matter-of-fact, like a disinterested observer, as if all the emotion had been squeezed by the experience and there was none left for the retelling.

'We failed. They shot him. Now . . . it's all over.'

She reached the end and stood staring out across the Wall. He went across to her and kissed her gently on the back of her neck. 'You did your best, Katherine. You'll be all right, you'll see.'

'But I won't, Harry,' she said, turning to face him, her mouth working hard to find the right words. As she did so, Harry noticed the first tell-tale wrinkles of age which had appeared above her upper lip. It was as if she were growing old in front of him. 'I've lived all my life in this city. Somehow it's got a hold on me which I thought, with your help, I could break. But after tonight I know it's impossible.'

'We've got the rest of eternity ahead of us. You said so yourself, just the other afternoon.'

She shook her head gently.

'Katherine, there's a whole world outside Berlin just waiting for us. Everything is possible if we want it enough.'

'No, Harry.' She was clear, determined. 'I love you, really I do. You have brought back a happiness into my life which I'd forgotten existed. A special moment which I shall never forget. But . . . you remember the rose you gave me, the day we visited the cemetery?' Her eyes had a faraway look of distant times. 'It was such a small bloom, so beautiful. I thought it was the loveliest flower in the world, every petal perfect, reaching out for the sun as if it were grown just for me. It lasted for days. Yet even as we cut the stem we were condemning it. One final burst of life and joy was all it had left. That was my rose, Harry. That was me.'

'That's complete nonsense.'

'No, my love. That's the truth.'

'But you were so full of optimism. You said at last you'd managed to escape, now that the Wall was down.'

'But the Wall isn't down. The concrete and mortar might have gone along the Gap, but the Wall's still there, as cruel as ever it was. They shot a man tonight, murdered him, just as they were doing twenty years ago. There's only one difference – instead of bricks and barbed wire, now there are Americans.'

'Oh, God . . .'

'No, Harry. The Wall isn't coming down. There are Americans there right now, with weapons and orders to stop anybody crossing. I love you. But what you are and what I am will always come between us, like that Wall . . .'

No! Harry wanted to scream. This was unfair, unreal. That's not why he came to Berlin. He might be American but he wasn't going to be condemned with all the rest. He was Harry Benjamin, not just a number on a passport. He was better than that!

'They're playing with us, Harry. They knock the Wall down, then block it up again. They talk of peace, then treat us like pawns in their great game. It's always been like that in Berlin. You learn to live with it.'

'I can't accept that.'

'Of course not, which is why you can't accept Berlin. And why you and I, Harry Benjamin, are not meant to be. Don't you see?'

She was not crying, but her cheeks were wet. She kissed him lightly on his lips, and then ran to the bathroom, leaving him lost in his confusion. Did he see? Of course he didn't see! He didn't see why Katherine should hold herself to blame. Or why he found it so damned difficult to be in love with a Berliner. He didn't see why his father's hatred should manage to linger on, years after the bitter old man had gone to his grave. Or why this damned city seemed to have the power to crush people, to chew them up and spit them out before moving on remorselessly to devour others.

But most of all he didn't see how the hell Schumacher had known on Monday what the CIA in Berlin hadn't learned until the afternoon of the following day: that the Wall might be rebuilt in a few days' time. Everywhere he looked, every stone he turned, there lurked Schumacher.

He stood stunned, confronting the seemingly irreconcilable demands of his feelings for Katherine and his doubts about her husband. Warfare raged within him, pulling him apart as he struggled to discover whether personal emotions or professional ambition held sway. As she came back into the room, face washed and hair groomed, looking calmer and composed, he still didn't know.

She walked over to him and rested her head on his chest like a weary traveller leaning on an oak for comfort and support. As his arms went around her, the words came out without any clear direction. 'I won't let you give up on me.'

'I'm not giving up on you, Harry. I'm the problem, not you.'

'You mustn't blame yourself; it wasn't your fault.'

'Then whose fault was it?'

'I don't know . . . no one's. It was one of those things which happen and you can't control. Fate, destiny, if you like.'

'That's exactly what I'm talking about. Nobody's fault. Just destiny.'

Harry stood silently, trying to find the right riposte, but he couldn't. His doubts collided with her certainty, and lost. 'Who was he . . . your runner?' It wasn't a conscious decision to ask. He knew the dangers of where it might lead, but something deep inside and very powerful urged him on.

'I don't know . . . just another man from Leipzig who had to get out in a hurry.' She shook her head disconsolately, trying to throw off the question and the pain.

'If you like, we could contact his relatives through our diplomatic channels – see if there's anything we could do, let them know he didn't suffer.'

Her large, trusting eyes were raised slowly towards his face. 'That would be kind. I'd feel so much better . . . but I'm not sure who he was. I have only a name – Gerd Brünner. Someone Edward knew. It isn't much to go on . . . '

It was enough, Harry thought. Schumacher again.

'Leave it to me. We'll find him.'

'Thank you, Harry.'

He felt like a complete bastard. Even as he held her and was receiving her thanks, he was thinking of himself, trying to tease information from her to feed his suspicions. Yet there was still the other side of him: passionate, honest, a little ashamed. He would never know whether it was honesty or shame which forced from him the next words.

'Katherine. Promise me you will remember one thing. I love you.'

There was no response from her for several moments, until a look of quiet contentment spread slowly across her face, soothing away the anguish.

'That's the first time you've ever said you loved me, Harry Benjamin. I'm sorry you've wasted your love on someone like me . . . No, not wasted,' she hurried to correct herself. 'Like our rose, it can never be wasted,' she said, her voice full of tenderness. 'And I promise I shall never forget.'

TWELVE

The Kremlin

'Tell me,' stormed Andreyev, 'I've got to know.' There was a cold fury in his eyes, the like of which his private secretary hadn't seen in all the years he had worked inside the Kremlin. This was a new Andreyev, scowling, merciless, like an avenging angel with thoughts only of retribution. The secretary began hesitantly, knowing all too well the fate of those who bore bad tidings.

'As you instructed, sir, orders were given that incidents were to be avoided at any price along the borders with West Germany and West Berlin. Appropriate formal requests were made of our comrades in the East German security authorities. They were ... curious, but highly co-operative,' the secretary hastened to add, knowing how sensitive the East Germans were to such blatant interference from Moscow. Everyone knew the reality of the Soviet puppet masters, but the East Germans were insistent on maintaining the pretence that it was they who pulled the strings along their own frontier.

'Co-operative? They shoot some stupid bastard in front of the cameras of the entire fucking world and you call that co-operative? Stop shovelling pig shit. I want the truth. How in the name of the Holy Mother did they manage to receive those instructions and then go out and start a shooting war?' Andreyev bawled. At less stressful times the hapless secretary might have remarked on how, during moments of crisis, Russians continued to appeal for divine support, even after three-quarters of a century of state-decreed atheism. Yet idle sophistry seemed irrelevant with a General Secretary covering his blotter in rabid spittle and you the only other person in the room.

'The orders were issued all along the border, Comrade General Secretary – read to every border patrol before going on duty. But . . .' The paper in his hand from which he was reading fluttered with agitation. '. . . it appears the dead man was no ordinary *Flüchtling*. He was *Stasi*, a senior member of the East German security forces, an agent for the West who had been under suspicion for months. I am told . . .' – he was trying as hard as possible to deflect the blame or punishment on to those who had provided the information – '. . . I am told that *Stasi* officers went to arrest him, but he escaped and fled for the border with certain top secret documents, and that while he was in the process of escaping a member of the pursuing *Stasi* patrol decided that incalculable harm would be done to the security of the German Democratic Republic if the traitor and his papers were to fall into Western hands . . .' He was gabbling now, trying to get it over with. 'So under the standing instructions relating to the apprehension of deserters . . . they shot him.'

'Dead, of course.'

'I'm afraid so, Comrade General Secretary.'

'And the name of the officer who shot him?'

'Not yet known, sir. Apparently the *Stasi* are undertaking their own enquiry since they regard it essentially as a . . . an East German matter.' The secretary's misery was complete.

'With the fraternal assistance of our colleagues and comrades in the *Komitet Gosudarstvennoy Bezopasnosti*, no doubt?' Andreyev hissed. The pedantic details were important.

There was no response beyond another uncontrollable quivering of the sheet of paper.

'So it's a neat little cover-up between the security services. Everyone covering each other's back.'

'But the enquiry is at the highest level. The chairman of the *Stasi* himself has taken charge of the investigation,' exclaimed the secretary, unsure whether the KGB *in absentia* was likely to be more or less dangerous than contradicting the General Secretary to his face.

'You stupid peasant! Who do you think was his classmate in the KGB training college at Khodynka Field?'

The paper fluttered to the floor as the secretary found himself incapable of controlling his fingers, and he ducked down in order to retrieve it and avoid the question. He need not have bothered; Andreyev provided his own answer.

'That big black-hearted bastard Bykov,' hissed Andreyev between clenched teeth. 'He's the one behind all this.'

'Surely not,' protested the secretary, petrified that the KGB bugged the Kremlin as well as every other government office in Moscow.

'I didn't get to sit behind this desk by being a complete cretin. I may not be able to prove it, but as sure as hell is hot I know it's Bykov. And for the first time I know where we all stand.'

He looked contemptuously at the secretary. The creature would have to go. He was clearly as much in awe of the KGB as of Andreyev, and there was no longer any room in Moscow for divided loyalties. But for the moment the trembling bureaucrat was the least of his problems.

Andreyev's lips moved, muttering words which were

meant only for himself, but he no longer cared who else heard them. 'I only hope enlightenment hasn't come too late,' he whispered.

Berlin

Harry went down to the basement area where the support services were housed as soon as he arrived in the office on Thursday. He hadn't ventured into this part of the Mission before, but he found the man he was looking for bending over a work bench taking apart the control unit of a television monitor. The German was around sixty with a shock of receding white hair and glaring, combative eyes staring out from behind half-moon glasses. There was something of the mad professor in him, and Harry was intruding.

'Achh,' the old man said without waiting for Harry to introduce himself, 'I waste half of my time repairing these *verdammten* sets. If only they would buy Japanese – so much more reliable. But no, German televisions it must be, and German televisions aren't supposed to break down. Doesn't matter that they're not really German any more; built by those cabbage-head Turks and Yugoslavs using Taiwanese parts. But if the label says it's made in Germany, that's all that matters to those idiots in Procurement, and I'm left to fix the damage.'

It was clearly a standard gripe, delivered without any pause in his deft dismantling of the equipment which he now proceeded to attack with a small electrical screwdriver. Only when he was ready did he peer over his half-moon frames to inspect his new arrival.

'And who are you? Haven't seen you here before,' he demanded. This was his empire and strangers were fortunate to be tolerated, let alone welcomed.

'Benjamin. Harry Benjamin. I've been here only four months and I've never been down to your territory before — Herr Selter, isn't it? I'd be grateful for your advice if you've got a second.'

Harry had summed up the old man's vanity well. Any recognition that a snot-nosed American foreign service officer needed the help of a local Berlin employee was always well received. He waved a hand to indicate that Harry should take a stool next to his work bench and went back to prodding at the control unit.

'If you want help, you're in the right place. What can I do for you, Harry Benjamin?'

'The escape attempt last night . . .' began Harry.

'Interested in that, are you? Came over myself in '61, just before they built the Wall,' the old man sniffed, as if to establish his credentials. 'Could tell you a thing or two about escapes, I could.'

'Do you have a video of last night? I was told you keep copies of all the news programmes.'

'For a month. Longer if there's a need. But what do you want with the shooting?' Harry may be an executive officer, but down in the basement he would have to explain himself before he got what he wanted.

'Something about it seemed odd when I saw it on the early morning news. Have you seen it? Didn't you think so?'

'Odd?' the old man squeaked. 'How do you mean odd?' But his curiosity was aroused and already he was taking a video cassette out of its cover and cueing it up on the screen.

'Look — here he is, coming out of the shadows and running across the sand.' Harry turned the volume up so they could hear every sound. The old man didn't usually tolerate his equipment being touched by anyone else, but his attention was already absorbed.

'Listen . . . Just one shot. No dogs after him, no shouts of warning. Just a single bullet. Not exactly standard operating procedure, was it?'

'What's your point?' demanded the old man sceptically.

'I'm not sure – yet. What sort of weapon do you think was used?'

'Well it wasn't a hand gun,' the old man mused, stroking a stubby chin. 'Too far. More like a sniper's shot with the AK-47. That's standard army issue. They use 7.62 shorts. One round from that can pull a man down at more than 500 metres. Smash through his chest like piss in the snow. I've seen it happen many times.'

'Okay. Then tell me this, Herr Selter. Can you show me any sign of the injury?'

The tape had wound on. The victim was face down in the sand, but the twisted angle of his back could have hidden any bullet wound. Yet now the border guards were turning him over on to the stretcher and about to cover him with a blanket, but for an instant his whole back was exposed. The telephoto lens shook a little, the harsh night lighting bleached most of the colour from the screen, but the picture of the body being turned was clear even if momentary. There was no sign of blood, or of any bullet wound. The old man stopped and rewound, playing the scene once again in slow motion until he froze it at the vital frame. He stared at it through his spectacles, then over his spectacles, and finally rummaged about on his work bench for a magnifying glass to make one final inspection.

'Nothing there,' he sniffed. A look of suspicion

crossed his face as he stared at Harry with renewed interest. 'What are you after, anyway?'

Harry ducked the question, and turned back to the frozen picture. 'Anything else odd? About the guards?'

The old man studied the screen intently, shaking his head. 'Regular border guards, so far as I can see. You can tell from the green and silver piping on the uniform.'

'Run it back a little,' Harry instructed. 'Just about there . . .'

'Hah!' The old man whistled through the gaps in his dentures as he took in what Harry meant. 'Hadn't noticed that before. You mean the civvy tagging along in the background . . . well, send me to the Russian front. A civilian giving orders to border guards in no-man's-land?' The German raised a cryptic eyebrow. 'Means only one thing: *Stasi*. What the hell were they doing there?'

Harry thought he knew, but he wasn't about to tell a crotchety old blabbermouth in support services.

'Come on, Rossi. It's not much to ask, is it?'

'Look, Benjamin, the Virgin Mary's put the finger on you. You're so hot I break into a sweat just being in the same room as you. The answer's no, so bugger off.' Rossi had another hangover and wasn't in the most tolerant of moods.

'Frank, listen to me. I don't want to get into any security files. I don't want to get anyone into trouble. I certainly don't want to remember our night out at – what was the name of the club again? You know, the one with that gorgeous fellow with the big tits and feathers and . . .'

'You wouldn't dare. You'd be in it as deeply as me.'

'Frank, I'm already in it. I can't get in any deeper without drowning. And anyway, I expect Mrs Rossi would be much less interested in what I had been up to while she was away than her old man's activities.'

'You couldn't be such a bastard,' said Rossi, uncertainty flooding every syllable.

'Not if you run this simple little check for me. Gerd Brünner's the name. Probably early forties. Lives in Leipzig.'

'You're vermin. You know that, Benjamin?'

'I'm also hungry, Frank. How soon?'

'Sundown, ratface.'

The White House

'We've got to do it, Leo. I can't ignore that sort of pressure. How on earth can I fight that?' Michelle pointed despondently at the television screen, which was showing yet again the final moments of the dash to the Wall.

Grossman felt Michelle drifting away from him. The media were unanimous, and they outnumbered and outgunned a single presidential adviser.

'You fight it because it's there, because you're the President, because it's wrong and because if you don't you're dead.'

'But every editor in the country is now screaming for me to do something about it. Look at the *Post*. "A treaty which does not include an end to death at the Wall will have no moral foundation. It would be less a way of bringing the world to peace, more a convenient cost-cutting exercise between superpowers which continue to carve up the world for their own convenience . . ."'

'Morality? They talk of morality?' Grossman, the

311

arch-exponent of power politics, knew that the discussion was venturing on to impossibly marshy ground. He felt all the certainties of the last three and a half years beginning to be sucked under, disappearing into impenetrable ethical mists. He needed to blow them away, and quickly. 'What the devil do they think your job is — a choirboy singing their hymns? You are President of the United States, not the blessed Pope. You serve the national interest and leave the saving of souls to others!'

'But the *Times* says it won't support the treaty without the demilitarization of Berlin.' Michelle's voice was resigned, flat, no fight left in it. He'd seen the latest opinion polls, too.

'You can't do it. You've got only three days left to settle the treaty. We can't throw it away now.'

'We can squeeze more time out of them. You yourself said they need the treaty as much as we do . . .'

'What if they don't? You'll have thrown it all away for one stupid, cretinous, suicidal East German. He's already the small change of history. In a week's time the world will have forgotten about him, while you will be announcing the signing of a great new peace treaty. Can't you see that garbage at the Wall is irrelevant? *It doesn't matter.*'

Michelle shook his head uncertainly. He wasn't convinced.

'Sign the treaty. Forget the Wall. Go and campaign as a great international statesman. Fight the election in Nebraska and Idaho and let the great American public decide — you've still got a great chance. But if you decide to fight the campaign 4000 miles away in Berlin, you'll be as dead as that poor bastard there.'

Grossman was being uncharacteristically coarse, overreaching himself, his lack of detachment showing.

He knew his position was weakening with every wring of Michelle's agitated hands.

'It could be the action of an even greater statesman to campaign as the man who stood up to the Russians . . . destroy and dismantle the Wall . . . get rid of the Iron Curtain . . . the final barrier to peace and freedom in Europe . . .'

'We don't want a reunited Germany. Nobody wants a reunited Germany!' – Grossman was shouting now, his voice strained, close to cracking – 'Nobody except the Germans, and they don't count. You reunite Germany and the whole course of European history, perhaps world history, will change. It would be the dominant power in Europe. The French, the British, the Italians, they don't want that. It would destroy the status quo and neither we nor the Russians want that. A reunited Germany would be an ambitious Germany, and everything which we have built in Europe since 1945 would collapse under its weight. They lost the war; they got what they deserved. For God's sake don't mess about with it now. The Wall must stay. Don't you see?'

Michelle sat passively, pondering. He could see many things, none of which he liked.

'Try this. If you throw a spanner into the treaty negotiations, they will fail. Do you think you stand a better chance of getting re-elected if you have the treaty, or if you fail to get it?'

'Signing a treaty which makes us look as if we've been pushed around by the Communists would be even worse. If I've got no votes in Berlin, I've sure as hell got none in Moscow.'

'New York. Think New York: 36 electoral college votes. Could be completely decisive. It's got nearly two million Jewish voters. How many do you think you'll get if you tear down the barbed wire and reunite the Fatherland? The barbed wire across Germany came from around the camps at Dachau and Buchenwald and Auschwitz. Leave it where it is!' Grossman offered up a fevered prayer that the weight of history – his history – would count for more with Michelle than the ton of telegrams and letters which had been flooding into the White House.

'There are 53 other states and territories, 500 other electoral college votes and 150 million other voters. What of them, Leo?'

'Ignore the pundits. Tough it out. Tell the world that your first reponsibility is to Americans,' Grossman pleaded. He was on the verge of desperation, feeling the treaty and his own place in history slipping irretrievably through his fingers. There was real pain in his eyes as he felt the burden of generations of bitterness towards Germans and all they stood for pressing down on his shoulders, and the ghostly voices of six million souls insisting that he must not forget – or allow Michelle to forget.

The President was looking out of the window across the panorama of the capital city which he had grown to love and regard as his own personal property. Suddenly it was all so insecure.

'I'm not sure, Leo. I'm just not sure . . .'

Berlin

'Why are you wasting my time, Benjamin?' Rossi didn't even look up from his newspaper and mug of coffee when Harry walked into his office.

'*Que pasa, amigo?*'

'You're not my *amigo*, you're a complete asshole. D'you know it takes five times as much work to prove that someone doesn't exist than being able to find him and get photos of him screwing his old woman? A complete waste of everyone's time. I am not a happy man.'

'Tell me about it.'

'There are three Gerd Brünners in and around Leipzig. One's an old man of over ninety. Practically dead in his socks. The second's his great-grandson, named in his honour, who's still sucking at his mother's tit. The third lives just outside Leipzig – except he's twenty-one and doing military service. So you see, your Gerd Brünner doesn't exist. Asshole.' He returned to sipping his coffee.

Harry lowered himself gently on to the edge of Rossi's desk, his body responding in slow motion as his mind wrestled with the pieces. A body without any sign of injury. A man who didn't exist. An escape which wasn't genuine. An international incident that was nothing more than a theatre piece in front of a world audience ... Could it really be? He kept coming back to Schumacher, a thread which somehow ran through all the mysteries he'd found in this city. Everything the Berliner had touched turned to grief. He had thrown inflammatory speech after bloody riot and economic blockade in order to defend the rights of Berliners – or so he had led everyone to think. But this? For the first time Harry began to be dimly aware of a greater plan. Not peace in Berlin, but confrontation which would destroy not only the arms talks but *glasnost* and all its creators. Schumacher wasn't working to knock the Wall down but to keep the bloody thing in place, to build it stronger than ever.

'And you can get your butt off my desk, Benjamin,' grated Rossi, returning his attention to the sports page.

'Yeah, of course . . . sorry. Thanks, Frank,' mumbled Harry. He walked off in a daze. How was he to make anyone believe his wild theories? He couldn't get near Schumacher himself or any of the Mission records which might support his case. All he had was a jumble of coincidence and suppositions, a fuzzy piece of video-tape – and Katherine, a woman he loved, whose grasp on her future was as tenuous as the future of the Gap. To have any chance of catching out Schumacher would risk breaking that grasp and the destruction of Katherine herself, leaving her with no husband, no support, no future, no hope.

Harry knew he had no choice. You didn't get choices in Berlin, only sides. And Harry had never doubted which side he was on.

THIRTEEN

Berlin

Harry had death on his mind. Gerd Brünner's, his father's, even his own. The optimism of youth had always decreed that he was immortal, but somehow Berlin had squeezed that out of him. All things must end; the question which Harry pondered was when.

He had returned to the Jewish cemetery. It was full of late evening light and the songs of birds, the abundant colours of early summer seeming to overpower the memorials and tombstones. But these colours, too, would fade and die – just like the rose he had picked for Katherine – and all that would be left were the tombstones and memories.

He wondered for a moment if any of his relatives were buried here. His father had always talked about going back to seek, but in the end had never dared for fear of what he knew he would find. Life was unfair, and life in Berlin seemed particularly so. He thought of his father, oppressed by the guilt that he alone had survived, and insistent that Harry carry his burden into the next generation; of Miss Pickerstaff, who was little more than a cog without a soul in a machine which had no mind, whirring on in the direction it was pointed regardless of where or why, rolling over anyone like Harry who got in its way; of Schumacher, whose entire life had been a deceit, who had no friends only allies, and who was nothing more than a marionette in a world made by others; and of Katherine, who deserved so much yet who had been granted so little, who asked only for the chance to love, but even when she found it had discovered she couldn't hold on to it.

And Harry Benjamin, what of him? Could he escape being crushed by this city when all the others had failed? Did he have a value or was he just a number, another pawn on the Berlin chessboard to be moved around in patterns dictated by others? Who was Harry Benjamin anyhow? He stared around the cemetery, and the gravestones stared back at him. So you think you can beat the system, they seemed to say? Like all the other poor bastards who now rot under your feet? Fool!

But if I end up as dead as you what have I got to lose? asked Harry, throwing back their challenge. He was supposed to toe the line and stop loving Katherine, that's what the system demanded. Screw them! They hadn't beaten him yet. But which was most important to him – nailing Schumacher, or being with Katherine? If he had that choice, he didn't want to make it. Perhaps the system would win after all . . .

He heard the creak of the graveyard's old iron gate as it opened to let someone pass. He knew it was Katherine. She had come, as he had asked. He hadn't been sure she would; it was the first time they had met since the shooting at the Gap, and since Katherine had been dragged away from him by her doubts and her memories. Now she walked into view along the pathway which wound around the cemetery. The sun shone from behind her, seeming to blur her edges and turn her into a spirit – beautiful, ethereal, immortal, not quite of this world. He rose from his bench to greet her and reached out for her hand. It was cold. She was holding back. As her face appeared out of the sun, he could see the lines of exhaustion and demoralization around her eyes and at the corners of her lips. She seemed to have withered. The sun had lied.

'Hello, Harry.' Her voice was low, tired. 'How have you been.' It wasn't really a question, more something to fill the distance. Was small talk all they had left?

'I've missed you,' he said.

'And I've missed you too, terribly. But it's something we have to get used to . . .'

'I'm still not willing to accept that. We have plenty of time. I'll wait.'

'We have no choice, Harry. Some day you'll see what I am saying is true.' She cast her eyes around, searching for something to say which would change the subject. 'Why did you want to meet here?'

'Because this is where you first persuaded me that we could bridge all those gaps between us.'

'Where you picked that beautiful rose for me. I remember.'

'And because I need your help.'

She looked at him sharply, a frown biting its way across her forehead.

'This was where you first told me about your escape ring. You asked me to say not a word to anyone about it, and I've kept my promise. But now I need to know more. I need to know more names of people you have helped across.'

'Why?'

It was the question he knew she must ask, but he still had no clear explanation. He couldn't tell her the real reason yet he didn't want to lie, and anyway he hadn't come up with a suitable lie which sounded in the least convincing. Research into refugees? An instruction from on high to gather more information about them? He knew it all sounded unconvincing crap.

'Why?' she repeated. 'Is this something to do with

319

Gerd Brünner? Have you been able to contact his family?'

'Not yet, I'm still trying. But I need more names. All I have is Brünner and the Jakobsohns here. I need more.'

'I don't understand. What for?'

'Katherine, I need to know. And I can't tell you why, not yet. I want you to trust me. I know how you feel about the ring. I won't betray your confidence.'

'But . . .' She was bewildered.

He was staring deep into her eyes to reach her, trying to convince her. He could see the suspicion lurking there; he had forced her into a corner, now she was thinking that he was no different from all the rest. 'Remember what I told you when we last met? I asked you to remember that I love you. I do love you, Katherine, and I'm asking you to trust me.'

'Is it about Edward?' she asked. Did she have her doubts, too? He could see the turmoil going on within her as she tried to unravel what this all meant.

'There have been so many of them over more than twenty years, Harry. I can't remember them all. There's only one list, locked up in my safe at home.'

'Give me just a few names you can remember. Something for me to go on.'

'I've never done this for anyone . . .'

'Do it for me!'

'But why?' She sounded exhausted.

'Because you love me.'

'You want to trade love for a few names?'

She looked at him as if she no longer recognized the man in front of her. But at last he could see the fight draining out of her tired eyes. He might not have convinced her, there was still the suspicion, but she no longer had the energy to resist. In an exhausted monotone, she plucked five names at random from her memory, and Harry could feel the pain which each revelation gave her.

'Is that enough?' she asked wearily.

'Thank you. I know how much . . .' The words seemed to fail him. 'I do love you, Katherine.' He leaned across to kiss her, but drew back. Judas had finished with a kiss.

She hung her head unresponsively. It was not the victory over her doubts that he would have wanted, but it was the only one he was going to get. It would have to do.

Dzerzhinsky Square, Moscow

The lights were burning bright behind the grey stone façade of KGB headquarters on Dzerzhinsky Square. All along the third floor where the chairman had his suite of offices there were signs of activity – if the old man hadn't left, none of his staff dared leave either. Conversations went on in many rooms off the light green corridors as his deputies and other senior officers tried to unravel what was going on. A series of highly placed diplomatic and military staff had been scurrying in and out of Bykov's suite all afternoon looking sombre, and now fellow members of the Politburo had been seen entering or leaving Bykov's private lift. Bykov was holding court. None knew for certain why, but it was clearly of the highest importance.

Chernov, the most powerful of Bykov's six deputies, caught the chairman's principal assistant as he was taking a leak in the enormous, echoing washroom set aside for the junior staff on the corridor.

'Okay, what's up?' he demanded.

The assistant hadn't seen Chernov coming and jumped in surprise as the deputy's voice boomed around the white porcelain surrounds. It had been a very trying day, his bladder was bursting with endless cups of tea and his nerves were stretched tight.

'I really don't know, Comrade. And in any event, I'm under the strictest instructions not to discuss matters with anyone.' His nervousness showed. He had been caught at a disadvantage, even more so as the zip on his new East German suit jammed as he tried hurriedly to put himself in order.

'You can't even tell a deputy chairman?' asked Chernov in a voice which revealed just how displeased he was to be flouted by a junior clerk.

'Eh . . . I'm afraid not, Comrade. Not even you. Chairman's personal orders,' replied the flustered junior, desperately trying to unjam his zip. He didn't like having to defy a deputy chairman who might well be his boss one day and who would not forget the slight. His misery became complete as the zip burst completely in response to his violent tugging. He was defenceless and embarrassed, desperately wanting to find some way of bringing the deputy chairman back on side. He looked anxiously around to check that no feet were protruding from under any cubicle door.

'I suppose . . .' He blanched as his words bounced back loudly from the tiles and echoed around the large room. His voice dropped to an exaggerated, hoarse whisper. 'I suppose, Comrade General, that there is no harm in telling you what will be widely known tomorrow in any event.' He glanced around nervously once again. 'An extraordinary meeting of the Politburo has been called at Chairman Bykov's request for Sunday.'

'At Bykov's request? For Sunday?' exclaimed the

General in astonishment. Both events were more than sufficient to have the gathering described as extraordinary. 'What in hades . . .' he barked, on the point of bullying the hapless subordinate into submission and disclosure, but suddenly he reined back. Something very big was in the offing. He recalled the fevered speculation which had been dominating the gossip in the quiet corners of Dzerzhinsky Square concerning the bitter divisions within the Politburo, and how such open factionalism couldn't last. He thought of all the eminent figures who had trooped into Bykov's office during the afternoon. He recalled that the Second World War had been declared on a Sunday. He scented blood in the air.

'Tell me. What was the Comrade Chairman doing when you last saw him?'

The secretary considered the question for a second, carefully weighing whether the answer could in any way be deemed treasonable. 'He was looking out of the window across Marx Prospekt,' he said cautiously. 'He was . . . singing.'

'An old Georgian battle song, if I know our beloved Chairman,' Chernov said, giving a cold smile.

'Why . . . yes, sir.'

That was enough for the General. Moscow on Sunday sounded like a very dangerous place to be. He resolved to leave early for his *dacha* and put plenty of distance between himself and whatever Bykov was up to. He turned his back on the secretary and began to lather and wash his hands with meticulous care.

The secretary at last saw his opportunity and left in search of a safety pin.

Berlin

Harry looked at the phone, willing it to ring with an urgent piece of business or some other distraction. It stayed silent. He counted to ten. Still nothing. He argued with himself once again that he should go around and talk to her in person, but he dare not risk running into Schumacher. He had no further excuse not to call; there was nothing to change his mind. He lifted the phone, feeling as if he were pulling the pin on a grenade, not sure where it would land, knowing only that it was certain to do immense damage when it did.

'Hello. This is Frau Edward Schumacher. Who is speaking, please?'

As he listened to her use her formal married name, Harry thought he heard the sound of the pin springing away.

'It's Harry.'

'You're not supposed to call me at home.'

'Is Edward there?'

'No. But . . .'

'Katherine, listen. Listen carefully. The five names you gave me. There's a problem.'

'What do you mean, a problem?'

'Two of them . . .' He took a deep breath. If they ever discovered he had told Katherine, they could lock him up, too. 'I've had all the names checked through our security files. Two of them are known to be doubles — agents working for the East.'

'That's a bad joke.'

He was silent, and slowly the earnestness of what he had said began to penetrate.

'What are you saying?' she said, her voice now shaking.

'We've known about these two for some time. We didn't know they had both come across using your ring, that there was a common link.'

'Who is "we", Harry?' but her tone suggested she had already guessed. He had never told her precisely what he did at the Mission, and she had never asked. It hadn't been important – up till now. He didn't bother to reply.

'Katherine, listen very carefully. I believe your escape ring was used for many years as a cover to smuggle over agents from the East among the genuine refugees you brought across.'

'Impossible! If that were the case either Edward or I would have known. Everyone we brought across was thoroughly checked out by Edward beforehand . . .'

'Precisely.'

'Harry, tell me you aren't serious.'

'I'm completely serious. Remember Gerd Brünner from Leipzig? He doesn't exist. It was all a sick show for the television cameras, designed to undermine the troop negotiations.'

'This is complete madness.'

'Have you ever asked Edward how he made his money, trading in the East? Have you ever asked yourself why he was so much more successful than most of the others?'

He could hear nothing but silence down the phone. 'Katherine, I believe Edward has duped you. All these years he's been an agent for the East. He's used you and the escape ring.'

'Just like you've used me.'

Her words cut through him like fire, burning away the careful self-control and authority he was trying to maintain. He had sensed something like this would happen; it was why he'd been so reluctant to make the call.

'No, Katherine. I love you. You must believe that.'

'I don't think I believe in anything any more,' she replied in a strange, distant voice. 'I suppose you suspect me, too.'

'No. If I did, why would I be telephoning you instead of coming round to pick you up with a platoon of armed soldiers?'

'Because you want something.'

'Because I love you, Katherine. Like I've never loved anyone before. I would have done anything to avoid bringing you misery like this. Tell me you understand.'

'I understand all right.' Her voice was cold. 'Now what do you want?'

He wanted to protest again, but the tone of her voice told him he was wasting his breath. 'I ... I want the rest of the list. We've got to check the rest of the names.'

'You want me to betray Edward,' she said quietly, accusingly.

'It's Edward who has betrayed you, can't you see? He's betrayed you and for all we know countless poor bastards who were trying to get across only to find the border guards waiting. Christ, for all we know he might have betrayed Peter!' It was a dark, evil thought which only his desperation forced out of him. He shouldn't have, but he was running out of ammunition. He was in danger of making a real balls-up of this.

'Katherine, I'm not being very good with words but you must understand. I love you. I'm not lying to you. For your own sake, you have to listen. If this were the last time we were ever to talk to each other I'd still not change a word. I must know that you believe me!'

326

He waited for her response, but all he heard was a long, slow sob of torment. Then the phone went dead.

Schumacher's car drew up outside his home in Charlottenburg. He felt like a stranded mariner in the eye of a hurricane. Everything around him seemed natural and normal, but he knew it was just a matter of time before chaos of an indescribable kind overwhelmed him. His hands had been trembling uncontrollably all morning, and the walls of his office at party headquarters had seemed to be closing in and about to smother him. He had to get out. He needed a drink – he very much needed to get drunk. And he still had enough sense of self-protection to come home to do it.

Katherine had heard him pulling up, and was waiting for him. She was seated in her favourite chair, holding a piece of paper in front of her. She said nothing as he crossed to where the crystal decanters stood and poured himself a large brandy, the glass beating out a tattoo as his unsteady hand rattled the decanter against its rim. He drank without respite until it was finished before refilling the glass and turning towards her. It was only then he noticed her wall safe was open, the door ajar on its hinges. She was staring at him in a curious, almost alien manner.

'What's up? What's that?' he enquired, waving his glass at the sheet of paper, his other hand thrust deep into his trouser pocket to control its shaking.

'How many of them were false?'

'What are you blabbering about?' he snapped, showing neither interest nor understanding.

'How many of those we brought across the Wall were traitors?'

Suddenly he was taking her seriously. 'What sort of idiocy is that? What the hell do you mean?'

327

'I know, Edward. I know what you used the ring for all these years. To smuggle across Eastern agents. To hide them like maggots among all the genuine refugees, in sensitive jobs where they serve their masters – your masters.'

'That's lunacy,' he blustered.

'I *know*, Edward. You betrayed me. Used me,' she said, her voice rising in anger.

'Never!'

'Don't lie to me,' she shouted, her voice showing she was on the edge of losing control. 'These lies have got to finish. You've deceived me all these years, and I'm not going to take any more of it!'

He took her very seriously now as he found himself being stared at by a .22 calibre semi-automatic, the one she kept in the safe and took with her when helping with escapes, just in case. She had never had to use it, but he knew she could. He had to play for time, give himself a moment to think. This was a moment he had always known would come, some day, but all the foresight in the world hadn't prepared him for it. Trying to look casual, he tossed down the rest of the brandy and moved slowly across to refill his glass. Katherine's free hand was gripping the arm of the chair, the whites of her knuckles revealing her tension, yet the barrel of the gun was rock steady, covering him as he moved. She was too excited and far too deliberate for him to take chances.

'How did you find out?' he asked, trying to sound matter-of-fact.

'They're on to you, Edward. They'll be here shortly, I suspect, and that will be the end of it.'

'Who, exactly, is on to me?'

'The Americans. Harry Benjamin.'

'Harry . . . Benjamin,' he whispered slowly, comprehension beginning to fill his bloodshot eyes. 'The young American . . . your lover?'

'She hesitated for a fraction of a second before responding. 'Yes.'

'So betrayal is mutual.'

'Don't fool with me, Edward! It's nothing like the same. You've betrayed me from the very start. For all I know you were betraying me even before we mét!'

'Why are you telling me all this? Why not just wait until they come to arrest me?'

'Because there is one thing I have to know from you.' Her hand tightened around the gun, her voice carrying an edge of ice. 'Did you warn them of Peter's and my escape? Were they waiting for us?'

'Jesus Christ, no!' Schumacher protested. Even in his alcoholic state he could still perceive the avalanche of revenge and fury which was about to descend on him. 'Not that! I couldn't . . .' He realized he was gambling for his life and that he might have only seconds left.

'Never in my life have I caused anyone's death. Certainly not Peter's. And the baby . . .' It was time for his greatest gamble. All his faculties were racing, like a chess player wrapped up in an end game who had run out of time and must dash the pieces across the board by instinct, with only his ingrained sense of survival to guide him. He made his move.

'Katherine, you will hate me for this, but there is something you must know. Your baby . . .' She flinched at the very mention. 'Your baby . . .' He was having difficulty with the words, knowing that one false move would unleash the avalanche. 'Your baby didn't die that night with Peter. He survived.'

For the first time the barrel of the gun began to waver.

'He's alive and well, an architect in the East.'

Her mouth had dropped open in astonishment. She

had never completely lost hope. The tiny bundle hadn't moved, even as she watched its father dying beside it . . .

'Alive . . . ?' She could scarcely form the word as her lips trembled. 'And you've known all these years?'

'Yes.'

'You bastard!' she screamed, bringing her other hand up to grip the gun.

'Listen, Katherine, you must listen. How could I have told you without betraying myself? They would never have let you have him, anyway.'

'Scum!' The look in her eye told him that he had only moments left . . .

'You can have him back! If – and only if – I'm there to demand it. They owe me, after all these years. You can be reunited with him – if I'm there to demand it. You'll never find him on your own.' The barrel of the gun still trembled at him. 'My life for his, Katherine. Do you hate me enough to sacrifice your son as well?' The barrel began to droop slightly. 'If we both get across the Wall, I guarantee you will be safe, and brought back together with him again. It's your choice, Katherine.' He gasped for breath, his move completed.

'Choice? What choice do I have? All these years, all these wasted years . . .' The anger had gone, there was now only abject misery and bewilderment. The gun dropped into her lap, her body sagged. Schumacher was back in control.

'If they are coming for me there's not a moment to spare. Be very clear about one thing. If I don't get across, you'll never see him again. We must move fast. There are one or two things I must get from my safe . . .' He moved over and relieved her of the sheet of paper and the gun. She didn't resist.

'. . . And I have one last telephone call to make.'

*

As he heard the phone go dead Harry's whole body seized. It seemed an eternity before he could feel his heart beating again and was able to take a deep breath. He sat motionless, frozen in time, his feet and his thoughts made of clay. He struggled to review the alternatives: could he be wrong after all? Was there a simpler, more innocent explanation? It made no difference. Whichever direction he came from he still arrived at the same point. Schumacher was a double-dealing shit, and with his hands on the complete list Harry finally would have the evidence to prove it.

Then why was he waiting, wasting time? What was holding him back? He shook himself free from his thoughts. He needed the list. He must get to Katherine. 'Car pool?' he barked into the phone. 'I need a car for Charlottenburg – immediately. It's urgent . . . five minutes? Can't you make it quicker? I said urgent!'

He slammed the phone down in frustration. Just as she had slammed the phone down on him. Only now did it begin to sink in how she must feel. Betrayed by her husband. Her devotion of all those years to the escape ring made a mockery, and worse. And Harry – what had she said? – had 'used' her, 'just like all the rest'. He had dismissed it at the time as an unintentional outburst – it was patently untrue, wasn't it? But gradually it began to dawn on him how it might look from her point of view.

'Another five minutes? You said that five minutes ago. Don't you understand this is *urgent*?' So what if he were the lowest of the low and there were many other more important people to take care of. Why couldn't they get it through their thick heads that, single-handedly, he was about to uncover a major security scandal which would go down as one of the most brilliant intelligence coups in years? 'Forget it! I'll take a cab!' he shouted at some nameless and blameless voice from the basement car pool who was only trying to do his job. He grabbed his jacket and scrabbled in his desk drawer for some loose change for the taxi. Balls! Did everything have to be so damned difficult? He couldn't even get a car! Still, after tomorrow they would be chauffeuring him all over town . . .

The door opened and Miss Pickerstaff came in. Hovering in the background, just outside in the corridor, were two soldiers with immaculate creases and very noticeable sidearms.

'Benjamin. Not thinking of going anywhere, were you?' She was smiling once again, yet the eyes were as dark as thunder. 'You know, from the moment you arrived I had you down as a meddlesome cretin. But until now I had no idea just how complete a cretin you are.'

How on earth was he supposed to respond to that?

'Could we do this a little later, do you think? I've got something important . . .'

'For you, Benjamin, there is no "later". You're going nowhere.' The two guards moved across the door to block it. Harry's jaw dropped in astonishment.

'I told you to stay away from Edward Schumacher. I told you to keep your nose out of trouble. I told you to report to me on every move you made in Berlin. I told you it was your *last chance*. Are you really so naïve that you thought you could fool me?' Her voice was full of ridicule that he should have dared to try. 'So now you are busted. Out. Finished.' She was relishing this bit. 'And these two gentlemen are here to ensure that your files and papers are secured, your office is locked, and you are thrown off the premises and out of the Mission. Permanently.'

'I . . . I don't understand,' protested Harry.

'My instructions to stay away from Herr Schumacher were absolutely clear. They didn't mean you should run off and bed his wife!'

'Katherine . . . how did you know?' he gasped, overwhelmed.

'Because Herr Schumacher just called me from his home to let me know. It seems his wife has confessed the sordid news to him. The sole redeeming feature of your behaviour is that you're not denying it. Saves all the trouble of a formal enquiry.'

'But you don't understand.'

'Oh, I understand all right. You're weak. Couldn't keep your grubby hands to yourself. They try to vet moral degenerates out of the system at Langley, but for some reason the worst seems to come out of people like you when they're posted abroad. Still, I'm glad we managed to catch you out before you had the chance to do too much damage. So these two gentlemen will supervise as you remove any personal belongings from this room, relieve you of your office keys and identity cards, and escort you off the premises. You have forty-eight hours before your one-way flight back to the States.'

She turned to leave, trying none too hard to avoid looking smug.

'You don't understand. Schumacher's a spy.'

'Not that one again,' she snorted with contempt. 'Be sensible. Try to act like a man.'

'Listen. Just listen for a second!' He banged his fist down hard on his desk, rattling the lamp and spilling paper clips everywhere. 'You ignored it when I told you Schumacher's business was built on official help from the East. You refused to believe that he might be working for them as well as us. But try closing your eyes to this. Schumacher has been running an escape ring from the East for more than twenty years. Using real refugees as cover, and smuggling in agents under our very noses.'

She was turning away again in dismissal.

'Don't take my word for it. Ask Rossi! Schumacher also organized last Monday's escape attempt at the Gap when the man was shot. Do you realize how much damage that's done to the Geneva talks? Unfortunate coincidence, wasn't it? But although we all heard the shot and saw him go down, there were no bullet wounds on him and he was picked up by the *Stasi*. The videotape proves it. And the escapee – Rossi checked him out – doesn't exist. Don't you see? It was all a set-up!'

'Do you really expect me to believe that a local Berlin politician is single-handedly trying to undermine East–West relations?'

'Not on his own, no. But he's a key player. Think of the speeches. The march down the Kurfürstendamm. The boycott. Now this bungled and incredibly badly timed escape. Just think!'

'This is ludicrous, this little game of yours . . .'

'Why is it ludicrous? Because it's been played under your nose for years and you didn't recognize it? What do you expect in Berlin, a rule book?'

She was blushing and flustered now, outraged at his personal attack but unable fully to comprehend the magnitude of what he was proposing. She went quiet for a moment while she summoned up the words to lash him. Harry took his chance, now slower and more deliberate as he tried to offer her another way out.

'I know all this to be true. There's proof. It's a list of all the escapees who've used Schumacher's ring over the years. I'm certain it includes a large number of agents. We can break one of the most significant spy rings of recent years in West Berlin. All we need is the list.'

'Which is where?'

'With Katherine Schumacher. I've just telephoned her to warn her about her husband and to tell her I'm coming to collect the list.'

'You did what? You telephoned the wife of a man you claim is an enemy agent, and tipped her off?'

'We're wasting time. You already said that Schumacher is at home. Even now he may be . . .'

'You say Schumacher is a spy. You've been sleeping with his wife. Now you tip her off. Has it ever crossed your mind that she could be in it, too?'

Damnation, of course it had, no matter how much he loved and trusted her. He knew that was why he had found every excuse to give her a little time, a little warning. Just in case. He couldn't bear to see Katherine hurt any more.

'I know she's not part of this,' he said defiantly.

'She's obviously told him of her relationship with you. What makes you think she's not at this very moment telling him all the rest? Escaping. Thanks to you.'

'I . . .' Words failed him.

'Worm! I shouldn't be throwing you out, Benjamin. I should be having you locked up!'

'Either way we shouldn't be standing here. We should be over at Schumacher's house, getting the list. If we don't have the list, we have nothing.'

She was silent now, considering, confused, uncertain what to do. He could tell by the way she looked at him that she didn't believe him.

'If I'm wrong and this is all just my vivid imagination,' he continued, 'the fault is mine, not yours. You won't be blamed. You'll simply get the excuse to take me to an even higher window before you throw me out.'

Something in what he said seemed to inspire her,

offer her some relief from her doubts. 'Sergeant!' She turned to one of the guards. 'I want my car and an armed escort ready to go in two minutes!'

The sergeant snapped to attention and ran off to do her bidding.

'So you believe me . . . ?'

'The armed guard is for you, Benjamin,' she hissed. 'I'm not letting you out of my sight until we've got to the bottom of this.'

She was as good as her word. Harry sat in the back of her car, sandwiched between two unsympathetic soldiers, while she rode in the front. A jeep with two more soldiers followed. It took them only twelve minutes to thrash down Clayallee and arrive outside the house. But by that time it had been nearly half an hour since he had talked to Katherine, half an hour since Schumacher had arrived home . . .

There was no answer at the front door but the door at the back of the house was unlocked and two of the soldiers swiftly began making a sweep of the premises. 'In here, ma'am,' one of them soon beckoned. It was Schumacher's study. The desk was a mess, with drawers open and papers strewn everywhere. A wall safe gaped open and empty.

There was a cry from a second room. 'Another one in here!' They ran to find a soldier placing the contents of a further safe carefully on to a polished mahogany table. No papers, although evidently there had been, judging by the empty document folder. Instead there was jewellery, with rows of pearls and the elegant diamond and emerald necklace Katherine had worn on the evening Harry had first met her; some old and dog-eared photographs; an empty magazine for a .22 calibre. And a red rose, pressed and dried, and still full of fragrance.

'So where's your list, the proof you promised?' demanded Miss Pickerstaff.

There was nothing to say.

'You tipped her off. You deliberately let her get away.'

Harry picked up the rose, and laid it carefully across his open palm. 'She's not part of it. It's Schumacher you want,' he said quietly.

'They'll have gone for the Wall,' she said, ignoring him. She picked up the phone and seconds later she was barking instructions into it for a priority stop-and-seize on Schumacher and his wife at all crossing points. 'Do whatever you have to. Detain them at all costs. They are not to get across!'

She turned slowly and deliberately away from the phone towards Harry. 'Sergeant, place this man under close arrest.'

FOURTEEN

Berlin

The youthful German policeman on duty at the Invalidenstrasse crossing point cupped his hand over his ear in an attempt to drown out the noise of the passing traffic. Someone was shouting at him through the crackle of his personal radio.

'Who? Schumacher and his wife?' He had never met Edward Schumacher, but the politician's face had appeared on too many news programmes in recent months for him to go unrecognized. He looked across to double-check, but it only confirmed what he had already seen. There had been very few vehicles through, what with the boycott, and every new car with its occupants had helped to lift the monotony and received close attention. 'Schumacher and a redhead drove through less than a minute ago. I can see them now, waiting at the checkpoint . . . What? Stop them? Too late. They're already over the line, surrounded by border guards!'

He watched as Schumacher's BMW meandered slowly through the chicane of concrete bollards and barriers designed to slow down and halt vehicles trying to crash through to the West. There was only one car ahead of them. The border guards were methodical, slow, inspecting documents, vehicle registrations, driving licences, car boots. They were obviously bored, one of them even getting down on his knees to look under the car, grateful for the exercise. Eventually it was waved through, the final red-and-white barrier rising to let it past, and then it was Schumacher's turn. Two guards examined the BMW, while a third took their various documents inside the ugly concrete guard house.

'Turning up like tourists, Edward? I thought at least you would have a military guard of honour.' Katherine made no attempt to disguise the contempt in her voice.

'You don't believe I would have survived so long if every border guard along the Wall knew who I was, do you? As far as these idiots are concerned I'm just another humble West Berlin businessman and politician.'

'I thought you telephoned ahead?'

'No. That was something else entirely . . .'

A sense of calm and security had taken hold of Schumacher. He noticed that his hands were no longer trembling, and he smiled in contentment and relief. He was back home at last, safe. For the first time in his life he had no need to be in fear, and nothing any more to hide.

'When can I see my son?'

The question punctured his euphoria. It disturbed him. He didn't look at Katherine; he offered no reply.

'When can I see him?' Her tone was insistent now. She had seen something, some mark of evasiveness, a slight twitch trembling around his lips, and after all these years she recognized the signs. 'You're lying, Edward, aren't you? You're not going to let me see him!'

No need to be in fear, and nothing any more to hide . . . For the first time in their lives together it was the moment to be honest with her.

'Your son died at the Wall the night you came across. Yes, I lied to you.'

She had been sustained only by the tension and the hope, by the reawakening of a dream she had never

339

dared let die for twenty years: that her baby lived. Now, in an instant, it was all gone. Her face drained, her shoulders sagged, the spirit and fight which had been within her crumbled to dust and was blown away.

'Why?' she whispered. 'Why did you have to lie to me? Why did you let me believe?' She was pleading with him, willing him to take back his words and tell her that it was a cruel and senseless joke, but knowing all the time that the deception was finally over.

'Because I needed your co-operation. You had a gun on me, remember?' His fingers closed over his pocket to reassure himself that the weapon was still safely in his possession. 'And we needed you over here, safe in the East, while we find out precisely what you know. Your knowledge, whether you are aware of it or not, could put a lot of my friends at risk. We have to give ourselves a little time to reorganize and get them back to safety. So I regret you will have to be a guest of our glorious People's Republic for a little while. I'm afraid the people will insist.'

She didn't respond.

'I'm sorry, Katherine. After all these years . . .' He didn't continue. There was little point in trying to find words which could never sufficiently explain or console. He was talking to a shell. Katherine's features were ghostly, haggard. There was no sign of life left in her face. Her eyes were glazed, unfocused, trying to peer into a distant past which now seemed to be lost for ever.

The guard still hadn't come out of the blockhouse with their papers; they were taking their own sweet time. Schumacher peered through the window and saw two of them gesticulating in their direction. They were inspecting an identity card, and looking closely at

Katherine. *Sheisse!* A *Flüchtling*. A Wall Rat. A refugee who had fled illegally from East Berlin many years ago and who was now trying to get back in. Of course they were suspicious.

He would have to explain the situation to their senior officer. Still, there was no rush. He had all the time in the world.

The small group of onlookers presented a pathetic sight. The soldiers stood dejectedly around the jeep, gesticulating and arguing among themselves. Ahead of them on the white line painted across the road at the very edge of the checkpoint, Miss Pickerstaff stood alone, slowly clenching her fists in rage and frustration as she watched her prey less than a hundred yards away, so close yet too far for her to lift a finger to prevent their escape. All Harry could do was to look on in bewilderment, squashed between two military guards in the back of the car, an impotent and uncomprehending onlooker. There was only one small barrier to be raised before both Schumacher and Katherine would be lost to him for ever. He wasn't sure which loss he would feel most keenly.

'Bring him out here,' instructed Miss Pickerstaff. The guards hustled Harry out of the car.

'Your bird has flown,' she muttered between gritted teeth. 'And your alibi with her.'

'She's innocent, I tell you. He must have found some way to force her.'

'Look, Benjamin! Use your eyes. Are you trying to tell me she's putting up a struggle?' They could both see very clearly that Schumacher and Katherine were sitting totally passively in the car, waiting to be waved through. There was no struggle, no angry words, no sign of protest.

'It's not what it seems. I know she wouldn't cross willingly.'

'Give it a rest, Benjamin. They're gone and the game's up. We'll just have to make do with you.'

He could see what she meant. He had managed to convince her that Schumacher was a traitor, but instead of accolades he was under arrest, accused of assisting him to escape. His career was in ruins, and Katherine was about to pass from his life for ever.

He could see her, or at least the back of her head. It hung down, dejected. As he looked he knew this was not a woman about to achieve happy release, more a woman about to be cast into damnation. She was innocent, he knew, no matter what they would say. But he couldn't save her, any more than he could save himself. He saw her head lift slightly and begin to turn. She wanted one parting look at the West, at everything she was leaving behind. Her life had now come full circle and she was back where she started, in misery, alone.

As she turned, her eyes met Harry's. He saw a flicker of recognition – he saw love there, too, he was certain – before it died, leaving only a hollow, haunted expression, like a soul peering out of the inferno. He was watching her being destroyed right in front of him.

He would never thereafter know precisely why he did what he did next. Was it for Katherine? Or for himself? All he could focus on was the haunted look in her eyes, and know he would never be able to live in peace with that memory.

The jeep was less than thirty feet away, with the driver standing up behind the wheel to get a better view of the border post. Harry hurled himself at the soldier, knocking him off his feet and right out of the vehicle, leaving Harry as the sole occupant and in the driving

342

seat. He was only yards from the other guards but he had the advantage of surprise. By the time they had heard the driver's shout of alarm and comprehended what was going on, Harry already had the jeep started and in gear. He released the handbrake and clutch together, and the squeal of tortured rubber drowned their shouts of protest as the tyres spun on the ground before gaining grip and propelling the vehicle forward. As the others rushed towards him one of the guards unholstered his gun and waved it in his direction, but couldn't get a clear line of fire. Harry found himself hurtling towards the checkpoint. The last thing he saw before he passed the first barrier was the look of astonishment on Miss Pickerstaff's face as she turned to see him at the wheel of the jeep bearing directly down on her. He passed within inches, and above the roar of the highly revved engine he could just make out her high-pitched squeak: 'Shoot him! Shoot him!'

But it was too late. He was already hurling the vehicle around the first bollard, the four-wheel drive giving him the ability to force his way through the carefully prepared chicane much faster than an ordinary vehicle.

On the other side of the checkpoint, the shouts of alarm and sound of scorching rubber could be clearly heard. Every guard on duty in the East turned to see the cause of the commotion, to discover a US military vehicle racing through the checkpoint and away from a group of US soldiers, one of whom was waving a gun in protest. This was not a situation the East Germans were used to; they had never known of anyone trying to escape to the East before. And in any event, if the US military were trying to stop him, even shoot him, the man must have something very valuable in his possession. So confusion reigned and not a gun was drawn in the East.

The concrete and steel chicane was meant to slow vehicles down for the customs check, not stop them completely. That task was left to the massive iron doors and steel barriers which at the press of a button could be thrust across the would-be escapee's path. But they had only been placed at the Western end of the checkpoint as the final impediment to flight from the East, and Harry was already past those. The other barriers had also been designed with the simple logic of preventing flight in one direction; no one had seen the necessity of planning for the folly of a military jeep bursting through in the other.

The border guards watched, paralysed with uncertainty as Harry wrenched the jeep around the last concrete bollard, thrust up through the gears and headed straight for Schumacher's BMW. He was squeezing as much speed as possible out of the jeep and concentrating on forcing the vehicle through the narrow passage of the checkpoint. It was only a small slip of the hand as it wrestled with the steering wheel, but Harry was already doing forty and accelerating when he nudged the side wall and started to climb. The jeep, already defying the laws of the East Berlin authorities, now also seemed to defy the laws of gravity and leaped sharply into the air.

Schumacher turned in his car seat to make out what was going on, and could scarcely comprehend what he saw. Less than fifty feet away a US military jeep was flying through the air, headed straight for him, with a demented Harry Benjamin as its pilot. Schumacher knew what this was. They were after him. A snatch squad, about to pounce, desperate to haul him back to the West.

The jeep arched gracelessly through the air and Harry had to fasten with all his strength on to the steering wheel to prevent himself being thrown out. The sights of the checkpoint performed a crazy ballet in front of him, his backside parted company with the seat and he had no control, waiting for the vehicle to make contact with the ground once again. When it did so it hit with a force which tried to drive his whole body back through the chassis and scrambled his senses. He felt as if his spine was six inches shorter and he could taste warm blood in his mouth from the lip he had just bitten. But these were the least of his concerns. His only thought was that he must almost be upon Schumacher.

Harry's jeep rammed the BMW from behind with a sound that would have done justice to a Detroit wrecker's yard. Metal ground on metal before being bent and torn, and glass was smashed and shattered. The jeep's engine died and the BMW was shunted several yards forward, its rear-end reduced to a concertina of warped bodywork, gaping holes where the brake lights had once been, and an exhaust bent askew and trailing on the ground.

This was the moment when one of the guards decided that, whatever was going on, it was time to regain control of the situation. He pushed the panic button and the alarm sirens began their anguished warble as heavy metal poles shot across the roadway and the solid iron doors on the checkpoint's western end came thumping shut. By this time, however, the only effect was finally to obliterate any view which Miss Pickerstaff still had of the mayhem. According to the designers, the checkpoint should now have been secure. But Schumacher was taking no chances. He thrust the gear stick forward and pushed his foot to the floor, even before he had released the handbrake. Five litres of carefully crafted German horsepower burst into life and the car took off, swerving crazily, trailing a thick cloud of blue smoke and firing off sparks as the mangled exhaust was dragged beneath it. The car had not reached any great speed by the time it hit the red-and-white steel pole which served as the checkpoint's first – or, in this case, final – barrier. The pole was set into recesses carved out of thick concrete pillars standing either side of the roadway and intended to thwart the most desperate of drivers. But yet again desperation had been conceived as a one-way concept. When the BMW hit head on but in the wrong direction, the windscreen shattered into a thousand crazy fragments while the barrier's heavy-gauge hinge, designed to be of sufficient strength to withstand the impact of a truck travelling East to West, simply popped its mountings and fell to the ground. Within yards the barrier had been pushed to one side and the BMW, with Schumacher struggling to control it, was setting off down the broad expanse of Invalidenstrasse.

Harry was on automatic pilot, his rattled brain still not recovered from the jolting, but he could see the BMW beginning to career away from him. He was losing it. He twisted the keys in the ignition and heard the engine spring to life – thank God he had only stalled it. He could see a border guard raising his AK-47 and waving it at him and after the fleeing BMW, but still there were no shots. The orders to avoid bloodshed along the border at all costs had been quite specific and, anyway, the guard had no idea what he would be shooting at. Harry left him to his doubts, and set off after Schumacher.

He was driving down a broad, tree-lined avenue, one of the central avenues of the old city. It wasn't busy, the typically light traffic of East Berlin consisting of a sprinkling of clapped-out Ladas, Skodas and Wartburgs with the occasional coach and battered tram. The tiny, fragile-looking East bloc saloons moved slowly along the badly rutted streets, and the BMW and chasing jeep were forced to swerve in and around them, leaving bemused drivers in their wake waving fists and punching their car horns in anger. But Harry was too intent on his quarry to look back at the chaos on Invalidenstrasse.

The BMW should have had him slaughtered for speed but for some reason was having trouble pulling away. Then Harry saw a plume of smoke swirling from the nearside. The torn and battered bodywork was leaning on a rear tyre, slowly eating into it with razor-sharp teeth. They had gone several hundred yards and the jeep, crashing through the gearbox, was beginning to gain on the BMW, hobbled by its rear tyre and through having to lead the way through the moving traffic. Harry glanced in his mirror, expecting to see half a division of troops and border guards bearing down on him, probably headed by Miss Pickerstaff, but as yet there was no sign of the convoy which he knew must be setting off in hot pursuit.

He looked ahead to see Schumacher wrestling with the wheel and making a sharp right-hand turn; Harry changed down to follow. With a squeal of protest from his tyres he came off Invalidenstrasse and into a series of narrow streets packed with old tenement buildings which led into a tangle of squares and side roads. Schumacher knew what he was doing, and already there was no sign of him. Harry began to feel the tingle of panic rising within him and he dashed recklessly around several corners, hoping that luck would choose the right course for him. He tried to listen for the sound of Schumacher's engine above the pounding of his own diesel and even detect the pungent smell of burning rubber to guide him through the maze of streets, but it was no good. He jumped on the brake and brought the jeep skidding to a halt at the next intersection, standing in the driving seat and desperately searching in every direction for some sign of the trail. There was nothing. Harry had lost him.

Less than 150 yards away, hidden in the embrace of a side street and behind a conveniently parked car, Schumacher watched. His eyes were bulging and he was sweating profusely, rivulets dripping down his brow and off his chin. Although the BMW was stationary, the whites of his knuckles gripped the steering wheel with ferocity. His hands had started shaking again, uncontrollably.

With his attention fixed rigidly on the sight of Harry punching the air in frustration, Schumacher had all but forgotten Katherine at his side. She was in another world, participating in a different life inhabited by Peter, the baby, the parents she had lost so many years ago. It was a world she could believe in, with true affection and without deception, a world she would rather she had never left. Only slowly did she wake from her own dream and rejoin Schumacher's nightmare, and begin to remember why she was there. She had no recollection of the chase, of the reckless pursuit away from the checkpoint. But she could see Harry's frustration, and the fear and loathing which flecked Schumacher's features, like a prisoner facing his hangman. And as she looked once again at Harry desperately searching the streets, she realized that the hangman was about to be cheated, that Schumacher was getting away . . .

The prolonged blast of the car horn snatched at Harry's ears like a call to spurs on a hunting pipe. Schumacher's lair had been unearthed. Moments later the battered BMW sprang into view and fled down the street. The pursuit was on again.

348

The BMW had a couple of hundred yards and a set of traffic lights on the jeep. Harry just kept his foot down, picking up speed through the red lights and knowing that every intersection was a spin of the roulette wheel. He survived this one, but heard the screech of brakes and the sound of crunching metal behind him as an innocent but unlucky East Berlin taxi driver reached an early end to his day. Harry didn't look back. He followed Schumacher round another junction – he was gaining on him now – and as he did so he heard the wail of sirens, loud and close by. They must be on his tail at last.

'Oh, shit!' he screamed as an ambulance, all flashing lights and red crosses, came out of a side entrance not twenty yards in front of him, completely blocking the road. As he closed in at frightening speed on the driver's astonished face, out of the corner of his eye he could see all the signs of a hospital – one of East Germany's major medical facilities in Tucholskystrasse, had he only had time to realize it – before he mounted the pavement and ploughed his way out of control between street lamps and hospital wall. There was enough room – just. The wing mirrors had gone and the spare jerry can was bouncing along behind him, but by some miracle there were no pedestrians around. The ambulance driver would recover; so, he hoped, would his badly shaken patient.

Harry bounced back on to the roadway and was once again in pursuit. The buildings on cither side were becoming increasingly impressive now, grand affairs whose architects had successfully wrapped them in imperial pomp and splendour to inspire future generations. This was the very heart of the old Reich, the Berlin which Harry's father would have known so well, in whose streets he would have grown up and first learned what it was like to be a German – and been told that he could never be one, no matter how hard he tried. It was the Berlin of Kaisers, of Führers, of Generals and of *Macht*. There never had been a place in the heart of Berlin for little people, the ordinary folk.

Harry ignored the historical niceties as he drew closer to the BMW. More smoke was pouring from the tortured rear tyre and with his right hand Schumacher was having to hold Katherine away from the controls. She was fighting, just as Harry knew she would! He screamed for more speed out of the protesting diesel.

The two vehicles burst like champagne corks on to Unter den Linden, Berlin's historic central artery, the gathering place over the decades of international orchestras, diplomats, opera stars and marching armies. It was the city's broadest boulevard, tree-lined, magnificent, self-indulgent, which led all the way from the socialist creation of Marx-Engels Platz at one end to the unmistakably imperial majesty of the Brandenburg Gate at the other. Many of the city's most famous institutions crowded its flanks, from the 'Red' town hall to the Soviet embassy itself. There was no chance here of the pursuit going unnoticed.

Schumacher struggled to direct his car around a line of stationary traffic, his wheels and brakes locked in protest, while Harry took the direct route across the central divide, taking to the air once more as he hit it and scaring witless an oncoming *Vopo* motorcyclist. The policeman and his machine parted company, continuing on quite separate paths until the motorcycle, spinning like a dervish top, rammed a parked car and burst into flames. The ensuing inferno soon engulfed neighbouring cars and a plume of thick, acrid smoke poured into the sky. Now the whole world knew where Harry was. Traffic came to a stop as drivers braked in

350

amazement and skewed their vehicles across the road and into each other. It took Harry less than ten seconds to get across Unter den Linden. It would take them hours to clear up the mess.

As quickly as they had burst on to 'Linden' they had disappeared and soon were among the narrower streets of a residential district, one which had once been part of pre-war Kreuzberg. Now Harry was right behind the BMW; he was only feet from his quarry. He could see Schumacher frantically wrenching at the wheel. Katherine seemed to have stopped her struggle, and was slumped against the passenger door. The front windscreen was entirely gone, the rear one cracked, the back end looked like a war zone and the rear tyre, so long under siege, had finally surrendered. The BMW was now running on its wheel rim. He had them – almost. But the streets were crowded and narrow, full of pedestrians, cyclists and the other clutter of urban life. Little children were playing, old women shopping and gossiping, lovers holding hands and strolling carelessly about. There was no way past, no way to force Schumacher to stop, so long as he kept his head and to this route.

A ludicrous thought flashed through Harry's mind: what the fuck was he going to do even if he did manage to stop them? And what were the *Vopos* going to do when inevitably they caught up with him? An hour ago he had been in his office in the US Mission. Now . . . ? He would figure it all out once he had stopped them – if he could stop them. Time, Harry realized, was not on his side. The forces of authority would by now be descending on him from all directions. It was only a matter of minutes before they caught up with him. And then it would all be over.

Schumacher swung left. Whether he intended to, or

whether it was simply a response to the demands of a rear wheel which was beginning to seize, not even he knew. But they were in a market square, lined with rows of stalls selling everything from vegetables and fruit to work tools and second-hand clothing. This was a people's market, where they bought and sold and bartered and dickered – and Harry realized this could be his last chance. They raced through an avenue of stalls, people scattering to all sides, and ahead Harry could see space where the stalls gave way to the open square before running into yet another series of small, narrow streets. That was where Harry had to stop the BMW, where he had to pull ahead and force Schumacher to one side. He swung out from behind, but was immediately forced back to avoid a line of women queueing for bread. Once more he tried, yet again was forced back. The open stretch of market square was just up ahead now. He had one last chance.

As the jeep pulled out, Harry could see all sorts of containers and baskets of produce piled high in his way. But no people. He could see no one! He pushed his foot yet again to the floor and ducked while boxes of fresh tomatoes, apples and cherries cascaded over the top of the jeep as he carved his way through the stock of a fruit stall. At the very last he hit the stall itself, a solid wooden construction which gave way only reluctantly, and the wheel bounced and spun in Harry's hands. The jeep nosed into the BMW, forcing it off its path until, locked together, the two vehicles rammed head-first into a building at the edge of the square and came to a bone-shattering halt.

Schumacher was thrown against the steering wheel and his head hit the few remaining shards of the windscreen. He was badly winded and concussed, the glass leaving two angry cuts across his forehead. Harry was thrown clear over the side of the jeep and his hands went up to protect his head. It worked too efficiently. When he hit the ground he heard something snap, and his right arm went limp and useless. There was no way he could throttle Schumacher now. He found his right leg had also been caught as he was thrown clear, and there was an ugly red patch spreading beneath a rent in his trousers. Only Katherine appeared to have escaped unscathed, but the shock of the last minutes was still with her. She sat motionless in the front seat, seeming neither to know or any longer to care what was happening to her.

His right arm was numb and his leg was on fire, but Harry had lost none of his senses. As he rolled clear from the wreckage, he could hear the sirens in the distance. This time he was sure they were meant for him. And for Katherine. He tried to get up, but stumbled. It felt as if his right leg was caught in a mantrap; the more he tried to move, the more he thought it was going to be ripped clean off.

Schumacher was beginning to stir now. Soon he would have recovered, Harry would still be crippled, and another lousy idea would have come to a sticky end. He could almost hear Miss Pickerstaff: 'Another complete cock-up, imbecile!' As he lay there, he decided he would give almost anything to listen to her nasal voice again, berating him, just one more time . . . The ripping pain in his leg brought his thoughts rushing back to reality.

'Run, Katherine. For pity's sake run!' he screamed. She looked around at him, her eyes hollow, aged, uncomprehending. 'Katherine, please! Get away. While you can. Run!' She was in no condition to understand, but neither could she resist. In a state of shock, the only message which came into her mind was the one

Harry was screaming at her: 'Run!' She almost fell out of the car and gave him another blank stare of incomprehension.

'Run, Katherine!'

She began to stagger off. Walking at first, but as her limbs responded to the garbled commands of her brain, she broke into a shuffling trot. Harry watched as she stumbled down the street, not knowing where she was headed, aware only that she must get away.

By the time Schumacher had come to, a small crowd had gathered. His eyes began to register as he was lifted from the car by two men, whom he tried to push away as understanding and pain flooded over him. He shook his head to clear his thoughts, and noticed with horror the blood seeping down his brow. He saw Harry lying a few feet away clutching his leg with Katherine running away down the street, and snarled with fury. He shoved at his helpers once more; they insisted, mistaking his fury for the aftereffects of concussion until he drew the hand gun from his jacket and brandished it at them. He had no trouble from them now.

His eyes wandered from Harry to the fleeing figure of Katherine, then back to Harry once again. Another snarl. He raised the gun, and Harry found himself looking down the barrel of the .22, behind which a twisted expression threw together all the wild emotions of guilt, jealousy, and above all loathing at having been cheated. Harry knew that Schumacher intended to kill him. He could see the German's fingers tightening around the gun, but he couldn't move. Yet the gun was. It wavered and trembled furiously, wobbling more as Schumacher tried to tighten his grip. The aftereffects of the crash and the exhausting years of inner turmoil combined into a storm of protest within Schumacher's outstretched arm, and he could not aim the gun.

Harry lay there, watching the ball bounce around his roulette wheel. Schumacher's eyes flashed away from Harry to the increasingly distant figure of Katherine, and back to Harry once more. He'll shoot me in the balls first, just for revenge, Harry told himself. He was petrified, hypnotized as he watched the swaying barrel waver all around and over him. The wheel was slowing down.

The gun flashed, and Harry flinched. But there was no pain. Schumacher had missed, even at such close quarters, the bullet burying itself a good foot from Harry's head. He stepped closer to try once again, but his arm was shaking uncontrollably, the gun performing an even more exaggerated death dance above Harry's head. Schumacher's raging eyes bore down, then glanced away once more down the street to Katherine. She was getting away. 'Bastard!' he screamed in a voice full of self-pity and self-hate. He couldn't do it. He wanted to, desperately, but he couldn't. He didn't have sufficient control. For the last time his trembling hands had let him down. He set off after Katherine.

Harry watched him go. The wheel had stopped and he had won, but already it was spinning again. And this time it was Katherine at risk. The threat to his own life had paralysed his reactions, but the thought of Katherine galvanized him. He gritted his teeth, cried with agony as his leg demanded that he stop, and began a slow, gut-wrenching hobble after Schumacher.

Katherine did not know what she was doing. She was running, that was enough. From what she wasn't totally sure, to what she had no idea. Images crowded in upon her — of Edward and Peter, the baby, a life of misery, Gerd Brünner, Harry's room overlooking the Wall and its big brass bed. She hated her life with its pain, its lack of meaning and its incompatible demands. She had only one wish now, to be back, womblike, in the embrace of Peter, the only man who had ever loved her without question and without compromise. She remembered how they had met, how they had first touched and kissed with such innocence and inexperience, and how they had both laughed through their youthful embarrassment. She thought of Wannsee, how he had laid her down beneath the clear night sky on a bed of sweet pine needles and loved her. She remembered the pain and triumph of bearing their son, and how complete a woman she had felt. And as she ran blindly along the streets, through alleys, past buildings and around corners, suddenly she thought she remembered all this, too . . .

It was dark now. Dusk had fallen and finished, although in their mad chase no one seemed to have noticed. But it was as yet far from over. Bystanders in doorways and on street corners watched in disbelief as a middle-aged man waving a gun ran down the street, followed by an unarmed pursuer with blood staining his trouser leg and a useless right arm. Surely this was fantasy, some form of stunt? What would the pursuer do if he caught his quarry – bite him in the leg? Harry knew how futile his actions seemed but couldn't resist the impulse. Schumacher and Katherine: his enemy and his love. Where they went, he must go also. It overcame the pain, the logic and all thoughts of self-preservation. He had no idea where he was, where this insane chase was leading, but he had to try to keep up with Schumacher wherever he was headed. Harry didn't shout – what was the point? And he needed all his breath for the chase. He was falling behind, his strength beginning to fade as the blood seeped down his suit. He put his head down and concentrated on summoning every last ounce of resistance to overcome the demands that were being screamed at him from all parts of his body. He mustn't let them get away! Then his weary eyes looked up again, searching ahead for Schumacher, and he saw a cold glow filling the night sky. He was no longer lost. God, no! Anywhere but this! He cried with anger and frustration as he knew the race was nearing its end.

She was here, that night, with Peter and the baby. It was in the dark shadows of this very building they had lain in wait for the right hour. It was where she had suckled the infant to sleep, held him in her arms, wrapped him and loved him before delivering him up to Peter. For the last time. She remembered how Peter had smiled at her, reassuring, strong as always, had told her he loved her and had kissed her. Goodbye. It had been just around the corner of the brick schoolhouse. Here. She had looked one last time at them, and he had shouted. *Don't look back.* And in all the years of loneliness and mourning since then, she knew she had failed his final instruction. She had always looked back. At first she had felt she had cheated death, but now she knew otherwise: death had cheated her. Had deprived her, condemned her to the purgatory of a half-life without them. Better, much better, a good death than only half a life, of waiting, of looking back. But now she was back, to where she had left them. She could still feel their warmth and their love, as though all she had to do was to close her eyes and reach out, and they would be there . . .

Schumacher staggered to the corner of the school-house around which Katherine had disappeared. His years of living off the fat of capitalism and with the grinding fear of betrayal had taken their toll; only his interest in self-preservation had driven him on. But he was not ready for what greeted him as he scrambled around the final turn. Ahead of him, floodlit as every night, standing out in the darkness, was the Killing Field.

As he blinked to restore his night vision against the glare, he took in all its parts: a simple sign telling him he had reached the border area and ordering him not to proceed, alongside which ran a continuous low barrier marking a track patrolled by guard dogs, and beyond, hiding the strip where so many had died, a broad stretch of finely raked, level white sand gleaming harshly in the floodlights. And across the sand Katherine was walking, slowly and deliberately, leaving a trail of footprints to mark her way.

'*Gott in Himmel, die Mauer,*' he gasped. He had never been this close, not from the East. He helped so many *Flüchtlinge* but only now, for the first time, did he sense what terror it must have struck into those who had resolved to cheat it. The shadows in which he stood were cold like a graveyard, inhabited by ghosts, and in the darkness it was as if nothing had ever changed. He could almost smell the presence of the hounds, waiting to savage anyone they might catch. And then the broad stretch of sand like a huge, floodlit arena, a no-man's-land on which the human body might be a target, with no place to hide. And there was Katherine, walking into its very heart.

His eyes began to adjust to the contrast of deep shadows and scorching bright lights, and he was gripped once more with panic as he realized that beyond this stretch of killing field no longer lay a wall which cut him off from the life he had just left, with its secrets, its double-dealing and its treachery. Instead, there was just a hole, a dark cavern waiting to swallow him. It was the Gap. And Katherine was headed towards it, back to the West, with her secrets and her revenge. She must be stopped! Where were those blind drunkards of border guards? Why hadn't they seen her? They would let her get away!

He ran along the perimeter strip towards a guard post, shouting and waving his arms to draw their attention. 'Stop her! For Chrissake stop her, you fools!' The two soldiers within the post were arguing furiously, pointing to each other then away at Katherine. One had the telephone in his hand, trying to shout down it at the same time as remonstrating with his companion.

'Shitheads!' Schumacher screamed. 'Stop her!'

One of the guards pointed his rifle at him. *'Halt! Nicht weiter!'*

'Not me, *Dummkopf*. Her!'

Katherine was now nearly halfway across, still walking on steadily, unhurriedly, oblivious of all around her. Schumacher screamed his fury and frustration at the guards, who responded to his invective only by waving their rifles increasingly aggressively in his direction. He could stand it no longer.

'KGB,' he bellowed. It was the first time he had ever described himself so, had ever dared let his secret slip. 'She must not be allowed to get across!'

But the guards remained unimpressed and even more confused. Their orders were clear, and had been reissued and re-emphasized since the shooting earlier that week. Any soldier who so much as waved a gun barrel in the direction of the Gap without specific authorization from a senior officer would wish he'd been sitting on the charge when they had blown the Wall. And where were the bloody senior officers when you needed them?

'KGB!' Schumacher shouted again.

It had some effect. They lowered the guns trained on him, but the arguing continued.

KGB: the cause which Schumacher had served ever

since he had been a man. For which he had lied, cheated, condemned men and women to death in the killing fields, had led a double life of deception and complete devotion. Now, as his service reached its climax, it was all beginning to unravel. The lie he had lived was going to be exposed. His secret would be revealed and his colleagues put at risk. And all because Katherine had been a whore, like his mother, and slept with an American. In a life of betrayal there was no room or sympathy for others who also betrayed. Particularly whores. And Katherine had betrayed him. As a whore.

Harry stumbled around the corner of the schoolhouse on the point of exhaustion and collapse; he had no more physical reserves. Whatever happened, he knew there was nothing more he could do. He blinked in the light. He could see Katherine walking across the sand. And he saw Schumacher lift his arm, and aim carefully at her. He had no breath left to scream, or do anything except watch it all unfold in front of him. Schumacher fired – one, two, three times. Harry could scarcely believe it. He'd missed.

Katherine hadn't seemed even to notice. She was in another time, long ago, years before these shots were fired. She had reached beyond the halfway point now, nearing the other side. The bullets had missed; she had survived. Then suddenly she stopped. She stood still, head bowed, hands clasped in front of her. This was the point where Peter and the baby had died, where she had last left them. She had arrived.

The scene seemed frozen in time as the onlookers struggled to comprehend what they saw. This wasn't an escape. But what was it? The guards stood nonplussed. Harry tried to reach out, call out, but couldn't. Schumacher still had his gun held out in front of him, but he knew he was too far away to be effective with a small hand gun. And in the distance beyond where Katherine stood, behind the remnants of what had once been the Wall, pushed back by steel barriers and guarded by US soldiers, a crowd of West Berliners stood in horrified silence while TV cameras captured the scene for millions who could not be present.

It all seemed to happen in slow motion for Harry. The pain and loss of blood were too close to gaining their victory. He was like a puppet with strings cut. He could only watch as Schumacher flexed his arm once more, walked from the protective shadows of the perimeter into the bright spotlights of the killing fields to cut down the distance between himself and Katherine, and began firing as he walked.

At last the crowd along the Gap could see the full picture as a man emerged from the far shadows, firing. Why was she just standing? Why wasn't she trying to protect herself, escape? Couldn't she see the danger behind her, getting closer? 'Run! RUN!' the crowd began to scream in encouragement. Even the US soldiers joined in, waving their rifles and helmets and raising their voices in support. With each shot from Schumacher's gun, the shouts of defiance grew even louder, washing across the death strip and reaching far into East Berlin. Only Katherine seemed oblivious.

Then her head came up, rising slowly, looking at the crowd, seeming to recall a scene from long ago. 'On! ON!' they shouted. *'Don't look back!'*

She took a faltering half-pace towards the shouts of the crowd, towards freedom. 'Come on! COME ON!' they screamed, many in tears of frustration and joy as they saw her waking from her dream. But she had been here before. She seemed to hesitate once more. Another shot rang out, and she fell to the ground.

Silence descended along the Wall again, as it had

always done in the instant of death. Only the faint click of magazines being fitted on American M-16s and safety catches being released hung in the night air. 'Steady-y-y-y,' bellowed the Lieutenant. 'Remember the orders.'

'Fuck the orders,' muttered a GI. He had Schumacher square in his sights, and had to live with his conscience as well as the orders. With a gentle squeeze of the trigger he fired a single bullet. It went straight through the heart and out through a fist-sized hole where previously the spine had been.

Just before the pain finally beat him and he collapsed into unconsciousness, Harry forced out one word which echoed all the way across the killing field.

'Kather-i-i-ine . . .'

EPILOGUE

The White House

Michelle took the telephone call shortly before midnight. He was alone. Grossman had wanted desperately to be in on this one, but the President felt he had been on the receiving end of too much of the professor's advice recently.

'Mr President, I believe we both know the facts. I also believe we both know their significance.' The voice on the end of the phone sounded tired and saddened, but firmly in control.

'Mr General Secretary, it must be clear to you that I cannot sign any treaty with you at this time. Not with that hanging over our heads.'

'Perhaps it will come as little surprise for you to learn that too many of my colleagues within the Kremlin also believe such a move would be – untimely, shall we say? Not wrong. Not never. But not now, not for the moment.'

'I understand. We had our chance. Somewhere along the way it all got messed about.'

There was mutual respect in the voices, a sense of loss shared.

'A period of stability, perhaps, learning to trust each other again. Time to let doubts and tempers cool.'

'I'm not sure I have a lot of time,' responded Michelle.

Andreyev understood. His doctors had told him that he, too, was fighting a losing battle, against an enemy which was even now eating its way through his belly.

'We each have our own electorates. We have no right to expect gratitude. It was a pity that we also seemed to run out of luck.'

'I pray there might still be another chance. Maybe our successors . . .'

'Yes, our successors. There is a young group of reformers here in the Kremlin, headed by a man called Gorbachev. I have high hopes. Perhaps they might be able to pick up the pieces . . .'

'At least we both survived, Mr General Secretary. We had better luck than those unfortunate people at the Wall.'

'Yes, the Wall,' sighed Andreyev. 'The Wall. You understand, Mr President, what must be done?'

'I fear history will not be kind to us, Mr General Secretary. They will say we missed our great opportunity.'

'Perhaps the wiser amongst them will say we created the opportunity for others.'

They were both silent for a moment, contemplating the verdict of future generations which both of them knew would not be kind.

'In any event,' continued Andreyev, 'it's scarcely our decision any more.'

'Neither of us has any choice.'

'No choice at all, Mr President . . .'

Berlin

The sun rose on a new day, and trucks full of materials and equipment began to appear at the Gap, accompanied by East German military engineers. As US troops held silent onlookers at bay and a priest led a small group in prayer, the engineers began rebuilding the Wall.

'They will never pull it down for us, Lothar. Never,' one young West Berliner muttered to a friend.

'Then it's up to us to do the job for them. One day. Soon.'

'Let's make it very soon . . .'

MOSCOW

There was a sharp knock on the door of the apartment in Kutuzovsky Prospekt, in the block where most of the Politburo lived under conditions of great luxury and even tighter security. The building was designed so that no one should get in, or out, unless they were supposed to. Bykov opened the door himself; he had been expecting the call. It was almost time for him to have been at the opening of the extraordinary meeting of the Politburo, but he had known since the telephone call which had woken him in the middle of the night that there was no point in even thinking about it. He had written a few personal letters, put on his full-dress uniform complete with medals and insignia, including the red-tinged medallion of the Order of Lenin and the simple gold star awarded to him as a Hero of the Soviet Union – not so bad for a country boy from the mountains of Georgia, he reflected – and waited.

'Comrade Bykov,' the General at the door said – no title, no deference, Bykov noticed, just formality and quiet insistence – 'you are requested to come with me.'

'I understand,' Bykov responded. 'I assume the armed guard behind you bears the same request?' He gave a wry smile to show there was no personal ill will. 'Comrade General, allow me just a second.'

The General was about to protest, but Bykov's tone was still that of the chairman of the KGB and brooked no argument. Anyway, the old man was co-operating . . .

The revolver shot from the room into which Bykov had disappeared told the General he had been sadly mistaken. In death, as in life, Bykov was intent on cheating them.

Berlin

It was not the most graceful exchange the Wall had ever seen. He was simply a package, being handed over with crisp salutes and shallow courtesies by guards who succeeded in ignoring him almost completely. He could have been a bundle of dirty washing for all the attention they gave him.

Harry hadn't been expecting this; they had told him nothing when they had brought him a fresh set of clothes and a razor earlier that morning. Now he was limping across the old iron bridge across the Havel at Glienicke Brücke, his arm in a plaster cast and sling, realizing that the far side of the bridge would bring him back to safety, to the West. He hadn't expected what was waiting for him there, either. At the bridge's end was gathered a crowd of press and TV journalists, lenses trained four-square on him, while in front of them beside a black Cadillac draped in the Stars and Stripes stood the US Ambassador. The senior diplomat held out his hand in greeting as Harry hobbled towards him, retreating in some embarrassment as he realized that Harry could do no more than wave a left hand awkwardly in his direction.

'Welcome home, Benjamin,' he beamed broadly, turning to smile at the cameras and usher him into the back of the limousine.

Home? Harry considered. No, not home. Not here.

'What's all this for?' Harry enquired, nodding towards the gaggle of cameras.

'Whether you like it or not, you're an international celebrity now, Benjamin.' There was just a hint of a pause. 'For your own information, we don't like.' Inside the car the Ambassador's tone was cold, the smile gone.

'I don't understand.'

'We have to put up with this circus. They think you're some sort of hero, but don't let it go to your head. From Washington's point of view you have single-handedly ballsed up the most important diplomatic initiative of the decade. You're not popular in the White House, son, or anywhere outside of editors' offices.'

'But Schumacher was an agent. He's been betraying us for years. I uncovered it . . .'

'Langley shares the view of the White House. You stepped out of line, and just got lucky. We'd have been much happier to keep Schumacher playing "doubles" if we could have held on to the treaty. We might have turned him, used him against the opposition. If only you hadn't got him shot.'

There was a pause. Harry's leg was throbbing again and his head felt dizzy. He was having trouble taking this all in.

'There's even a high-level opinion within Berlin that it may be you who's the real "double",' the Ambassador continued, taking care to keep his tone neutral and not to take sides.

'Me?! Working for them?'

'Schumacher was coming to the end of his line, anyway – so the reasoning goes. You exposed him, but only after you'd tipped him off. You get yourself beaten up a little by the bad guys . . .' – the Ambassador nodded towards the bandages – '. . . and handed back across the border like a returning hero. The best cover a "double" ever had. That's how some of your colleagues think.'

Images of Miss Pickerstaff swam in front of Harry's eyes. She was smiling.

'Anyway, there are those who want you to know they will never forget what happened in Berlin. Officially they can't prove a thing, not yet at least. You're a celebrity, after all. But they want you looking back over your shoulder for the rest of your career, remembering . . .'

To hell with them all. He would remember anyway. He would remember this city of sorrow, with its pride, its madness, its memories which had haunted his father and which would now haunt him, if he let them. He could never forget the Wall, of course. But most of all he would remember Katherine, and he would struggle hard to remember only her smile, her warm green eyes and the light in her face when, for a short while, she was happy.

He hoped they would let him keep the dried red rose that had been in her safe, and one of those old, cracked photographs they had found alongside it, of a young and radiant Katherine, a tiny baby wrapped in christening clothes, and a proud father looking on. Together.

Harry, too, would spend time looking back.